TKEN
HUNTRESS

FROM INTERNATIONAL AWARD WINNING AUTHOR
KIA CARRINGTON-RUSSELL

CRYSTAL
♦ PUBLISHING ♦

DEDICATION

To all my readers, friends and family
Thank you so much, without you and all of your support I wouldn't be where I am
today. Thank you for being my pillar on darker days and the light of every celebration
and new release of every world I pencil to paper.
Your support and love is what guides me to pursue my dreams.
Thank you.

NEW WORLD

The pressure of a new world is limitless.
There is no expectation of a future;
when the past has been so carelessly destroyed.
Society's former glory has been taken.
Now we must survive and try to maintain numbers.
The world seems abandoned.
But in the dark monsters lurk.

I am a Token Huntress.
I will find the humans who remain,
And with great pleasure will destroy all vampires.
I am the vision of the new world.
I am Token.
I am Hunter.
Do not become my prey.

PROLOGUE

HUMANS HAD CRAFTED the first hunters in 2016, and for a very specific purpose: to stand against vampires. Our creation had been considered a success and the last standing hope of humanity's survival.

The presence of monsters lurking in the dark had been scary tales passed through generations pre-existing times prior to modern society. When vampires announced their existence to the human leaders in a grand gesture of settlement and equality in 2010, they were deemed as a consequential threat. Though their existence had been addressed in privacy and shadows for some time, the mere audacious proposal to live amongst humans with equal rights was considered preposterous.

They were deemed humanity's focal threat, and their existence was to be eradicated. The humans formed a temporary treaty, to keep the vampires in the shadows for a few years longer while they best approached a feigned agreement to keep the few leaders, known to be a part of the Vampire Council, at bay. This was in hopes of finding the best introductory way to announce and involve them into the twenty-first century—though the humans had no such illusions. What they didn't realize was the vampire's numbers and superiority that would soon outmatch the war they would bring upon themselves. Trickery and berated beliefs were humanities undoing.

In those few years of shadowed negotiations, in the silence, we were made. Scientists had concocted a sub-species of human. Young vampires had been trapped, studied, and tested, these experiments starting in the year 2012. That was officially reported, though any hunter worth half their salt knew it predated long before that.

Synthesized blood and cell mutation from vampires had been injected into human test subjects. The first subjects were claimed by the virus, which turned them into vampires themselves. The injection deteriorated every cell in the body, reforming it into the identified virus stricken black cells of vampirism. The change in mutation only evolved the test subjects to have an immediate desperation and thirst for blood to survive. However, the thirty-first human subject to be tested was a success, and the first hunter had been born.

Selective DNA combined with the capabilities of advanced technology resulted in a new breed: the hunters. We matched the vampires in almost every way. Although we functioned and looked like humans, we were a different race entirely. We were exceptional in every way, sight, smell, hearing, speed, strength, stamina, and endurance beyond humanly possible. We healed quickly, and our bodies required less maintenance to sustain, such as food, water, and sleep.

However, we did lack a natural empathetic ability. Emotion was not something we entertained, or perhaps our mission was so ingrained into us that we acknowledged from a young age sentimentality would only slow us down. Although we looked human, our notable differentiator was our florescent eyes and unique gifts exclusive to each hunter. Whether it was the gift to bend metals, commanding wild animals, or controlling flames, scientists had created something that their theories and papers could never entirely understand. But those gifts were what enabled hunters to stand confidently against vampires.

At the same time, in the technology era, the twenty-first century, humans also attempted to craft military robots. Though the prototypes were deemed the way forward with impressive weapons on hand, they were inferior compared to even young vampires. They didn't have the speed or the tactful advancements to match them.

Before the second wave of robots could be trialed, the vampires covertly provoked an already brewing war amongst nations, and the start of World War III began in 2017. Amongst this, as humans fought between their own beliefs and egos, the vampires took advantage to overthrow humanity in a synchronized attack across the world.

The military was stretched in every continent. The dividing nations had already suffered damage and disease following the nuclear bombs, mass deaths, and general havoc. That was when the hunters, still deemed as only prototypes, and a small army was deployed. In 2019, survival camps were posted and guarded by the hunters for the remaining human population. A small secondary army was dispatched to fight amongst the war. Few of those camps remained, having lessened in numbers and standard over time. By the 2020s, the world's natural resources were depleted. Electricity, water, and conventional gases were sabotaged by both parties.

The wars changed the world beyond recognition. Nuclear weapons had changed the face of the land. Pollution increased dramatically in civilized society's final decades. A thick layer of dust and fumes cushioned the earth's surface, preventing the sun from penetrating our atmosphere as it once had. The lack of light enabled vampires to roam freely. They could now prowl the lands in both night and day. The technology era fell.

It was in the 2030s that the Hunter Guilds were structured. Their role was to raid for supplies and to find surviving humans. Any humans that were recovered were transported to safety. Any vampires found were killed on sight.

Within that decade was when the first generation of hunters was born, not created in a science lab, but born of nature's natural accord. Though the children had fluorescent eyes, throughout their childhood and teenage years, they showed no apparent gift until their eighteenth birthday. Only theories could be rallied because the hunters lacked in any reasonable explanation, their manmade craft went beyond science. Though, there was a theory amongst Guild leaders. Perhaps it was the only blessing passed to the hunter gifted children born into a world of war. They were gifted time so they could mature into an adult and understand their role without perplexed and uncontrollable powers that would be deemed as a military advantage. Perhaps it was nature's way of making sure our species survived. After all, imagine a baby lighting everything on fire. If a child was born without the eyes of the hunter, they were cast out amongst the human camps to live a normal life.

It was once predicted that by the year 2300 the earth would be so hot that parts of it could not be lived on by humans. The drastic decline in the human population went some way toward stalling that process. The world went back to a more organic state, and the animal population grew. Animals that should have been extinct by 2100 multiplied uncontrollably. New, strange plants evolved that depended less on sunlight and water. Trees and vegetation grew where it could, creeping through the silent streets of deserted cities. Freshwater was rare and hard to procure. The oxygen in the air became thin as plant life struggled to survive. The world became a dark, sparse forest of abandoned civilization. Broken cities grew gray and dangerous. Lurking in this new landscape were hunters, humans, and vampires, as well as an abundance of animal life. The species at the top of the food chain was uncertain.

In 2115 the human government—who at the time still had some authority over the hunters—attempted to take back military control of a place called the 'White House,' in a land then recognized as 'America.' Some humans resented the leadership the hunters were asserting over the survivors, others feared them. The government still had many weapons they'd been storing and utilized in a last attempt to regain their lost civilization. Many vampires, humans, and hunters alike were wiped out in this last act of rebellion. This foolish action allowed the Vampire Council to dominate the war. It was the humans' final failure. This was when communication between the human government and the hunters ceased completely. Hunters took control both of themselves and of the responsibility to build and protect the remaining human population.

It wasn't until the late 2200's that the Guild noticed a change of estranged behavior in some vampires. Usually, they were strategic, intelligent, sharp, and restrained. However, some of them lost their humanity, deranged and devoid of any intelligent approach, and would seemingly hunt and feast on anything with little control, we titled them- the sabers.

Now, in the year 2341, we continued our ambition to protect the remaining humans and take down the Vampire Council. Although the humans created us, we acknowledged they were incapable of looking after themselves. It was for their own good that we were in complete control of their well-being as we were made to be. Our camps were evidence of this. We nurtured them and ensured their survival as a species. It was, after all, embedded mechanically into our genes.

Amongst our hierarchy and fellowship, there were always a few elites who were positioned as leaders of their small raid groups of between six to eight members. These hunters were superior in organizational skills, fighting, speed, talent, stamina, and war tactic and would lead their team beyond our walls. They were known as Token Hunters.

At eighteen, it was an honor to be named Token Huntress as one of the youngest announced hunters within my Guild.

CHAPTER I

THE STAGNANT AND dusty smell of the underground classroom was getting on my nerves. It was stuffy and boring to say the least. I looked at the small window that peered down into our class at the back of the room. I was desperate for the outside world and fresh air. The small window shunned any form of sunlight coming through offering the intended impression of imprisonment. What little light could seep through the dirt-covered glass only highlighted the dust particles that floated lazily above the heads of my equally bored classmates. The small room seemed crowded, yet there were only ten of us in total. The hunter to my left desperately tried to stifle a yawn, feigning interest in the class.

At the front of the room stood our teacher, Miss. Femine, who spoke nervously and under inspection by our formidable Head Huntress, Miss. Campture, who stood at her side. There was only one exit door positioned next to the large chalkboard, and, almost metaphorically, Campture blocked it. She often came to check up on the classes. We were expected to be knowledgeable in all fields, and Campture monitored our progress like a hawk. Our education didn't cease until we reached thirty years of age—only then were we deemed intellectually competent. Her radiant yellow eyes rested on each of us in turn. Her long snow-white hair was as stiff as the air in here, and her frown lines were visible from four desks away. Miss.

Campture's eyes locked on mine as she telepathically overheard the insult. I diverted my gaze, certain I'd been busted. Every hunter had a gift and hers, unfortunately, was the ability to read minds.

I tapped my fingers lightly on the leather garter that was strapped around my hips, trying to distract myself from any further thoughts while she stood in the room. I focused on my fellow hunters instead. They varied in age, from eighteen to late twenties. All of their eyes glowed iridescently as they upheld more attentiveness than usual. Their unique eyes were the physical feature that claimed them as hunters from birth— the defining feature that differentiated them from the defenseless humans. I'd watched all of them discover their gifts and abilities on their eighteenth birthday which would ultimately assign them into the division within the Guild they'd work.

All of them had honed on their special ability unique to them that immediately showed itself on their eighteenth birthday with telltale signs. Ever since they'd been mastering their gift. Well, everyone's except mine. I fixated in Femine's, direction pretending to listen as I revisited that all too frequented memory of waking up on my eighteenth birthday to discover my fluorescent purple eyes permanently washed into a dull gray, no gift apparent, and a void to be left in the wake of my mother's death on the very same night. I stopped thinking about my creeping suspicions around my mother's death with Campture in the room.

I'd only been permitted to stay within the Guild because I was born hunter. They also couldn't deny my ability and superiority in combat. I was the most skilled in my generation of hunters. I excelled in both raids and in battle. My speed, stamina, strength, and tactical projections in battle were unprecedented. Undeniably, I was the best of the younger hunters we had within our Guild.

Campture's cough snapped me out of my idle thoughts. She was intently staring at me. I really hated that she could read my mind. I trailed my gaze over the bulky arms of my boyfriend, James, who sat in the front row. We had been 'official' for a little over two years, the label mostly for his sentimental desire. His blond hair had been recently shaven, standardly as he did every month on the same day. He must've felt my gaze because he peered over his shoulder, worriedly staring at me with his fluorescent green eyes. An agitation rose in me, as it always did when he looked at me so pitifully. Since suspicion amongst the Guild surrounded my eighteenth birthday and death of my mother, he looked at me the same, as if I were a fragile, flightless bird. We no longer agreed on much. Instead of retribution and revenge—he believed in reservation and safety as if I was some weak animal that needed to be protected within the walls. And despite not being dependent on an exceptional gift, I was announced Token and was far superior in many ways.

I turned my gaze to Femine as she raised a weapon called a *chainsaw*. We'd heard of them before—they were tools from the past. The weapons craftsmen had now reformed them, utilizing them as a suggested weapon. Tanya, a huntress whose ability allowed her to harness electrical currents, had obviously been put to use. At first, the Guild wasn't sure how to use her ability; after all, the time of electricity had long passed. Now, at sixty-five, she harnessed one of the most invaluable gifts within our Guild.

Femine hoisted it with little effort. A former raid member, she now mentored the new generation, though the muscle in her arm and delicate movement exhibited the warrior she was once, and still was. "The chainsaw was commonly used in the twentieth century to cut down materials such as trees and wood. However, after some adjustments, we've supplied it with enough battery life that it'll be useable for a few days before needing to be recharged. Does anyone have any comments on how they think this may fair in battle?"

Corso, a hotshot, spoke out like he always did. He was one of those *I-know-everything* kind of guys, and sadly, James' best friend. "It would be awesome," Corso enthused, unknotting his legs from atop the table. It was the only time he'd shown interest in this class, despite Campture's leering presence. "It could last the duration of a typical raid. We could use it to cut down supplies swiftly, and it'd leave some pretty severe damage in a fight. You could easily target and dispatch a vampire's arms or legs if you don't have immediate time for their heart or beheading. I think it's an exceptional new development." Corso leaned back into his chair and folded his arms smugly. *Kiss ass,* I inwardly thought.

The only way to truly kill a vampire was by beheading or piercing their heart. The idea that fire and sun were the only methods to kill them was quickly scratched out in the 2000s—because at some point, they had evolved. Sure, their skin melted in the flames, but it was a slow process, and they'd find a way to extinguish the flames before it took any real effect. And the sun, well, no one truly knew how long it'd been since they could walk out into the sun, and it was something that wasn't accounted for in the technology eras war.

I pushed away part of my golden-blonde fringe that was bothering my eyes. The strands had strayed from my tightly bound braid. I deliberated between fixing my hair and entering into an argument. Though, I could never miss a chance to be right.

"It's impractical," I stated. Corso's head whipped around, his fluorescent red eyes raging. He hated being challenged, especially by me, what he deemed to be the mutt of the group that could still kick his ass.

"Esmore?" Femine prompted.

"It's slow, bulky, loud, and can only be used at close range. No better than a blade or sword, weapons that *can* be administered into the chest quickly. Our only advantage is that we can match the speed and strength of vampires, so why would we use a weapon that could slow our movement down? We've been using the same tools for hundreds of years. In what world would something so heavy and bulky ever be practical in a fight? We're not out there to display new gadgets or to show off that we can revive useless items that should have been left to rot. Most of the vampires out there are far older than that, they know how a chainsaw works. We're living in the year 2341. We shouldn't be attempting tricks; we should be sticking with what has kept us alive all these years."

"I could easily use it in a fight and would have a far greater kill count than you," Corso said viciously.

I gave him a smile that didn't reach my eyes. "You couldn't stab yourself with your own knife even if you fell onto it," I said, and then looked back to Femine. "This isn't about who kills the most, this is about practicality and keeping ourselves alive out there." This was our first basic rule in training and yet hotshot here always had something to prove.

"That's all it ever is to you, isn't it, Esmore? Keeping yourself alive?" Corso sneered. "My, what a huntress you are. I intend to kill those vampires who slaughtered so many of our kind. But it's okay, you can hide behind me if you like." He shrugged his shoulder and dismissed me.

I briefly looked at James, who was practically begging me to stop through gaze alone. Only two months after my mother's death, and following the death of our Token Hunter, Drue, I was put in charge as Token Huntress of the new squad. Although a lot of the older hunters didn't much enjoy the announcement and role change, I had since brought everyone back safely, with zero counts of death on my team. I wasn't a huntress to dare in gamble play or risk taking. The survival of my team was paramount. "Then may I make a suggestion? On the next raid, you lead, Corso. I mean, it's not like I know what I am doing as *Token* Huntress. Why don't you and your chainsaw take center stage?" I mocked. "That's what you want isn't it, a moment to show off how big and strong you are?" We locked eyes. It was like watching an animal be ensnared in a simple trap. His red eyes glowed at the thought of being in charge.

"I will. Miss. Campture, did you hear that?"

"Esmore," Campture growled.

I never asked to be Token Huntress, and it had taken me some time to adjust to the new responsibility, especially when dealing with those who opposed my promotion considering my lack of gift. Despite my disposition, I wasn't willing to risk my teams' lives which meant as a newly founded team, we had the least amount of vampire strike rates and had no intel on the Vampire Council's location. But I'd rather the lack of vampire kills opposed to a death count of hunters shadowing my steps.

Campture shook her head, her icy silence breaking for the first time since stepping inside the room. "Corso, such a thing will never happen for you."

"Perhaps, though," Femine ventured, eager to please, "Corso could trial it in the next raid?" I diverted my gaze to the former raid member. I was shocked by Femine's push on the matter. Surely, she understood more than anyone the risks involved in using such a predated weapon.

A low knock on the door interrupted the thick tension. Kelf, an older hunter now in his fifties, addressed Miss. Campture. I honed my sensitive hearing pointedly toward their conversation. As they whispered and everyone began to chat amongst themselves, James rose from his seat. He approached my table and requested that the hunters sitting next to me move aside. I ignored him and strained on the conversation between Campture and Kelf with little remorse about eavesdropping. If it was private matters, they would've left the room.

"Two vampires have been spotted not far from our walls. They're alone, but the first raid team is still currently out," Kelf said quietly.

"Es?" James interrupted as he settled beside me. He used that tone when he wanted a heart-to-heart chat. It was usually a precursor to a long and bitter fight because I didn't like being told what to do.

I stood up, uninterested in enduring another one of *those* talks. "There's something I need to deal with," I said abruptly, grabbing my Barnett crossbow that I always kept close by. My leather pants swept past James' leg. He caught my hand and looked up at me with saddened green fluorescent eyes. I arched my eyebrow in challenge. Would he really try to stop me in my duty as a huntress, especially as his token?

"Be safe," he said hesitantly. I let a breath escape, trying to persuade the quick-rising anger to push back down.

"Always," I soothed, rubbing my hand over his shaven face and kissing him on the lips. I walked confidently toward Kelf and Campture.

"I never said that I wanted you to go," Campture lectured.

I dismissed her comment with the slightest flick of my head. We both knew that she did. Narrowing my gaze on Kelf, I asked, "Where are they?"

"Toward the river on the east, within range of our fishing nets," Kelf said, stepping aside.

"Thank you, Kelf." I nodded to Campture in respect. Although I had my suspicions about her secretive nature and bearing of news about my mother's death, I did respect her for looking after the Guild. We'd been hidden in this location for fifty years, with no threat of being found by an outsider. Not even other Guilds knew our exact location which was safer for everyone.

I curbed my thoughts around Campture, trying my hardest not to be caught out, and pulled into questioning as I speculated her character and my mother's passing.

I walked through the quiet and ghostly white walls of the corridors before turning toward the exit. If someone didn't know the tunnels in this underground system, they could get lost very quickly. Although our home dwellings were posted above ground, our basic training, classrooms, weapons, and storage units were below. I climbed the stairs quickly and stepped out into the dull sun. It was a depressing sight that greeted me. The metal walls were covered in organic moss and vines that kept our Guild well hidden. Though it served its purpose to protect us, at times it felt like a prison as opposed to a sanctuary.

I looked up at the dull gray sky. The bright blue was a rarity to see in these parts. The effects of pollution from long ago still hung in the air, an eyesore and disadvantage for humans and mammals who couldn't see through it.

The Guild Hunter in charge prior to Campture had sought this location strategically; there was optimum light where we were based, well, best as there could be. We were well hidden amongst the forestry, with a river on the east for fishing. The woods also provided a practice ground for hunters who were in the first years of their training. The roar of the river close by drowned out the sounds of our animals in the farming section of the Guild.

My eyes fell on some young apprentices who were training with bows. The youngest there was four, his bright orange eyes fixated on the target.

Rules, regulations, and principles were embedded in young minds from the start. From there on, various training and tests were administered on a weekly basis. Our teen years were the most torturous, with hormones and hierarchy in question, our skills were evaluated and judged every step. It was our gift that was the final nail in the coffin to what section within the Guild we'd be assigned. Some were prematurely selected for raid teams, having displayed efficiency for war tactics prior to the revelation of their gift. The others were segregated into less confrontational sections. At eighteen, we were no longer considered as apprentice hunters.

I greeted the three hunters who watched over the east side wall. They slowly opened the doors with thick rope, their bulky arms tightening as they pulled. One of the younger apprentices ran out after me, clutching my long sword. It wasn't overly thick, but it was elegant, and I could use it swiftly with as much damage as the bulkier ones.

"Esmore, you forgot this," she called, pushing it forward meekly.

"Thank you, Urabell. But I was informed of only two vampires." This information alone was enough for any raider to know that my Barnett crossbow would suffice, but the implication was lost on her. She glanced at me quizzically. Urabell looked to be only fourteen, and she was of lower intelligence than others her age. She would never be a part of any raid team, but perhaps she would excel in the cooking sector. I grabbed my sword and sheath, thanking her once again before she ran back toward the underground system. I stepped through the doors listening to them close behind me. Finally, I was alone.

I followed the small man-made trail that reached the fishing nets at the water's edge. I was always invigorated to be outside the walls and in nature, despite the dull coloring. The sun could be dimly seen behind the clouds. The trees were dire, near dead looking, and the leaves had stiffened in time, still attached to the branches in a sickly manner. A novelty I once had as a teen was envisioning what they might've looked like when they were beautiful and green like they had once been described.

A thick fog swept through the trees, settling on the land. The fog was far worse in the old cities. It streamed from the sewage pipes, even though they had collapsed so many years ago. The earth had lost its original beauty. The fog swept past my ankles as I walked even now. It felt like the land of the dead was stepping aside for the remainder of those who were living.

I stepped over a gaping crack in the ground that etched deep into the earth—the result of an earthquake. The ground shifted a lot more nowadays than it did in the technology era. It looked as if the earth was in pain with open wounds.

The last shipment of humans had been caught in a minor earthquake as they were carted to their new safe human camp. No one had been harmed. There were six of them, a large group, and although I found and saved them from a small herd of sabers who had sniffed them out, I didn't feel a loss as we waved them goodbye. We had a protective instinct for humans. But over time, it became merely a job. We held no special feelings for them. In fact, the more research I did, the more repulsed I was by their selfish actions. I would continue to do the task I was born to do until the day I died, but I held no respect for their kind. When found, they were transported to the camps we created for them.

Our camps were efficient, and, most importantly, safe. They cropped their own food, gathered their own water. Finding locations for camps was hard. Soil for farming was scarce. The human camp closest to us was connected to the same stream of water as our Guild. The humans then had to boil the water to purify it and make it drinkable. Every two weeks our transport team would go to them, supplying them with what we found on raids and what we had hunted for them. In the human camp, only a few could hunt properly. It made me question whether all human camps were like this, or if other Guilds across the world had to provide so much more to keep their humans alive. I'd never come across another Guild, though my mother had informed me of meetings and her time spent amongst others of our kind. We were scarcely scattered throughout the world.

I heard a splash of water and crouched to the ground. The vampires were ahead, not that far from me. I crept closer to peer at my unsuspecting prey. There was a female figure caught in one of our fishing nets. Her very youthful, glowing complexion implied she wasn't vampire, but a human. I examined them for a moment. The male vampire wasn't overly aggressive toward her. Instead, it seemed, he was using his elongated nails to cut through the net. He was obviously on the cusp of becoming a saber. Sabers were vampires of any age that had lost their minds. Once they became a saber, they couldn't retract their claws or fangs and held no rational thought. Their humanity left them, leaving a shell of a monster. At least the vampire members within the Council could control themselves slightly, but this kind was the worst. This one had not fully turned. I estimated he had about a week. Actually, I estimated he had about twenty seconds.

I stepped out from the bushes. The girl looked up at me, frightened. "Run, Chris!" she shouted to him as she noted the crossbow in my hand. I cocked my head slightly to the side in curiosity. Was the human trying to protect the vampire?

The pale, blue-eyed vampire turned on me, his fangs ejecting as he stretched out his fingers. I must admit that the absence of the iridescent eyes that marked me as a hunter often gave me an advantage. Usually, they didn't know who they were pointing their disgusting fangs at.

I pointed my crossbow at him. If I were only human, I would never be able to match his speed. I would never be able to pull the trigger so quickly. But human was something I was not, and pulling the trigger brought me much satisfaction. His instant, surprised expression startled the girl and she screamed. I had pierced him straight in the heart. He staggered before falling backward into the dark water. His pale skin turned a ghastly black as he floated limply. By nightfall, his corpse would deteriorate into nothing, polluting the earth further.

"Nooooo!" The human girl tangled herself further as she tried to reach him. Her scream pierced my sensitive ears. She thrashed in the water as she tried to swim toward him.

"You do understand what he was, don't you?" I asked her, mostly out of curiosity. I had never received this reaction from a human I had just saved from a vampire.

"I love him!" she wailed.

My eyes bulged at her confession, and then I simply laughed. It was a malicious and dry echo that found no humor. I strapped my crossbow to my back. She looked no more than sixteen. "Dear child, vampires do not feel. He was merely trying to eat you." Within seconds I was by her side, cutting away the fishing nets.

"Don't touch me!" she screeched, pointing her finger at me. "We only just escaped that horrible Council together, and now I have nowhere to go!"

"The Vampire Council?" I asked in surprise. "Where is it?"

She lifted her chin in an act of defiance but quickly crumbled under my intimidating glare. "I don't know," she admitted, looking back at the decomposing vampire corpse. "When we fled, he took me on his back. I was asleep. We just wanted to be happy..." she trailed off. "I loved him."

"You don't know what love is. We need to go now," I stated bluntly. What could she possibly know of love, especially with that of a vampire?

"With you...? No, you're a murderer," she whimpered.

"No, I am a huntress."

Her blue eyes widened again as she looked from me to the vampire's body. "But… your eyes?"

The mere mention of it insulted me. Was my skill not enough to show I was a huntress? "You either come with me now so I can have you shipped to your fellow humans, or you can be eaten alive out here." I looked down at the vampire's corpse. "Beside your *love*." I began walking toward the Guild. My job here was done. Whether the human followed or not, I didn't overly care. Though, I knew she would.

I paused momentarily, raising my hand in the air, gesturing for the girl to stop. I scanned the trees and honed my hearing, scattering it back and forth in every direction. I had the acute awareness of being watched. My stomach fluttered with an unknown sensation. I narrowed my gaze, feeling the presence that lingered a moment longer. Before I could step toward its direction, it faded into the background. I hitched my crossbow over my shoulder. Had I imagined being watched? My eyebrows furrowed. I'd never doubted myself before. I waited a few more moments, certain that we were entirely alone. I could only rely on the creeping suspicion that whoever or whatever lingered felt my presence and made themselves scarce. Still, to have someone or something so close to the Guild wasn't a good thing. I flicked my fingers at the girl, indicating that she could walk again. Even if she was sobbing after her so called beloved, I was certain she'd follow.

Whether vampire, hunter, or human, we all had something in common and that was desperation to survive. And, like a moth to a flame, she followed. Together we walked in silence toward the Guild. The hazy mist darkened as the sun slowly went down. Howling rang out as the most barbaric kind of vampires swept through the forest.

CHAPTER 2

I HAD TO slow my pace so the human could trail behind. She was fragile and frightened after her seemingly appointed guard and lover had been disposed of. We weren't far from the Guild. The girl would be fed, and by tomorrow the transport team would escort her to the human camp, where she would be looked after by her own kind. Without my intervention, she would've only lasted a few hours in the night.

"Where are you taking me?" The girl sniffled as she tripped over a log. We were so close to the wall already that I flagged one of the archers to open the gates. The clunking noise was heard before we could see the fog breaking ahead of us as the gates opened.

James was there, waiting patiently with his arms crossed over his chest. "Ah, thank goodness," he said, walking toward me. It agitated me that he would think something might've gone wrong. I was more competent than he was in battle. I would not be put on a pedestal because I was *his* woman without a gift, and he often pushed for that.

A fleeting memory returned to me as I recalled the first raid I'd been a part of at sixteen. My mother was standing in the same spot as the gates were pushed open and she greeted our group. Hunters limited their display of emotion, but my mother had come rushing toward me with a relieved smile. She wiped vigorously at my face where blood had splattered across it after Drue had stabbed a saber in front of me. It was only supposed to be a simple day raid, but it went on longer than expected, and we were forced to travel at night. We were attacked by a pack of them, but Drue had ensured all the apprentices were brought back safely. I pushed away my memories in case Campture was close by. Though I wasn't sentimental, there was an unfurling anger in me that rose when I thought of my former Token, mother, and even father. I looked into the distance and toward the solace place of our temple where the deceased had been buried. There I could sift through these uprising thoughts that welled, a lingering darkness of anger and inability to do anything to return those who I loved.

"Es?" James' words broke me out of my trance. I was staring at the place where my mother had once stood. "Are you okay?"

"I'm fine," I said, addressing the girl behind me. "We need to prepare her for travel tomorrow. I found her with the vampire. They were… together."

"Together?" James repeated questionably.

One of the guards attended the frightened girl. "She claimed she loved the vampire," I said with distaste. As ridiculous as it sounded, we had to take every word seriously after she claimed to have been held within the Vampire Council.

"She *loved* him?" James repeated in bewilderment. He shook his head. The girl must've been so brutally tortured within the Council that she became deranged and fixated on her captor. "Hey, Es," he said suddenly, grabbing my hand. "Before your duty on the wall tonight, come over to mine?"

Last time I had gone to his home, he wanted to yet again pursue the details of our future and voice his concern for me as Token Huntress. His new fixation to protect me behind the walls since the discovery of my lack of gift infuriated me. What initially drew me toward James was his strength and challenge. I respected him as a fellow hunter. I was sixteen, and we had both become flirtatious with raging hormones. Many of the younger huntresses wanted him. He was, after all, attractive and considered one of the rising hunters of our time, equally established like myself. I'd jumped at the chance to claim him as mine.

But after my mother's death, much changed. I didn't want to be 'just' his. I was my own hunter and hated the thought of someone else trying to control my life, especially someone who claimed to love me. It all came down to control. Only one of his parents was a hunter, so when he was born with his fluorescent green eyes, he was separated from his human mother. That was why he clung so tightly to the thought of a family- one I wasn't ready for. Now when I looked at him, he always seemed so sad. Although I put distance between us at times, I still cared for him- he was one of few I had remaining. I often fought with myself at how I mistreated him.

"We can do that," I agreed.

He smiled with relief, obviously expecting a different answer. "That sounds good. I'll see you then. His grip tightened around my hand as he pulled me toward him, kissing me on the lips. He cupped my face with a lingering look that insinuated he wanted me to stay the night.

"Hey, Es," Dillian called out, walking toward me. James and Dillian greeted one another briefly before James left. When James turned his back, Dillian looked between us and mouthed, 'All good?' I mouthed back, 'Tell you later.' We'd been close friends for years and sparring partners for even longer. He had iridescent pink eyes and long, black, shaggy hair, with four metal bars in his ear. He looked harsh and grungy on the outside, yet he was the most sensitive hunter I had ever known.

"I can take this one if you want me to?" Dillian said, gesturing to the frightened girl, who trembled at the sight of Dillian's rough exterior.

"Yeah, you take her. You're always best at empathetically assisting them in transition," I noted, adjusting the strap of my crossbow.

"You make it sound like such a system." Dillian chuckled to himself. Where most hunters had some empathetic capabilities, I found myself stifled at connecting with any form of emotion. I only understood duty, strength, and intuition. Before I could speak, Dillian interrupted, mocking me, "It is a system," he said, pulling a face and pretending to be a sillier version of me, one of which I had never displayed. I punched him lightly on the arm in a show of humor and zest. Dillian had always made my social cues easy to follow.

"I should report to Campture." I sighed. Though before I did, I wanted to clear my head of all these racing thoughts that were bubbling inside of me like a miasma. Why were they coming forward today after my months of training for them to stay down?

I looked toward the closed gates with the lingering impression I was being watched. I couldn't rein in on its exact location, but a powerful presence felt like it was overwhelming me and yet I picked up no trace of sound or smell.

"Cool. Are you on wall duty with me tonight?" Dillian asked, cracking his neck and pulling me out of my sudden fixation. "Es?" he said, clicking his fingers in front of me. He gave me an odd expression.

"Wouldn't miss it for the world," I stated sarcastically. It had always been one of Dillian's favorite catchphrases. I patted him on the shoulder. I needed a moment of silence before I reported to Campture. The girl behind me began crying as Dillian approached her. He might've looked scary, but he was one of the kindest and most human-like when it came to freely expressing emotion.

I knew I'd be reprimanded for not reporting to Campture straight away, but needed a moment of silence to squander these bubbling thoughts. While walking alongside the edges of the wall, most of those who were on guard ignored me, though some attempted to wave in greeting. I returned the gesture but chose to avoid the dining areas and main residential area, lacking in the mood to bump into anyone and discuss private concerns.

I rounded to the back of the Guild and toward our shrine which held our deceased. I was pleasantly surprised that I was the only one there at dusk. It was surrounded by a white picketed-fence, and the grass was always maintained and kept green. It was a symbolic measure: because of the fallen, everything can still live and grow. Near the small gates of the shrine were thick sticks with cloth wrapped around them. Beside them was a silver container of oil. I didn't have any flame to light or show my proper respects.

A small white-pebbled path led to the shrine. Beside it was various flowers that hunters had left behind in secrecy. It was a tradition created by humans. We didn't keep gravestones as they did. Instead, inside the shrine we had small silver-plated squares. Behind them was a small canister of the dead's ashes. We were educated in human tradition that some would spread ashes over their favorite spot or in a memorable place.

The circular room was four stories high. It was almost full and construction of a second building would soon need to commence. There was no roof to the shrine so the dead could bathe in the sun and moonlight whenever they pleased to.

I sat in front of the shrine on the green grass, arching my legs in front of me so I could lazily rest my arms on them. The wind attempted to lift my heavy braid and pushed the grass around me.

I sighed, staring into the tall building that held my father's and mentor's ashes and the scribbles of mother's date and time of death. I found peace in my solitude. This was the only life I knew, and yet I felt disconnected from it. I had adjusted to my dull clear vision, missing the haze of purple hue of my hunter's eyes. Ever since the night of my eighteenth birthday, I felt as if everything had changed and I was the one left to deal with the suspicions and hushed whispers around my mother's death and loss of my gift- whatever it might've been. Or maybe I was the first defected born hunter.

Elder hunters remarked I was the first hunter to have lost their iridescent coloring—the trademark stamp of our identity. They asked carefully of one another when I was propped on a stage like some foreign species, what to do with me: *If she is not a hunter, then what is she? What is her ability? What is her place amongst us? What right does she have to lead us into battle?*

This went on for a week after my mother's death, and I had become so quiet and despondent in myself that I didn't care for the fight until that rising anger that pitted my stomach every day, caressed me into reminding them of who I was. Even with no apparent gift, I was still stronger and faster than any of my generation and surpassed even those who once mentored me. It was never the title of Token I had been after, but it was the exaggerated push I needed to prove them my worth, and so no one within the Guild would dare come after me as if I were some mutt of the group that needed to be disposed of.

Much like I had suspicions of my mother's untimely death. My mother was not weak, and I couldn't fathom the report of her death. My mother's gift had been nicknamed 'The Corpse,' and was phenomenally useful in both fighting and healing. She could submerge into a creature's body and replace their organ with her own energy. That was only if she wanted them to live, of course. She had killed many vampires during her rein by simply touching them and pulling out their hearts. But she had saved many hunters and human lives as well by replacing their damaged organs or limbs with her gift of healing energies to replace their 'broken' part.

On the night of my eighteenth birthday, my mother had been called in to assist Kelf with a last-minute scouting task. Reportedly, sabers were nearing our walls, and they went to dispose of them. In my opinion this was suspicious considering Kelf hadn't been beyond the walls in a fighting gesture for years and there were guards posted nightly who could've dealt with such a small matter.

Yet it was my mother who had become overwhelmed and sacrificed herself for Kelf's sake. By the time a second squad had come for back-up she had been dragged away. For months I'd been pitied and motioned that I was dealing with denial. I waited for my mother's return because I couldn't believe that such a vile and mindless creature could drag her away. And yet everyone so readily accepted the report fixating their suspicions toward what was to be done with me.

Campture showed little care in the loss. Though my mother and her never saw eye to eye often dividing leadership and followers within the Guild, my mother wasn't an unruly type, but she wasn't afraid of voicing her own opinion either.

My father had been killed when I was ten. He was a leading hunter who assisted the transportation of humans amongst camps. Thirty humans were found surviving in a small cave underground. With so many humans to transport, two raid teams had to assist the transport team, just in case vampires caught their scents. Unfortunately, the Council had intervened, and both my father and another hunter were captured as they intercepted the vampires and protected the humans. By the time their remains were found—by my mother and Drue, no less—only a portion of their corpses were found and brought back to burn.

I held distant memories of my father. He had trained me on the sensory side of hunter skills, such as patience, listening, concentration, and keeping my temper intact. I was an aggressive child, but he made sure that I quickly pulled that into line.

It was my mother who trained me in hand to hand combat from a young age and then Drue, my Token Hunter, whose team I had joined at only sixteen. I had highly respected him as a mentor and a fellow hunter. He too had been killed by an attack against the Council. A specialized team had been created for the task, and due to speculation days after my eighteenth birthday, I wasn't able to join movement outside the walls for six weeks. I wondered if I had gone that day if it would've made a difference. That all too angry presence began to ride. If I were fighting by Drue's side, then maybe I could've evened the disadvantage.

After studying a small moving camp attached to the Vampire Council, the team swept in closer, hoping to capture and collect further information about the Council's whereabouts. But the mission had been a risk, and for once, Drue's gamble did not roll in his favor. After two days of fighting, Drue and his members had been dragged away and we never saw them again. All but one remained, who was left to live long enough to come back and offer a message. 'They are coming for you,' the deranged hunter had whispered over and over again as she rocked back and forth. She was locked in a cell for questioning. By the time Campture reached her for interrogation the huntress had somehow died. It was the day after, Campture named me as Token Huntress of a newly formed group.

I took a heavy sigh, releasing the clump of green grass I'd scrunched up in my hand. Ever since the day my remaining parent was taken from me, life hadn't been the same. I couldn't fathom or process the change that stirred within me. I became entirely blank, devoid of my attachment to my mother and only focused on strengthening myself to hunt the vampires who killed her and my father.

The sun had completely fallen, and now I sat in the cold darkness. I could hear footsteps approaching the shrine in the distance and decided it was time to make myself scarce and report to Campture. I rallied my internal walls, making sure not to let anything slip in thought.

I walked toward the tunnels, waving back at those who offered me a small smile and ignored those who narrowly stared at me with bright eyes within the dark. Most of the hunters with my Guild had come around to my difference after I had taken steps to prove myself, but others still made sure to watch me closely. Irregularity wasn't something that belonged within the walls of any Guild.

Instead of stepping down and into the tunnels, I walked up three flights of stairs toward Campture's room. Her room was the highest within the Guild, and only a few short moments later, I found myself at Campture's large steel door. She was reading a book at her desk, pretending not to notice my entrance. I made myself comfortable in the seat opposite. I liked to unnerve her, simply because I didn't trust her, much like she didn't trust me. I could sense it. Campture snapped the book closed. "You're late," she hissed.

"I apologize," is all I said with no reasoning, nor did I plan on giving her one. I expected her to press the matter further but instead, she snarled and rolled her shoulders back in an attempt to make herself look more poised. "What do you have to report?"

"It was only a lone vampire with a young human girl of perhaps sixteen years of age. I killed it, obviously."

She nodded with approval. As was protocol, if our spotters found something suspicious or there were vampires nearby, we disposed of them. However, I had to confess my undoing. Had I asked questions first and shot later, we might've been able to interrogate him further about the Council.

"A blunder indeed," Campture grumbled, biting the tip of her nail. I inwardly hissed at her intrusion on my thoughts.

"Though the girl might be useful," I added. I had done what most hunters would've done. Shot a vampire on the spot. Sabers were useless in any regard to try to capture. Their humanity had long forgotten them. However, the two other factions were ones that we needed to approach with caution. Some were a part of the Council: tactful, clever, civilized, and self-regulated. We'd captured and tortured members of the Council before, but none had told us of their location. Campture's ability was also useless. It seemed that, like us hunters, some vampires also had gifts. And whoever was in control of this Council was able to haze the vampires' memories so no one could enter and inspect their minds. The Council often hunted for humans and took them back to feast on. It was an even larger gain if they could get their hands on us living hunters. Crazed vampires alike had salivated at the thought of tasting our blood. Supposedly we tasted sweeter.

Then there were the covens of vampires. They weren't aligned with the Vampire Council, but they weren't sabers either. They loved everything dark about being a vampire. They were the rebellion within the rein of the Vampire Council who played by no rules, only respecting the hierarchy in their own coven. They were ghastly creatures who ventured through the land in large packs.

"We haven't heard of movement about the Council's whereabouts for months, so why now? Why so close?" Her yellow eyes were quickly on me as I left my thoughts blank. It was something I'd become accustomed to when around her. I knew her distrust in me would have her searching for something further.

"When I questioned the Council's location, the human girl couldn't say. Perhaps if *you* pursued this further. Maybe her mind hasn't been tainted by the Council," I mused.

"Very well, I will meet the child tonight and question her before she is shipped off to the humans," she said, dismissing me. I stood tall, before charging for the door. How sad for this young girl to run away from the vampire Council and to have truly believed that she loved a vampire.

"And Esmore?" Campture drew my attention before I walked out. "Vampires do not know love."

I trembled with annoyance. I had let the thought slip when I considered the human's words.

Campture continued, "That girl did not love the vampire. I will inform the humans that she is sick and needs attending to when she arrives."

I gave her a twisted smile, one that conveyed I did not appreciate her squirmy tentacle-like mind. Her mouth twitched in displeasure as she witnessed what I perceived her mind to look like.

"Leave," she demanded. I made my way down the staircase, clenching and opening my fist, trying to center my anger. I halted when the cool air brushed against my skin. I had entirely forgotten to report the looming presence I felt while in the woodlands. I looked back up at the tower where Campture no doubt was still reading her book. But maybe I had imagined things.

CHAPTER 3

I STALKED TOWARD James' small house, where he lived by himself. His father, another casualty, had been killed when James was young. Since my mother's and father's deaths, I also lived alone. I pushed away the sad thought, looking into the sky. The moon was dimly glowing amongst the clouds, and the screeching of animals beyond the walls had already begun. I could hear in the far distance their lives being taken from them as they were torn apart either by one another or possibly even sabers deep within the forest. The world had gone through so much, yet most animals were able to adapt and thrive. Although the resources decreased such as preferred plants and water, the animals either became extinct, adapted, or mutated. The animal population had peaked many years ago until more vampires had lost their humanity and turned into mindless sabers. Now many animals were extinct, and those who survived adapted. It made food scarce for us, and as the animal population dwindled, so did the humans. We kept live animals within the Guild in the farming section. But for a survivor out in the wild, finding animals to live off was more difficult.

The homes were built out of stone and positioned close to one another. They were small homes with very little space to offer, but still everyone had their own door for privacy. Mine was located further in the back, right next to the Guild's wall. Often if I couldn't sleep, I would climb the wall by myself and watch the mist as it swirled through the woods. Further past the houses, I could see the outline of our farm. It took so long for the Guild to find land that could be efficiently used for crops. We had a few animals such as pigs, chickens, goats, and cows. We even had six horses, with a foal on the way. The horses were now used only for transporting the humans. They were once used for the raids, but it quickly became impractical. We could easily match their speed, and they became a liability as the vampires and sabers began hunting and feasting on them. The many cries and squeals of sixteen horses in one large raid being taken down by a pack of sabers pierced my memories. I was only sixteen then, and Drue had lost three hunters as well. We had lost so much to learn so little.

The doorways were short, and tall hunters like Dillian often had to lower their heads to fit inside the door. James' house was in the middle of the row of houses. A few sticks with flames rested along the path for anyone who was walking around at night. Most preferred to be within their homes at this time, but some roamed the grounds restlessly. I greeted one of the older hunters in passing.

I opened the door to James' home, where he sat patiently waiting with a few slices of fruit on the small wooden table in the middle of the room. Our food was supplied at the eating quarters, but sometimes we were able to take some home with us, not that we had any place to store it.

There were only two chairs, a single bed on the left, and a narrow bench along the wall behind him. Beside the door were a few of his personal weapons. Although there was a section in the Guild where weapons were supplied, the raid teams were able to keep their own collection within their home. There were no windows and only the candle he had lit on the table brought light to the room. The only weapon I had in my home was my crossbow. Sometimes I took my sword as well, but that was the property of the Guild, although everyone knew that I wanted to handle that blade and unofficially it was mine. Most of the other hunters used the larger bulkier weapons, which was why some struggled to hold their ground against the Council's tactical members.

"How did you get on with Campture?" James asked. He had changed into a tight-fitting sleeveless shirt.

"It was as fun as ever," I said blandly, looking at the various fruit on the table as I took my seat. There was a heavy silence as I grabbed a grape and popped it into my mouth. It was an overly bitter batch, forcing me to impolitely spit it into my hand.

"You know after you left to eradicate that vamp, Corso was permitted to trial the chainsaw in our next raid," he said, biting into one of the plums. It was a cooler night than usual, and a cool breeze swept through the room.

"Well, that sounds wonderful. Yet another responsibility I will have to handle." They were wrong about the predated tool, and I knew it would end badly.

"I don't know why you and Corso don't get along," he tried to soothe me.

I looked at the stone wall, trying to push my agitation away. "Is this why you asked me to come here?" I was so sick of him lecturing me.

"No, I'm sorry," he said earnestly, grabbing hold of my hand. He stood up, pulling me toward him with a shy smile. "I've missed you lately." He wrapped his arms around my waist. I dropped my shoulders, forgiving him, trying to let the moment sweep through me. I wrapped my hands around his neck, following his lead. His iridescent green eyes brightly shone when the flame flickered.

His waist was firm against mine, and his chest felt warm. He leaned in, kissing my forehead. He began to roll a small piece of my golden hair between his fingers. "Do you know that tonight is our two-and-a-half-year anniversary?" he asked, kissing me gently on the lips. His warmth filled me, and I could feel it slowly trying to creep toward my cold heart. "I know you didn't remember, but that's okay."

He parted my lips, and his tongue found mine. He pulled me closer to him, his hands lightly playing with the hair behind my neck as he pulled me to him. We moved toward the bed, James laying me down on it as he looked at me endearingly. "I love you, Es," he said, finding my lips again before I could speak. His large body swept over me with warmth, and his cold hand slid under my shirt.

I kissed him back, enjoying the relief that swept over my body. I didn't have to think of anything else when we were like this. I could simply be with him.

"You should move in with me," he said between kisses. His mouth began kissing down my neck. I opened my eyes and stared at the dark roof. He had broken our moment of silence and just being. When James went to press his lips against mine again, I pushed his chest away. He stopped and looked at me in surprise.

"James, we've spoken about this," I said, exasperated. Why did he have to push such matters?

He gave me a cocky smile, trying to dismiss the uncomfortable atmosphere.

Propping himself up on one elbow beside me, he said, "C'mon Es, your parents had only been dating two months when they married." He smiled.

I watched him with little reaction, but that bubbling sense of irritation rose when he would continue to push. "My parents are not me," I said, now propping myself up on my elbows so he was no longer lingering over me. The mood was gone.

"No, they are not. But you know I love you more than anything. Let me look after you," he yearned, reaching for a locket of my golden hair.

I pressed my hand on his chest again, pushing him against the wall as I slithered from the bed. I gathered my crossbow that I had left beside the door.

"What, are you going to run out again?" He flustered angrily.

Why was he always like this? All he ever wanted to do was cage me. "I've told you before, I don't want to get married, and I don't want children. I am a Token Huntress, and I will not let you take that away from me," I said proudly.

"You are something else sometimes, you know that?" he said, infuriated. "I am telling you I love you and want to look after you, and all you do is push me away. Tell me what I am doing that is so wrong?"

Here it was again, the same argument had aroused itself. "You are trying to control me. I am who I am. If you are looking for obedience in a woman, then maybe I am not the woman you should be after. I imagine that is what you tell Corso and the others, isn't it?" I asked spitefully.

His eyebrows knitted together in infuriation. "Well, at least they listen to me. You have changed ever since your mother died!" he shouted.

The air went still as my sharp gaze reached his eyes. My jaw clenched as I tightened the grip on my bow. No words could convey my fury at him. If it were anyone else, I don't know what I might've done. One of the greatest lessons my father taught me was how to hold my outbursts. I nodded my head, pinching my lips firmly together as I considered this lesson. Everything that boiled in my mind, every destructive word… I could not continue this pattern with him, because I knew shortly I would not be able to hold my temper anymore. Inside a darkness, an emptiness, swirled. I did not yet know how far it would go. His words that hung in the air were enough of an invitation for me to leave. I had nothing to say that would be productive in this conversation. I still felt a pang of anguish in my chest, not at the thought of losing James, but at my mother's memory and having her death thrown in my face. I turned and left.

After slamming the door shut behind me and slipping into the cool air,

I felt something wet on my face. I touched my cheek, revealing a tear. I was bewildered by such mixed emotions. *Why, why are we still together if this is the outcome of our nights spent together?* I knew within myself I could not choose James over my duties.

I stalked toward the northern wall, where, tonight, Dillian and I were due to keep watch. Perhaps Dillian had some insight for me. He understood human emotions far more than I ever did. Maybe he knew the answer as to why I would shed a silent tear.

CHAPTER 4

"THERE SHE IS," Dillian called out as I reached the northern wall. The sky was now fully immersed in darkness, and only a small portion of the moon shone through. At night, the mist grew denser due to the coolness of the air. There was a loud gurgling scream nearby, indicating that an animal had been attacked. I took hold of the rope ladder and climbed to the top. Dillian held his hand out to help me up. He pulled me to his side, and we sat for a moment in companionable silence. He was focusing in the direction of where the noise had come from. Dillian was one of our greatest spotters. His gift was a rare one. We had only known four before him. His sight was intensified, far more so than even mine. The fog and mist were not an obstruction for him.

His piercing pink eyes relaxed as he turned to me with a smile. "Only two sabers, but they've already taken off in the opposite direction."

I nodded, happy with that. I placed my crossbow beside me as I dangled my legs over the wall, looking at the dim moon. Dillian had his legs scrunched up, his knees near his face.

"Did you guys get into another fight?" Dillian asked softly.

Now and then we lightly touched on our romantic interests, but most of the time we talked about anticipated combat and upcoming raids. Dillian was a part of my raid team. When we were searching for something specific or had to go near a city, he would accompany us. Although not the strongest fighter, he had a mind for tactics. In fact, it wouldn't surprise me if he was nominated to become a Token Hunter in the near future, simply because of that overly smart brain of his. I had been promoted at a young age because of my superiority in combat and fast resolve. It outweighed even the older hunters who couldn't match me in a fair fight. I had a natural understanding of leadership, delegation, and coercing a group of hunter's gifts to our advantage. Dillian, I suspected, would be promoted because of his quick wit and ability to overshadow warfare and I respected his opinion on our raids deeply.

"Yep," I dragged the word out, considering it.

"What happened?" he asked, his eyes falling on the foliage in front of us. He was scanning through the trees for unseen dangers. Very little usually occurred, but precautionary measures were what kept us alive.

"He keeps trying to cage me, talking about me settling down and having his children. He doesn't want me to be a Token Huntress," I said. "He threw my mother's death in my face and said I hadn't been the same since."

Dillian paused for a moment, tensing. His shoulders dropped. Whatever he thought he had seen was obviously nothing. His fluorescent pink eyes flicked over to me as he placed a reassuring hand on my shoulder before speaking. "In a sense, he's right. You have changed." Dillian and I never pulled any punches; we were honest with one another, which was why our friendship worked so well. There were no theatrics. We were comfortable. "But I don't think that is something he has the right to hold against you. Esmore, you are an outstanding hunter. Your abilities are far superior to those of any other here, with or without a gift. If you think he is trying to cage you, then you need to really speak out. Try and make him understand. The Esmore I know would never let herself get cornered, whether it is out on the field or even within the Guild. You have always spoken your mind, a quality passed down from your mother, maybe you need to stop holding back. You never did before your eighteenth birthday so why hold back the punches now?"

I considered this for a moment, my shoulders slightly sagging in defeat. Maybe such a relationship wasn't worthy of my time anymore. Although, thinking of James with another woman made me feel slightly conflicted. I found it hard to understand or engage my emotions. Ever since my mother died, there was stagnation within me, preventing me from functioning properly. I was just so numb.

Dillian roughed up my golden-blonde hair playfully. "You will figure it out, Esmore, you always do." He continued scanning over the foliage. We were often positioned on this side because it was more likely to be populated with sabers or members from the Council. In the very far distance in the north was a large city. It was probably about a six-day walk for humans, but for my raid team, it was about an eleven-hour run. When we approached the city, formerly known as San Francisco, we required to rest the night before entering or executing any attack. It was an unfortunate way we differed from the vampires. All they needed was a little bit of blood to rejuvenate themselves. As for us hunters, well, we still needed rest to replenish our bodies. Not a lot, but it was most certainly something the vampires had over us. They could go without sleep and rest for days. We had to be cautious in the cities as sabers often gathered there in packs.

I leaned back on my elbows, my legs still hanging over the wall. "How did you get on with that young girl?" I asked. It piqued Dillian's interest, as I often didn't ask about the humans I found. He turned to me as I continued, "She claimed to have loved that vampire." I glanced at him. I had never met a human that claimed to love such a hideous creature.

"I know, she told me you killed her lover. She will be all right. She was slightly dehydrated, but it's only a temporary condition. When I left her, Campture arrived. I assume she's searching through her mind to see if she can find the Council's location." Dillian pondered for a moment, looking unsettled before he looked behind us. He lowered his tone. "Do you ever think that we are treating the humans like cattle?"

I raised my eyebrows at him, surprised by this reflection. "How so?"

"I don't know, I've just been unsettled by it for a while. I know we are protecting them and taking them to safety. But take, for example, that girl today. She was terrified when you found her, not relieved. And those that come through here, they seem to be similarly affected. I know some seek us out, but they are terrified of being transferred to the human camps. I feel like we are just shipping them off. I never understood why we couldn't merge both hunters and humans together again, like the old days. I don't understand why babies must be taken from their human parents if they have hunter's eyes. I know that we do it for survival, for both the humans and ourselves. But the more humans we transport, the more unsettled I feel by it. I just… I don't think there is such a huge difference between humans and ourselves. I think they want to learn how to defend themselves just as much as we do."

"But they don't have the hunters' skill, stamina, speed, nor gifts to match that of the vampires," I replied.

"It's not about matching us, it's about defending themselves so they don't feel so lost and helpless. Some have survived for many years out there without us. I get the feeling they don't feel safe even if we put them into a protected camp. I feel like we are taking away their options and rights by forcing them to be there." His pink eyes were damp. I tried to understand his thoughts and his sensitivity toward the humans, but couldn't comprehend it. I cared very little for the humans, and that was something we both knew. He gave me a smile, dispersing the tension. "I know you probably don't get it, I was just thinking, that's all," he said, dismissing the subject. "How come Campture has been on your ass more than ever lately?"

I sat upright, doing as Dillian had before and looking behind me in secrecy. If Campture was currently investigating the young girl's mind, then she wouldn't have access to my thoughts. I took that opportunity to divulge my deepest conspiracies. "Dillian, I think Campture is lying about my mother's death," I stated bluntly.

"What?"

"Think about it, my mother was one of the most ambitious huntresses here. She alone took down packs of sabers at a time. In what reality would she be taken down so easily? Kelf hasn't gone on raids in years, so why was it him who left the walls with my mother? Campture and Kelf have been close for a long time, and both are very secretive. I don't trust the story they've fed me." It all gushed out of me. I felt selfish for offloading it to Dillian. Now he would have to be wary of his thoughts around Campture as well. But if I could trust anyone with my secret, it was him.

He inhaled deeply, considering this. "Have you told James this?"

"No, you are the first person."

"Good, don't tell him. Who knows what sort of trouble it could lead to? I know he's your boyfriend, but this suspicion will only get you into trouble, Esmore. I know you miss your mother, but you cannot state this opinion so loudly. It is a form of treachery to go against, or even be suspicious of, Campture."

I crossed my arms, my jaw clenching as I tried to not let infuriation rain over me. "So, you don't believe me."

"I never said that." His deeper tone grabbed my attention. "Your suspicions are a reflection of what I have been pondering on for a while now. But, Esmore, right now there is nothing that can be said or done. I want to tell you to pursue your doubts, to find out what really happened. But I'm conflicted in giving you such advice because it's unhealthy to cling so tightly to the past, especially if it puts your life in danger. I want you to be smart about this, be safe. And I am sorry, but I think I should deter you from speaking of this openly within the walls."

He began searching over the foliage again. He was only four years older than me at twenty-two, but he always seemed far older mentally. I couldn't claim him to be unsupportive because everything he said was true. How was it that I could speak freely with Dillian, but when it came to James, I was secretive about my true feelings?

I ruffled my hair, agitated. "How do you and Julia do it? How do you guys not fight?" I asked, thinking of his loving relationship with Julia. She was part of the farming section in the Guild. It was fitting considering her gift was the enhancement of plants. When her gift was activated, the mist within the Guild's walls lessoned. She was only small in size, fragile-looking, with big blue iridescent eyes and long wavy brown hair. Dillian and her had now been together for five years. They were sweethearts from apprenticeship. They complemented one another perfectly—they were both sensitive to the humans, and they held a strong attachment to family members. Julia was one of the few who cried when we lost hunters. Although her mother frowned upon her sentimentality, it was what attracted Dillian to her.

A wicked smile crossed his lips in answer. My eyes brightened at its significance. I punched him in his arm, playfully. His smile only stretched further. "I am going to ask her to marry me," he said proudly.

I couldn't help but mirror his smile. "Well, it's about time," I said. "When?"

"In three days. It's her brother's eighteenth birthday, so we will celebrate the awakening of his gift. I want to ask on that day after the ceremony." His eyes held a glimmer over their natural pink. It made me feel overwhelmingly light to see him so happy. Dillian most certainly deserved it.

Crunching noises pierced my ears. I stood up sharply, grabbing hold of my crossbow. My glimmer of happiness distracted me from my senses. With relief, I quickly realized it was not a vampire near the wall. The noise was coming from behind us.

The glow of yellow eyes settled on me first. I watched Campture walk toward us, her face stern. "I've just inspected the young girl's mind," she stated as she stopped in front of us. Kelf also crept from the shadows behind her, obviously having been with her during the process. "You are to take your team on an inspection tomorrow of the city. Although the young girl's mind has been muddled, and her memory of where the Vampire Council location has been erased from her mind, I was able to dig up some memories. They were of fog-filled streets. It was all I could unravel. With so much fog, it leads me to believe at some point she was taken through the city. Or perhaps she and the vampire who was accompanying her were fleeing from the city. The Council might be residing there, and if that's the case, I want an inspection team to investigate it straight away. Until now, we've had no real idea as to where their location is, but have suspected in previous years they might have been hiding within the nearby city. Find what you can and report back. You are looking for signs that indicate the presence of the Council. This is not a raid mission, and you are not to attack. Your mission is to gather what intelligence you can about unusual activity in the city. We must be certain to find them before they find us. Be prepared to depart from here upon sunrise. I will have Kelf debrief your team."

"Of course," I said elevated. A small glimmer of hope that I could fulfill my purpose as huntress rose in my chest. Campture nodded curtly to Dillian before both she and Kelf marched off.

"Well, it looks like tomorrow will be an exciting day," Dillian said, nudging me.

"Finally, Dillian, we may have found a lead to the Council," I replied breathlessly. This was what I had been waiting for since becoming Token Huntress. The fangs there were as good as dead.

CHAPTER 5

WHEN THE SUN began to rise, I was quick to change into my black leather pants and a sleeveless leather shirt. I strapped my crossbow to my back, adjusting the straps between my breasts. I adjusted my garter on my waist, which held four small knives then slipped a smaller one around my ankle, inside my leather boot.

The crisp air of dawn greeted me as I left my home. I was on my way to meet with my team in the weapons room. James was sitting outside my door, waiting for me. When I emerged, he stood upright, his proper raid attire on—full leather—with a few weapons equipped. "I was on my way to the weapons room as well," he said quietly, in consideration for the other, sleeping hunters. I ignored him, still angry over the argument we had last night. I stormed toward the weapons room, with James following in silence. It was easier for me to avoid the subject and wait for time to stretch over it than to confront the mixed emotions and relationship talk.

But James only ever wanted to talk about our relationship. Right on cue, he interrupted the silence. We had just reached the stairs to the tunnels, which were dimly lit by flames on the wall. "We need to talk about last night," he said, sure of himself. It was always the same thing. I wasn't ready to settle for children or marriage. At only eighteen, I couldn't help but feel like it wasn't anything I would consider until older, if ever.

I walked down the narrow hallway, tilting my head as I listened in on a few of the hunters within the walls, already decorating themselves with weapons. They looked up in unison when I entered. This room was cleaned daily, leaving the floor, ceiling, and walls pristine white tiled and spotless. There was a silver bench wrapped around the room, where weapons were splayed out as the hunters carefully chose from the selection. If a weapon was idly left lying around or misused, the punishment for that member was being locked up for two days without water or food. We were forced to show respect for the weapons in this room at a young age; after all, the room was our everything, our first line of defense. On my left were numerous swords, knives, and blades on display, ones that weren't regularly claimed. Most were held up by a few well-positioned nails. In the left corner of the room was a tall wooden box. It had many separators in it where the swords were usually hung, but they were already claimed. My sword was still there, as it was off-limits to any other hunter. In front of me was a large mirror where hunters could appraise their apparel.

The twins, Kora and Kasey, were already prepared for departure. Both were cleaning beneath their nails, looking bored as they leaned against the wall. Directly across from me, Teary, the eldest of the group, was assessing her arrows. Pac was pacing in the corner. There were usually eight hunters per raid team, including the Token Hunter.

Teary, a huntress in her mid-thirties, had many daggers strapped across her body, with her bow and arrows on her back. She was a rather large woman, very muscular and tall. Her muscular arms often challenged James equally in arm wrestles. She had long red hair tied into a tight bun at the back. Her fluorescent orange eyes were a symbolic reflection of her invaluable gift. Teary was able to manipulate fire, although she couldn't create it. If it was within the vicinity of her, she could bend it to her will. The closer the flames were to her body, the easier it was for her to control. When the flames were hundreds of meters away, far more concentration was required, and at times it left her open to incoming attacks. Teary tried not to rely heavily on her gift alone, so she incorporated it with her weapons as much as possible. She carried around numerous lighters with her, and all her wooden weaponry was pre-dipped in oil. The common lighter had been replicated by one of our hunters, Reece, who had a knack for manipulating gases, and understanding the reinvention of archaic objects from the technology age. The greater the explosion, the quicker she could claim the flames as hers, instead of merely enhancing a small flame.

Teary was one of the older women I didn't have issues with. Some of the older hunters felt resentment over my authority. I found her gift and her attitude very useful when ambushing vampires. I often had her cover the back of the group as the rest of us swooped in. However, before I became a Token Huntress, Drue was in charge, and he did not use this structure. Most of the time he forced her to be a part of the initial attacking team.

"Was Reece able to bottle you some more gas, Teary?" I asked.

She had an unfamiliar accent, it was very thick, and her voice was quite masculine when she spoke. "I hav' al ten in my packet," she said, gesturing to the carry-case at the front of her stomach.

"Tested and range-approved?" I asked. We had to test the repercussions of the explosions because other hunters would be surrounding. We couldn't allow for any of the others to be swept in by the flames.

"Te range is about forty meters for the largest one, but that is only in case of an emergency. Te others are standard, within a five-meter radius," she answered.

I placed a hand on Pac's shoulder as he paced past me again, attempting to slow him for one moment. He simply nodded, confirming he was ready to depart. His skin was tanned, and he had very small eyes. He had short spiked black hair that was dyed blue on the tips. He was slightly smaller than me, but his size did not reflect his strength or ability. Unfortunately for Pac, when his gift of speed awakened, the constant shakes never stopped. As our 'run in man,' he was fast—extremely fast. For about two years straight, I challenged him almost every afternoon, but I couldn't keep up with him. We often had him race through areas we were unsure of or had him quickly gather humans out of dire situations. But the speed contained in his body forced him to fidget as he tried to control his ability. Not all of us had such side effects, but some did. Because of it, he hardly spoke, and when he did, it was too fast to really understand. Despite this, Pac had married. He had three children now. Unfortunately, one of them was born human. It was rare for such a thing to happen, usually with two hunter parents the child would be born a hunter as well. But his second child was not. That child was his only son, and his green eyes were a dimmer shade of Pac's. Within a few days of the child's birth, they were forced to transport him to the human camp. Although they did not cry, I could only imagine their resistance toward it, but it was one of the Guild's many rules.

I eyed the twins as we waited for Dillian and Corso to arrive and complete the team. They were identical twins, Kora and Kasey. Both had cut their black hair short into a pixie style. It was often hard to tell the difference between them. If it wasn't for my keen sight, I could not have told them apart. The only way I could was to identify the small scar on Kora's chin. I still forced them to wear different colored chokers and bracelets so the team could effectively tell them apart. Kora wore blue, and Kasey wore green. I had to enforce this because they liked to play immature tricks on the other hunters. They were easy to work with on the team, but outside of attacks, investigations, and raids, they were terrible. The separate colors were also necessary because of their gifts. Both *girls*—and I call them that because of their immature attitude, despite their age of twenty-two—had majestic coral-colored eyes. We used them as our perimeter trap. Kora had the ability to take mobility away from creatures. Kasey was able to project that ability further and increase it. Often, we used their combined ability to entrap our prey.

They were still disgruntled about me becoming their Token Huntress because of my younger age and lack of a gift. As well as that, they were both infatuated with James, even though we had now been dating for a couple of years. Their gift was commendable and had many times protected us from gory outcomes. But their attitude was something I often had to contend with. They were replacements for two of the older hunters who were a part of Drue's team, and then mine. They were both in their thirties, and when it was announced that I was to be Token Huntress, they forced Campture to move them onto another team. There were only four teams in total. Pride and arrogance was an interesting trait amongst the hunter kind. Most of us didn't work well together because of that defect in our personalities. When we worked together, we were a tremendous team. But outside of that focus, we all grew very tired of being around one another.

A shuffle behind me began as James made way for Corso to stride in. His red eyes were glowing as he tapped his fingers on the chainsaw strapped around his back. A buckle was secured on his stomach to help with the weight. My eyes narrowed on it, my rage boiling. "What is that?" I asked savagely.

"I approved it," Campture said as she walked in with Kelf by her side. The black bags under her eyes indicated she hadn't had much sleep. "We need to trial these things, Esmore, if we are to enhance our Guild. I will not debate this further."

The air stood still as James gave me a warning look to bite my tongue. I crossed my arms, holding in my savage words. *That thing is impractical,* I shouted loudly in my mind, watching her wince as my amplified voice echoed in her mind.

Dillian walked in behind Campture, stopping behind her and giving me a warning glare. Behind him I noticed two young male apprentices. "What are they doing here?" I asked sharply.

"Esmore, I warn you of your tone. You seem to have forgotten your place. This is Tori and Fam. Although they are only sixteen years old, their skill and speed are the best of the apprentices thus far. You will be taking them on their first raid."

"But we are going in to see if we can find traces of the Council. I can't take in two apprentices. What if we are confronted by a pack of them? It's another two lives I'm responsible for."

"We can look after ourselves!" One puffed his chest out at me. He had fluorescent brown eyes and blond hair that was cut short. The other puffed his chest out as well; he had a similarly cut style of black hair, with very pasty white skin and white eyes. I gritted my teeth together as I inhaled the boys' scent of testosterone. They hadn't even aged enough for their gifts to awaken.

"They are good in combat," Campture said after having read my thoughts. "And the point of this investigation is not for you to engage or confront a fight, but for surveillance. Really, it is a superficial task which they can easily be a part of."

"Did you really think that the Head Huntress would waste an important task on a newbie like you?" the apprentice with blond hair said smugly. I recognized him as the son of one of the older hunters who had been on my team before transferring because of my announced role. This apprentice thought he was far greater than he actually was and I wanted to quickly deflate his ego.

"Let me tell you two something, you little delinquents," I said, pointing my finger at them angrily. "You are to stand down and remove yourself from the high horse you are on. You will show respect to these hunters and huntresses before you." I raised my eyebrows as they both quickly adjusted themselves. Neither could meet my gaze. "You *will* do everything you are asked to, and without complaint. More importantly, you will never speak back to me, your Token Huntress, ever again."

"Yes, Ma'am," the one closest to Dillian said.

"Esmore," Campture growled. "You are to see me after this inspection. I've given you too many warnings about your intolerable behavior."

Dillian interrupted the tension before Campture or I could argue any further. I remembered much harsher words being spoken to me when I was an apprentice, but too often now when I had something to say, Campture would find a way to punish me for it. She truly hated me, and her yellow eyes were always trained on me and everything I did. Yet she was the one who promoted me to Token.

"This is Fam," Dillian said, grabbing the young apprentice with the white eyes and nudging him forward. He had been the one who was easily influenced by the other boy.

"And I am Tori," the other boy with the blond hair spoke up, slightly pushing his chest out again.

"You've given me children," I said in annoyance.

"Do you forget so quickly that this was once your situation when Drue took you out on your first raid? You will take them, no matter what you think about it. This is an order," Campture said dismissively.

Dillian gave me a fierce look which clearly said, 'No more.' It was hard to bite my words as I looked around to my team, agitation rising again as I stared at the chainsaw strapped to Corso. Having Corso on my team caused me great displeasure, but his gift was commendable. His skin could excrete acid. He was the slowest on the team; his hunter senses never seemed to have developed as much as the others, but his gift was easily used in situations of sudden torture if we needed to learn something quickly. It was also useful in preparing traps; if there was water in front of us and we needed to put some distance between us and the sabers, he could easily excrete acid into the water, burning the flesh of those who followed. I believed he was permitted to my team because of James' preference. Although James had no huge say, he did have Campture's interest if he needed something. He abided by the rules and regulations without fail. *Who could have asked for a better hunter?* I thought inwardly as I looked at him.

Grabbing my sword, I looked over my team. Usually, it was eight, but now it was ten. I couldn't help but look at the apprentices again begrudgingly. "Hurry with your weapon selection, we leave now. Depending on your speed, we may camp an hour away from the city before surveillance tomorrow. Everyone is to take the usual positions. Dillian, James, and I at the front. Teary, Pac, you both take the sides. Kora, Kasey, and Corso take the back. As for you two apprentices, you are to stay at all times within this boundary. You are not to change position, and you will not argue about it. Where we are going, we may come across a pack of sabers. You are to be on guard, and, most of all, quiet."

With that, I was satisfied that everyone would quickly gather their equipment and follow. I smoothly walked past Campture, my eyes conveying my mistrust in her judgment of the situation. I had a lingering feeling that having these two apprentices *and* the chainsaw as Corso's weapon was not going to lead to a pleasant outcome.

CHAPTER 6

THE MIST THAT steamed from the ground was cooler during the mornings. The already dead leaves that littered our path were shrouded in dew. Although I imagined a normal human would feel such coolness of temperature, I was comfortable in my sleeveless leather shirt.

We were greeted outside the gates by the transportation team. It was a small carriage with only two horses to pull it. A team of four hunters surrounded the cart. One sat at the front with the ropes to control the horses. This was the main mode of transportation now, although we could use the vehicles used until the 2150s. But of course, their loud noise drew too much attention from vampires. Also, it seemed a waste to place our supply of gas that we found on raids in such vehicles.

"Good morning, Esmore," the Token Hunter of the transport team said. Golipse was always polite; he was different from the rest of his moody team. Perhaps it was because he was older. He had also been well-acquainted with my parents, and because of that, I assumed he often went out of his way to speak to me. He had wiry white hair and milky white eyes. They were once white, but the haze over them now clearly indicated blindness. He had once been a part of the raids, but at the young age of twenty-four he was ambushed by the Council, and other members, including his Token Hunter, were killed. He was kidnapped and tortured for information about the Guild's location. Luckily for my mother's raid team, Golipse's gift was sensory, so he was able to feel the surroundings around him with exceptional awareness. He was also able to distort them. So, when my mother's team was close to where his kidnappers had taken him, his gift rang a siren of sorts, sending signals to her. They found the young Golipse and killed the members of the Council that had taken him. Unfortunately, his sight was already destroyed. They had dropped acid into his eyes; fortunately, it hadn't further reached into his body through his bloodstream, which would have killed him entirely.

The older we aged the more we learned about our abilities. Golipse was not only able to sense his surroundings, including if vampires approached them, but he could also disturb the environment. That meant that if he felt a vampire approaching, he could distort the surroundings, so we seemed invisible. This was a necessary ability to protect large cargos of supplies or human transportation. Although old and blind, he was still a fierce fighter from his many years in the raid team. Now looking into his white glazed eyes, I questioned how he must have felt when moved to a different team. It was unusual to happen, once you were selected for your position you would usually stay in such a place until your death. But Golipse, well, perhaps they took pity on him and pushed him into the transport team. Ten years after that, Golipse was now Token Hunter in that division.

"And a good morning to the fine Dillian as well," his smile stretched wider. Dillian was not too far from the carriage, folding back the thick material to reveal the young girl I had found yesterday. She shook vigorously from the cold even under her thick clothing. Her eyes lit up when she saw Dillian.

"You will be safe," he reassured her. His remorse and open display of emotion was something I often had the urge to hide from others. I couldn't understand Dillian's anguish over humankind. Empathy was not something another hunter would fail to notice. Often, I had to shield Dillian from the others, so they would not stare at him in mortification as he soothed the humans. Mercy and kindness were not common traits amongst our kind. Although I didn't understand, I would not attempt to stop him either.

"Be quick today, Golipse. I feel that the air may be far chillier this morning. Perhaps we're due for some rain, something which we cannot afford to be trapped in," I said, looking into the sky. Although through the trees I could see a glimmer of light, it was almost non-existent. If we were caught in the rain, this trip could go wrong quickly. The rain only heightened and thickened the fog, leaving some of the hunters almost blind. The uneven terrain also meant that it would probably flood.

"You don't have to inform me, young one. I can feel the moisture in the air against my skin," he said with a crisp smile. I felt foolish after I'd said it, of course he could. That, after all, was his gift. I was informing the wrong person entirely. I wished him a safe journey as he transported the human to the camp. The large doors creaked shut behind us. Golipse and his members started at a quickened pace on the southeast trail. With the horses' at full pace, they would arrive there within two days. Although they would have to walk day and night in darkness, it was unavoidable. We couldn't have the human camp and our Guild so close together in case vampires found either one.

"Let's move," I said, taking the lead. Although the apprentices seemed clumsy, they fell into position quickly. Once out of sight from the Guild, I breathed in heavily, slightly tightening the straps on the small bag I carried. We all wore a bag that held a few supplies for the nights that we would have to stay out in the open. Inhaling deeply once more and soothing my raging nerves, I looked at James and nodded to him. It was now time to quicken our pace.

It was something the Guild had taught us at a young age. There was running at our natural speed, which was still faster than any human, and then there was our heightened speed, which took an extreme amount of concentration. We had to train our minds on every movement of our bodies, shifting our muscles forcibly and in sync to propel us forward. It was exhausting, but something we had to do to cover more ground without horses.

The trees around us became a blur, the cool air tingled against our skin as we jolted heavily through the thick fog. We had to concentrate on every step to avoid stepping into the gaping cracks in the ground. As I suspected, the fog began to thicken, which led me to believe that it was soon to rain.

There was something odd about running together. Because everyone's senses were heightened, our movement and flow became attuned. If one quickly halted the others immediately did so as well. One scattered and unfocused individual could easily throw off the rest of the group. I wondered if vampires had a similar unison when they ran in packs. Much to my surprise, my initial judgment of the apprentices as weaklings was incorrect. They in no way affected our progress on foot.

Slowly, heavy spots of rain began to splatter. Until the black sky above us opened to a pelting storm. The fog had thickened, and I struggled, even with my keen sense of sight, to watch where I led my team, who were heavily dependent on mine and Dillian's direction. We were almost entirely pillowed in white. It had been raining for some time, and we'd run straight into the middle of the storm. Small streaks of blinding light flashed across the hazy colors of the sky. A loud bang rattled the ground, sending a quivering jolt up our legs as the lightning struck close by.

I felt one of my member's concentration stammer, startled by the flash of lightning. I quickly spun on my heels, collecting the young apprentice, Fam, in my arms as he tripped over a slippery mud pile. Instantly, everyone halted as I did. It only took a moment of distraction to land us on our ass in the real world. My strained eyes looked down at the startled apprentice as his white eyes scurried over where he imagined my face might be. Although I was holding him, he couldn't see me through the fog. "Thank you," he stammered. I tilted him back to standing. Only Dillian and I could make out shapes in front of our group. And now that everyone had reached their limits, we had to stop.

The rain dripped off my lips onto the muddy ground beneath me. I searched through the slight outline of trees. We couldn't run any further in this storm, we'd have to wait it out. I looked around at the others who did a similar sweep of our surroundings, I doubted they could see past their hands. I could not lead them so blindly. Although I believed in my ability to lead them safely, I couldn't be so selfish as to force them to run without their sight. "Dillian!" I shouted over the rain. Dillian knew what I wanted from him, and he projected his far keener sight into the distance. He was locating the closest place that offered cover nearby.

"Esmore," James said from behind, remaining in his position. His wet hand slipped over mine, and he grabbed me firmly. "Do you really want to stop here? At only midday?"

His question and anticipation were valid, the less ground we covered today meant the more we'd have to stretch tomorrow. And already our pace had slowed down significantly because of the rain. I reassessed my team. I could not risk them. Before I answered James, Dillian responded quickly, as if answering James.

"I can see an abandoned barn ahead. The house attached seems to have been burned down, but the barn still has a solid foundation by the looks of it," Dillian shouted over the pounding rain.

"And the radius around? How far can you see?" I asked, walking over to him. I couldn't see as far as him, but to know what direction I was leading everyone in was a very good start.

"I'm sorry, Esmore, I can't see too far past the barn. The fog is limiting even me," he shouted as another cracking bang rang out, dropping most of the hunters onto their knees as it rattled through their bodies. The thunder echoed throughout the trees.

"Be on your guard!" I shouted at them. "We're going for shelter and giving today a rest." I nodded for Dillian to lead us toward the barn. Although our speed wasn't as great as it had been that morning, it was a pace that quickly delivered us to our destination. As Dillian had mentioned, there was a wooden barn, and it wasn't as small as I had envisioned.

I searched the surroundings, even after Dillian announced it clear. I nudged the door open, searching through the empty barn. There were a few rotted bundles of hay on the ground. It had been abandoned long ago. There was a small wooden ladder that led up to a thin plank of wood that lined the barn, with a few windows on either side. There were three windows that could act as our lookouts. Although water leaked from the old roof, the fog was not as thick inside, and we could comfortably rest in it. And best of all, there were no vampires.

I flagged to everyone that it was safe to enter. The rain pelted against the shards of remaining glass in the windows. I had Dillian, James, and Corso each take a post by them. In such thick fog and rain, we'd have to be cautious of sabers or vampires looking for shelter as well. They could hunt by smell, and if they caught a waft of our scents, we'd be at risk of an ambush.

I rested my bag beside me, taking a seat on the hard wood beside the entrance. Kora and Kasey gathered in the center with the apprentices, who already looked exhausted from only half a day's run. I placed my crossbow beside me, took my sword from my sheath, and held it loosely by the handle as I pointed the tip to the ground. I wasn't at all happy with this holdback. We would now have to wait yet another day to venture into the city. I crept my gaze up the young apprentice, Tori, who walked over to me with a tight expression.

"We aren't tired. Just because Fam had a small fall doesn't mean we have to stop. We are fine and rested," he protested. I tightened my grip around my sword, annoyed by his insolence.

"Little apprentice, I did not stop because of you or your friend. We stopped because I ordered it so. And you simply do as I say," I said harshly. "How do you think you will get along in a raid team with such an attitude, once you are no longer an apprentice? Do you think other members will allow your tongue to speak so immaturely?"

"Immature, have you even grown breasts? Look how young you yourself are… you…" Before I could teach the child a lesson, Teary's firm and harsh grip dug into Tori's shoulder, slamming his knees to the ground as she held him. Her foreign accent was even thicker when she was angry.

"Ye little maggot, ye'll say no more. Esmore is one of te brightest Token Huntresses we av' within tha Guild. Ye will learn respect, boy, before I teach ye a lesson. Ye are far better off if it is me, than her herself."

Although I kept my stern expression, I was pleased by her kind words. It was nice to have someone say such a thing, especially a hunter who was so highly regarded by Drue in our previous group.

"She doesn't even have the eyes of a hunter," Tori snipped, trying to regain his composure. I allowed a demonic laugh to pass through my lips. I didn't have the greatest sense of humor; my smiles and laughter had quickly vanished after my mother's death. But getting a kick out of teaching a young apprentice a valuable lesson was an opportunity I couldn't let pass.

I drew both of their attention with my laugh. Teary momentarily paused as well. "Do you know why my bright purple eyes turned to a dull gray, young apprentice?" I said, cocking my head to the side and looking at him as creepily as I could. "Because on my eighteenth birthday, when my gift awoke, a demon form of myself appeared, and when it did, I consumed it entirely, its fiery wicked hair leeched out the color of my eyes as I engulfed it. Now, I do enjoy the hunt and the taste of fresh meat. At times, I often love to rip apart a saber's flesh, just for the enjoyment of my taste buds."

"You're lying!" he spat, but as he said it, I could see the faint hint of uncertainty reach his eyes. A small smile pressed at Teary's lips as well as Pac's, who watched from a distance. Kora and Kasey rattled the young Fam with their own malicious story. Of course it was a lie, but one which might deter the young apprentice from annoying me for some time now. And I couldn't deny that at times I felt something dark within me that felt foreign, perhaps what might be considered a demon.

"Well, you shall see," I said in a haunting whisper as I looked toward the door.

"Now ye've done it, ye best be going back into the safe company of ye friend Fam, better safe than sorry I say," Teary said, pulling him back toward the others. I peeked from the corner of my eye, noticing that although he pretended to be resistant, his feet quickly scuffled away from me.

After agreeing on the rotations for guard duty, the others rested. Sleep was something far from my mind, and so I stayed at my post even after

James insisted on taking my place. My team's safety was my responsibility, and it was not something I took lightly, not for any amount of sleep. I opened the door slightly, leaving my thoughts behind. I watched carefully through the thick fog and rain, making sure nothing would venture nearer during the night.

CHAPTER 7

A FEW HOURS later, Kora and Kasey happily woke the apprentices, who were not used to such early mornings. The girls kicked Tori and Fam in the stomach, perhaps not as gently as I would've hoped. Both of them had a mischievous grin on their faces, ready to kick again before they stirred.

After almost a full night of rain and lightning, the fog began lifting, and only dew remained. Stepping outside, we saw with relief that the early morning sun peeked through the trees. We were lucky no vampire smelled us out during the night.

"Find your positions again. Today there can be no delay. I expect we'll reach the city by midday. Pac, by the time we can see the city, I want you to do a run-through ahead of us. Dillian, keep your eyes sharp ahead. Kora and Kasey, be prepared. If the rain affected the city's fog, we might still encounter a pack of sabers during the day." Though sabers were sensitive to the light and habitually only hunted nocturnally. "If we come across a pack, I want you two to focus on locking them in. And everyone, remember our priority is to find clues about the Council's whereabouts. Be alert and try your hardest to remain in the shadows," I instructed.

Everyone quickly assumed their roles, and once again we ran together as swiftly and efficiently as we had the day before. The sun caught up from behind, silhouetting our shadows in front of us. Hours flew by in what seemed to be a merge of colors and a stream of wind. When we could see the city on the horizon, Pac disappeared into the distance with lightning speed. Minutes later, he reported back that he couldn't see any movement on the borders. He was only ever to approach the borders—I couldn't risk him going into the city alone.

We paused at the border, where an old, shattered tarmac road led into the forgotten city. During the last world war, this area was known as 'San Francisco.' There was a sign that stated it as we walked on the cracked road toward the city. This was one of the cities that hadn't been heavily bombed. It was the eastern and southern states of the former 'America' that had suffered the most damage.

I imagine San Francisco was once beautiful. Remains of magnificent buildings towered in the distance to form an elegant skyline. The city was mostly surrounded by water, but the rising sea had swallowed the edges of it to the west. I could hardly see the tops of the buildings through the mist that rose from the ground. Even through the fog, I could see that the city was built upon sloping hills; its buildings nestled on streets that gently rose and fell in height.

The mist was worse here because of the sewage pipes, and I could hear a constant wheezing noise hum through the city as if the earth itself was sick. The cockroaches grouped in huddles as they scampered into the cracks of the ground. Many buildings had burned down, but some still remained. I scanned the streets ahead warily. The road was lined with broken glass, discarded materials, and rats. The smell of unhealthy gases pained my nose. There were charred walls and shop fronts where fires had once been lit. Many bullet holes were embedded in the walls. Wiring hung from large poles. I was informed these were *electricity poles*.

It seemed the humans had overindulged in everything; life was in no way difficult for them. I would even say their spoiled ways were the reason why the remaining humans had no survival instinct whatsoever. They could not hunt, fight, or even tend to crops. These inadequacies alone greatly reduced the humans' numbers after the fall of the technology age.

"We will take the streets in the south and then carry through to the north. We'll camp an hour out of the city at nightfall, and tomorrow we will search more thoroughly in the other parts," I said, adjusting my bag straps loosely and retrieving my crossbow from underneath. Just for reassurance, I held firmly onto the handle of my sword to make sure it was also still there. Everyone else gathered their weapons. I grimaced in annoyance when Corso grabbed his chainsaw with a smug grin.

"Are we to gather supplies if the opportunity presents itself?" Teary whispered from behind me. Although this was not a direct order from Campture and we were only there for surveillance purposes, such an opportunity couldn't be missed.

"Nothing large, and no one is to stray from the group without my permission. Only take things so light that you can pack them in your bags. But remember, our priority is to gather information."

We crept through the dark streets, keeping tight to the decaying buildings' walls, becoming more cautious the deeper we went into the city. We wouldn't walk into the central parts of the city today. The city was so large, we could be here for days living off the packaged food in our bags. Once supplies ran out, we would have to return to the Guild.

We often raided this area in search of human survivors, but we'd never made progress on locating the Council here. Some hunters suspected they resided here, but after months of searching, we had to focus on other parts. Perhaps previous teams had been closer then they realized. This was my second time leading my team into the city, and it was something that brought me great distaste. Unsettlement lingered in the air. Our gaze collectively stretched over the vast emptiness, and a swift breeze that swept through the buildings added an ominous feeling of disorientation. Our eyes and ears strained for movement, and the slightest noise, such as a cloth trapped in broken glass, would cause us to stop in alarm, and assess.

We hurtled around a large building. A shadow's movement within the building across from us took my attention. I gestured for the group to halt, and they formed a silent wall around the window frame. Shards of glass edged from the frame. I wrinkled my nose at the pungent smell which emanated from within. I hesitated to walk in, wary that a group of sabers could be clustered inside. Tori obviously decided this was the time to display his bravery because he stormed past me to the entrance's wooden doors. I didn't have time to reprimand him because he'd already taken his first step within the building. Without hesitation, I followed him angrily. I flagged everyone to keep tight, and we cautiously crept into the lobby. A dusty chandelier was the only remains of the building's former glory. There was a counter on my right which had sustained obvious fire damage. On my left was what looked to be the silver doors of a large kitchen.

I halted everyone, raising my hand for them to stop. I trained my hearing on the sounds from within the building. Tori was near the stairs and for the first time found hesitation in his next step. I didn't dare make any loud noises in case nearby vampires heard the echo. It was a dark room, but I now realized what I had seen in the window.

"Sabers!" Pac yelled.

As he screamed, a saber jumped onto the chandelier before plummeting to the ground. After it hit the ground, many more crept from the dark shadows. I shot one in the chest with my arrow then aimed for another that jumped from above. It used the chandelier to deflect my arrow and lunged to the ground—I shot it in the chest before its back legs landed. Swiftly taking aim, I shot another two in the chest as they ran out from the kitchen. Just as I had dreaded, we'd walked into an entire pack of them.

Kora had raised her hand to the smaller group of sabers that continued to spill out of the kitchen and Kasey enforced her gift by tightening her grip on their mobility. The sabers were locked in their trap and couldn't move. Their eyes frenzied around. Kora released her grip, and the sabers could move freely once again. They charged at them but slammed into the invisible wall Kasey still had them frozen behind. Kora slashed down a stray saber outside the trap who dared to ambush her twin sister. They were trapped. Pac ran along the circle, quickly cutting them down. They fell to the ground, their bodies lumping into blackened flesh as they began to rot. The smell of death already filled the room.

Corso's loud chainsaw pierced my sensitive ears as I continued to shoot more oncoming sabers. Why is there a pack so large? Teary's scream echoed through the great room, grabbing my attention as I turned to see a saber's large fangs driving deep into her shoulder. Her blood splattered everywhere.

Corso ran for her with his chainsaw, swinging it at the saber's neck, but as I predicted the weight of the chainsaw was bulky and slowed him down. Before the saber could tear into Corso, James skidded in front of it, stabbing it in the chest with his sword. Another pounced on James, its fangs only drew a pinch of blood on his neck before James' exterior hardened to metal and broke the saber's fangs completely. It squealed in agony before James adjusted his handle and stabbed the saber in the chest.

I shot a saber that prowled the two apprentices, who, although were deflecting the three sabers that encircled them, clearly now understood how far out of their league they really were. I could tell by their expressions that although they fought fiercely, they were both surprised and frightened. This was what we trained for. Unsheathing my sword, I charged for them. One used its elongated claws trying to slice at my chest. I deflected its hand, the remains of what might've been a female vampire squealed as her hand flung in the air separate from her body. She snarled at me, those elongated fangs defiantly tugging down her cracked and filth retched face. Her long hair was matted into clumps of mud, and she only had a moment to gaze at me with slitted black eyes as I pierced my sword into the gristle of her throat. Her dark blood spurted over me as she paused for a moment, trying to gasp for air. I dislodged my sword from her throat and sliced defiantly, beheading the saber.

Easing around its body as it slumped, I stabbed into the next saber's chest, avoiding its claws which aimed to burrow into my face. The figure's chest blackened around my sword as the rest of its skin sagged and took a black tinge. I tugged my sword out of its chest, the echo of its body sloshing to the ground. Another saber attempted to jump on me from the swinging chandelier. I twisted myself awkwardly, anticipating the angle which she would fall on my sword. Though she fell, it wasn't directly in her heart as I'd anticipated. She was suspended on my sword as I hoisted her up. Her nails barely missed scratching at my face as I flicked her to the side, across the room. Her body skidded with black blood pooling from behind her. When she looked back at me I shot my arrow bang on target in the center of her eyes and then the second, a fraction higher to where my sword had gutted her. As soon as I hit my second mark, her body began to decay into an amounted mass.

A loud snap echoed through the room as I witnessed from the corner of my eye, Fam's neck being snapped by a saber. Fam's eyes were wide as his life dimmed. The saber roared in triumph, trying to quickly drag him away as Tori chased after him. My inner rage erupted. No one had ever died under my watch. The moment was only slight, but enough to switch my controlled self to that seething and barbaric raw rage that my father had always tried to oppress.

I enhanced my speed and was instantly in front of the saber, slicing through the arm that clung so tightly to Fam's lifeless body. As it wailed in pain, I cut off its other arm and then one leg. It dropped before me, and I could feel myself growing in sadistic rage as I towered over him. Although it was obviously about to die, it still tried to have one last bite, its overgrown fangs dripping with blood from where it must have bitten into Fam's body.

With my other hand, I raised my bow to his chest, shooting him. From there I aimed at every saber within the dark lobby. I shot one and then another. My arrows shot quickly, as, in my rage, everything was heightened, and there was no distraction from me meeting my marks. My need for blood was far greater than I could ever admit to anyone. I wanted to see their blood drip and watch their bodies decay. I wanted to behead every single one of them and keep their heads as trophies. They should have never challenged me nor attacked my members. This protectiveness was by far my greatest strength. And when tempered with, when what I was protecting was threatened, I could not contain myself. This potential was what made me a Token Huntress.

The sound of the chainsaw pierced my ears, and then the scream of Corso followed. He was in front of the large silver doors which led to the huge kitchen. One of the sabers had grabbed hold of his chainsaw and in a swift movement, cut it through Corso's leg. James, who was cutting down sabers as they scrambled down the stairs, aided his friend, bringing his sword down and plunging it into the saber's chest. It went straight through, and with James' control, the tip of his blade stopped right before Corso's face. The others fought in the corner of the room, holding off the sabers that billowed from the darkness of the kitchen.

Atop the stairs were eight sabers trapped within the invisible walls that the twins had placed them in. It was Dillian and Pac who protected the girls from the oncoming sabers. I took my aim. One, two, three… I let the count pass through my lips. All eight were quickly shot down. A scuffle took my attention as I noticed a saber dragging Fam's dead body to a door underneath the staircase. *It dares to feast on my apprentice's body*, I raged internally. Chasing it, I noticed the path it took was a dark back alley, one which had very little light. This one was a lot faster than the average, and I realized that it was leading me into a trap of further sabers that lingered in the alleyway. Torn and shredded curtains in the windows on either side of me twitched. They were even hunting me from the buildings, following my steps. I wasn't deterred by numbers. I would retrieve Fam's body.

Simultaneously, two sabers jumped out on either side of the two-story buildings. The first I shot with my bow, the second I shoved my sword into its chest fiercely, before flicking it off with great strength against the building. I heard the splatter of its already decaying body as it slid down the wall.

Ahead of me were another two. One side-stepped me, leaving me open on my side. Its claws cut against my stomach lightly, giving me the opening I needed to swing my sword up at him, dragging it deeply up its stomach to its throat. I clobbered the other one over the head with the back of my bow, following through with my sword, piercing it in the chest.

I quickly caught up to the saber that dragged away its feast. Taking aim, I shot it down and grabbed Fam's body from its filthy clutches. I took him in my arms, close to my chest as a pack of eight sabers surrounded me. They were gurgling in glee at what they considered easy pickings. I had once read up on an extinct animal called 'hyenas.' The sabers reminded me of these creatures. I let out an enraged growl. Not because I feared them or could not handle them, but because I could not look down at the face of Fam before his body got cold. A whistling noise pierced my ears. A dart came toward me from up high in the buildings. I threw my body over Fam protectively as I felt the dart graze past my left arm as I dodged it.

A small gas cylinder tinkered beside one of the sabers, followed by a match. The small boom was quickly controlled by Teary, who instantly wiped around a clean sweep of flames. A few daggers were thrown, and the sabers dropped dead around me. The immediate heat instantly forced my body to sweat. I searched through the thriving flames in the direction of where the dart had grazed past me. The evidence of it was also caught in the crossfire of the flames. Atop one of the buildings a shadowy figure stood, wearing a long leather jacket that flapped in the breeze. I was being watched. I went to stand, to pursue the cloaked figure, but a wave of dizziness hit my body and slightly buckled my legs. I looked at the small graze on my arm that was left behind by the dart.

The flames receded, and Teary reached my side. She watched momentarily my firm grip that didn't loosen on Fam's body. She clutched at her own shoulder wound.

"Is this poison?" I asked Teary, attracting her attention to the graze on my arm. My body was already fighting back its effects, though it could've been dangerous if the dart had met its mark and embedded into me.

Teary assessed it, squinting, and gave it a sniff. "It's a form of paralysis, there is a slight infection already crisping at ye skin. It'll soon affect ye whole body. We will get ye out, Token Huntress," she said, adjusting herself to lift me. By now James and Tori followed her.

"No. Burn it out now," I ordered, still eyeing the rooftop's shadowy figure. They still watched on. And yet I couldn't find myself to order anyone else to follow. I was compelled that this was something personal. That I would have to catch them myself and return the favor.

"No!" James shouted. I gave him a steady look which forced him to stay back. I didn't care about a scar. Teary didn't question my decision, quickly lighting a flame and edging it over the scratch. She had to dig deep with her flame so the poison wouldn't stretch any further. I held my poised expression as the burn quickly crisped my skin, fixated only on the figure that had poisoned me. *And who are you?* Despite their advantage on the rooftop, they made no further attack against us or more specifically, they did not attempt to attack me once again. I assumed it was a member of the Council. They had previously attempted such methods, trying to kidnap and torture other hunters for information on the Guild's location. Yet, this figure did not move, and for whatever reason, none of the other hunters had detected its presence. It felt like the same mysterious presence that I'd been feeling the past few days- watching me.

I slowly stood. The poison on my skin had been burned away and the flesh melted with it. The shadow on top of the building took a step back and vanished. I was tempted to pursue the vampire, but when I took one small step forward, I was pulled from my fixation and reminded of the cold dead body still clutched tightly in my hands. *My team.* I had to make sure everyone else was all right and return Fam's body to the Guild before any other sabers or vampires alike smelt him within the city.

"Let's retreat," I said, looking at Teary's shoulder which still bled. James slowly reached for Fam, and much to my discontentment, he was taken from my arms. I didn't show the displeasure of Fam being taken from my grasp, not wanting to waver on my firm expression. This ambush had been bad.

We caught back up to the others who waited cautiously within the building. Many of the sabers' bodies were seeping into the carpet. My steps slowed as I walked in to find Dillian holding Corso. His leg badly mutilated. Already the others had found some reasonably clean cloth and strapped it tightly over the wound, but his blood still dripped onto the floor. We were in a horrendous state to run through the forest. So much blood would surely attract more vampires.

My facial expression further hardened as I saw Pac within Kora's and Kasey's arms. Five stab wounds to his chest. But Pac was so fast, I couldn't fathom how he might've been killed. As if reading my mind, Kora's voice rang out. "He protected us from three," she simply said. Death surrounded me like the calamity of the past few months. But these were the first under my watch and command. I had failed. It was my fault for not being there to protect them. I looked at Dillian for some form of reassurance, but he only reflected a pained expression. I couldn't seek such refuge in James, who was aiding his friend, and also cautious of his advantage on twisting any show of emotion I might have.

"We must retreat." My voice was only a shadow of the fierce tone I had earlier. "We must return to the Guild, and with only death to show for our efforts."

CHAPTER 8

W E HELPED OUR fallen members through the streets of the destroyed and long-forgotten city. We were on edge and cautious about the creatures that might follow. Corso contained his screams, mostly because he was nearly unconscious. He was bleeding severely, the thick red seeping through the bandages and leaving a trail in its stead. He wouldn't make it even if we ran at our heightened pace as a group. We were quick to reach the city's outskirts, stopping for only a moment to regroup properly. Our first goal was to get out of the city, especially because of the trail of blood we left behind enticing the vampires who might sniff it out. Why the lone vampire didn't follow us I wasn't sure, but I couldn't sense his presence close by any longer.

I assessed Teary's neck; it was a clean bite—no venom had been injected—I was relieved to know she wasn't at risk of being turned. That was how vampires continued their steady stream of population, by injecting their venom and turning humans and sometimes hunters alike into vampires. Sabers had no control of their venom, and it was likely they could accidentally turn anyone. The 'changing' as vampires liked to call it looked painful and could last for days as their body ate away at itself, died, and was reborn. However, for hunters, the transition was only a few hours, already being partially fabricated from vampires, it didn't take our kind long to submit to it entirely. We'd tried to save our own kind many times before with no success. There was still so much we had to learn about the vampires and their ambitions as their world was unclear as they guarded their secrets as tightly as we did our own.

"Esmore, he won't make it," James said breathlessly, looking between Corso and me. "You need to run ahead of us with him on your back. You can get there within half a day, I know your speed. You need to take him back to the healers at the Guild. We have no other choice." Although he covered his emotion, I could see the worry in his eyes for his friend. And although it pleased me that he voiced his confidence in my ability, I was hesitant.

"I cannot leave you all," I replied. I didn't want the team to break up any more than it already had.

"We cannot waste any more time," Dillian replied. There was a large cut above his florescent pink eyes. "He's losing too much blood, Esmore. Sabers may follow. If you carry Corso, it's not us they will follow, but you. We will be safe, and you can outrun them. It's his only fighting chance."

Dillian understood my thought process and struck true with each word. If I stayed with them and continued to strap Corso to my back, effectively, it could be worse for the group as a whole. I peered momentarily at Corso, who was dipping in and out of consciousness. I draped him over my shoulder. James grabbed a rope which was in my bag, quickly strapping him tightly, yet awkwardly, onto my back. There wasn't much height difference between Corso and me, and his weight didn't affect me in the slightest, though his one dangling foot would drag. I needed to make sure I could still swing my sword with my right hand, and still lift with my left hand and shoulder as I strapped my Barnett bow to the front.

"I love you," James said, kissing me on the lips and stepping out of my way.

"You are to bring Pac and Fam back, and all of you are to return alive. No breaks, be wary," I ordered. I was hesitant for another moment, risking the chance of not seeing them again. No, my team was strong. They would make it back. I nodded and vanished in a swift swirl of fog.

My steps echoed in my ears as I ran through the trees. Running at speed caused the noise of the wind to irritably whistle in my ears with the thumping of my ever-steady breath. At this pace, I would easily make the full day's run within a few hours. I wasn't as fast as Pac, but I could muster a far greater speed than the other hunters, including the older and respected Token Hunters. My eyes burned from the fog and wind that ambushed them.

Gradually, I became tenser. For the past five minutes, I could sense footsteps following me as it steadily crept to night. I was being hunted. I had no doubt that it was sabers who had been sleeping somewhere deep within the forest before catching a whiff of Corso's bleeding injury. It did not concern me in the slightest. I was confident I could take them out within seconds, they were mindless beasts after all.

My speed didn't waver. Moments darted by, and the terrain began to change slightly. Footsteps approached closer as they ran on all fours, their breathing heavy. I could hear them clumsily chasing after me. The barn where we had stayed only the night before was left in my wake. I needed to get rid of the sabers before I reached the Guild. I enhanced my sight, no longer straining through the foggy dark. They were upon me.

A saber jumped from the high treetops on my right. I raised my Barnett bow, shooting it down, and then the second one that followed. Three had surpassed my speed, carrying Corso had slowed me, if only slightly, but I refused to untie the rope that bound him to my back.

They challenged me head-on, ejecting their vile, long nails as weapons. I cut up the chest of the first one, impaling it as hard as I could. My force was brutal enough to force it back, but it was able to streak three talons across my cheek. I was limited in free movement with Corso strapped to my back.

I shot the second saber with my crossbow. It took me only a second to nock a new arrow. As I balanced it in one hand, I hacked my sword across the third saber's neck, shocking it for a moment. My sword didn't slice its head completely off. While it was stunned, I plunged the sword deep into its chest. Already I could begin to smell the stench of their corpses.

Corso mumbled something under his breath, still drifting in and out of consciousness. I couldn't twist around to look at his leg, but if the sticky wetness on the back of my leg was any indication, he was still bleeding. If he were a human he would've already been dead. Although we didn't heal instantly like the vampires, it helped in the long fight against death. If I made it back in time, he'd still be struggling for his life. That end battle would be his to fight.

On my left, two sabers attempted to ambush me. One tripped over a log and then crawled at me on all fours like an animal. I shot the first and then the second. I filtered through the ominous sense and lack of noise behind me. They were all dead.

Corso mumbled under his breath again. I couldn't make out the words, but it sounded like the same gibberish he always spoke. Corso and I never saw eye-to-eye, but I still would do everything in my power to protect and keep him alive. I slightly readjusted him on my back, briefly looking over my shoulder to scan if anything else followed. Though nothing pursued me, I had that nauseating sensation that I was being watched. The image of the figure standing on the roof halted me to a dead stop. I searched in the direction but couldn't hear or see anything. Was I being paranoid? Corso mumbled again, evoking my priority on the urgent matter.

I picked up the pace once again, taking a heavy exhale and refocusing my acute senses. I couldn't delay any longer or take any unknown or longer routes. I was already racing against time. The fog surrounding me billowed away as I breezed through it. A few more hours passed and much to my delight no other vampires followed. Over the last hour I could feel myself depleting in energy. With only a mere twenty minutes left of my run, Corso's mumbling became fainter.

A startled scream ripped past my lips as acid started to drip from Corso's skin onto my shoulder. The right side of my body buckled under the intensity of the pain. Corso's gift was turning against him and excreting acid from his body. In consequence, it now dripped over me. Smoke sizzled from my wounds. I couldn't move my stiff shoulder. With my remaining arm, I strapped my crossbow back over my chest, scared I would lose control of my arm entirely and drop it. I gritted my teeth. There was no other way I could carry him.

Soon his chest began to secrete a slow-burning stream of acid, causing it to smolder through his shirt and onto my back. My legs buckled and I held my scream of anguish in. I could feel the tiny pin-like droplets burning away at my back, one tear at a time. Breathing heavily, I tried to block the pain. *I have to save him*, I reminded myself. I focused on my breathing and desperately accelerated the last of my energy back into running. My legs buckled a few times when the acid dripped onto the back of my calves. It was affecting my willpower as my muscles began to spasm. I dared not think about the long-term effects it might have on my body as I pursued only one goal. I would return Corso alive.

I could see the gates and attempted to wave my good arm and sword for them to open. "Open the gates," I bellowed, my voice uncharacteristically cracking. The two hunters atop the gates looked surprised but commanded the hunters below to open them. I ran through the tiny slither of opening, past the hunters, and straight into the tunnels. I almost buckled in relief when I saw the white-walled infirmary. I rushed into the room, placing Corso on the first bed I saw, more forcefully than I intended to.

I quickly moved toward one of the tall wooden stands that held the white coats. I wrapped one around me before the nurses could properly understand what was happening. I still flickered across the room at high speed and flicked my golden blonde hair from beneath the white coat's collar. I couldn't let them see my wounds, because if they did, they'd advise Campture and that was something I didn't want. She may very well deem me unfit to go back beyond the wall to find the others.

Within those few seconds, the two nurses—who had been quietly enjoying their tea—panicked. They sprang into motion as soon as they saw Corso's bloody body on the bed. Droplets of green leaked from his skin as perspired drops sizzled and melted through the mattress. If it weren't for his hunter blood, he would most certainly be dead by now. We could heal efficiently, but the body couldn't heal an amputated limb.

"We were attacked by sabers. His leg was cut through with a chainsaw," I began to explain quickly. I was irritated by the festering burn on my back and neck and adjusted myself uncomfortably. The two nurses both looked at me blankly; of course they didn't know what a chainsaw was, it was a trial weapon. "The weapon he was attacked with had a metal jarred exterior. It can cut through solid wood and obviously flesh. The weapon works in a rotary motion."

That was all the information they needed to start busily handling him. "This is Corso; we have to watch his acid. We need to put him into a coma. It'll stop the perspiration of acid from his skin," the older nurse said. All hunters, no matter their Guild department, were aware of one another's gifts, especially the infirmary members. She jabbed a needle and injected an oddly colored liquid into Corso's arm. The younger nurse began tearing away the heavy bandage wrapped around his amputated leg.

Part of it was still dangling. It looked as if the acid was assisting Corso's survival by burning away the rest of his leg. When the huntress tore off the remaining scraps of bandage, his green festering wound was secreting thick acid, trying to erode his bone away.

"Token Huntress Esmore, are you in need of assistance?" the older nurse with white eyes asked, catching my attention. It was then I realized how tightly I strapped my arms around myself, trying to contain the shakes—the repercussion of Corso's acid affecting my muscles, making them spasm.

"No, I'm fine. Do what you can for him. I'll be taking my leave now. Thank you both," I said, nodding my head in respect before leaving.

Struggling to lift my crossbow, I rolled my right shoulder. At least, I was able to freely move my right arm which always held my sword. I quickened my pace out of the tunnels and stood at the front gates impatiently.

"Open them," I said to the two guards, who were surprised by my sudden appearance. They looked at the white robe I wore with suspicion.

"I think not," Campture's voice rose from the shadows. Kelf followed behind her. I shot a harsh glare toward the guards who had already alerted her of my arrival. This would only make it more difficult to leave and find the rest of my team. "Why are you wearing a robe?"

"My team is still outside beyond the walls. We've endured heavy damage, and I could only bring back one. I will report to you when I return with the rest of my team," I said, prompting the men to open the gates.

"No, you will report to me now. Your team is strong enough to return on their own," she said sternly.

"I am their Token," I retorted savagely.

"You, Token, have already abandoned them," Campture said, narrowing her yellow eyes on me.

"I had no choice, I had to save Corso. Because that ridiculous chainsaw weapon was permitted to be used as a trial weapon, it had been used against him, and he suffered severe damage. We lost another two after being ambushed by a pack of sabers. I will not witness the death of anymore," I said, clenching my hands, trying to stay my nerves around Campture as she delayed me further.

"It's not about what you want, Esmore," Campture glowered. I imagined my rebellious nature reminded her of my mother and she had always been quick to squander it. "You don't have a choice. If you leave these grounds, there will be consequences."

I felt the anger swell inside of me, like a savage animal clawing its way up through me. This image came to mind, and I felt myself slipping out of control. Whatever this creature was that showed itself from time to time, I wanted to aggressively push back and was tantalized by the idea of ridding myself of Campture entirely. It wasn't so much a direct thought but a nauseous wave of knowing. Campture took a step back, startled by whatever she might've seen or heard in my mind.

I took a shallow breath, reminding myself of the lessons my father had taught me. *Contain those thoughts and dark intentions… breathe.* Calming the darkness that bit at my insides, I focused on Campture again.

Campture's lips tightened at my internal anguish. She drew breath to speak, but I wouldn't stay just because she said so. My allegiance was only to myself and the safety of my team. I bolted for the unsteady rope ladder on the north wall where Dillian and I were often placed on guard. My left shoulder was almost useless now. As soon as I reached the top, I flipped myself over the high wall, and landed on the other side, regretting it as soon as my knees took the impact of the heavy jolt. The fog swept around me, unsettled by my sudden jump.

I scrambled on the forest floor to get back up. I narrowed my eyes to the direction in which my team would be in and then began running for them in the dark night. Repercussions were something I'd consider later. I couldn't risk the chance of losing anyone else because Campture wanted to follow her own twisted set of rules and regulations.

After a clumsy two-hour run, I eventually found the tired group, their pace slow. Much to my relief no more had been lost. Fam's and Pac's bodies had become paler. Dillian tiredly carried Pac and James carried Fam. The others formed a protective formation around all sides of the group. Dillian was struggling with the weight of Pac so I asked to carry him. James was one of the strongest in our Guild, mostly because of his gift. He didn't struggle or sweat in the slightest under the added weight.

"They are doing what they can for Corso now," I answered James before he even had to ask.

"Why are you in a white robe?" Kora asked, looking me up and down.

"And how did you return to us so quickly? Didn't you have to report to Campture as well?" Kasey interjected.

It was protocol; of course they would question how I arrived back to them so quickly. A report of this magnitude would have taken hours. I would have to tell her every little step we had taken. There would be meetings, inquests, lectures. It was evident that I'd ignored such a protocol after dropping Corso in the infirmary. Very few defied Campture, and she would not take it kindly. I held my blank expression without response. I shuffled to take Pac. My lack of response and detail when not required was something my team was very used to, but James knew better.

"What did you do?" he moaned.

"Is this really the time?" I snapped, rearranging Pac on my back. "We need to get back to the Guild."

The slower pace gave me time to reassess all that had happened. It pained me to search my fellow teammates' eyes to see very little emotion there as we carried our fallen comrades. I was upset to know I had failed them in so many ways. This was why I preferred to work by myself because then it was only my life at risk. I would not show the others, but I truly cared for their safety under my guard. My mother had engrained that being a Token meant to show no emotion or self-doubt in my decisions. That weakness, even such as mourning loss, would not be respected amongst our kind. I took that in my stride, becoming every bit the savage Token that was expected of me.

CHAPTER 9

UPON OUR ARRIVAL, the gates were opened immediately. Despite our bloody entrance, hunters within the Guild mirrored the same disinterested expression, fixated on their tasks. Even when they glanced over at the two dead we carried on our backs, they showed little interest. Only one small child ogled and pointed, but when she did, her mother ushered her back into their home. Our existence was purely to train and fight. Only in death were we released of this task and even then, it was almost as if we barely existed.

"Esmore, perhaps we should visit Campture straight away and ask that whatever punishment she has decided upon to be lessened. The longer you prolong, the worse it will be," James said. He was always like a pet when it came to the Guild. He would follow, and he expected the same from me. Well I suppose most hunters were like that. To follow orders and not question were our mantras. Had it not been for my upbringing with my mother who had a very audacious outlook, perhaps I would've been the same as them. And though my mother might've been considered wild in her time, and my father even ushered for her to lower her tone, he would still stand by her. The loyalty that should be upheld within any family. That had been my raising.

"First of all, James," I spat angrily, "I will go to the families of our fallen to report their loss and to offer my apologies for not keeping them safe under my leadership."

Before I could continue arguing and list off my numerous irritations, Dillian stood beside me, and pressed a warm smile at James. "I'll take her straight to Campture afterward, James," he said reassuringly as he went to take Fam from him.

James held tighter onto the body. "*I* will go with her," he said possessively.

"I don't want you to come with me. I can handle Campture on my own," I gritted out, trying to suppress my rising anger. It was the same creeping sensation I had with Campture. After being riled in the events and ambush in the city, it was harder for me to suppress. I was imploding at every small flick that antagonized me. I noticed the odd exchange between James and Dillian. Surely he didn't see Dillian as a rival? Reluctantly, James handed over Fams' body.

Dillian and I walked toward Pac's small home first. I had worked various raids with Pac for almost two years and was honored when he decided to stay on my team even after Drue's passing. I'd never envied Drue when he informed the family of their loss. I now felt like it was my responsibility and no one else's to knock on their door as he once had and with only a corpse in hand. Dillian and I were silent as we approached. It was as if we were gravely walking to our own funerals. I tapped on the door lightly, struggling as I briefly forgot about my left arm's immobility. Dillian gave me an inquisitive look.

Had I been gifted time, I would've led her to the temple and offered her a respectful passing for her husband's death. But that was time I wasn't afforded, and instead, I had to bring his lifeless body to her doorstep. I didn't want to chance Campture finding me before I sought her out. She might make a scene and reprimand me publicly about disobeying orders. Though I knew I would still be punished, this wasn't the time for such trivial matters as her pride being shaken and making an example out of me.

Pac's wife opened the door, her eyes darting to her husband's body. She did not move nor did her face change in expression. She gestured to raise her hand toward his face but retracted it quickly, curling her delicate fingers into her palms instead.

"I'm sorry that I let this happen. He fought fiercely and protected fellow members of the team. He was heroic," I said. She nodded her head stiffly, still too numb to show emotion. She did not reach for his face again, but instead held both hands to her stomach. There was a noise coming from inside. I assumed one of her children must have woken.

"Very well, I will inform our children. In the new day, we shall pay our respects. And where will you keep his body?" she asked me.

My body stiffened at the emotionless and transactional reply. I recalled the day my mother crumbled before me when she brought back my father's body. I wanted to shake and slap her, to scream at her, 'your husband is dead.' But her movement was typical, this was what was expected of us. And yet, within the pit of my stomach, it made me nauseous. This custom was not right, yet I could never voice such an opinion.

She looked at Dillian as a few tears piled in his eyes. He was one of the most sensitive hunters I knew. Most hunters did not appreciate such free expression—neither did she. Did she see it as a weakness in Dillian to cry so easily and be pardoned from the hard manner we all adopted? Or did she feel weak within herself and envious for being unable to break, to let such emotion surface?

"I will bury him at dawn," Dillian said. "At our shrine, alongside Fam."

"Very well," she said, agreeing on the place and time before closing the door on us. The small light from her singular candle vanished when she closed the door, and I felt myself harden in the cold breeze. I let myself slip into the darkness, far more comfortable with little emotions. At least there it was an abyss of silence.

Dillian led me to Fam's home, which wasn't far from Pac's. It was daunting to walk around at this early hour in the morning. Hardly anyone was awake. He lightly tapped on the door, and within a few moments, Fam's mother appeared. Her throat tightened, and she clenched her jaw at the sight. Instantly a tear dropped before she looked away into her home. She quickly wiped it away, calling for her husband.

When Fam's mother turned to face us once again she had covered any sign of her previous expression. It was as if, even in front of her husband, she could not show such affliction. She was not as emotionally bound as most, and I could see the artery in her neck noticeably tightened with every breath she took. Her bottom lip quivered slightly. She fiddled her hand over her face in an attempt to hide it.

"Your son…" I hadn't the time to finish before his father cut me off.

"We would like to keep our son here until morning, then we will bury him at the shrine," he said. His voice was rough, and he reached his hands out to take hold of his son. Hesitantly, Dillian handed Fam over.

"Thank you for returning his body to us." And with that, Fam's mother closed the door. Once again the singular candle's light was taken from us, and we were left in the dark.

"I'm going to take Pac to the shrine. You can assist me before you confront Campture. It's up to you, I'm not going to hold you back from your decision, but you do know you're prolonging your inevitable punishment. All because you're doing something so human," Dillian gritted out murderously. Dillian wasn't a boisterous rebel, but I never liked leaving him in his current state. Though I considered leaving him to take Pac on his own, I couldn't find myself walking in the opposite direction. I'd already disobeyed Campture in so many ways, what was another few moments?

We walked to the white picket fence area with maintained green grass. Near the small gates of the shrine were thick sticks with cloth wrapped around them. Beside them was a silver container of oil for giving light. Dillian held two flames while I carried Pac.

In the center of the four-story circular shrine was a large oval stone. This was where we would set alight our fallen hunters, turning them to ash. Usually, only the closest to the dead would witness it.

Already a few sticks were laid down on the stone. A member of the Guild who maintained the shrine had already been made aware of Pac's and Fam's death. Tomorrow they would be burned, and their human soul would be set free from this destructive world of everlasting war.

I recalled the words of a huntress who became sick in her old age. She began to misunderstand everything and forget who everyone was. It was called *dementia*. She was the only huntress to suffer from a human disease. Still, there were no answers. When she and I paid respects to her grandson, she looked at the scenery peacefully. She questioned loudly why we fought so hard for a world that was already broken. She said she couldn't wait for the day she was set free, and that she didn't understand why everyone clung so tightly to such a monstrous world. It had been such a human thing to say. I could imagine that some humans also thought this. But she was not human; the disease made her think unconventionally. Shortly after that, she died, but her words had stayed with me ever since. Carefully, I placed Pac on the stone. I reassessed his lethal wounds, still so disheartened.

"There is nothing you could have done," Dillian said, placing a strong hand on my shoulder in reassurance. I winced slightly at his touch, grabbing his immediate attention. I shuddered at the touch, but it didn't hurt as much as I had initially anticipated. "What have you done to yourself?"

I pulled the white robe back to assess my left shoulder. Dillian raised his flame to it, offering me the other one. My lips slightly parted in surprise. My skin was healing.

"Corso, in his unconscious state, had been dropping acid on me when I carried him." I shrugged the white robe from my back. "What can you see?"

Dillian assessed it, poking his finger through the holes of my leather shirt. "If these holes were created from Corso's acid, then you are healing somehow at a rapid pace, Esmore."

I flicked my plait, readjusting the white robe to reveal where I had forced Teary to melt a part of my skin. Now only a small red blemish appeared. "It's healing," I said, just as surprised. It had been such a long time since I was seriously injured in any way that my healing rate came to me as a surprise. Dillian reached for my white robe, pulling it over my arm and covering me up.

"You need to get rid of those clothes. It won't go down well if you are healing in such a way without explanation. If you were burned by Teary's flames and infected by Corso's acid, you should not be healing so rapidly, especially without scars. It will only heighten suspicion around your huntress eyes, Esmore. You can speak of this to no one," Dillian said sternly. Dillian had a curiosity toward the change of my huntress eyes and what it meant, but he was also protective of any uncertain outcomes concerning me.

"I know," I agreed. I repeated the words to myself as I took a seat on the bottom step.

He sat beside me, stroking his hand through his shoulder-length black hair. He often did this while thinking. "You can't tell James," Dillian said assertively. It was an odd warning considering he knew I told James very little compared to what I told him.

"I know," I said tiredly. The full two days finally caught up, and my body felt fatigued. "I haven't trusted him entirely, if ever, but especially not now after his reaction to everything," I said, annoyed by his very name. I looked at Dillian from the corner of my eye as he studied me carefully. "When you are around Julia or even parted from her…" I trailed off, not knowing how to carefully voice my question. I came up with no unclipped way to say it. "Do you ever feel like you are enemies?"

"No, never, Esmore, that's not a companionship. I love Julia and would do anything for her. I would risk my life for her."

"I would risk my life for James," I objected.

"No, Esmore, you would risk your life for anyone because you do not fear death." His words rang true. It made me reflect on the darkness and anger I felt as a child. All that my father had helped me suppress was now resurfacing again.

"When Campture told me I was not to leave the Guild, I felt something within me, something… dark. It felt like an animal rising within me. Hatred fueled me, and I wanted to see her hurt and watch her blood splatter. Sometimes I feel that way when challenged by vampires, but it was the first time I'd ever experienced it against my own kind. There is a feeling inside of me I cannot explain. The same darkness sweeps within me every time James challenges me, and I don't know how to control that anger. When I look at James, and when I feel him touching my skin, I want to push him away. I feel as if that anger is instigated by both him and Campture. In my heart, I don't feel as if it is right anymore. I have a longing beyond these walls which I cannot explain properly." And I wondered if it had anything to do with my mother's death. Had I grown suspicious of everyone here because I wanted to go out in search of her, still unable to believe in her death?

"You're very talkative tonight," Dillian remarked, his eyebrows perked. I usually was so careful and limited in words. "Do you mean to say you have a longing for another?"

I went to object instantly, but nothing followed. I thought about this for a while. There was no one I was fond of, and yet, I felt something stir within me as if somebody had created a change. For some reason my thoughts instantly narrowed on the person who had shot the dart at me from the rooftops. I quickly scratched that from my mind.

"I do not long for another, but I do long for *something*," I said, holding my hand to my chest and gesturing outward as if trying to convey my meaning. "And James… he is not a part of that. He wants to ground me, hold me, force me to be a minion of the Guild. I can no longer simply *be*," I said, realizing what I was about to say.

"Esmore, if you cannot speak to him openly, you shouldn't be in that relationship. To me, it sounds as if you feel like you are bedding the enemy. And if that is indeed how you feel, then that is not the bed to sleep in."

"But right now, my blood boils. I feel like everyone is my enemy. Not just him. But certainly not you."

Dillian took a heavy sigh. He placed his hand over mine in reassurance. "It has been a long day for all of us. You'll find a way to make peace with this."

Maybe he was right. Well of course, Dillian was always right. His hand tightened over mine as his facial expression contorted. "What's wrong?" I asked. He forced his hand to his face, tightening his grip around his forehead as if in pain from a sudden headache. He breathed heavily, removing his hands and opening his eyes, looking forward as if possessed.

Suddenly, I felt a creeping presence. I retracted the sword from my sheath that rested beside me and raised my Barnett crossbow. I searched past the shrine, the tops of the trees, and past the great wall. I couldn't see anyone, but I could feel them. Hunters had an eerie sensation when foreigners were close. But for some odd reason, even though the presence was faint and very far away, I was being led in that direction. It was drawing me in. I had to stop myself from stepping forward, almost having been mesmerized by some unknown allure. I was conflicted as to whether I should give chase to the presence that beckoned me from within the forest or stay by Dillian's side. Something horrific was happening.

"Go," he said through a harsh cough. His eyes were darting across as if he were reading rapidly. "It's our duty." Behind us, in the distance I could see James, who now stalked toward us. He would find Dillian and take him to the infirmary. With Dillian's permission, I ran toward the southside wall, where, for some reason, the guards were not on duty.

I scampered up the ladder, standing tall on the wall and searching through the trees, prepared for anything that would come. I dared the follower to show themselves. I still couldn't see them, but I felt drawn to them, knowing where their shadowy presence was in the forest. I jumped off the wall, inflicting the same jolt of pain in my knees as last time I jumped.

I dashed through the trees nearing the fishing nets. It didn't take me long to halt and behold the sketchy presence that had been eerily bothering me for days. Near the fishing nets, in the only patch where the moon shone, was a figure. He was crouched with his back to me, washing the clear river water over his face. His jacket was identical to the one that had fluttered on the rooftops after I had been shot by the dart. And his overwhelming presence was all the same. This was the same vampire.

I aimed my Barnett crossbow at him, infuriated to realize I'd been followed from the city. He had got the better of me. Although I stood with weapon aimed, he was hardly fazed. He looked at me casually over his shoulder. He passed his hand through his shaggy black shoulder-length hair, tucking it behind his ear before smirking in my direction. In the moonlight, his unblemished skin seemed even paler than most. One blue gem hung from the piercing in his left ear and glistened under the moonlight.

"You're a part of the Council," I seethed. My hands shook when I confronted him. I tried to control my shaking that tempted me to put my weapon down. I could hear the pulse under my ears, and my very breath was a rackety clamber within my throat. All of my senses were uncontrollably and acutely heightened in his presence. Was I frightened of him? Surely not. Was it something else? I'd never known fear before. There was a strength radiating from him I could not understand.

He twisted only slightly, his jacket opening further to reveal his chiseled stomach and pale skin. He wasn't even wearing a shirt. Another blue caught my eye. He wore a leather necklace with a similar blue gem dangling from it. His gray eyes held an intensity that captivated me from further moving. His stark black hair and pale skin were in opposition to each other, yet magnificent at the same time. Was it fear that rattled me or... *excitement?*

He finally spoke in a tone that felt like it could be as silent as a pin dropping to the floor but as powerful as a wolf's growl. "Oh my, aren't we rude. We don't ask for names anymore? I must confess, I am disappointed by your manners." I couldn't recognize his foreign predated accent, but it sounded very proper, very old.

"What have you done to my friend?" I demanded from him. I was certain Dillian's sudden pain was caused by this vampire. I gathered my wits about me and held up the Barnett bow in a threatening manner.

"Now, accusations never get us anywhere, young Token. Where are your eyes?" he asked inquisitively.

"You shot me!" I accused. I still couldn't understand my body's resistance to pulling the trigger to shoot him. I needed to capture him, I convinced myself. I needed answers. If he were my link to the Council, I would have him.

"I hardly grazed you," he said childishly, sweeping through his hair again. He didn't deny it was him that shot me from the rooftops. "If you had come with me quietly and willingly I wouldn't have to pay you a special visit here. I didn't think you'd be so dramatic as to melt your skin away because of it. I'm abashed you deem me as some kind of animal?" As he said it, a cocky smile pulled at his lips, revealing his fangs.

I shot the arrow at him but he easily out-maneuvered it, his speed far greater than I anticipated. He was coming for me. I braced my sword up in defense, but he was already behind me.

His words were a cold puff embracing my ear. "I do not want to fight you, Esmore," he growled. I struck my sword behind me, but again he had anticipated my moves. My heart raced. Never had any vampire been ahead of me.

Again he was behind me. His hands grabbed me from behind, and he held me firmly, his chest hard against my back.

"You looked sexier in your leather. White garments don't suit you." I felt his cold fingers lightly brush over my neck. I sucked in my breath, unsure as to whether he was going to rip out my neck or if he was attempting to seduce me.

All of a sudden, I was very alone. I spun quickly, no longer able to feel his presence. He'd vanished. I looked down at my white robe. He had slid down part of the collar, revealing my shoulder. His lingering touch trailed down my shoulder. I grabbed the robe, covering myself in disbelief. How did he know my name? Why did he flee?

"Esmore!"

James burst out of the forest, startled by my rattled expression. I quickly concealed my confusion. I looked into the forest again, in search of the Council vampire whom I'd just come in contact with. How did he know my name? So many questions bombarded me. My entire body thrummed with an unexplained excitement, and my breath came out in staggered breaths. His face kept flashing in front of me as he lingered on my mind.

"What happened?" James said, coming to me and pulling me close to him. Instead of flinching, I accepted his embrace. My head rested into the warmth of his chest as I battled with myself. *Who was that, and what is this strange feeling that he has left behind?*

CHAPTER 10

JAMES LED ME back to the front gates of the Guild with his arm comforted around my shoulder. I felt like a stray, like an animal that had been abandoned by their owner and was taken in by another. I was familiar with James, yet when I walked within the walls everything felt different. *What is this sudden change?* Something had frightfully woken inside of me, and I couldn't fathom what the change had been.

"What did you see out there?" James prodded. I thought of the mysterious vampire I met, reminding myself of why it was I went there. Wasn't he doing something to Dillian? Dillian only started acting bizarrely when I could feel the presence of that vampire.

"Where is Dillian?" I demanded, coming out of my haze.

"Do not answer a question with a question," Campture lectured sharply as we walked into her room. I hadn't even noticed James leading me up the stairs. I threw a contemptuous look at James. Of course he and Campture were in cahoots. "You jumped the fence against my orders twice in one day," she seethed. "What do you have to say for yourself?"

Again, I felt an unfamiliar strength rise within me. I didn't know exactly what to report, as I had not yet concluded on anything myself. I couldn't entirely understand why that vampire chanced a meeting with me and then simply let me go.

"Why are you wearing this robe?" she questioned, marching toward me. I stepped away, on reflex more than anything. Why didn't I trust her? She growled at my step away, narrowing her yellow eyes on me.

"Take your robe off!"

"Es…" James trailed off as if trying to soothe the situation. In that moment it only made me feel even more disgusted by him. He always wanted me to play by the rules. He never supported me or sided with my 'estranged' beliefs or questioning of procedures. I tore the white robe off, revealing my damaged leather attire. They both ran their eyes over it feverishly as if witnessing a tremendous secret being revealed.

"When I carried Corso back he began to perspire acid onto me," I explained quietly, trying to contain the beast inside of me that wanted to emerge. I felt trapped by them, cornered as an enemy, as opposed to being their comrade in any way. It was only now that I noticed Kelf also standing in the room. I felt disorderly and groggy as to how I got here.

"What's wrong with your head?" Campture grimaced in rage as she took another defiling step toward me.

"Nothing," I replied both angrily and confused. I touched my face, expecting to retrieve blood from a wound. There was nothing.

"I cannot study your thoughts? It's the same barricade of distortion as those who have been in contact with the Council."

The accusation startled me. I processed her words. *How was that possible?* I traced through rational thought. Was Campture becoming senile or did it have something to do with the mysterious vampire by the river? Did *he* jumble my mind? James didn't intervene or move when Campture advanced on me.

She stretched her long fingers toward me. "Do not touch me!" I hit her hand away from me. The loud smack of defiance echoed in the room. Her fluorescent yellow eyes grew very thin. My instinct interjected as she tried to touch my mind to connect with me. My inner voice was very clear at that moment. *I do not trust you.*

"Miss. Campture, I think a lot has happened today, maybe we should—"

Kelf was quickly cut off by Campture. "Hold her in the cell!" she demanded.

I stood there breathing slowly, trying to contain what it was within me that eyed her neck, wanting to rip her voice box out. If she couldn't speak then she couldn't command. If I resisted or lashed back in any way I would be outcast, or worse, killed. I tried to grasp onto rationality, I wasn't allowed to disobey the Head Huntress. *They are my people*, I reminded myself. Whatever punishment was to come would not last long and would only be an example so others didn't fight back in such a way. *I am a Token Huntress. All will be well. This is where I belong.* But such a savage and foreign part of me couldn't respect her for treating me this way. It was as if this darkness that swirled inside of me was finally finding a voice of its own- one that I could no longer suppress by using my father's techniques.

The hunters who guarded the door crept in and surrounded me cautiously. If I wanted to, I could have escaped. James looked at me, unsure of what he should do. I gave him a look which told him to stay back. He was the last person I wanted touching me. I tried to hide the savage smile that wouldn't dare reach my eyes. She was daring enough to command my fellow hunters to tie me up.

"I do not need to be tied down like an animal to be taken to a cage. I can walk myself." I spat on the ground at Campture's feet. The rising savage part of something foreign uncurled in my stomach, delighted at the dishonorable act. I could no longer pretend to respect her as my Guild headmistress. They couldn't keep me in a prisoner cell forever. *I am a Token Huntress, and I have done nothing wrong. She can't hold anything against me.* Until I was free, I would stay silent until she decided to stop treating me like the enemy.

I walked to the cell which was close to the north side of the wall in a separate underground tunnel. It was separated from the other tunnels that housed the training, education, infirmary, and eating areas. At the end of the tunnel were three different cell rooms.

The first silver door was opened for me. There was only a chair and small window up top. This was placed in here to serve as a discomfort to the vampires we kept. Usually, they were tied to the wooden chair, which was the only thing in here. It was directly positioned under where the sun would shine during the day. We tied them with silver rope—it was the only thing that truly affected their strength substantially, and the silver burned them. It was one of the few objects that we could use against them which decreased their will to fight. One of my fellow hunters closed the door behind me.

I began pacing the room with my arms crossed over my chest, thinking about the day's events. I again looked at the scar that should have been on my arm after Teary burned it, but nothing was there. How had I healed so rapidly? I thought of the vampire from the Council. How had he been so much faster than me? I punched the wall in rage. How had everything fallen apart so quickly? I retracted my hand, noticing a small trail of blood from where I had busted my knuckles. I refocused. A member of the Council knew where we were. This could destroy us and yet I was now locked in a cell, unable to tell anyone.

I leaned against the wall and closed my eyes for only a second, but my body's exhaustion quickly put me into a deep sleep.

There was fog everywhere, like always. But this time it was thicker and trailed over the water where our fishing nets were. I looked closely, noting that this was the exact spot I killed the vampire who had been a part of the Council and was with a human girl. Lurking in the river was the same shadowy figure I had recently met. He was washing his face, whistling a tune I'd never heard before. The moon shone dimly, causing the wet blue gem on his left ear to sparkle.

I wasn't alarmed, and my hands didn't grab for my weapons. Here, I was at ease with him. I searched my surroundings, unsure of what was happening. "Is this a dream?" I asked, my voice echoing in the enchanted forest. It felt as if we were the only ones present and that no one else existed. I couldn't hear forest animals or others nearby. Right now, it was only him and me.

"You could call it that," he said, looking over his shoulder with a smile.

"Did you do something to me?" I asked. Campture could no longer read my thoughts, and that happened after my confrontation with him. It was odd… I felt so soothed, so *human*. I felt vulnerable yet safe at the same time. He slowly walked over to me, the water dripping over his face and muscular frame. A few droplets from his dripping hair landed on his leather jacket. A small line of water trailed down his stomach, illuminating his abs.

I could not describe the exotic intensity that swirled around us. In this place we were familiar with one another. I hungered for his touch. It was as if we were lovers reunited. In this dream world, I was encompassed by his smell, his allure, his everything.

"Your eyes are greedy," he whispered with a playful smirk. He walked closer to me, the fog sweeping around him. When he reached me, without hesitation, he reached for my face and cupped it. He pushed aside my golden fringe, looking at me longingly. "You are ravishing."

I stared at his beautiful lips as he spoke, undeniably mesmerized. Something was enticing me to pull him in. He grabbed my hand and pressed it against his hard chest. His skin was cold, yet somehow I felt electrifying warmth.

"You are so cold, yet you feel warm to me," I said in a distant tone.

"That is because you are my familiar," he said, his thumb stroking my cheek. His thumb trailed down my cheek and my neck, before stroking along my collarbone.

"We have met?" It all felt like a distant memory or a dream that I'd be entrapped and had no ambition to run away from.

"No, Esmore, our souls are familiar. We are of the same."

His words made no sense to me, yet I lingered upon every word. He did feel so familiar. There was a fierce connection I couldn't entirely understand nor deny. My hand trailed slowly over his chiseled stomach, stopping near the belt of his dark blue jeans.

"But I don't even know your name," I said, fully captivated by my desire. His hand lightly brushed over my breast as he pulled me in. He held me endearingly as he leaned in to kiss me.

"My name is Chase." His words thinned into a whisper before I could feel our lips touch.

Hitting reality hard, I jolted up from where I was sitting against the cold wall. I was still in the cell. I looked above me, remembering my dream. "What the f-" A loud banging noise broke through the silence. I straightened myself and noticed the sudden rash that had spread across my body. I looked at my skin, noticing it wasn't a rash at all. I was simply too hot and had goosebumps plastered all over my skin. I stood, listening as someone walked down the stairs toward my cell. I held my head high, waiting for the accusations they would soon throw at me. The sooner this was over, the sooner I would be able to inform them of the immediate danger we were in. The sun shining through the window informed me that it was now day. I must have slept all night.

Campture walked in with her lips pursed tight. She, too, held her head high. "You need to go out to find more information." I knitted my eyebrows in confusion. "It seems as though one of your members, Dillian, has yet another specialty in his gift. He can foresee," she said as she avoided eye contact with me.

Kelf was standing behind her, looking at me respectfully, like he always did. Kelf didn't hold the same bitter distaste for me as Campture did. He was one of the first to nominate me as Token Huntress.

"Dillian cannot foresee the future," I said suspiciously. He could only see long-distance.

"I thought the same, Miss. Aguire. I thought he was playing mind games… trying to relieve you of your punishment. But, after connecting with his mind, I saw the same visuals that he did. And it is not a lie. He was very clear about the few members who should go. And you, Esmore, were one of them."

"And you will let me go without punishment?" I asked, almost not believing her words. Her lips tightened again, and I could see one of the veins in her neck protrude.

"We had to send another raid team out yesterday morning. The transport team did not return. We had another team follow afterward to make sure the human was untouched. Both teams have yet to return."

There was silence for a moment. I thought about Golipse, who was a part of that team. It was a very stormy day indeed, hopefully it didn't give the vampires the advantage. "I see. So, have you revoked my Token title yet?" I said with arrogance, folding my arms over my chest.

Her gaze locked with mine. I could sense her rage boiling. Whatever it was she wanted to say, she held the words back. It must have infuriated her that she could not read my thoughts. After my odd dream, I had suspicions that the vampire I'd met by the river might've had a role to play in blocking Campture from inside my head.

"Foresight is a very powerful gift. You all have your part to play. This is how we will find the Council. I will not let your attitude or almighty pride get in the way. You cannot simply dismiss a Token. But you have disappointed me greatly," her tone thickened. "And there will be punishment; you will not come out of this unscathed."

I did not take her threat lightly. I knew when I returned there would be consequences for defying her. But at least now I knew Dillian was safe, and we might have the upper hand in the fight.

"When do we leave?" I asked. My body was now rejuvenated. I was ready to attack the Council. Finally, we had the chance.

"Now."

CHAPTER II

I QUICKLY CHANGED into a fresh set of clothes, not any different from my usual leather pants, boots, and long leather shirt. I met my team in the weapons room.

The team was smaller than what it had been only yesterday. Kora and Kasey looked at me suspiciously, Teary indifferently, and James pouted angrily with his arms crossed over his chest, not able to make eye contact with me. Dillian looked tired, the bags under his eyes evidence that the foresight took much out of him. But it didn't break his spirit, and he gave me a weak smile when I walked in. A part of me knew he would've been worried about my lockup. James shot Dillian a murderous look. I couldn't help but want to walk up and slap him for his stupid jealousy. When we returned from this mission, I would have to deal with him accordingly.

To my surprise, Tori was standing with everyone, his arms crossed over his chest, mimicking James. When he looked at me, it was not with his usual contempt. His eyes were filled with respect, and he now looked like a man. I was saddened to know that such terrible circumstances had to happen for him to respect me as his Token.

"What of Corso?" I asked. Everyone looked down, except Dillian. I inhaled deeply, preparing myself for what they would now say. I had failed him. The tally of members who had died under my charge had grown. Were we out of our league? I internally slapped myself. *No. I have never, and will never, doubt my skill or that of my fellow hunters.* This was because Campture permitted him to use such a stupid weapon from the past.

"His leg had to be amputated," Kasey explained nonchalantly. Her upbeat tone bothered me. I gave her a pointed look. She shrugged her shoulders at me childishly. "What? He could have died. It's good that it's just his leg."

"He is still battling for his life, though," Kora interrupted, slightly more seriously. "It's all up to the infirmary team now. We did what we could. I doubt he'll be a part of this team anymore. How could he possibly fight with only one leg?"

Their blatant disinterest in Corso's outcome irritated me. And yet this was how we had all been programmed and how we were meant to be. If you couldn't fight then you were of no interest within our group. Swallowing this, I nodded, thanking them. I felt almost sorry for the loud-mouthed Corso—he lived for the raid team. But now with only one leg, who knew what would happen to him?

"Status update on the transport team?" I asked. Campture was vague in her descriptions of their whereabouts; she would usually go into far greater detail.

"Nothing yet, no one has returned. We ain't yet sure if it was delayed, if they are in hiding, or if something else has happened," Teary answered.

"Can you not foresee them?" I asked Dillian. He looked at me as if he had only just walked into the conversation, his mouth slightly open. He looked horrible and so awfully tired. I was hesitant to take him on our outing.

"It doesn't work like that, Es," James said. My gaze must've been harsher than I anticipated because he dropped his gaze to the ground.

"I am still trying to understand it myself," Dillian interrupted tiredly. "It's kind of like, I'm being shown things. I don't get to choose, they just happen. I saw a few things and pieced them together over the night with Campture, who could see the same as me when she read my mind. Everything leads to the exact hunters and members of this team going back into the city. There we will find a Council member, fight off a few more. It will be a challenge, but everyone will be unharmed. This is what will lead us to the right information about where the Council is stationed. This much Campture and I clued together."

This was good news indeed, but I couldn't help being suspicious of his 'new found' gift. Suddenly, Chase's image flashed into my mind: the water dripping over his lips, his stone-cold abs... I closed my eyes in irritation. Why am I seeing him? When I opened them again, everyone was looking at one another cautiously, and then eyes were on me once again.

"Teary, what have they supplied you with?" I asked, dismissing their looks and walking over to assess the items in her bag.

"The same as last time, except I was given three grenades as well."

I thought about this for a while. *Grenade.* The word rang a bell. She pulled one out from her bag, and I held it up to the team. "These were used a few times when Drue was Token. They are effective when there are a lot of vampires surrounding. All you do is pull this pin. They have adjusted these ones, however. Last time they used one, another hunter was blown apart because they were too close. Now there is a time limit on them. So once the pin is pulled, ten seconds is allowed. Everyone, make sure to run for cover if this weapon is used."

"Esmore?" Tori called, walking toward me with my sword and Barnett crossbow in hand. His head bowed reverently as he offered the items to me. I now looked at him differently. I could tell by the way he looked at me and moved around me that he held respect for me. It was reassuring to know he didn't hate me because I was unable to protect his fellow apprentice. His gift of my weapons was a token of that respect. "Campture wanted me to give you back your weapons."

I took them from him with feigned indifference.

"Well, if that is all, we will leave at once. I saw no clouds, so this will be a full day's run. We won't stop until we are at the edge of the city. We will rest there for the night. If anyone cannot come, they must speak up now. Dillian's gift is new, and we have yet to test its reliability. I will not hold it against anyone if they don't feel up to it."

I had Dillian in mind as I said this, he looked terrible, and I hoped that he would stay behind. But no one stepped forward. Dillian deliberately ignored my eyes, knowing that statement was intended for him.

"Well then, move out."

We paused periodically twice. Each time I called for refreshments and a small break, mostly for Dillian's sake. He would never admit it, but he had been struggling with our pace. I didn't know how this new foreseeing skill of his worked, but by his exhausted expression and sunken eyes, it took a lot out of him, I could tell that much. I held the utmost respect that he didn't ask me to stop and continued to persevere.

As I kept an eye on James broad back as he took the front position of our group, memories flashed of when we first began sparring and taking an interest in one another at sixteen. At first, it was to train and test our skills against one another as we were both at the top of our classes, but then things flourished into something more. It was enjoyable to have such a tough opponent. All the female apprentices wanted him. I couldn't help but be flattered back then. Eventually it became more, and we started a relationship—one that was seemingly happy and playful. But slowly the sparring stopped as he began to see me more as his girlfriend than a worthy challenge. Shortly after that, when my hunter's eyes vanished, it seemed he only wanted to conceal me, like a damaged animal. Looking back at it all now, that was when the problems began.

We navigated our way through the forest. There was very little fog to interfere with our sight and no vampires to be seen. When we could see the outskirts of the city we set up camp. We'd stayed in this lookout once before. It was a good location: a cave on the side of a hill. It gave us a visual of the city, but no further as the fog lurked over the ground and into the distance. We took turns to stay on watch, two at a time. It was Teary and James who were to take the first shift, followed by myself and Dillian, but looking at him now, I'd insist he sleep instead. Kora or Kasey could take his shifts.

Tori walked over to me, tightening his leather jacket around him and puffing his chest up. He had seen me watching Dillian closely. "I can take over Dillian's shift, if you would like, Token Huntress," he offered. I considered it for a moment. He had proven himself to be a very gifted apprentice when we had last fought together despite his rash movements that had us ambushed in the first place. I didn't care to reprimand or guilt him, he would live with his demons. And it would be a mistake he'd never make twice. Looking at Dillian, who was searching for his water bottle, Tori was a much better choice for now.

"That would be appreciated. Please inform Teary of the change," I asked, tapping him on the shoulder in thanks as I walked past him.

I could feel James' gaze on me from afar as I crouched next to Dillian. He looked paler than usual. "How are you fairing?"

He rubbed over one of his eyes before scratching his head. "I've had better days, but I'll be okay after a few hours' sleep." He dropped his tone to a whisper only he and I could hear. "How are you? You could cut the tension with a knife."

I took a seat beside him on the rocky ledge, looking out toward the city. The land had almost engulfed the sun. "Which form of tension? My imprisonment by my own kind, my boring relationship issues, or my confrontation with a Council vampire?" I deadpanned. I knew that no one could hear. Campture could not read our minds from so far away. Here, we were free.

"What!" Dillian exclaimed in a hushed tone. He bent his knees awkwardly to his chest, eyeing me from the corner.

"A vampire followed us from the city. He had been the one to shoot me with a paralysis dart. Last night, when you had your first... uh... vision, I was confronted by the same vampire on the south. He was faster than me, stronger than me, and held a power I'd never felt confronting a vampire before." Despite all that, it hadn't been the part that frustrated me the most. "Dillian, he knew my name."

Dillian didn't hide his shock. His lips parted in surprise as he tried to absorb this new information. He looked behind us, making sure no one could hear. James was scraping his sword down a tree trunk to sharpen it as he watched us warily. Right now, he and his monstrous jealousy were the least of my concerns. He had no right after how quickly he had turned on me last night all to appease Campture and her orders.

"What did he want from you? Did he try to kidnap you?" Dillian asked cautiously.

The more I thought about the vampire's actions, the more I realized they were not threatening. He didn't even carry a weapon which was somewhat offensive now. Did he think I wouldn't be a challenge? I pondered over his motives for a while, pausing as the image of him popped into my head again. The water sliding over his chiseled abs. His wet, glistening black hair. I refocused myself. How filthy of me to admire him—a vampire.

"He only asked me about my huntress's eyes," I finally said. Dillian didn't interrupt as I continued my train of thought. I remembered him saying we were... *familiars*. "He said we were familiar, but I've never met him before. What do you think that means?" I asked, rattled by my inability to decipher it. Did he mean that we were acquainted or did the word *familiar* hold a far greater significance to vampires? My stomach tightened with desire at the memory of his cool touch.

I slammed my hand angrily into the ground. Dillian flinched in surprise, and I looked at him apologetically. I tried to suppress my thoughts. The sudden ache of my knuckles was the only thing taking away my lingering thoughts. *He is not a man*, I reminded myself. *He is a disgusting vampire.* I growled, irritated. *What spell had he cast on me to make me seemingly… infatuated with him?*

"Did you tell Campture about this?" Dillian asked. At my hesitation, his eyes bulged in disbelief. "Esmore, there was a Council vampire outside our Guild. They know of our location. What if they ambush us now? How could you not tell her that?"

Everyone looked up as his volume rose in the last sentence. Luckily, they didn't know what it was he was yelling about. He regained himself, pinching his nose. "Sorry, I'm tired. But, Esmore, you know the potential consequences of this. There are people back there who are unprotected. People I care about, even if you don't."

I was ashamed of my actions. What could I say, I didn't have time? I wanted to figure it out myself first? There was no excuse I could use to justify it. And the more I thought about it, the angrier I became. Why had I not told her of him? Before recently, I wouldn't ever hold something like that from her, even at my most defiant. I felt like my mind was tricking me.

I rested my hand on his shoulder, deep in thought. "Don't worry. I promise I won't let anything happen. Rest, Dillian." But I was tormented by my own insincerity. Why was I now keeping dangerous secrets when it risked not only me?

CHAPTER 12

I DIDN'T DARE sleep that night in case my mind drifted like it had the night before when I was confronted by the vampire who went by the name Chase. I didn't want to dream of him in such a grotesque manner. I hated how my body ached for him. I should have shot another arrow when I had the chance. I was sitting on the edge of the rock, scouting the trees below. I had the daunting sensation that Chase was still watching, and I couldn't decipher if it were reality or paranoia. I couldn't help but feel a pull toward him, and I tried my hardest to suppress it.

James took the opportunity upon wakening to advance on me. He sat down beside me. "Es, we have to talk…"

"You betrayed me yet again," I solemnly said. "Your head is so far up Campture's rear end that it's almost comical. I cannot trust you," I said defiantly. In a way, I hated him, yet there was something that stopped me from saying what I really wanted. I realized I feared being alone- entirely. Though James angered me, he was all I had left. Was that selfish of me? I preferred doing everything on my own, so why would such a thing bother me?

"I only tried to protect you. If you would have just listened, Esmore, everything would've been okay," he said exasperated. "You always run your mouth or do something that's against protocol. How do you expect me to stand by you when you won't listen to my reason?"

"I do not take orders from you. You don't own me, you don't control me, and you certainly cannot protect me, from any punishment from within the Guild walls or out here. I had so much respect for you once," I said harshly, rising to leave. He caught my hand, and I was angry at him for it. Before I could act on that and hit his hand away, the reflection of something caught my eye.

I looked deep into the trees, suspicious I had seen Chase pull back into the woods. If anything reflected, it would be the blue gem of his earring or necklace. I was disturbed by how much attention I paid to his jewelry. There was nothing there; was my mind making things up? I could no longer feel the pull of his presence. How undone was I becoming?

"Es," James said, reminding me that he still held onto me. "We need to work this out, I know we can." He took my hand, kissing my knuckles gently. I stared at him, unmoved by the action. I had enough of talking and only wanted to focus on the mission. I would deal with the calamity of this at a later time.

"We'll discuss it when we get back to the Guild," I said, retracting my hand and walking away.

Upon dawn, everyone woke almost simultaneously. Kora and Kasey yawned, covering their faces with the thin blankets provided. Dillian looked much better. His skin was no longer a ghastly pale. I'd hoped that he was taken by a deep sleep and wasn't interrupted by his new found gift.

"Okay, we keep tight in formation. Kora and Kasey, you two take the back; James and Teary take the sides. Tori, you are center; Dillian and I will be frontal. If anyone hears or sees anything, stop the group immediately, and we find cover to observe."

Everyone was prepared, but I caught sight of slight resistance. Though none of us would show our weakness, it had only been days before that we'd been ambushed in this exact same city. If I hadn't looked for it, I mightn't have seen it. An unsteady group was something we couldn't work with, and I hoped that by the time we reached the city everyone would have refocused themselves.

I gestured for everyone to move out. In our favor, the sun was seemingly bright today, forcing the sabers deep into the darkness of buildings and sewers. Though it wouldn't affect their ability to attack us, they were exceptionally sensitive and uncomfortable in the sun. I didn't like walking into the city with no factual evidence or reasoning besides Dillian's premonition. It seemed too convenient. But if both Campture and Dillian believed in it, I would take his word for it. After all, it had been the biggest clue we had in years to finding the Council.

At our accelerated speed we were on the edge of the city streets in minutes. I held tightly onto my sword with my right hand and my Barnett crossbow with my left. I flicked my fingers in the direction right to us, gesturing to search this side of the city first. The challenge we faced was although Dillian had foreseen us being in the city, there was nothing specific to look for. We had to simply hope we would stumble into the area where we were meant to be aimlessly searching for our next clue.

After walking around a quarter of the city, we were becoming frustrated. "If I may speak?" Teary whispered. I approved. Teary had been working the raid teams for a while, so her advice was greatly appreciated. "Perhaps we need to go further in toward the center of the city. I doubt that the Council would be on the outskirts. If anywhere, they would be hidden somewhere in the middle. Perhaps we need to split up to cover more ground."

I considered her idea but was adamantly against being separated. We might've been able to cover more ground, but there was an ominous sensation creeping over me in the silent and hollow streets of the long-forgotten city. "We'll go deeper into the city, but we stay together. I don't want to risk another ambush from the sabers." Even if we were better prepared this time, we were also smaller in size now.

Teary nodded in agreement. We walked further into the city, the eerie silence howling in the way of a breeze coming through. Deserted, much like it always had been. I'd only ventured into the heart of the city once. And at a later date, in the same area was where my Token Hunter, Drue, was killed. It was dangerous in the center because of the clusters of tall towers. It was too easy for the team to be torn apart, and it would take us longer to escape into the outskirts if we had to flee. A silent wind brushed through the city. On this side, there were very few bones and remains of corpses. On the west side, where we'd just come from, however, a large amount piled up, and cockroaches infested the streets.

It was reported when the vampires overpowered the humans that most had enough time to escape. The east side was a richer area and population who were given priority. The rest had not made it in time. I imagined that if it were only one hundred years since that era, the city would reek of death. But now, three hundred years later it was a ghost town. I couldn't picture its former glory. Street posts had bent over time and were now dipping eerily over the dark streets. The roads had large cracks in them. Most windows had been shattered. Droplets of stained blood had not been wiped away entirely despite the thick layer of dust and grime covering the streets. And this was considered the cleaner part of the city. The other side's fog was thicker, and it crawled densely around our ankles.

A flicker of motion grabbed my attention, and I arched my Barnett crossbow into that direction, only to realize it was a shred of curtain flapping in the wind outside the window. Still, it was unsettling that the buildings survived and remained even after all this time. It made me consider how selfish the human race had been and how congested their population must've been living in rooms atop of one another. Although the vampires were revolting creatures, they weren't the ones to blame for destroying the earth. Humans, however, monopolized the resources and drained the earth dry. And ironically, their technology was no match for the simple fangs of vampires.

We searched cautiously around the buildings and what were once glorious parks with captivating fountains. Dead trees remained, some were still barely rooted underneath the cement and others had fallen over, ripping up cracks and chunks of ground with them. Fog misted over the paved edges of the waterfall that had slowly deteriorated over time. I wondered what significance these areas meant to humans and whether it impacted their day to day living or if they were only for visual stimulation opposed to the dull buildings they had once thrived amongst. I wonder if humans saw this all now, what they would think of their once luxurious existence.

Continuing to search through the abandoned park, we could see a large bridge in the distance. Its structure was still mighty and stood strong as it was pillowed with fog. I hadn't yet had the chance to see it up close, but it was something Drue openly admired. Out of curiosity, I wanted to look down at the still water passing underneath. I wondered if it had been abundantly full of water in those times. Was the water sparkling clear or a dirty grotesque color then as well?

Movement caught my eye. Near the water fountain sat a figure. I raised my Barnett crossbow. It was a girl who sat in a wheelchair. I furrowed my eyebrows in confusion. What was a girl in a wheelchair doing here? I looked to Dillian, who was skeptically looking between her and me. I flagged my team to spread around the girl in a circular formation. She must be human. Kora, Kasey, and Teary distanced themselves to the left. James, Tori, and Dillian kept to the right, as I kept my position at the front. Slowly, with my Barnett crossbow held high, I walked toward her. The others surrounded her quickly waiting for my go-ahead.

After walking through cracked paths and dead grass, I was only a few feet away from her, but she seemed not to have noticed. She was facing the water fountain, looking at the shattered cement heap. In her hand, she held a small yellow flower. Looking around the area, I couldn't see one living plant she might've plucked it from. She was wearing a pale blue dress with long sleeves. She also wore a purple scarf, partly concealing the red-gemmed necklace she wore. It reminded me of the one Chase wore in a different color.

She was humming to herself, and when she looked over her shoulder, it was me who was more startled by her calm composure. She was pretty, with pale brown eyes and a ghostly white tinge to her skin. She was noticeably sick with some form of illness. Her hair was long and golden, but as a breeze swept through it, it moved unnaturally. She was wearing fake hair. Under her eyes was a ghastly brown color. This girl was dying of some sort of disease.

"Hello?" she said, her voice raspy. I looked at the positions my team members were in, unsure of what to do under these circumstances. I didn't care much for humans, but this girl, she struck me as odd. How could she be in the middle of the city by herself in such a weak state, without having been attacked yet? I considered how we could possibly take her to safety. She looked too fragile to move. She was so tiny, and she looked to only be in her mid-twenties.

"What are you doing here?" I asked suspiciously, still searching our surroundings, waiting for a trap or ambush. Was this girl some sort of bait? Although I already knew she was not a child, her presence gave off a very innocent vibe.

Suddenly, I was overwhelmed by many presences closing in on us. I raised my crossbow in the direction of Dillian and shot behind him at where a vampire crept from the shadows. Council vampires. My team broke into action, fighting off vampires who attacked them. *This girl was bait.* I looked at her angrily, wanting to kill her.

A ghastly snarl ripped through the air drawing fellow vampire's attention. The Council vampires were holding back one of their own, pinning him so he couldn't freely move. The vampire they held captive was blond-haired, bronzed complexion, with blue eyes, and average in build. But as the others struggled to contain him, I realized despite his average frame, he was far stronger than them. While they held him in position, I couldn't let the chance slip to take out such a powerful vampire.

Aiming for his chest, I shot an arrow. He busted the faces of two of the vampires who held him and snapped the neck of another who tried using a sword against him. He dodged my arrow, growling savagely. Before I knew it, he was already in front of me, his speed incomprehensible. He backhanded my crossbow away from me and moved to grab my throat, but I narrowly dodged it, taking hold of his arm and swinging myself over it.

I balanced in a crouching position, aiming to strike my sword through his chest. Before I had the chance, he kicked me across the face, knocking me along the gravel. I quickly collected myself, having to focus intensely on his next move. His speed was the same as Chase's. I inhaled deeply, summoning the darkness which always fed and enhanced my senses. *I can and will kill him.*

James ran toward him with his sword. The vampire grabbed him around his neck, and I took the moment of distraction as my opening. James' skin hardened into metal. The vampire growled as he was unable to snap it. James was a decoy, a maneuver we'd used plenty of times before. He threw James into a distant tree, the bark exploding around him at the impact. The vampire moved so he stood in front of the girl who sat in the wheelchair. She looked down as she toyed with the yellow flower in her lap.

Even when I conjured all my strength, his speed was unmatched. I aimed my sword for his chest. He grabbed my blade with his hands, blood spurting everywhere, his eyes now savage on me. He threw it away in one swift movement, grabbed my throat, and was ready to rip out my heart. His large fangs were already covered in someone else's blood still dripping in thick clumps. Had he bitten into one of his comrades? I couldn't breathe nor did I gasp for air. I would not fall so far as to want mercy from his kind.

Before he plunged his fangs into me, a hand stopped him. My heart pounded, yet I was not scared to face my anticipated death. A swift movement was made, and I fell to the floor, holding my throat and coughing for my first desperate breath. Whoever had grabbed his hand, tore him away from me. I looked up at the all too familiar leather coat. It was Chase. My body thrummed wildly at the closeness of him. His back was to me as he faced the vampire who had almost killed me. Did the Council really have such old and strong vampires right under our noses this entire time?

"Don't touch her. She's mine," Chase snarled, holding two swords.

"She threatened Whitney!" the other vampire spluttered and spat a mass of blood onto the ground.

"Tythian." The small voice of the woman from behind him broke the tension. "It's okay, we can go now."

He buckled to his knees in front of her, cupping her face gently. "I'm sorry," he whispered to her. "I did not know they would use you for this." She gently caressed his face. Amidst the unsettling noises of weapons scraping against one another, it seemed to them that nothing else mattered as they gazed into one another's eyes devotedly.

"Let's go home," she said with a reassuring smile. I was mortified how comfortable she was in the blood war that raged around her.

Before I could stand, the vampire had grabbed her chair, and with lightning speed, they were gone.

Chase turned to me, his fangs not as large as Tythian's, but I could see he too was an aged vampire compared to most we confronted. "Esmore," he whispered. Before I could run for my sword to use it against him, he had already vanished, leaving me behind.

Kora and Kasey were the reason he'd fled. They had advanced on him, trying to entrap him. For whatever reason he hadn't tried to kill them. He simply hid amongst the dark. I could still feel his presence close by, but it felt as if he were only watching. Not fighting, but just watching how everything would play out. Realizing Chase was gone, they focused on another three vampires, entrapping them as Dillian and Tori covered their backs. One by one, the girls trapped more. There were so many of them.

Teary was fighting off four. They all seemed like young vampires, Tythian and Chase being the exceptions. They lacked in strength and speed, some still trying to find bearings on their enhanced abilities which made them easy pickings for my team. We could equally challenge vampires that were no more than one hundred and fifty years old. After that it became difficult to compete against a vampire who had lived for so long.

James was now by my side. He had gathered my Barnett crossbow and sword for me. I used my arrows instantly on a vampire who ran for me, piercing his chest. He crumbled to the ground, quickly decaying. I roared in anger at how easily the previous two vampires had overpowered me. I sliced through another vampire, cutting down his throat and through his belly. I cut across another's head, slitting his throat and puncturing his chest. I raged again, feeling myself fill with hatred and a need to see their blood. I cut off one's arm, plunging my sword into its chest, driving so deep into it that after a few steps I had nailed it to a tree. It slumped around my sword, its skin turning black. I pulled the sword out, watching it as it began to decay.

A huge fire lit behind me. Teary was controlling the flames, sweeping over the ten vampires that encircled her. There must have been one hundred vampires creeping out from the shadows of tall buildings. This had been a well-thought-out ambush. James grabbed one vampire's throat and then another as it ran from behind him. Smashing both their heads together, they shattered from the impact. He grabbed his sword from the ground where a vampire must have previously knocked it out of his hand. He punctured both in the chest before they could heal.

I could feel the presence of many more coming from the distance in overwhelming numbers. I located Teary. We were becoming outnumbered and the only way to take out that many vampires at once was to use the grenade. As if knowing what I was thinking, James ran to Teary as she continued to sweep her hand in elegant swirls, lighting vampires who grotesquely screamed in response.

In the distance, a vampire stalked toward Teary. He, too, was strong and old and was holding some manner of hierarchy as the other vampires followed him in a structured line. James pickpocketed one of the grenades from Teary's pack and pulled the pin. Inwardly, I counted the short seconds in my head. *Ten, nine.* Teary continued to control her flames, still engulfing the many around her. *Eight, seven.* Two vampires came at me. I quickly thrust my sword into them, before shooting an arrow into another vampire who jumped at me from atop the rubbled fountain. *Six, five.* James threw the grenade toward the small army that stampeded toward us.

The leading vampire swept one hand across and toward Teary and James. A gust of wind extinguished her flames and pushed them both back. They went flying. The wind caught Dillian, Tori, Kasey, and Kora as well as they smashed into a nearby building and buckled forward from the impact. The gush of wind had splattered even their own kind who were in range of the single-handed attack. Somehow, this vampire had the gift to control wind. The grenade flung into the air was being pushed toward my team.

Four, three.

With all the speed I could muster, I ran for them, catching hold of the grenade in the air before it tinkered to the ground beside where my team caught their bearings. I ran toward the oncoming army of vampires, focused on getting the grenade as far away from my team as possible. I threw the grenade toward the vampires.

Two, One.

The grenade exploded into an array of blasting colors and shattered far more than just the anticipated amount. In one quick flash, a burst of dust swept over me with the chasing burning flames that encased my body. I was engulfed in darkness. In the remaining moments of my life, I heard my name whispered by an angelic voice. I had never imagined the afterlife might've sounded so tempting or sweet. With no regrets, I realized it was my time of death and the journey of what might await me beyond.

HOLLOW DARKNESS

The darkness which was bestowed upon me at birth,
has edged into my very soul.
My father whispered those haunting words and lessons,
making sure I would never reveal that clawing beast.
Father, you and mother are now gone.
And I am the shell of an adult now.

The world I fight in against vampires is offering a power which we
never thought I'd know.
I can feel it rising, and with it I feel the taste of pleasure.
My skin shrieks to be free of this taint, but I can feel the beast within
me, smiling.
I am Huntress, but within me, I can feel this darkness.
Father, what if it consumes me?

CHAPTER 13

T HE CLOUDY DARKNESS I was shrouded in slowly began to clear. I
mumbled something under my breath, startling and waking myself
up. My eyes felt sticky as they fluttered open. I was in an unfamiliar
room. I shot up, wincing at the surprising amount of pain that followed. I
looked down at my body, which was covered in deep cuts and gashes. It
seemed odd that they were so deep and yet they didn't bleed. It looked like
an animal with sharp claws had attacked me and savagely taken chunks of
my skin.

I suddenly realized I was not alone. I reached for my weapons, but they
were nowhere near. The room I was captive in was large and looked like a
basement of sorts. I sat in a large king-size bed with a wooden frame. Above
me was a small window where no light shone in. I had the eerie sense that was
because it was night. There was an odd material hanging in front of me. I tried
recalling its name; it was a type of lounge bed from the technology era. We had
studied many trivial things like this at the Guild. It finally dawned on me. It
was a 'hammock.'

I was mortified to notice that many faces were looking at me in the way
of tiny dolls. Rows of them were stacked on a tower of six silver shelves. It
looked like there were many more rows behind. Their heads rattled slightly
when a small breeze swept through the room. They were creepy.

"They're called bobblehead dolls," a familiar voice said as he crept out of the shadows. Chase walked up to one, lightly tapping its head. It began to bobble fiercely.

He wore dark blue jeans, which were torn to shreds and a long leather jacket. The material hung in threads. I could see his muscular legs through the cuts, toned and strong. A small line of hair trailed from his belly button to below his belt. I flushed in anger at my admiration. *He is a filthy vampire,* I reminded myself.

"You kidnapped me," I spat angrily, regaining my poised demeanor. I'd never show my weakness to a vampire.

"Pardon? No. I was the only one who tried to save your life," he corrected me. The glimmer of the blue gem on his ear grabbed my attention as he stepped forward. I was disgruntled by how comfortable I was in his presence. I flushed with fury, knowing I had to kill him. I had to kill all vampires. I searched around, looking for what I could use as a weapon against him. Perhaps I could kick in the wooden bed, splintering it and using it as a stake.

"Esmore, your hunters abandoned you. They left you for dead when the grenade went off. I swooped in as fast as I could, but you had already been gunned down with shards from the explosion."

I idly looked down at my wounds. They did look like the repercussions of such an event. The memory painfully crept up on me. I recalled my self-sacrificing motions with no thought behind it. I'd run with the grenade to save the others without hesitation. Chase's torn jeans were much the same as my tattered clothing. Part of my breast, stomach, and inner thigh were revealed, and a foreign sensation of exposure crawled over my skin. I tightened my jaw. Whatever this wave of nauseating emotion was, I didn't like it. I'd never experienced an oddly thrilling mixture of self-consciousness as well as allure. I hated every moment of feeling something after going without emotion for so many years. What I hated most was this particular vampire who evoked such feelings.

"If that's the truth, then I should be dead!"

"Wow," he mocked. "You are so depressing. I thought you would at least idolize me or something after I saved you."

"You kidnapped me!" I spat savagely, hiding my pain as I moved uncomfortably.

"I saved you, at least admit that," he said. I searched the inside of the room, once again looking for something I could use against him as a weapon. But my body ached with an exhausted fragility I'd never known, and I questioned if I could get anywhere quick enough to evade him. As if knowing what I was thinking, he went serious again.

"Esmore, you should be dead. Hunters don't heal like you do." He slowly walked toward me. My body stiffened of its own accord. I maintained my gaze on his enticing gray eyes that refused to look away from me. There was something that nagged at me as if he felt familiar. It felt as if we had known one another long ago. My body craved his touch. My mind was repulsed at the thought of it, yet my body sang out for it. Despite everything I had been taught and raised on, my body felt no fear of being in his presence. If anything, I felt empowered by it. I tried to find my logical form over the confusion of feelings that bombarded me. He sat in front of me, on the edge of the bed. "But I am glad you are not." He reached a hand out toward my face as if going to cup it.

I was confused by my body wanting him to touch me, but my instinct to kill him. I slapped his hand away from me with a determined look. "I am not your pet," I said dryly. "You should have let me die."

At my words, he seemed disheartened, and his shoulders slumped slightly. At the same time we noticed my hand was now bleeding. The force I applied to hitting his hand away reopened one of my wounds, its thrumming pound engulfing my entire hand.

"You're so savage, I love it," he said humorously, changing his demeanor entirely. I couldn't gather my thoughts on his personality, which turned quickly from intense to, well, energetic. "Let me wrap something around that." He walked into a room that was behind me. I looked through the partially opened door to see a bathroom.

"I don't need your help!" I snarled, wanting to be anywhere but here. Why didn't he leave me to die in the explosion? I hated how much he rattled me. I'd never felt such confusion, not since my mother died.

"Oh, I'm not doing it for you, Esmore, because I know how much you despise me. For now," he said with a cocky smile. "But in all seriousness, those are my bed sheets your hand is bleeding on, so I would like you to keep your blood to yourself. It tempts me too much. You smell so sweet, and I'd rather not play this tempting game right now."

I glowered angrily. How dare he suggest I was food?

"I promise I won't touch you." He defensively raised his hands. His movement caused his jacket to open further and reveal more of his glorious muscles. "Not unless you want me to. I am old enough to fight my cravings,

Esmore." The way he rolled my name in his mouth alone seemed to give him great pleasure. I said nothing, so he continued to fill the thick tension in the air with more talk. "You know if you have a small taste of my blood I can heal you much faster than your hunter blood can."

"Absolutely not!" I spat in disgust. Before I could throw further words of reproach at him, a banging on the door began. I refocused my killer instincts. Chase had brought me back to the lair of the Council. Before I could hide, Chase had already grabbed me at lightning speed and hid me behind the door of the bathroom. He covered my mouth with his hand so I couldn't make a noise. He had me pinned against the wall so I couldn't fight him. His speed had once again taken my breath away. I could sense he was aware of his strength and held me carefully.

"Chase, I know you are in there!" a rough-sounding male shouted, banging on the door again.

"Don't leave this room," Chase whispered to me. His face was close to mine, his hot breath mixing with my own. Suddenly he realized our closeness. His eyes clouded with a very different expression. My body was responding to his touch, even though my mind screamed at me, infuriated. He licked his lips, staring at mine. The lingering feel of his fingers on my skin sent shudders of faint hotness through me. My body wanted more.

The vampire shouted again, breaking the trance we were in. "I will break down your door. You have to report to him now!"

Doing the only thing I could to remove his grip on me, I bit Chase's hand hard, drawing blood. He loosened his grip on me, slowly taking his hand away from my mouth with a small smile, finding my defensive bite comical. "Please, Esmore, do not leave this room. No one here can know you're a hunter. They will kill you." Hesitantly, he stepped away from me, assessing me carefully like I was an animal ready to break free. But I couldn't move; he had stunned me. A smile came across his face as he licked the small bite marks on his hand. Already they had healed. "Well, it looks like you did have a taste for my blood after all."

Before I could voice my repulsion, he was gone. I heard the slam of the door behind him, and suddenly I was very alone. The bathroom had a claw tub on the left-hand side, on the right, a toilet, and a long marble white bench with two basins. I hurried over to it, looking into the large mirror. I gasped at the single droplet of blood that lingered on my lip. I smeared it away with my hand, hoping I hadn't ingested any of it. Looking down at my hand in amazement, I saw my wounds had begun to heal. The pink scarring vanished, and my skin returned to its plump state.

My hands shook from anger. I had never felt so powerless in my life. Never had my mind and body been so at odds with one another. On that thought, never had my body desired anything so desperately. I pressed myself to the basin, looking at the claw bathtub, deep in thought. I questioned what happened to my team. *Please let them be alive.* I measured the distance between them and the grenade. It was far enough for them to have escaped the explosion. And it should have been large enough to wipe out the majority of the vampire Council army.

But I couldn't recall anything after the explosion. I thought myself dead. I remembered an angelic voice calling to me, and I now pieced together that was only the whisper of my name from Chase's lips as he collected me into safety. Well, his version of safety. After all, he had taken the brunt of the blow, possibly being the only reason I survived such a blast. Anger flashed through me again. Darkness was rising from the pit of my stomach. I closed my eyes, calming my thoughts so I could push back the vile darkness that so quickly rose to the occasion from my short temper.

I rested against the basin. If Chase reported to someone, it might've been the vampire who had the ability to control the wind. He was the leader who led the small army that ambushed us, perhaps he was this district's Council leader. Or maybe he'd been killed in the blast, and there was another in charge. Why had they gone to such great lengths to bring a substantial force when we were only a small raid team? And what of Dillian's foresight? How had Campture and him interpreted it so poorly? Though the predicament wasn't ideal, I had still managed to infiltrate the Council somehow. It would be a missed opportunity if I didn't delve further and gather as much information as possible. Perhaps Dillian's premonition hadn't been all for nothing. I decided to follow Chase. Whoever he was reporting to must've been someone of importance within this Council.

I looked down at my exposed body. It would only draw further attention if I walked around like this. I planned on being a shadow that no one would notice, but if I were spotted, I didn't want my appearance obviously sticking out, indicating that I'd been removed from the explosion. Humans were brought into the Council all the time. If a vampire smelled me, they would assume I was a human as well. I wasn't yet sure what they did with those humans, but in any case, my smell wouldn't be unfamiliar to them so I hoped that worked in my favor. It was our eyes that so easily gave us away as hunters and I was at an advantage there.

I surveyed Chase's room. In front of the bathroom was his bedroom that contained the king-size wooden bed, hammock, and rows of bobblehead dolls. There was a wooden desk and a black leather chair in the corner to my left. Beside it on the right was a small room, which looked to be a closet.

I jumped over the two steps leading into the room. I'd been correct. There were numerous leather jackets and other clothing neatly folded in their allocated spots. I snagged a long leather black coat, throwing it over my shoulders and tightening it around me. I wanted to take away any suspicion if I was caught. Not that I considered this much of a cover up, but it'd have to do. I had no intention of being seen.

I searched around the room for anything that could be used as a weapon. I kicked in the closest leg to the wooden desk, snapping it at the base. The wood moaned. I ignored my audible wince at the exaggerated movement. Luckily there were only a few notepads and pens on the desk, so the lost leg was no strain on the table. Honing in on my tracking skills, I reached for the door handle, only to be quickly surprised. I didn't need my tracking skills, oddly enough. For some reason, I just felt and knew where Chase was. I furrowed my eyebrows in both frustration and confusion. What had he done to me? He hadn't even yet told me his name was Chase. I was just assuming that from the dream I had. I breathed in and out harshly, trying to contain my rising anger as once again I felt that darkness stir within me. I counted slowly like my father had raised me to do if my temper or anxiety became too overwhelming. I never understood what it was that tried to appear on the surface, but it was something my father had taught me to push down. I'd never dared ask any other hunters if they struggled with the same inner turmoil. It was something my father made me promise to never let surface, so I knew it was a secret. But that secret was trying it's hardest to now be exposed. Whatever it was, I needed to get rid of it. And so, I thought of it doing exactly that, and slowly, but at my command it receded, and I was left alone with a clear mind.

I opened the door slowly, peeking through the small gap. I evaluated the hallway for a moment. No one was out there, but it was awfully bright. The walls were painted white, and very bright white lights shone from the ceiling. It wasn't at all what I'd expected. I had always considered the Council to be damp, dark, and filthy. There were blue porcelain vases with white roses in them against the walls.

I could only see in one direction, daring to peek in the other I slowly popped my head out, looking to my right. I saw with relief that no one was there. In that direction of the hallway however, was a line of doors, perfectly measured apart from one another. I wondered if this might've been the rooms of fellow vampires, just as I had been creeping out of Chase's. His room was one of the first in the corridor I now stood in. I scurried out, pressing myself against the outer wall of Chase's room. At the end of the hall was an open space with white marble floor and a running water fountain. It was the first I'd ever seen. The water collapsed over the painted rock perfectly and almost in a soothing gesture. It was beautiful. Down my left was another hallway with more doors. Perhaps more rooms? I suppressed my urge to investigate further. I had to find Chase and who he was reporting to.

Snagging ahold of that odd tie that linked me to him, I let it guide me. He was northeast to me. I looked across the room again, expecting to run into a vampire, but no one came. A creaking noise startled me from down the hallway where someone was opening their door. I ran across the white marble floor and hid behind a large white statue that did its best to cast any form of a shadow in this brightly lit room. The statue was of a creature with stripes on it. It had large canines and claws. If recalled correctly, this was once called a *tiger*.

I crouched lower behind the statue waiting for the two vampires to walk past. I wondered if they didn't pick up on my scent because they were so used to the smell of humans within the Council. Or perhaps they felt so safe within their walls that they didn't care to detect any abnormalities. When I suspected the vampires were completely gone, I followed a few more steps down the hall and was stifled around a corner. In the center of the hallway were two large wooden doors that were closed. I somehow knew Chase was in there. I looked around, trying to find a way in besides the front doors without being noticed.

Looking up to the ceiling, I noticed there was a small white pop in square. I was sure that would lead me into the roof where I could move around unnoticed. If I was lucky there'd be another opening just above the room where Chase was. I jumped onto the head of another statue. This time it was of a white wolf. I balanced on its head and jumped, pushing the square into the roof without a hitch. Jumping for the second time, I pulled myself up into the darkness just before another three vampires walked around the corner. Quickly, I replaced the white square so they wouldn't notice a hole in the ceiling. When it was closed, I felt comfortable in the dark space. I exhaled, somewhat relieved to see something not painted white. It all just seemed far too clean.

I quietly crawled along the interior roofing. To my left there were a few piled materials such as wood, fabrics, and paint. It was a small attic of sorts that looked to be used more as a storage space than anything. It boggled my mind to think that these vampires were so organized. With luck on my side, there were also many entry points just like the one I'd squeezed through to scramble inside. I opened the first one on my left, which opened into the hallway again. Closing it, I traced the familiar tug that connected me to Chase and opened another square which acted as the door in the roof. Looking down, I was noticeably in the same room as Chase. Even with exceptional hearing, I was still too far away to eavesdrop on the conversation. The room was audaciously large and the height of a two-story building. There was a steel ridge underneath me that ran around the room's infrastructure. Securely fastened to the steel ridge were colored spotlights that weren't switched on.

This room was very different from the clean and pristine staging of the hallways. There was a large booth at the front, which had two large discs on the top. I'd recalled this archaic object being called a DJ booth. The room was decorated in an antique manner. The room was almost a mockery of the clubs that humans had entertained themselves in long ago. In the center was a large wooden dining table opposite to the wooden throne where the vampire who had ambushed us with his army, sat.

The vampire who challenged me directly, Tythian, burst through the doors. I took advantage of the loud noise as a distraction, falling onto the floor as quietly as possible. I rolled to the right of me, hiding behind one of the lights. I was now in earshot to listen in on their conversation. Not that I needed to be any closer to hear Tythian's rage vibrate and echo throughout the room.

"Fier, how dare you use Whitney!" Tythian roared.

So, the vampire in charge was Fier. The man he addressed, Fier, wore a black suit and watched Tythian with great intent. His hand rested on the side of the large wooden throne.

"Actually, to be on the factual side, she nominated herself," Fier said, now placing his chin on his closed fist.

"She's sick!" Tythian roared.

"She is just a human! If you wanted her status to change you would have turned her by now. She is merely a pawn to me," Fier blatantly said. The statement outraged Tythian. He grabbed hold of a wooden candle stand nearby, throwing it across the room in anger. It smashed to bits against the pale gray walls. Vampires began to surround him, taking a protective stance around Fier. I wondered why he hadn't changed the human if he displayed such ownership of her. Older vampires with enough control could turn humans into their own kind. Even then, it was more common in the technology age for humans to be turned into vampires because there were more humans to feed off. But very rarely now were they changed.

"Do you dare come in here and challenge me? How dare you, after I found you and saved your life?" It was me who showed you kindness and brought you back to humanity, and me who has allowed that girl to stay here!" Fier said, spit coming from his mouth, his fangs had slipped out in his rage. His fangs were not as large as Chase's or Tythian's, forcing me to wonder if he was younger. So why was he in charge?

Chase watched from the sidelines, unfazed by the commotion. As if feeling my gaze, he looked in my direction. I hid further behind the light. Tythian went silent, clenching his fists before leaving the room in a rage. He seemed oddly protective of that human woman, Whitney.

Fier summoned Chase forward to speak with him. A small breeze swept through the room, brushing my plaited hair over my shoulder. I looked to the right, realizing there was an open door. How had I missed that? There were staircases close by that I could use instead of using the interior of the roof to move around.

Fier lifted his nose in inspection, his eyes quickly narrowing on Chase. "I can smell a human," he said brazenly.

"Yes, I'm so glad you noticed actually. I found myself a wee little human on my last walk through the city, perhaps you can smell her on me," Chase said light-heartedly as if sporting a new range of clothing.

"No. I can smell her presence in these surroundings," he said, gesturing around the room. The vampires in the room began looking around uncomfortably. I hid further behind the light.

"Well, you see, she is kind of fat, so perhaps you can smell her literally all over me, she has a large surface area," he said, spreading his hands out wide. My mouth gaped open.

"I don't have time for your jokes today, Chase; report to me what happened!" Fier demanded. He began to pick at beneath his nails. I found it ironic that he wanted an official report despite being there amongst the attack.

"We had sixty-five casualties," Chase began. It seemed like he was cautious of how he phrased what he was saying, aware that I was close by.

I was adamant he knew. If I could feel his presence, did that mean he could feel mine? "All of the hunters had enough time after the explosion to escape. Their grenade screen worked, and we took considerable damage."

They're alive. I sagged slightly in relief to hear my team had escaped, especially that both Dillian and James were alive.

Fier roared in outrage. "Find them! I want you on the outskirts now! Report back to me in six hours!" Fier demanded, sounding more like a child throwing a tantrum. Wind whistled through the room as his rage heightened. Much like Teary's ability to manipulate fire, he could somehow do the same with wind. Vampires with gifts weren't unheard of, though it was rare and we didn't know where the origins of their gifts came from.

Chase gave a half-cocked smile in compliance. Then he vanished as he left the room in a quick departure. My eyes darted across the room but couldn't keep track of him. The other vampires turned to each other, whispering amongst themselves as they walked out of the room. Suddenly, I felt a heavy presence loom over me. His blue gem necklace dangled beside me, and I realized I was not alone. Chase had known where I was the entire time. "Boo," he whispered.

Before I could rebel in any way he grabbed hold of me. He had me tightly bound in his arms, sweeping me through the door, then through the hallway and back into his room. His speed was exceptional. It was comparable to my fallen teammate, Pac. He laid me onto his bed before I even took my next breath.

"Do you understand the serious predicament you just put yourself in? Do you know what would've happened if you were caught?" he asked, yet he didn't seem entirely surprised.

I raised myself onto my knees so I was no longer lying on the bed. I still held firmly onto the wooden leg as a weapon. His movements were quick, and it rattled me to know I couldn't compete with him. After vigorously pacing the room, he came at me. On instinct, I raised the wooden leg to his chest.

I was now on my knees, my back to the wall as I tried to cower further away from him. He didn't come at me aggressively. Suddenly, his breath was inhaling mine, and his gray eyes silenced my movement. He looked down at my breasts, where I firmly held the end of the wooden leg. If I had the confidence I would have scrambled off the bed to break the tension of us staring at one another, but I couldn't escape his gaze. The small piece of wood was all that I held against us in my defense.

His eyebrow lifted in challenge, and before I knew it, his speed had taken me. He took the weapon from my hand and bound my hands together above my head, pinning them against the wall behind me. It wasn't threatening, but it was as if he was proving that even though I had a weapon, I could easily be trumped.

My breath was taken in the swift movement. His eyes looked over me, over my breasts, down my stomach and legs. "You look good in my jacket," he growled. I sucked in a sharp breath, still surprised by how quickly he overpowered me. He leaned closer against me, his chest now lingering against mine as he assessed my eyes and stared longingly at my lips. My heart raced at his proximity. My body craved for him to touch me.

Slowly he released my hands. One of his hands trailed down my arm. I slowly retracted them and folded them over my chest, uncertain of what was happening. *I cannot be attracted to him. He is a vampire*, I tried to remind myself. But my body ached for him in a way I couldn't entirely understand.

"I'm sorry," he said quietly. "I just lose my senses when I'm around you." He looked away from me, running a frustrated hand through his hair.

My mind came up blank. I didn't know how to respond. I was still trying to break away from the overwhelming sensation of desire my body hungered from him. Something aggressive emanated from him that my body responded to, yet I knew he would never hurt me. It went against everything I was raised to believe. As I watched him dip his head into his hands taking a shallow breath, I wondered if, like me, he was battling off this mysterious urge we felt around one another. It was as if when he got closer, when he touched me, it was intoxicating for us both.

"Just, please, don't risk such trivial things without my companionship. You cannot fight all the vampires here within the Council. There are three vampires here older than me and some with their own gifts. If they want you, Esmore, they will have you." He rose from the bed, lending a hand to help me off. I hesitated to take it, instead standing on my own. He fidgeted with the back of his neck before taking off his leather necklace.

"Wear this while I am gone." With a swift movement, his hot breath was on my ear as he stood behind me and gently placed it around my neck.

"Why?" I asked, placing my hand on the smooth gem. My logical side wanted to rip it off my neck as if a Vampire was branding me, but another part of me almost treasured the gem's cold feeling.

"You'll find it's different in the vampire Council than outside in the woods, Esmore. Here in the Council, vampires fight over their humans.

This is the only way I can protect you. If any other vampire approaches you, this claims you as my property. Before you kick and scream at me, I know I don't own you, nor will I ever try. But the way it works in here, it'll be the only way to deter any vampires from showing further interest in you. Think of it as a gift. I know you're not my property nor would I ever look at you like an item. But here, other vampires will. You don't want to draw attention to yourself, do you?"

It was very different from the way James fought over me and claimed me as his. He idolized me as precisely that, property. Yet Chase made it clear this branding was only to deflect other vampires' attention. "They will recognize it as my necklace. And if they dare touch you, they will know the consequences. I have to deal with another matter quickly, so please stay in here until I return."

I slowly turned to him, and as I spun around I was unable to avoid my arm brushing across his shirtless stomach. Suddenly, my hair blew in my face, and I heard the click of the door. He had already vanished, and I was now alone.

He is a grotesque vampire. I cannot stay, I thought as I fumbled with the smooth gem he had given me. I sat by the window idly for a moment, trying to comprehend my thoughts. I focused on my logical side because everything else in my mind was a jumble. *I was now in the perfect position to infiltrate and learn of the Council's inner-workings. I could single-handedly be the informant who would change the hunters' strength in this war.* But, like a double-edged sword, Chase also knew the location of the Guild. I was unable to comprehend why he'd saved me and brought me back here and why he hadn't reported the Guild's location to his leaders. Was it something he would use against me? What ulterior motives did he have to keep me pent up in here? What infuriated me even more was my body's yearning for his touch, yet my mind in every sense was telling me to kill him.

I flicked his necklace away, having now realized I was fidgeting with it in comfort. I starred at the little bobblehead dolls in a new light. If I could rip one of their heads off and file it down, I could keep it as a small weapon. I could search the Council's hideout while Chase was gone. Why he thought I'd respect his words in any way was beyond me. This was my chance to make a difference. Finally, I could avenge my father's and mother's murders. I could kill as many of them as possible. But for now, without my weapons, I had to be smart.

CHAPTER 14

I T TOOK ME a few hours to build the courage and decide on my next move. I'd tried to find an escape route within the room, attempting to rattle the bars on the small open slit above the bed. Even if I could somehow rip them from the walls, I wouldn't be able to fit through the small gap that led out onto the street. I paced back and forth, irritated. I concealed the wooden leg—my makeshift weapon—inside Chase's long leather jacket I wore.

After attempting to rattle the bars, I jumped off the bed and walked over to the three-legged wooden desk. Inside the small drawer were a few items such as inks, quills, and a letter opener. I almost scoffed as I examined the letter opener. *And how many letters did Chase receive?* I rolled it over my fingers in thought and sparked a brilliant idea. I wondered what a good job it could do on the little bobblehead dolls. I walked over to them, cautiously, and still surprisingly creeped out by them. They seemed to chatter amongst themselves. I'd never seen such a modern item that made me feel squeamish to approach.

There was an eeriness to them with an array of different faces that stared back at me. Some wore capes, some wore large-brimmed hats, and some wore exquisite dresses. A small breeze swept through the window above sending another wave of chatters between them. I grabbed the first one closest to me, which had a red mask across his face. I tugged on the head, ripping it from its body.

Sitting on the bed, I took the letter opener to the doll's shoulders and began chiseling it down into a small pointed edge. It might not be the most effective dagger I've ever used, but it was better than nothing. Impressed by my work, I grabbed another four and did the same, placing one small dagger in the inside pocket of the jacket. Searching through Chase's clothing to find a belt, I tightened it around my thigh, slipping the other daggers into it and shuffling slightly to make sure they didn't stab me as I moved. It wasn't the garter or weapons I was used to, but it would do. I tightened the leather jacket over me, concealing my still torn leather shirt and pants. Surprisingly, my leather boots managed to suffer very little damage from the explosion.

I threw the hood of the leather jacket over my golden hair, concealing most of my identity.

I hadn't yet seen any humans walking around or locked in rooms but assumed surely they would be imprisoned somewhere within the Council. The vampires searched for humans as frequently as hunters did. I imagined they were storing them somewhere close by. Since the human girl I'd saved only days ago hadn't offered us much information, I wanted to see with my own eyes and study the inner workings of the Council. Every vampire and human we tried to interrogate had been tampered with. Their mind had glazed so not even Campture could penetrate it and read their most profound thoughts or secrets. By being here, I hoped I could find the reasons behind that. It could be a skill we could develop and use ourselves.

I quietly opened the door, peering to my left and then to my right. I considered it odd that I hadn't seen many vampires freely walking around. But it was night. Perhaps this was when they went on their raids, choosing to compete with the sabers of a night time. It'd been some time since I'd seen Chase and I no longer felt his presence close by. I could only pray he wasn't leading his team to the Guild.

Depending on the information I found tonight, I would try to find a way to escape and return to the others. I wondered if they stayed close to the city or went to the Guild to report to Campture. It was a solemn thought knowing they thought of me as dead. After seeing the numbers in Fier's army when we were ambushed, I hoped they returned to the Guild and reported to Campture.

We'd now learned two new things. One, we had confirmation that the Council did reside in the forgotten city of San Francisco; and two, their numbers were larger than we initially considered. I wondered if other Guilds that were not within our district were up against Councils with so many vampires as well.

What I couldn't fathom was why they'd used so much of their military power and force against our small raid team of hunters, it seemed excessive. I wondered if Dillian's premonition had been a trap somehow or we were lucky that I was brought directly to the Council where I could move freely.

I pulled the hood down further, concealing my face as I stared down. I headed left again like I had last time. I was startled by the small person who blocked my path. It was the young woman, Whitney, who had been the bait to our ambush. She sat staring at the water fall blissfully over the fountain.

I was engulfed in fury when I saw her. It was because of her that we'd been so caught off guard. It was only the night before this woman had been the undoing of my team. She began wheezing a frail cough amongst the silence. Only the trickle of the water washing over the statue in the fountain made a noise.

She looked over at me with a faint smile and raised her hand for a small wave. Why was she waving at me, was she deliberately provoking me? I pulled down the hood further, looking around again. No one else was near, we were alone. I approached her, and, as I did, she focused on the water fountain again.

"I'm sorry about the other day. For what it's worth, I heard your fellow hunters made it out alive," she said before I even reached her. My back stiffened as she said, 'fellow hunters.' If a vampire walked past and overheard that, any attempt to have disguised myself would've been in vain. I could pass as human because of my eyes, and I wanted it to stay that way. Noting my stiffness, she raised her hand to me apologetically.

"Don't worry, I won't tell anyone what you are. But you know, you're in the wrong place. If any of the vampires found out…" her voice was weak, and she gave out a deep cough again. She was very sick from whatever illness she had. Thinking of the attachment the vampire, Tythian had for her, I wanted to understand why she was here freely moving within the Council. She was human, and he was vampire. Yet, he'd been so protective of her. Perhaps they were territorial about their human meals, but even then, she was so weak that I couldn't understand how her blood would give him any strength.

"You're human…" I began.

"I understand," she said, tightening the scarf around her neck and readjusting the fake hair she wore. "As a hunter, you wouldn't understand why a human like me is a part of the Council, right?"

I stood there in silence as if answering her question. Well, yes, that was one of the many questions I had for her.

She smiled timidly. "I've never really been able to talk to someone like this about Tythian and how he saved me. It's nice." Another warm smile stretched over her face as she seemed to be recalling a distant memory. But then the shadows under her eyes became prominent, and she seemed almost sad. "Tythian and I first met when I was fifteen. At the time, my father and I were trying to find refuge, in fact, we were searching for a Hunter Guild, or just hoping to stumble upon one of your raid teams, and hoped to be taken in. One night a pack of sabers attacked us. My father was torn to shreds in front of my eyes," she paused momentarily. She weakly smiled, trying to hide her transparent sadness. "It was Tythian who saved me before they turned on me. I've tried to explain to a hunter before how I feel toward Tythian, and they laughed at me. From my understanding, hunters aren't the saviors I thought they'd be. Ever since that day, Tythian has looked after me. To me, he is my everything. He has been for the last ten years."

The sincerity in her voice angered me. How could she hold such feelings toward a vampire? "You know he'll drain you." I was rehearsing what we'd been told since a young age. Our teachings from within the Guild didn't prepare us for every circumstance, but I couldn't understand in any shape, why a vampire would keep such a sick human, especially under the pretense of them having some sort of humanly relationship. I'd never heard of a case where a vampire carried a human around with them for ten years.

"Tythian would never do that. He's old and has far greater control over his cravings than most vampires. I am his familiar, he would never do anything to harm me, and it'd be almost shameful to feast on me in such a way."

Familiar. I recalled Chase once saying that to me in my dream-like state. He'd claimed we were familiar. I hesitated to ask her what it meant because I had a profound desire not to know. As if that explanation would change me in some weird way. What I needed to focus on was finding out everything about the Council, and if this girl was so freely speaking, then I would take advantage of it.

"I love Tythian with all my heart," she said with a warm smile, red blushing over her cheeks. Her pale-brown eyes reflected a sadness of sorts as she watched the water trail down the statue.

"Vampires don't know how to love. He doesn't love you in return. They're savage beasts. They've pillaged and killed most of your kind, torturing and eating humans. How could you love such a monster?"

"We all face death some day. It just so happens they need us to survive, and from the stories Tythian's told me about humans in the wars, we were not much better. We were simply weaker. I do not fear death," she stated abruptly. They'd clearly brainwashed this girl. "I'm already dying and am at peace with that. I do not fear death, in fact, I welcome it."

I pondered on this for a moment, looking at the fragile girl from the corner of my eye. Recalling from the first time I met her and the commotion that surrounded her, she certainly hadn't seemed scared—of us or the vampires.

I decided to play along with this game for a moment. "If Tythian loved you, and you are dying, why hasn't he turned you into a vampire?" I asked, recalling the great displeasure it brought Tythian when Fier asked him the same in their argument. If he really wanted her forever he would've turned her by now, surely she knew that. She was being manipulated. But she only smiled in response.

"Tythian has wanted to change me for many years; after all, I am his familiar. But I don't want that. Death is a part of life; it shouldn't so often be challenged. My body has been made fragile, and I can feel myself slowly deteriorating. But with Tythian by my side it makes it all okay. It's a very human experience and being gifted ten beautiful years with him is more than I could ask for in a lifetime with anyone else. He has respected my wishes, and I look forward to when I pass on. I've accepted it and have no desire to cheat death."

She was at peace with death, all because Tythian had made her life worthwhile. The notion almost sickened me by how brainwashed she'd become. I questioned if there was anyone I could feel so happy with. When I thought of James, such sentimentalism did not come to mind. I was repulsed. But when my body touched Chase's, feelings triggered. I felt odd and challenged. I flushed in rage, annoyed that my thoughts had trailed off yet again to Chase, whom I had to hate. Even when I despised him, my thoughts continued to sporadically turn to him.

Whitney began giggling at my expression. "You're a hard woman to read, but I can see that already you are questioning everything you've probably been taught as a hunter. The bad guys aren't as bad as you've been made to believe."

It wasn't entirely true, but I was absorbing the information and attempting to make my own calculations on some things. I wanted to take in everything I could even if it was delusional words from a sick woman before I escaped the Council. "Do all humans walk around as freely as you, or are they all chained to a wall like swinging blood bags?" I asked. She grimaced at my way of words, but I wanted to use provoking language to shock her into realizing the very inhabitants she claimed as her home.

"Vampires are not as evil as us humans once believed. The Council is a civilized structure. They capture humans, but only to ensure their own survival. Hunting for animals doesn't suffice. They don't kill the humans unkindly in here; it's the sabers that do that. Yes, some humans are killed, but that is usually by the younger ones who lack control, and there is a penalty within the walls if a vampire drains a human completely. And usually, if it is a vampire with no political power, they too are killed. It sends out a pretty big warning shot to anyone else who is considering it. The humans live freely within the walls just like me. Like a trade-off, their blood is in return for the Council's protection from the sabers, which live outside."

"And that's why you're alive, because you are Tythian's meal?" I asked. I was surprised by how willing she was to answer my questions. She seemed fragile, but not silly. She knew what information she was providing me with and how it could jeopardize the Vampire Council. So far, besides Chase and Tythian, she was the only one here who knew what I truly was.

A noise from behind sharpened my senses. Two vampires were walking toward us. Before I could speed away to a secure hiding place, she grabbed my jacket's leather cuff. "You're safe with me, just keep your hood low so they cannot see how pretty you are," she smiled.

I hesitated. It could yet again be another trap. But even if it were, I felt secure with the weapons on me to fight off two vampires. And I needed to gain this woman's trust if I was going to learn any more. She'd now lived within the Council for ten years and was voluntarily feeding me the information to any of my questions.

I stiffened beside her, and rested my other hand to the opening of my jacket closest to one of my wooden bobblehead daggers. I stared at their feet as the two vampires walked past. I anticipated the change of their stance or toes to point in my direction. But they simply continued walking without hesitation. After they were long gone, I pulled my hand away from my weapon.

"Vampires don't jump humans in passing," she giggled. "Most humans are safe to live here. Some are kept longer than others. If a human puts the structure into jeopardy, such as trying to convince a vampire to turn them, or trying to injure a vampire or another human, then they're discarded. Some vampires grow attachments to humans and claim them as their own so other vampires don't drink from them. A few have fled with their human lovers if they cannot claim that specific human as only theirs. It's Fier who gives the okay for certain vampires to have their own human. If it isn't approved, the human's blood gets shared equally with favoritism not allowed."

I narrowed my eyes on her as she said, 'human lovers.'

She looked up at me, intrigued. "I've heard hunters can be more merciless by shipping humans off to camps. Although a few hunters still protect them, I've heard of other humans feeling like sitting ducks, and some even escaped and were surprised when found and brought back to the Council. Most have a misconception about the ways and believe they'll be dragged off and torn from limb to limb. Sabers do, or sometimes coven members. The covens are hard to manage because the Council has no control over them. I mean the sabers lost their minds and humanity, but covens are the worst in my opinion," she scoffed. "They choose to toy and devour humans in grotesque ways. In this world we live in, humans are becoming extinct, and when that happens, everything will die off. Our race might not be important, but we're essential to the survival of so many others. We've shaped this world to undeniably go into extinction. So, I think there are heavier concepts to wrap our heads around than me loving a vampire who feels compassion and cares for me in return. We'll all die eventually, it's just a matter of when," she said, deep in thought and looked up at me with a small smile.

"Oh, look," she exclaimed softly, "Chase gave you his necklace." She pulled out her red one from underneath her scarf. "Tythian gave me mine when we first met as well. It means I am his and it keeps me protected from the other vampires." Her eyebrows furrowed for a moment. "Chase has never given his necklace to anyone or kept a human for himself. Does that mean you are Chase's familiar?" There was that word again.

I felt an unnerving presence. Someone was watching us. Suddenly Whitney perked up. "I can sense Tythian is close, that must mean their raid ended sooner than they thought. After a few days of being here, everyone will know you, and you'll be able to walk through the halls freely into the human sections. If you'd like I can show you around?" I was almost surprised by her openness to want to show me more and provide more information. Furthermore, pretending I was a simple human was a dangerous concept to those who she might be fooling as well. Why had I even been brought here to hide under the lie of being a human?

Whitney continued. "I'll be here tomorrow. Most of the vampire raid teams go out during the day to find humans, the others usually rest. The humans mostly come out of hiding during the day, so it's the most practical time for you to look around. I could keep you company if you would like?" She began adjusting her wheels and pulling away from me. Her little arms seemed to struggle with the motion. I nodded my head in accepting her offer. If this woman was willing to show me around the Council as some tour guide, I was certainly not going to decline it. Though I still had suspicions about how easily it was being offered.

I was disturbed to feel that I too could sense Chase was close by, presumably with Tythian. Looking at Whitney again, I wanted to ask her what this talk of 'familiars' was about. But later, when it was just her and me alone, not in earshot of vampires who might reprimand her for feeding me their secrets. It was best to stay inconspicuous and out of sight. Especially the vampire Tythian, who had once tried to kill me and knew me for exactly what I was—the enemy. I wondered if this was somehow a twisted trap. If so, Whitney's innocent act was very convincing.

Whitney and I parted ways, and I walked back toward Chase's room. Chase was somewhere back in the building, and I considered it was best not to be busted twice for escaping, though I didn't understand why he didn't treat me like a prisoner and lock the door or tie me up.

The lingering presence I felt earlier became stronger. I was getting confused as to whether it was Chase's or something else. My senses were starting to jumble in enemy territory as I became hyperaware and sensitive.

I hesitated at Chase's door, looking down both sides of the hallway. I had the creepy sense that someone was watching me. I placed my hand on the door and at lightning speed, not giving me the time to pull out my wooden leg in an attempt to defend myself, a male grabbed me and dragged me into a room numerous doors down. He threw me against a wooden dressing table, closing the door behind him. The back of my head smacked hard against the wood as I smashed into the dressing table with no balance. I gritted my teeth only being offered a brief glance at the vampire who in many aspects was more powerful than me. The Council seemed to have been hiding very powerful vampires under our noses this entire time. He was a bulky vampire, with very small pin-drop sized and lustful eyes. His fangs dripped with saliva; the size of his fangs validating my previous suspicions- he was an old vampire.

"I do like fresh meat, what a rewarding treat to stumble upon you and my, how pretty you are. Perhaps we can have a little fun before I drain you completely. I'm sure no one will notice if a new little mouse went missing." His voice had a very heavy and thick accent.

Despite his age and impressive strength, I was a proud hunter, and I would not become the meal of some repulsive vampire. I moved my neck back and forth slightly, rattling off the impact of being thrown across the room. Now this might be a challenge. I almost smiled in glee. I pulled the wooden leg out of my jacket, prepared to use it when I created an opening to pierce his heart.

The vampire smiled wickedly. "I do like foreplay, dear," he said, raising an eyebrow. My advantage was he thought I was only human.

I inhaled deeply, focusing on his movement carefully. I heightened my senses so I'd be able to track him as best as possible. He charged for me. I spun to the side, next to the full-length mirror to move out of his way. I smacked him over the head with the wooden leg forcing him to propel into the closet. His own momentum did worse damage to the piece of furniture than when he had thrown me into it. He looked back at me in surprise, now realizing that my speed and strength was not that of a human. He had underestimated me.

"Filthy hunter!" he spat sharply, now coming for me. In one swift movement, I moved behind the mirror and slammed it onto him. It shattered into thousands of pieces over him. He scratched at his eyes, trying to rake out the small shards that impaired his vision. I clutched for my handcrafted daggers, slamming one into the side of his neck. Before I could plunge another blade into his chest, he grabbed me around the throat, lifting me against the wall. My feet no longer touched the ground, and I desperately gasped for my next breath. I hit him in the face with the wooden leg twice, even managing to break his nose. In one swift movement, he knocked it out of my hand, pinning me harder against the wall. His face began to heal, and the bleeding wounds of his eyes disappeared.

His green eyes looked at me, hungrily. "The element of surprise might've tricked me once, Girlie, but never again. What a treat for me," he said, arching his head back to plow his fangs into my neck.

He was suddenly thrown off me, his grip so tight that I was flung with force as well. Before I slammed into the wall on the other side of the room, I was caught in mid-air. My hands wrapped around Chase's neck as he angrily looked at his fellow Council member. The vampire snarled at him grotesquely. Chase only stood tall, with me still in his arms radiating a confidence and power I could almost taste. I was almost mesmerized by this majestic being that had such an effect to draw the darkness of a room into him.

"You saw nothing in here," Chase commanded. "You will never touch her again. You are lucky I didn't kill you. Are we very clear, Gardar?"

His shoulders slumped slightly, and he took on a blank expression. "Yes," he said, sounding brainwashed. Suddenly it appeared this Gardar, had amnesia. His anger had vanished entirely. He looked around at his room, surprised at the mess it was in.

Just like that, we were gone as if the scene had never happened. Chase lowered me onto his bed, my hands still lingering on his bare chest underneath his leather jacket. "I told you to stay in here."

I pushed him away. "What was that back there?" I demanded from him. That vampire had no recollection of any of our fight. Was Chase the one who could manipulate minds? Was he the one preventing Campture from reading and fiddling in peoples' minds, because perhaps it was Chase who had already been in there? I found it no coincidence that after I made contact with Chase that Campture couldn't read my mind afterward. And my attraction for him was very likely the same kind of trickery he'd just displayed toward Gardar. "You brainwash people."

His serious demeanor vanished as he looked at me, skeptically. "Brainwash? I didn't even think that was a word a hunter would know. Please, I don't employ such cheap tricks. I manipulate, imply, slip into people's unconscious states and interject." He said it as if it were two different things entirely.

"You've brainwashed me! That dream I had of you the night after we met *was* because of you! You have never even spoken your name to me, yet I know it," I said. My mind and logical self told me to run, but my body wanted to grab the edge of his jacket and pull him into me, wanting a taste of that power. The thought of it tangled in my stomach, making me feel disgusted in myself.

"You... I didn't. I only interfered with the outer layer of your mind so the Guild mistress could not see our meeting or gather any thoughts you had of me. She needn't know I was so close. And the hunter who had the gift to see long distance…"

"What did you do to Dillian?" I demanded, pulling out one of my daggers and preparing to pounce on him. I knew he'd done something to him, the timing had seemed almost too perfect.

He only raised an eyebrow. "I may have sent him a little nudge in regards to believing his gift was more profound, and what he thought he might've been seeing. Just small stuff. That is how *my* gift works. I can manipulate anyone I desire. I needed to lure *you* to the city and considering he was one of the few you spent most of your time with, I decided to strategically use him. In my defense it was for your own good, you weren't safe there. And, well, because our meeting was so uninspiring, I came to you when you were dreaming. But in those dreams, you had full control as well. It was you who tried to kiss me," he said with a suave smile. "I was a little bit disappointed you didn't try to dream of me naked," he said, arching a playful eyebrow. I stared at him, abashed. He sighed, defeated and evidently discouraged.

I threw the dagger at his chest, enraged by his trickery. He caught it between two of his fingers, tsking at my actions. Again, I could feel something rising within me. I went to pull out another one of my daggers, but my fingers fumbled and shook.

I tried to push the lurking creature down, but this time I was really struggling. The entrapment only heightened my senses. I was hyper-aware of the vomit trying to creep up my throat, burning me, every inch as my darkness rose, swelling inside of me. It felt like whatever anger was within the pit of my stomach was starting to take on tendrils and shift upward to escape. I couldn't let this darkness consume me, not now. Whatever it was it was evil. Much like Campture did when this first happened to me, Chase watched me, surprised. What had happened to my face for him to react in such a way?

"Esmore, you need to calm," he said, holding his hands out to me. "Why did your eyes flash purple?" I looked up at him, equally surprised. Purple, that had once been the color of my huntress eyes. "Esmore, I can sense whatever it is that's rising within you, and it doesn't want to play nice with me. You need to calm down."

I felt like a wild animal. I wanted to rip his throat out, yet there was a gentleness to his words that almost slickened over the monster within in an attempt to restrain it. Though the rest of the work would have to be done by me. Chase took a step forward, and I fumbled back from him. My throat felt dry, and my gums ached. I tried breathing deeply but was overwhelmed by having let the intensity sweep over me for too long.

"It's okay, Esmore," Chase said, holding his hand out to me. I was stuck under his words trying to cling to them to ground me before I was completely taken in. Whatever was creeping forward rattled me into a state of fear. This creature fed off that. "Esmore." His soft word repeated. I felt the light touch of his hand against mine, feeling like a serum spreading through my whole body. I could feel Chase with me as if touching my mind and reassuring me. If he could manipulate people's thoughts, then perhaps he was helping me, caging this beast once again. He held tightly to one of my hands. I could feel the creature completely fold within my stomach, responding to Chase's demand. He cupped my face.

At first, he stared into my eyes, but when I refused to look at him, he stared at my lips instead. Longingly, I inhaled deeply, knowing what it was he was about to do. My body longed for his touch in its most primal state. I couldn't even think rationally any longer. He slowly leaned in, his other hand trailing up my forearm and holding my waist beneath my leather jacket. Before our lips touched, I pulled away regaining my senses and thought.

Sadness filled his eyes from the rejection. The beast was now gone, and I had once again gained full control of my body. "I have a boyfriend," I exhaled, confused that in this moment, it was my only line of defense.

"I know," he said, stroking my jawline. "But you were never meant to be his. I've seen how he treats you, like you are a mere object. I would never treat you so unequally," he said, gritting his teeth.

"You're a vampire," my breath came out staggered. When Chase touched me, when his hands lingered over my hips, I actually felt emotion, compelling, and enticing.

"I am a vampire, but I'm also your familiar," he said, his grip tightening on my waist as his thumb trailed over a part of my bare skin through the shredded leather shirt. "And I, Esmore, want to know what you are. I've known hunters for a long time, and I've never seen anything quite like you."

I considered the beast that had almost crept out from my darkness. I was a hunter, yet the creature within felt dark and impure. *What was inside of me that was so desperate to come out?*

"I don't know," I said honestly. Suddenly aware I was revealing myself to be vulnerable, I pushed Chase away, holding the leather jacket tightly around me. He looked down at the handcrafted dagger I had made.

"Did you use one of my bobbleheads for this?" he asked suddenly, his demeanor was now childlike again. He raced toward his shelves. "No, not Batman," he whined. "If you feel like you need weapons just ask me, but please don't attack my collection again," he desperately pleaded grabbing the parts that remained of his dolls mournfully. I rolled my eyes.

"It took me forever to find that one," he mumbled as he mourned over the remains of it. He took a sharp breath in, and I was surprised not to see him shed a tear by the way he reacted. He mumbled a few things under his breath and walked toward the shower. "I need to be alone," he grumbled. He took his leather jacket off, revealing the tension of the muscles beneath his skin. He began to undo the belt on his dark leather jeans. He stopped for a moment, his hand still on his belt. Slowly he slid it off, arching a suggestive eyebrow at me. It was like someone had clapped in front of my face as I realized I was staring at him the whole time. I looked away from him, walking toward the hammock.

He is vampire, and I am hunter. We were natural enemies, I continued to remind myself on replay the entire time he was in there.

CHAPTER 15

S WAYING IN A hammock was a nauseating experience, so I lay within it limply. It gave me the time to cocoon myself within my mind and thoughts completely. I wasn't yet sure why Chase had brought me here or why he let me freely roam the halls. He'd brought me into the enemy's territory, claiming it was for my own wellbeing because I wasn't safe amongst my kind within the Guild. I'd never required anyone's protection nor did I need an outsider's opinion on it. I could protect myself, whether within the Guild with their strict rules, or out in the wild where vampires roamed. But when Chase said it, there was a seriousness to his tone that I didn't want to push. I didn't want to ask him why he had suspicions that I was in danger because his opinion ultimately didn't matter, and I didn't want to be anymore brainwashed than what I already felt.

I couldn't rest knowing I would only have a few more days, maybe even hours, before I would have to figure out my way of escape. I had to get out of here and return to the Guild with all the intel I'd gathered. If other vampires within the Council found out who I really was, I'd be tortured. I was gambling with my life.

My biggest hurdle would be convincing Chase that I cared for his companionship in hopes it'd provide me more freedom and a way of passage out the doors. This necklace I wore was seemingly meant to ward off other vampires, yet it didn't deter Galdar by any means. Taking out Chase one on one wasn't an option, he was more powerful than most of the vampires in here, which meant physically he'd be able to overpower me. I had to be cunning in the way I'd move around him.

I had to prepare for the moment I escaped, I'd have to warn the Guild, and we'd have to prepare for battle. I had no doubt Chase would lead the Council to our walls if he hadn't already. It might even mean after all these years of living and our location being secret- we would have to relocate. I hoped they hadn't already over swept my Guild, and I had no way of knowing until I escaped and saw it for myself.

That night, Chase insisted I sleep in his bed while he took the hammock. I had to start playing the role of 'pet.' It was to my advantage that he underestimated me and didn't tie me up, and so I decided not to fight him on every minimal command. Even though we slept apart, I couldn't sleep with his presence so close, and I found myself frustrated by not being able to focus on my escape. Often, I found myself lifting my head to look at him, but then he would do the same, and I would roll over, irritated. This happened a few times. It wasn't out of curiosity, it couldn't have been. I was growing angrier at the thought of how many mind games he must've been playing on me. I was also inexplicably conscious of bedding in the same room as a vampire where no restraints were involved. It was a preposterous notion yet was my unyielding reality.

I didn't get any sleep that night. I idly stared up at the window, where I could see a small mist of fog swirling above the street. I could see a glimmer of the outside world and yet I couldn't touch it. It was an unnerving silence slumbering within the city. In the Guild, I would hear all forms of screams and birds hoot throughout the night. I couldn't even hear sabers hunting which forced me to wonder how tight and wide their security stretched.

As we had comforted into sleep, Chase informed me that a team had been sent out to find leads on the disappearance and whereabouts of my raid team. The only information they had was traces they might've ventured toward the southeast. If that had been true it meant they weren't going in the direction of the Guild. I didn't know why Chase was telling me this, and if I was in some form of twisted intel-gathering game. Maybe he was trying to befriend me so I'd entrust the Guild's darkest secrets instead of stringing me up and torturing me.

I had remained silent when he told me, in conclusion, he told me he didn't know why Fier had become obsessed with pursuing my team. When we entered the city he sent out an order for us all to be detained alive. Chase enabled that and led us right here. I made sure to hold onto my composure. I wanted to keep hold of my ability to move freely for the time being and tried not to read any further into what was probably lies.

What did make sense to me was that I never fully believe Dillian had suddenly acquired a new extension of his gift. I believed and trusted Dillian, but the situation had been superficial. And by extension, Chase had tricked Campture into deploying us. Which meant it was highly possible the Council already knew of our Head Huntress' gift and abused that so we fell into their trap. We were wide-open and exposed at the Guild. So why hadn't they yet attacked? What were they waiting for? What information were they hoping to extract from my teammates? Or was it because they wanted to find out our location through them? But Chase already knew the site. I looked back up at him. He opened one eye peeking back at me. I sighed, frustrated, and shuffled back into the bed. I could sense the smile that stretched on his lips.

When I thought of my team's safety, I thought of James. An ill feeling stirred in my stomach. I wanted to know if they were safe and alive. Just because the Council had seen them escape, it didn't mean they could survive so long outside the Guild's walls. We only packed our bags for a certain amount of nights, and the elements outside the walls and in the open were dangerous. Why hadn't they returned and reported to Campture? Perhaps for precautionary measures. Maybe they were cautious that the Council knew they survived the blast.

Slowly, I watched the shadows of night turn into the shine of day. I had hardly slept in days, and my body began to crave it. I was drunkenly aware of my surroundings. How many more days could I last before it would affect my performance? Could I demand from Chase to let me leave? Who was I kidding? He was a deranged vampire who thought he was keeping me safe from my own people. A kidnapper wouldn't give his victim an explanation or an honest motive. I repeated these trains of thought in my mind, but when I looked at his peaceful resting face, all of those thoughts receded. The hatred I built up for him had gone. And so, I would have to fight myself internally again to raise the hatred having momentarily forgotten what he truly was.

As he woke, he stretched out into his hammock lazily. His yawn was loud as he began to rub his face pleased with his night's sleep. I was amazed he was able to sleep within my presence, and even more surprised that I hadn't tried to dagger him during the night.

"Good morning, beautiful," he said merrily.

I sat up with a scowl on my face, unappreciative of his comment, only to find him checking himself out in the full-length mirror near his three-legged desk. He arched an eyebrow in my direction, now realizing I thought he had meant me. "Well, you too," he winked. "I am going to get you some clothes so you aren't walking around in my leather coats like a weirdo. Might I suggest while I'm gone you have a bath as well, you kind of stink. Everything you need is in there," he paused for a moment as if in thought. "Well, everything but me." At my mute reaction, he smiled. It was the exact response he'd expected. He swept through the room and was already gone. I exhaled angrily once again at how my body wanted him, by his words alone could I lose my trail of thought. I hadn't blushed in many years. It was such a rare hunter expression, being overcome with such a sexual intention.

He had been right about one thing though, I did need to bathe. And now that I was alone, I couldn't help but feel the desperate pull to the sensation of hot water on my skin. The water at the Guild was often cold by the time I used the shower late at night. I became accustomed to it. But to now be able to bathe in it, well, that was something I did look forward to.

It didn't take me long to figure out how to use the claw bath. Dipping my toes into it, the water scalded me, but I couldn't help but find relief in it as well. I peeled the dirty and sweaty clothes off. I undid my plait, the luscious curls greasily sweeping around my face. I washed my hair vigorously. I dipped my head under the water, trying to ease my train of thought. So many things kept trailing over one another. I was never like this. I was always so sure in both my thought and actions. Never did I feel such a trivial thing as doubt. If I wanted something, I took it. But now it seemed as if I had no idea what it was I wanted. Chase made it very hard to keep a clear mind. This was never what I had thought would happen when I finally infiltrated the Council, and I had to continuously remind myself of my objective.

Chase returned with some clothing, placing them near the door where I could collect them myself. He had lingered near the door for a while, unsure as to whether he should walk in to place them on the basin. I hadn't told him not to, more so as a test. How odd for a vampire to be considerate?

The clothing was not to my taste and reminded me of what Whitney wore. It was a long, green flowing dress with long sleeves. When gathering it, something hit the floor. Chase had placed a garter and two knives in there. Three small sharp daggers were also a part of the package. He was serious about me not touching his bobblehead dolls.

I walked out, uncomfortable in the free-flowing attire. Never had I worn such a thing in my life.

"Aww, you look so pretty," Chase commented, sitting on the edge of his bed with one leg folded over the other. "What? You need to tone down the 'I can kick your ass' attitude. There are only a few vampires here older than me. For the most part, I know you can handle yourself with the rest. But I don't want you catching anyone's eyes, and you have to play the role of weak human to make it easier for us both. Vampires also find hunter's blood to be a delicacy which is why I had to erase Gardar's recollection of you being a Hunter. I gave you those weapons, but, just in case, please be smart about it."

"I wouldn't be in such a situation if you hadn't brought me here," I said coldly.

"Well, that is very true, but regardless, I know you are benefiting from this. You are thinking, 'I will find out everything I can, and then I will go back to my Guild, where I stupidly think it's safe. I will tell them everything I know, and they'll embrace me as a hero, and we shall eradicate the whole vampire race. I shall lead it with my very own sword,'" he said in a ladylike, mocking tone.

I didn't even sound like that. Before I could swallow back my fiery words, he approached me, now very serious. I held my ground firmly. I had my weapons out. I could defend myself far more efficiently, even against Chase. But when he took his next step, I was mortified that my body voluntarily stepped back. It was unbearable to stand so close to him. Now I took another step back of my own free will. I hated the pull he had over me. *It must be a gift of enticement or something… he must be brainwashing me with his gift.*

His shoulders sagged, and he didn't take another step toward me. "I just wanted to tell you that you look beautiful with your hair out. You're like a golden bird. You're right in front of me, yet so untouchable and spectacular at the same time. Esmore, I will not let you return to the Guild. When I say it is not safe, I truly mean that. I have seen it all before."

"In a premonition?" I mocked. I didn't take kindly to flattery, yet my breath became uneasy at his words.

"My sweet, Esmore, I cannot prophesize things, my gift doesn't work in such a way. I have, however, lived for four hundred and thirty-one years. I am far more accustomed to the world of hunters than you with your short eighteen years. The hunters are not a loyal breed. If they have an inclination that a hunter is treacherous in any way, they kill them on the spot. Most of the murders are unjustified, and whatever information tipped them off was usually later found to be incorrect. I guess in a way the hunters are very similar to us, but I wouldn't allow them to do that to you. I intervened that night when we first met because I already knew of the mistrust that Guild mistress, Campture, had in you."

"Why did you follow me? You shot a dart of paralysis at me. You were planning on taking me hostage," I said sternly. I felt very unintimidating with my long-flowing dress, so I crossed my arms for added effect.

He laughed lightly to himself at that. "I did, and I had every intention of bringing you to Fier. We were to take the Token Hunter. And I had every intention of doing so. But then, well, it's probably going to sound corny… When I shot the dart I purposefully missed. I just had to see your face. You felt me, as I did you. You knew of my exact location, and when you looked at me, I looked at you like I do now. You were like a golden bird: so close yet untouchable. And I understood you were important, but I didn't understand how. So, I was intrigued and followed you, only to find out how close you were to death within your own Guild no less, so I had to intervene. I meddled, and you should be grateful for that."

"I was not near death," I retorted. I could protect myself from anything.

"Esmore, let me explain to you what would have happened because I have seen it far too many times in my lifetime. Your kind is very predictable and very untruthful. Your young are raised on lies and mechanical beliefs from the technological era. Even though you hold so much hatred for vampires, you are so very much like us. So very much like humans throwing around their power and strength." Chase shook his head as he realized he had rambled on to another topic, and refocused on telling me what he predicted. "Campture had you locked up. Within those next days, she would have created a conspiracy about you; how you are involved with vampires, misleading your Hunter Guild. She would have used the deaths of your fallen members as proof of that."

I shook my head, but he continued, unperturbed. "Your boyfriend, whom you pretend to love so much, would not be loyal to you. When I watched you both, it seemed like your relationship was a label. I know you can feel the same desire around me that I hold for you. That isn't anything your boyfriend could ever provide you, and you can't deny me that. Do you know how hard it is for me to control my urges around you?"

He now looked at me lustfully. I couldn't help but feel empty as if those words he spoke punched me in the stomach and took everything with it.

Because he had been so blatant about it, in this room and by myself I could confess I no longer loved James and wasn't sure if I ever had; I was just so used to the attachment. And I couldn't deny my body's pull toward Chase. Which confused and enraged me more.

"My relationship has nothing to do with you," I said. "And you ran off subject." Although I didn't entirely enjoy his ramblings, I entertained them, reminding myself to absorb as much information as possible. I'd never spoken so freely with a vampire before. It was at my advantage.

After a moment of silence, he continued. "Your boyfriend would have pleaded your case for about half a day, but then would have been convinced of the same conspiracy. He has an unnatural want for you, Esmore. It's not love he holds, but a profound sense of entitlement. Whatever happened to him a long time ago has made him now believe that he owns you."

I thought of his childhood. He was taken away from his mother. He always begged me to live with him, to leave my position as Token Huntress, to wed, to have children. Could it be as severe as Chase let on? But I was fine; I could always look after myself. But to have an outsider's perception of what I already feared sent me deeper into those dark thoughts. Did James really believe he controlled me?

"He would have pleaded with Campture for, say, a day at most. By then he would have been convinced that you were a traitor. He would have come and offered you an ultimatum: to live with him as the mother to his children, under his protection, or you could choose death.

"Your best friend, Dillian, would have been outraged. Despite the low emotion levels of hunters, you had a few who would stand up in your defense. The woman who can control flames would have been first. She would seek out Campture on her own. On her next raid, this huntress would be 'accidentally' killed by her own kind, but they would claim it to have been sabers.

"Unfortunately, the little apprentice, Tori, I believe it was, would be a witness. They wouldn't kill him, but he would never be allowed on a raid again in punishment. Your best friend, Dillian, would face a decision: defy them and die, or say nothing and stay with his girlfriend. Of course, he loves her very much, but he would still fight for you. He would openly be killed in front of all. He would be an example to other hunters not to interfere. You would then be killed."

Still, with my arms crossed over my chest, I entertained the theoretical scenario. In truth, I could understand his thought process on the matter, and although I wish I could have dismissed it as a lie, I couldn't. I already had my doubts about Campture. I didn't trust her after my mother's death. I suspected she had made me Token both because I was one of the best warriors, but also to keep me close. I wish I could laugh in Chase's face at the words he spoke, but all of it seemed sincere. This had been the longest time I'd been away from Campture's clutches, and it gave me time to freely let my thoughts roam when I had for so many years learned to be silent and obey, in case she would hear my most inner suspicions.

"And this is what you suspected would happen?" I asked dryly. I didn't want to give Chase any power by suggesting I believed him.

"Esmore, I would not lie to you. I brought you back to protect you. For now, this is the safest place. I know it seems unlikely because you're surrounded by what has been the enemy your entire life. But the difference is, if they only think you are human, I can protect you from both the vampires within these walls and the hunters who want to execute you within your own home. I cannot protect you behind the walls of hunters. Although I would have tried it in a heartbeat, if my manipulation to bring you to me didn't work."

"I cannot be kept as a pet," I spat angrily. Even the mention of James had irritated me. Men thinking they could do as they pleased or that I needed to be rescued and saved. I would have to return to the Guild. I couldn't fathom how he genuinely believed the only place I'd be safe was the home of vampires.

"I would never treat you as a pet, Esmore. For now, please have faith in my actions." He reached out for my hand. "For now, let us stay for only a while longer until everything calms down. If this is not a place you want to be, we will find a way to leave. I'll follow you to make sure you get out safely if it's something you so desperately want. But know there will be consequences if I do such a thing."

I considered this for a moment. I had comments to make, remarks to shoot him down. But I could not voice them. For what reason would he sacrifice all he had for me? The thought of him following me sent a warmth through me which was as scary as it was deadly. His hand slowly intertwined with one of mine, unlocking the firm grip I had across my chest. I froze at the touch, uncertain of how to react. My mind went blank. He simply held it and leaned down to kiss my forehead. A shudder of warmth spread over my forehead and, like I had noted before, I actually felt something when Chase touched me. It was almost overwhelming as I hadn't felt such a feeling in so long. His other hand stroked my cheek and trailed down my neck. He lifted his necklace away from my throat so that it was no longer tucked into my dress, and visible.

"There is so much I want to share with you. But I'll wait until you are ready and want that," he promised. I could feel the heat radiate between us. It was like a swirl of tension, pushing us together. I could feel my legs wanting to give way to him, and desire heating me.

I stared at his lips, longingly before catching my inner damaging thoughts and desires. I pulled away from him. I could not, even to James. I could not be unfaithful until I could tell him my feelings were no longer valid. My mind scrambled again. Why was that my issue here? The more significant problem was that Chase wasn't a man or hunter, he was a *vampire*.

"Tythian and Whitney are the only two who know your true identity. I'm convinced that most won't recognize you from the blast considering most were wiped out, and Fier was never in direct range of seeing you. After much arguing with Tythian, he has agreed to say nothing. He is older than me, but we have lived together for a long time—he is someone I can trust. But as I said, he doesn't take well to those who threaten Whitney. I've also been informed she will be showing you around. It shocks me that you found her so quickly. But be careful around her. Tythian and I are close, but if you insult her in any way or push her for too many answers about the Council, he will not take it kindly. He is very protective of her."

"Because she is his familiar?" I asked.

"She told you about familiars?"

"Well, no, not yet, but…" Before I could demand the answer from him, he cut me off.

"I'll tell you soon enough. But for now, let's go out, and I'll show you the big bad vampire lair," he suggested, his fingers waving in the air spookily. "And, if anyone asks, you are *mine*." His tone was so sharp that his sudden mood swing had even me intimidated. "I know you don't belong to me, Esmore. But please, if anyone asks, you must state it. It's the only way within the walls I can keep you protected… you must be bound to me."

I didn't like the idea of being bound to any vampire. But to make it out of the Council alive, I bit my tongue. There were vampires here who could overpower me separately, and I was hugely outnumbered. I already had a taste of what Chase's speed and strength were like. I was now growing wary that I wasn't as strong as I had once thought, well, not in comparison to the older vampires. Especially not in comparison to Chase.

CHAPTER 16

Walking out into the white halls, Whitney and Tythian were already waiting in front of the water fountain. It seemed Whitney had a fascination with water features. This was her favorite spot to sit and simply stare. Tythian noticed us first. Chase went tense and stood in front of me. Tythian was the only other vampire who knew my identity, and it was apparent he didn't like that I was within the Council. Though I would still keep vigil in case another vampire had seen my face the day we fought in the city center.

Whitney then noticed us, patting Tythian's hand lightly in a reassuring manner. "Don't you ruin my friendship for me," she said playfully with a light smile. He looked down at her, his hand tightening around hers. His eyes glistened in adoration. His blond hair was slicked back smoothly, seeming very golden against his tanned skin. He was wearing black pants and a white buttoned shirt.

Chase stood next to me as we had come to a halt in front of them. It gave me a moment to admire the difference in not only Tythian's and Chase's style, but age as well. It made me question a trivial matter such as why Chase seemed to be the only one who never wore a shirt and only a leather jacket. I swept my eyes over his hard chest and impressive stomach that protruded with unnatural muscle. He was a slender build but in no way deceived the eye that he was weak. When my gaze reached his hip bones my thoughts went hazy. He found my eyes, a cocky smile twitching at his lips. Although my expression was bland, he knew I had been staring at his perfect body.

When I compared both men's style, it was immediately apparent there was a very large age gap simply by the way they dressed. Although Tythian looked to be in his mid-thirties, there was an atmosphere around him. He was much older than Chase, possibly the oldest one here. I would have to ask Chase later- curious but also mindful that Tythian might be the hardest vampire to take down.

"I'm sorry about the attire," Whitney said sheepishly. "You see, I always have to wear long dresses. It is more comfortable for me because I get very cold, very quickly. Chase asked me to find you clothes as we look the same size. It was all the clothing I had in my closet."

"Do not apologize, Whitney. She should be grateful," Tythian interjected sharply. A low growl erupted from Chase in some form of warning. His fangs were already bared, and Tythian followed. Though his were larger, Chase didn't back down.

"I said not to, Tythian," Whitney said, slapping him on the arm lightly. The exertion of it forced her to cough into her hand. Chase caught and held my hand so I would not run to her aid, merely letting me watch. I hadn't even noticed that I'd stepped forward. I was losing my mind here. I was showing displays of human compassion.

"Whitney," Tythian said, dropping to his knees in front of her. He rested one hand on her back, the other holding her hand tightly. "Let me ease the pain for you, please." His tone was begging. She continued coughing hoarsely. Tythian's eyes scattered over her, he was suffering himself.

"I'm okay," she panted. She looked back at the water fountain. It was as if she had forgotten what she was doing. She looked back at Tythian, placing her hand on his smooth jaw before stroking it. Her eyes were filled with such love that I was suddenly reminded of Chase's hand holding mine, and I let go. Never did I think I would see such a display of affection between human and vampire in this lifetime. I wanted to deny it, but as they stared into one another's eyes, I knew their feelings were real.

"Please help me make this a wonderful day. I like Esmore," she said, her voice fragile. She reminded me a little of Julia, Dillian's girlfriend.

"Anything for you, my love," Tythian responded, kissing her knuckles. He stood, resting a kiss on her forehead before turning to me. He tried to soften the hatred in his eyes and took on a disinterested expression. I knew that look all too well. It was the same one I adopted many years ago.

"Well, first of all," Whitney clasped her hands together. "I bet Chase has forgotten that you actually need food to survive, so let me take you to the food hall." When she mentioned it, both Chase and I looked at my stomach, forgetting that I did actually have to eat. So much had happened over the last few days that I had completely forgotten and lost all appetite.

"Shit, I knew there was something I forgot about keeping a pet human," Chase teased. I raised my eyebrows at him in challenge. I was no one's pet. Yet I was not angry at him for the comment, accepting it as playful. I looked forward to Whitney again, once again surprising myself with the level of comfort I had with such an emotional response.

Tythian pushed Whitney in her wheelchair. He turned down the hallway on our left. Along the wall on the left were numerous doors as we walked at a steady pace. I wondered if they were the rooms of vampires also. A few vampires had walked past us and looked at me hungrily. A few times Chase growled, checking my chest every time to make sure that his necklace was showing around my neck. A few vampires had even let their fangs slip, covering their mouths in apology as Chase's larger fangs came out nastily.

"Don't scare the young ones; they can't help it that you brought a human in that smells so appetizing. It was your choice to bring the wrong kind of human," Tythian said with his nose pointed in the air.

"It's not like I had a choice in the matter," Chase said, stretching back his arms and revealing his perfect chest as his leather jacket pulled back. Again, I couldn't resist letting my eyes trail down each and every muscle. His body was splendid and very alluring.

"What do you mean by that?" Tythian asked. He caught me staring at Chase hungrily. I looked away, angry for letting myself slip. The longer I was with Chase, the more my rational thoughts fled. I became primal, only thinking of one thing; what his skin would taste like on my tongue. To be able to touch him, breathe in his scent. To kiss him and…

Tythian looked between Chase and me before continuing. "Is she your—"

"We can discuss this another time, surely. All I need to let you and Fier know is that she is my human to feed from, no one else's. That is all that should matter," Chase snapped, no longer as relaxed. "But I will tell you this: she ruined my Batman bobblehead doll."

"That one took us almost a decade to find!" Tythian complained, now showing a far less mature side. He was very serious about it. Another two vampires walked past me, studying me intensely. It was then that Chase grabbed my shoulder and pulled me into him, eyeing them warningly. Their pace quickened as they scurried away. I considered popping out from under his shoulder but weighed the options. There would be far worse consequences for me, especially with Tythian within the same room. So uncomfortably, I stared forward, allowing this intrusive vampire who had become infatuated with me to rest his arm over my shoulder in a juvenile claiming manner.

"I remember when I first saw your bobblehead collection," Whitney announced, still looking ahead as we came to another intersection in the huge white underground lair. How many vampires dwelled here? Tythian led us into the right hallway, where at the end there were two large wooden doors. "I screamed when I saw them, they were so creepy," Whitney giggled. She turned around and laughed at the look on my face. "I had the exact same expression on my face, creepy little things. But it makes sense. His mother started that collection for him. So, it has been the only thing connecting him to the era that he was born. You should see Tythian's collection, it's—"

"Nothing," Tythian said in a bored tone, cutting Whitney off. She looked up at him with pouted lips. He gave her an even smile and brushed back part of her fake hair where some had fallen into her eyes. I side glanced Chase. His mother began collecting them for him. I'd never even considered the prospect that a vampire had a mother, though they were human born so it made sense. I wondered if she was a vampire as well. Before I could ask, Chase loosened his grip on me and stretched his arms back again. I was so relaxed that I had forgotten that he still had hold of me, deterring other vampires' admiring looks.

"Oh, so we can talk about Chase's collection, but not Tythian's," Chase said childishly.

Tythian opened the large wooden doors, revealing an enormous white room. There were eight long tables, each of them hosting twenty chairs each. On the right side was a large open kitchen with benches. There were mountains of food already placed on top of the dividing bench that came between the food hall and kitchen. There must have been forty humans in here at least. Some of them were already eating their food, and others chose from the dishes on the dividing bench. All of them stopped eating and talking amongst themselves for a moment to stare at us. None of them seemed disgruntled by the fact that two vampires had walked in, and then

I noticed that there were already a few vampires in the room, sitting beside humans.

"I don't understand," I whispered to Chase. Why would the humans be so calm with the vampires in here? They were the enemy.

"Some vampires prefer to keep one human for a while. They grow an attachment to them, whether it is because of sex, blood, or companionship. Most humans come around to it quickly. We have better shelter, facilities, and food for them here, and it's much safer than them living out in the open where the sabers or covens could get to them. Because of our Council rules and regulations, we don't torture or objectify humans. Just as you are finding fewer and fewer humans every day, so are we. We need to limit ourselves and ration the blood supply. Animal blood isn't the sweetest, so we try to enjoy humans in moderation."

I looked in revulsion as one woman was talking to the vampire across from her. The female vampire that sat beside her was drinking from her wrist as she did so casually. It was disgusting. Fools, all of them. This reminded me why I had very little respect for humans in the first place.

"What do you feel like eating, Esmore?" Whitney asked me. Noticing my tightly locked jaw, she continued, "Perhaps we'll come back later when there are less people. I'd love to show you the gardens."

I took her cue to snap me out of my angry haze. "The gardens?" I repeated, trying to look away from the creatures that I hated so much. Chase was watching me warily. Whitney smiled, urging Tythian to proceed. He led us around the tables as others not so discretely watched us. It was obvious I was new. Most of them had dark hair, so when I walked through with my golden-blonde hair I stuck out noticeably. They all watched, even the vampire who was feeding off its companion. I eyed her evilly, wishing now more than ever I had my bow and sword.

There was one large glass door in the corner of the room. Tythian opened it for us, taking us out to a pavement. There were two male humans playing with an orange ball. One side-stepped the other and skillfully threw the ball toward the hoop. It sunk in and he scored himself a 'two-pointer.'

"This is called *basketball*. It's an old game. It's only the Council here within the city that has brought such an old game back, the other Councils we meet with don't usually partake in such games," Chase educated me. The way he said it provoked more questions from me.

"You interact with the other Councils often?" I asked him, still watching the men play. Tythian led us around the corner on the right. There were vampire Councils all over the world, but we weren't sure whether they kept in communication with one another.

"It was only five years ago when the Council's last met. We were known to be the smallest, but since, we've been gathering and growing in numbers. I dare say in the next few years our numbers won't be as small."

Above us glass windows covered the whole roof. It was a dreary day. Dark clouds covered the sky and blocked the sun. Although it should have been dark in here, it wasn't. There were bright lights shining along the roof. "Where do you get the power for all this?" I asked, lifting my hands and gesturing to our surroundings.

"We have light and hot water here because of the solar panels. It was a technique used in the technology age, and probably one of the few which they actually got right. The humans realized they were heavily polluting and destroying their facilities too quickly, so they created this. We have only had these for four years now. We used to go by fires and were relatively primal. But Fier wanted something more stable. We went on many raids to try and find other solutions. But much of the material has been either taken or wiped out. However, the city proves useful for finding such things. And Gardar, you met that vampire only yesterday..." He paused. The only vampire I had met was the one who attacked me. That was the vampire he intended to make me wary of. "He used to be a mechanic and techno wiz in the days of technology, so having him nest into our home within the past ten years has proven beneficial."

"You tell her too much," Tythian scolded.

"I tell her what I want to tell her," Chase replied.

I wondered if it was because of Tythian that Chase wanted to come. It was evident Tythian was no ally, not that I would consider any vampire ever to be my ally. When we were led around the corner, a small green strip of land came into view. There were many flowers. It wasn't overly large, but it was beautifully maintained. There was a wooden deck with a few tables and chairs and a few large trees. I paused trying to take in all the various colors and plants. I was used to the dead woods. I'd never seen so much green and colorful flowers.

"Because of the glass roof and the large walls, the fog can't get in. We never use fresh drinking water on the plants either. We keep the drinking water in storage in case, for some reason, we can't obtain more for a long time. This water comes from under the large main bridge in the middle of the city. You know it? It was once called the 'Golden Gate Bridge.' We're looking for a way to connect a hose and pump from there to here. But for now, we use those large blue drums," he directed my gaze to where three drums were standing next to the wall, "to facilitate the garden. Obviously, we can't grow anything too large here."

I gave him a side glance, questioning why he was telling me all this. He had already guessed why I was staying, and that was to report back to my Guild as soon as I was able to escape. So why tell me so much? He gave me a cocky grin, suggesting he knew exactly what I was thinking. I frowned, now wondering if he was listening in on my thoughts.

"I helped start these gardens," Whitney said with a gleeful smile as she played with a pink flower.

"You did a stunning job, my love," Tythian said, watching her with admiration. She gave him a smile and picked the flower, offering it to him. He took it and placed it in his pocket.

"Hey, do you want to see the training room?" Whitney asked me. This girl was making it too easy for me to uncover their foundations.

"I do not think that is wise, my love. You know what she is," Tythian reminded her patiently.

"I know, but she's Chase's familiar, so she won't do anything to hurt us," Whitney disregarded him. Tythian's gaze cut to Chase. I hadn't yet had explained to me what a familiar was, but by Tythian's response it was bad.

Whitney went to push toward the dining room's direction again, but Tythian firmed his grip on the wheelchair handles and began pushing her. I suppose he was leading us to the training room at Whitney's request after all. The amount of control she had over this vampire was startling. I never knew such a relationship could exist.

"The newer vampires are very clumsy. Since the sabers have been overpopulating, we've been required to recruit and build our numbers. A lot of them are trained daily. We need to protect ourselves from hunters and other covens. The more experienced ones, such as myself and Tythian, lead separate small groups when we need to find more humans or human supplies. Sometimes the sabers are close and hide within the dark buildings during the day. So, if it is suggested they are dwelling within the city, we go out to kill them. They can't smell the humans within here because we're underground and the fog on the ground interferes with their sharp sense of smell. A lot more have been coming closer frequently so we cut them down before they get any closer. Like ridding the city of an outbreak of mice really," Chase explained.

At this point, I was sure he was telling me all this in bragging gesture. We walked around the large tables in the dining room and then through the wooden doors, back to the intersection. This time Tythian led us down to the right. We entered another room through more wooden doors. But instead of being covered by the typical white walls, it was all glass. The larger room was divided into many sections. I saw an archery area, a boxing arena, and an exercise area. The one on my right was for hand-to-hand combat. Twelve vampires practiced with one another.

The next room on my left seemed to be some kind of torture chamber. Three vampires were tied to metal chairs. Fire was applied to their skin. They would scream for five seconds before water was thrown over them. Their healing quickly took away their wounds as they panted heavily.

"It's called the Tolerance Room," Chase said, breathing hotly over my shoulder as I stopped to watch. "Fire is the most effective. We train our vampires with pain so they are accustomed to it in battle."

One vampire was standing still against the wall. A vampire on the other side of the room threw a dagger at him which plunged straight into the other vampire's stomach. He didn't even flinch, closing his eyes as it happened. He inhaled deeply, refocusing, and nodded for another dagger to be fired at him.

"You seem kind of sadistic if you just stare," Chase said with a smirk. "Don't tell me you're one of those women who like it like this?" he said, clamping his teeth together to make a biting noise close to my ear. I looked at him abashed, but he only returned a cocky smile. Quickly he snapped out of his playful manner as Fier approached us from the other room. I prepared myself for the moment he might recognize me. All I had was a few mere weapons amongst rooms full of vampires.

Fier looked at me with an expression of surprise. "You told me she was fat," he said, holding out his hand for me to grab it. I did not move. I would never touch him nor kiss his hand, if that was what he expected.

"Sorry, she doesn't like it if anyone else touches her besides me, if you know what I am saying," Chase said, embracing me. His hand slipped around my waist. I had the urge to flip him over and slam him into the ground for fumbling his hands over me where they did not belong. I gritted my teeth, enduring it as I knew I had to act as human as possible. And like Chase said, I had to appear as *his* so I would go unnoticed.

"She doesn't seem to enjoy your touch," Fier said, his green eyes searching over my face. "She is beautiful," he continued, his hand coming to touch my hair. Chase pulled me tighter into his arms possessively.

Although I could've held my ground, I couldn't have done so without Fier being suspicious of me. I was grateful for Chase pulling me back. Fier arched an eyebrow at Chase in challenge. A small breeze swept through the hallway, making a low howl. The two vampires who walked with him looked at one another, slightly concerned.

"A little possessive, aren't we, over a meal?" Fier asked, his fangs now revealed.

"If I may speak with you privately, Fier, I would like to speak about important matters, such as the team's updated report on pursuing the hunters?" Tythian interjected.

Fier flicked a harsh gaze to Tythian's interruption. He growled and nodded at Tythian then looked back to Chase. "I'll be seeing her tonight at the rave, after all, that is where all young vampires take their humans to dry hump them," Fier said as he continued to stare at me.

"I am not a young vampire," Chase growled.

"It was not a question. I'll be seeing her tonight," Fier said, eyeing Chase before walking around us to speak privately with Tythian. Whitney watched them as they walked away, deep in conversation already.

I grabbed Chase's fingers, using all my strength to pry his hand off me. Small cracking noises began as I had him in a firm grip. He had to slowly dip to the ground to get away from me.

"Ow, what do you have, mutant fingers? That hurts," Chase said, now his carefree self again.

"Do not grab me ever again," I hissed, releasing my hold of him. I had to put distance between us because my body thrummed in waves of heat at his lingering caress. I was upset with myself for not being entirely repulsed by his touch. When he faced Fier in my stead, I felt protected. This was bad, and I had to break the spell.

"Ah, I see, you like it rough," he said with another playful smile. His comments didn't help my situation in the slightest. It was as if he knew it boiled my blood. I tried my hardest to hide my desire for him, but every time he touched or embraced me it became harder to push him away. The longer I stayed within his presence, the further I felt his world consuming me. I had to break away. I couldn't comprehend my yearning for him. I felt an odd desire for him within the pit of my stomach. His touch made me flutter. I was becoming nervous and suspenseful around him. Foreign signs of emotions and feelings I'd never known existed before. It was making me weak and almost human-like.

"Why the glass rooms?" I asked Chase, trying to take a more serious tone. I needed to dispel my tension. I made sure my voice was low enough for Fier and Tythian not to hear. The vampires who followed Fier were standing idly by the doors, holding them open for him. I now understood that Tythian used himself as a distraction so Fier stopped applying pressure on Chase. "And why does Fier ask you so many questions?"

Chase gave a half-cocked smile. "So many questions, and your next one will be: what is a rave?" he mocked. I stood there silently, and then he realized. "Oh, you really don't know what a rave is. Well, diva, the rooms are glass, so Fier can regularly walk through and check on their training and progress. In here, there are eighteen rooms." I looked further down the hall, which looked lengthy. "The two end ones are weaponry, and no I can't take you there, only vampires are permitted. A rave is, well, a lot of music, dancing, and lights stretching across the floor. This is something the vampires have enjoyed for many years. In the technology age, it was the easiest way to scout our desired victims for the night and toy with them for a while before we took them." He wasn't distracted by my horrified expression.

"Fier is Fier. He wants a lot of things and chucks a tantrum when he doesn't get them. I will not lie to you; I'm uncomfortable by how he stares at you, so please never approach him alone, especially without me. You just really stand out from the rest of the humans. It's everything from your golden-blonde hair, to your beautiful face, physique, smell, the list could go on. Even though we're vampires, we are still men, and you are beautiful, Esmore." His tone was sincere, but he was trying to cover the actual issue—Fier's interest in me could prove fatal. "But I think for the most part you would be okay when they begin to learn about your wicked personality."

"Chase, I want you here now," Fier commanded over Tythian's shoulder.

Tythian came to Whitney, bending himself on one knee to speak with her at eye level. "Whitney, I'll be back shortly, my love. Why don't you head back to our room and rest for a while?"

"I have to go also. Keep close to Whitney or go back to my room," Chase said seriously. He gave me a smile. "No hug?" he teased immaturely. I now understood that if Chase felt threatened or uncertain about something he would state the concern and then try to cover it with humor. Not that I wanted Chase's protection, but I was uncomfortable at the thought of him leaving. My stomach turned. I didn't understand this feeling. How could he so easily creep under my skin?

He hunched over, whispering in my ear, his hot breath spreading over my skin and blazing desire. "I'll make you fall for me; you will only wish you committed sooner. I'll show you what 'hard play' is my golden bird." Chase's lips brushed against my ear, and then he pulled back with a smile, assessing my rigid body. I had frozen on his words, desperately trying to bring forth my mature mind. But my body pulsed for him; it longed for his touch. And as he smiled at me hungrily, I knew he could sense that. If others weren't surrounding us, I think I would have been very tempted to take him at that moment. It was Chase who walked away, leaving me startled and hungry for more. That hungry darkness within me rose, now tainted with lust. I stared at his back as he strode away, hoping to burn all my fury into him in case he might combust. What spell had this wicked vampire put me under?

CHAPTER 17

WHITNEY LED ME to the water fountain where we had met earlier that day. "Don't worry, they won't be too long. It's probably just to inspect a part of the city or attend a Council meeting," she said with a smile.

"I'm not worried," I said irritably. As soon as Chase had vanished from my sight, I felt like I could begin to think rationally once again, and affirm my hatred for all vampires. Such a union between vampire and hunter could not happen. And I couldn't be unfaithful to James. But the longer I stayed within Chase's presence, the darkness within me grew, growing because of desire, instead of the anger it usually fed off. I don't know what magic or gift Chase used against me, but it drained me of all will power and clear thought.

Now that we were alone, I could finally ask her what all of this 'familiar' stuff was about, and why I kept being objectified as such. I assumed it was the notion of some kind of lovers, which we were not. I had to make sure that would never happen. However, the more I could find out about the vampire's inner workings, the easier it would be to unravel their empire. If this would somehow work in my favor then I had to know every small bit that was presented to me. And I suspected that this woman would lead me to many of those answers.

"What is a 'familiar'?" I asked Whitney. She smiled, looking down at her twiddling thumbs.

"I really can't explain it to you; it's honestly not my place. But you will find out soon enough. I do hope you plan to stay with us, Esmore. I often worry about Tythian. When I pass, I'm worried he won't cope, and I need someone I can rely on to look after him. I can't have him slipping over to become a saber after my death. In that sense, he is so fragile." I was disgusted by the deluded notion that I would stay here and especially to play happy family with her vampire.

"You just diverted my question with a request," I noted, watching as two vampires walked past, looking at me curiously. Never had I thought it would be possible to be standing in the middle of the Council casually chatting amongst these filthy creatures.

"So I did," she giggled to herself in amusement. "Come to my room, I think it'll be safer for you there until Chase gets back, you draw too much attention. No one would dare come into Tythian's room or Chase's, for that matter. So maybe I'm just asking for the company."

I had planned on freely walking around in an attempt to find new intel or bearings. But Whitney was right about one thing. I stood out. It discouraged me from venturing off, mainly because I hadn't yet found an escape route. And wherever Whitney was leading me would be a new part to the Council for me to explore. She was proving herself to be very useful. She'd lived here for many years, and without Tythian's eyes watching over us, I could ask her so many questions.

"It's this way," Whitney said politely as Gardar, the large vampire that had attacked me only yesterday, walked past. He paused for a moment, staring at me. He distracted himself and walked toward where we had come from. I wondered if he held a higher role within the hierarchy because of his age. It was bizarre that he held no recollection or hatred toward me from the previous fight. He simply kept on walking without hesitation. It made Chase's ability all the more frightening. What if he had used such trickery on me already and I hadn't even known? I pushed the thought away not willing to deliberate on what-if assumptions.

Whitney led me past the giant tiger statue I had hidden behind only yesterday. We walked past the wooden doors where Chase and Fier last met. They were now closed, making me question if they were indeed having a meeting. I followed her down the white hallway, where on the left only three doors were. She opened the first one, revealing a much cleaner and homely room in comparison to Chase's doll-collecting weirdness.

On my left were a small wooden table and a brown, soft-looking couch. There seemed to be a small wrap around kitchen with a wooden table and chairs. The flooring was white marble, and there were a few paintings of flowers on the walls. In the left corner was a large king-sized bed and on the right seemed to be where the bathroom and a walk-in closet were.

"I'll show you Tythian's collection before he gets here," she giggled to herself. "I thought it was strange at the start as well. But when Tythian explained it to me, it made sense." She was leading me toward the walk-in closet. When she opened it, I saw that many various colored silk formal shirts were hanging. *Hundreds.*

"Tythian is eight hundred and twenty-seven years old. So, after about two hundred years, he began collecting things. He explained that it made it easier to grip onto humanity. Every year there is an anniversary of some kind where you gift yourself with something. He said it made it easier to count the years, especially when humanity was literally destroyed. A lot of the vampires here still collect things, it isn't uncommon. Chase does the same with his bobblehead dolls," she said behind me as she waited by the door. I ran my finger over the silk of the shirts. A lot of them looked old, and the material was something I hadn't felt before. We wore practical clothes which hunters had been wearing for centuries. A different fabric grabbed my attention. Nine shirts were collected together. The style was much different from the others, and none had buttons.

"They are called 'sweaters,'" Whitney said, wheeling her chair to a stop behind me. The material had an odd image on the front, and I realized it was a flower. "I know they're not silk, but it's so hard for him to find them now. So ever since I met him, I've made this for him annually. I found how to create them in an old book Tythian stole for me from a library. Of course, he had to teach me how to read then. I create a special one every year."

Looking at them, I said nothing so I wouldn't offend her, but I couldn't imagine such a shirt on the proper and handsome Tythian. Yet for Whitney, I believed he very well might wear it. She pushed through two of them, revealing a box hidden behind them on a small shelf. "This is the one I am working on for him now," she said with glee, revealing an almost completed one. "I started it a little early this year, but I'll finish it while he's away sometime during this week."

She placed it back in the box she had removed it from and hid it amongst the clothes again. Walking out of the large room of shirts, I peered into the bathroom. In there, from what I could see, seemed to be a medium-sized tank, attached to it was tubing and a mask. Whitney noticed me staring and looked almost ashamed.

"It helps me breath when I most need it," she admitted, still staring at the ground.

"What is wrong with you?" I asked gently.

"Well, it's been very slow, I had medication for it that Tythian tried to administer, but it doesn't help anymore. He told me he saw it a lot in the eras before. He is almost certain it is a disease called 'cancer.' Apparently, in the technology era they could treat it, and most survived when aided by the medication. But now, there's no such thing." Suddenly she perked up, as if defiant against the sadness. "But that's okay, I mean my papa always told me that everything happens for a reason. And as much as I love Tythian, I have no fear of dying to be with my family again. So, I find no sadness in any of it, only for Tythian. He still cannot accept my decision, although he respects it, he doesn't want me to go."

"Why don't you let him turn you into a vampire?" I asked. Their love seemed undying, and as much as I hated the thought of Whitney being turned, I was curious as to why a human would not take such an opportunity. I had seen many humans offer themselves, wanting the chance of elongated life, one that could last for thousands of years. Some humans I had met wanted that more than anything. One would think a young woman who was dying would want that more than anyone.

"Because although I love Tythian, sabers were what killed my family. I could never allow myself to be turned into a vampire, to eventually turn into that exact same creature. I am peaceful, and like flowers, I'd even consider myself simple. I don't need a full lifetime, nor the possible chance of eternity to know that I am blessed to have life. I love Tythian, but I think defying death is not natural. I could never be disgusted by him, but I don't think I would have the will power to stay humane for hundreds of years. I mean, when you think about it, after so many hundreds of years, what do you think it is they live for? I couldn't imagine any goal that would need eternity to complete it." She looked at me innocently, seeking my answer. But I did not have one. Every word and question she spoke was true. What would take so many hundreds and thousands of years to accomplish? Could you really just 'be' indefinitely? Vampires could be killed, but they had the option to live a very long existence.

"I don't know," I said honestly. It didn't sit well with me that she didn't pass harsh judgment on the vampire kind, especially after what had happened to her family.

"Why did you come here, with Tythian, into where all the vampires are? Any of them could lose control and trigger into sabers." I asked.

"Well, at the time when Tythian saved me, I was drawn to him instantly, and honestly would have followed him anywhere. At fifteen, I was mesmerized by his handsomeness, but also by having someone so willing to protect me. Without my father, I was alone. When I began questioning everything, I realized it was wrong to hold a grudge against Tythian or any other vampire here for what had happened. Although they are a race and did overpower the humans, we live in a time of survival. It is what it is. None of these vampires within the Council took my family from me, it was sabers. I couldn't curse their race because of what some sabers or individual vampires had done. Tythian helped me realize that. I have seen a few vampires slowly turn into sabers here. Not all of them are so strong to hold on to their humanity. From what I have seen, sometimes it is too easy to be persuaded by a much hungrier side.

I have seen the signs of them being turned, and by then there is no hope for them. It's like a sickness that breaks them down and converts them. Some endure it for longer than others. But once it is noticeably there, most of them give up. Having sabers within the Council is a liability. They'd kill all the humans here, and it is known that the Council does not approve of sabers. They're the creatures that are further extinguishing the food supply, so the Council actively kills them. The other vampires can smell the sickness within those vampires who have begun to slip into a saber. They are killed before they can fully turn. Once that sickness has started it will inevitably claim them. They are creatures without purpose. All they do is kill. They are the darkness within vampires, not the vampires who live within the Council. But every vampire here could be affected if they don't keep to their humane side and disallow the hunger to take over."

She paused before continuing, gaging my interest—all of which I found fascinating. "For those who simply disobey the rules here, such as torturing humans, going on a blood frenzy, or even challenging other vampires, they're also killed. Liability to the humans' lives here is not taken lightly; they are, after all, the Council's meal source. We don't live in an age of human law, we haven't for over three hundred years. But here there is some structure and rules. I feel far safer in here than out there where there is nothing but death."

Whitney began coughing harshly into her hand. After hearing her words, I didn't think much more could be said. All of it was thought-provoking. It reminded me of when Dillian and I had spoken of such things and his concern for the humans. I now had an insight into what it was they actually feared. Although it was our task to save them and take them to the human camp, we didn't place much structure or reassurance for them. And here, looking at all the white walls and clean living, they were somewhat safer than in the outside world. Obviously, humans didn't feel safe without structure or security of some kind, and their payment was in the exchange of being fed off.

"Excuse me," Whitney gasped over a handkerchief she had pulled out. A few droplets of blood grabbed my attention before she hid it in her small hands, smiling at me. "I have a few items of food here, why don't we eat here instead of returning to the hall?" She positioned herself at the head of the table, offering me a seat next to her. She pulled out a few pieces of fruit from a small shelf which had very few items on it. There was a small bowl of fruit, a few bottles of some red liquid, a few plates, bowls, glasses, and cutlery. Her hands trembled as she tried slicing the fruit on a plate.

"Let me," I said, taking the knife from her and slicing thin pieces of the apple and then pear. After only taking one bite of the pear, the door opened, and Tythian and Chase entered. They had been lightly debating something that had been said at the meeting they had.

"What Fier says will go, but I must admit I am losing respect for his decisions lately. He is acting like a child who simply wants a bigger throne," Tythian said, walking over to the shelving and grabbing one of the red bottles. He poured the thick syrup-like substance into two thin glasses, and I then realized it was blood.

"Well, I guess we'll figure out what Fier is up to when it comes to it... we can't exactly challenge him, we don't have the numbers," Chase said seriously. He took the seat beside me, as did Tythian beside Whitney, kissing her on the forehead in greeting. I saw Chase looking at me from the corner of my eye, thinking the same.

"Don't touch me," I said sharply.

"Whaaat, how did you even know I was thinking that... you are too confident in yourself, my golden bird," he laughed.

"Stop calling me that," I said, annoyed by his erratic personality. But still, I was not annoyed by his taunts. He was no longer appearing to me as the enemy which sobered me up quickly. What was happening to me?

There was a long moment of silence. "I don't know why you keep her here, you're playing a dangerous game with both of your lives, Chase," Tythian said, now serious.

"I can look after myself," I said angrily. Around these three I didn't have to pretend to be a defenseless human. I was entirely huntress, and with great pride in it as well.

"Little huntress, you may fight well, and in fact I will commend you on being very strong for your age. But you are no match for the vampires here who have lived for hundreds of years, training, and surviving. And another thing that bothers me is why do you not have your eyes? I have never seen such a hunter."

"She can't answer you because she doesn't know why," Chase said protectively. I had never told him, simply because I hadn't the answer. Tythian continued to stare at me. I didn't have to answer, but I found no harm in speaking up either. It would be no advantage to them, and he could think me lying.

"I'm the only born huntress to have no gift," I simply said. I was not ashamed of this. I wasn't a cripple without it because I'd never known its power in the first place.

"And yet you are Token, why?" Tythian asked, sterner this time. He hadn't even doubted me. We were both getting agitated by one another's presence.

"Because she is super amazing and hot in leather," Chase said with a childish beam. He was trying to distract us like he did when confronting Fier. Did he always become immature when trying to dispel tense situations?

"I've worked and lived with you for many years, Chase, which is why I haven't killed her already, but know and understand the situation you have now put yourself in. I honestly can't fathom what you are to gain by doing this," Tythian said seriously to Chase.

"I think Esmore is very sweet, no matter what she is or isn't," Whitney interjected. Tythian looked at her for a moment, before apologizing.

"I am sorry to have spoken to your guest in such a way, my love," he said, kissing her knuckles.

Chase took a mouthful of the blood, his fangs shining as his lips parted for it. I looked away in loathing. They bottled it, how disgusting.

After a few hours of discussion and awkward tension, Tythian asked us to leave as Whitney began to tire. "Besides, I think it would be a fitting time for you now to go to this rave you are expected at," Tythian said, grabbing Whitney out of her wheelchair and placing her comfortably in bed. He tucked her in, feeling the warmth of her forehead and looking over her worriedly.

We excused ourselves and left their room, walking toward the large wooden doors they'd had their meeting in earlier. The entire process made me feel like an official prisoner of sorts. I was being dragged from place to place. Though Chase hadn't been hostile himself, or Whitney for that matter, it made me only acquire absurd theories for their selfish motives. Yet none of them sat well within my stomach, which I often trusted most. However, I didn't trust myself much in the presence of Chase who was forming all sorts of rewiring. "Stay close to me the entire time. Don't talk to anyone and don't get us into trouble. We are simply going to say 'hi' to Fier, and then we will take our leave. Besides, it's almost night. I have somewhere I want to take you."

"It's already night?" I said, astonished.

"Well, we did get up at mid-day, Esmore," he growled my name as if enjoying its taste. "Most of us wake at mid-day."

A thumping noise began irritating my ears as I felt a heavy pound under my feet. I looked around the hallway, assessing where it came from. What vampire could make such a noise?

Chase laughed at my reaction, gearing for an attack. "No, Esmore, this is a rave. It was something that was appreciated many years ago by our kind. We've only been able to project this in the past few years. This is how many vampires spent their earlier years," Chase said as we stood in front of the large wooden doors where the Council had their meetings. The thumping was louder. If I recalled, it was called 'music.' But it sounded dreadful and glitchy like someone kept scratching it and then bringing it back to an enormous loud bang.

Chase opened the door before me. My eyes widened at the spectacle in front of me. There must have been hundreds of vampires in the very dark room that was only lit by flashing colored lights. The room once seemed so large, but now with so many vampires it was crowded and stuffy. There were chairs and couches in certain spots where vampires lazed and some publicly fed on humans. The whole atmosphere seemed hormone-driven and intoxicating. Everyone had a sexual tension surrounding them.

Chase grabbed my hand, pulling me into the room. I didn't want to be a part of such a place. I fisted my hand, hesitant to be dragged into this display with so many vampires and only a few weapons to protect myself. I looked to the ceiling finding my quickest escape route. Not that I would know where to go afterward. I had to go along with Chase's crazy scheme. The music continued to bang and crackle on the dance floor. Most of the vampires dry humped one another in sync with it. There were six vampires hanging from the ceiling in what looked to be silk cloths. The dancers in the erected cages wore nothing but gold skirts. I was barged left, right, and center as Chase charged me through the mass of dancers. Some frolicked over their partners as if they were a pole, grinding themselves up against their leg and biting into their neck.

"I take it you've never danced," Chase shouted over the pounding music. I looked up at where I had once hidden. I was staring at the same lights once, only now realizing their purpose as an array of green blinded my sight for a moment. "What do you do in celebration for things, like if you just want to have an enjoyable time?"

I looked at him scornfully. I didn't have to hide my agitation of being in here. Someone's hips bumped into mine. Chase tugged me into his arms before I could release some of my tension on the woman who did. She looked at me in disinterest before looking at Chase, who held me tightly in his arms. It was more like he was strapping me in. I tried to use my full strength to get out of his grip. I resisted the urge to smack the back of my head into his just to be free. It was natural for me to do so when he held me in such a way, and I had to fight away the urge to defend myself. I was fighting against my reflexes. Despite this, I pooled into his arms very quickly, the tension releasing.

"Chase," the dark-haired vampire said with a velvet voice. She was very attractive, slender, and tall. "Is this a pet you now have? Was my blood not sufficient for you, or was the sex not fragile enough?"

"Oh, Tanya, I didn't even recognize you with a shirt on," Chase said with a laugh. "And yeah, she is *my* pet," he said, stroking the top of my head. His hard chest was tight against my back as his one hand pinned me harder to him, locking in my resistance. The woman snarled and stared at me as if she wanted to fight me then and there. I stepped forward slightly, urging her to try. Chase turned me around, leading me further into the dancers, dismissing the vampire.

"Oh, a bit of a tease for the ladies, are we?" I said, trying to provoke him enough so he would let me go. The room made me uncomfortable, and every bang of the music seemed to rattle the floor. The darkness within me seemed to stir to the erotic and distasteful beat.

"Hey!" someone shouted angrily. I looked to my left where a human lay dead on the floor. The vampire who had drained her completely was spotlighted instantly. Chase and I stopped walking, and he put a hand in front of me protectively, assessing what would happen next. Gardar pushed aside the crowds of vampires.

"You know the rules!" Gardar said. The other vampire pleaded for his life, but within moments, Gardar had bitten into his jugular, ripping out his throat. He plunged his hand into the younger vampire's chest and reefed out his heart. The young vampire slumped, the smell instantly filling the room. Everyone cheered as the vampire and dead human were dragged away.

For what Whitney had spoken about rules and sense of restraint, I saw none of it in this room. I wondered how much Tythian must have protected her to the point where she might've not seen these kinds of acts.

Chase grabbed my hand, hurrying me toward Fier, who sat in his large wooden throne. Finally, we reached the end of the crowd. Everyone began dancing again, and the lights were streaking through the room randomly.

In front of Fier, two female vampires with very little clothing on were on the ground kissing one another. "Now bite her neck," Fier commanded, aroused. The darker vampire bit the blonde-haired vampire's neck. She gave out a moan in pleasure. Fier watched intently, enjoying what they did. "Now, slide your fingers…"

"Fier!" Chase yelled over the music, grabbing his attention before he could proceed with his next demand.

With his head rested on his hand, Fier looked up, his eyebrows raised. "Ah, there you are, would you care to join me?" he asked. As Chase said nothing, Fier's green eyes rolled over to me. "How about you?"

"She won't be involved in any of that. I have only come to assert my ownership of this human," Chase said seriously. I wanted to drop him on the spot for claiming me as his. But looking around, I now appreciated that I would be in far more trouble. I also understood that although I didn't like someone claiming me as their property, much like James did, Chase only did it to dispel other vampires' interests toward me, which if anything might buy me more time to find an escape.

"No. I am fond of your human," Fier said, staring at me intently. "She is so supple, and she smells delicious."

"I request this out of respect for my mother. I won't let you have her. She is *mine*," Chase said, tightening his grip around my hand. I felt the tension rise between the two.

"You dare bring your mother into this," Fier growled. "For what, a human?" He paused for a moment, staring at Chase's hand, which was strongly bound over mine. He now raised a skeptical eyebrow. "You have got to be joking me... this cannot be your familiar?" Fier said seriously. He began to laugh. "A human, truly? My heavens, it is like a second Tythian all over again." He cackled, further wiping away tears. "How disappointing. Fine, I'll allow this, but you have two weeks to turn her or I will claim her as my own."

Chase and Fier stared at one another. Chase snarled in response. Suddenly a harsh wind howled past Chase's cheek, slicing his cheekbone. A small trickle of blood began to bleed before the wound healed instantly.

"Get out of my sight before I change my mind," Fier said, waving us away.

Chase led me through the crowd of vampires. My steps staggered over a body on the ground. It was another human who had numerous bite marks all over his body. He must have only been thirty, and there would be no justice for him. He was already dead. This was a very different version to the story-like dream Whitney had tried to sell me on.

Finally, we were out of the sordid room, and Chase slammed the doors behind us. I felt as if I could breathe again. Before I could finally release my rage at him, he spoke. "I won't let anyone hurt you, and I will not turn you against your will."

"I do not like being spoken for. I demand that you let me go."

"Give me three more days to convince you to stay. I'll show you the way out now, and in three days, if you don't want to stay by my side, I will escort you out. But you can only go with me, if you go alone you will be chased down," Chase said seriously. "I want to prove to you, Esmore, that you are not safe in the Guild. I know that all of this is intense and you're probably thinking about how I'm tricking you or something like that. So I want to show goodwill and take you to the large bridge that is still standing. That way I can show you the way out. Just know that if you try to escape me, I won't chase you, however there are many posts within the city, and you will be tracked and captured before you even make it to the outskirts."

I stared at him for a moment, trying to guess his ulterior motive. Why would he offer me such things? If he wanted to trap me then why would he show me the way out... unless it was a trap. I was skeptical, but when I looked into his beautiful gray eyes, I only saw sincerity.

"I am not tricking you, Esmore," he said patiently. His gray eyes were genuine as he dropped my hand and placed his hand on his chest. My eyes followed his movement to his hard chest. I was immediately angry with myself again for being so easily distracted.

"C'mon," he said, grabbing my hand and pulling me through the hallways. Obediently, I followed him, mostly because I was trying to flush out my hotness. There should not be sexual tension. The moral dilemmas of being attracted to Chase were excruciating. But my mind could not justify it; my body wanted action.

We walked past Chase's room, continuing straight. We then came to an intersection, and he pulled me right. I made sure to take note and remember every turn and detail. He opened a silver door that had very little light in the room. It was dark and secretive. But I realized that was because there were metal stairs in front of us. Two vampire guards were on either side of the door.

"I am taking my human out for a little," Chase reported to them. They skeptically looked between one another, but when Chase challenged them they stepped aside. Chase led me up the spiral metal stairs. If I were human I would not have been able to see where I was stepping. Maybe that was why this room was so dark because only vampires could use it. The darkness for me, however, was no issue.

After a short walk up the spiral stairs, we came across a small ramp connected to a door. It was a narrow ramp with no side bars. Humans would fall to their death if they misplaced their feet before even making it to the door. Still holding my hand, Chase pulled me steadily toward the door, as if I couldn't see where I was going. In front of the guards I had to pretend to be clumsy, helpless, and *very* human. When he opened it, the wind of the night brushed over my skin, like a breath of fresh air. It was refreshing and intoxicating to be outside once again. So, this was how I would escape.

"None of that," Chase said with a smile. "Please, give me three days. And let me take you to the bridge. I know you've always wanted to see it up close."

I had never told anyone of my curiosity over the bridge within the city. So it was probable he could listen in to my thoughts. I felt myself building in anger, but he only smiled sheepishly, rubbing his thumb over my hand. His touch ceased my rage. It conflicted and frightened me with a barrage of unknown emotion how much his touch alone could extinguish my angry flames. What tormented me most was that I had not yet pulled away or fled.

"C'mon, Esmore, the night will be ours together," Chase said sweetly as he stood by my side, his hand over mine. He began walking me in the direction of the large bridge. My mind continued to peak through glimmers of rationality. Fight or flight.

CHAPTER 18

WE WALKED PAST the water fountain where Whitney had baited us into the trap, and what should've been the place of my death. The after-effects of the grenade had destroyed everything in the surrounding area. Glass in nearby buildings had shattered and rained over the ground. The rusty light posts were thrown meters away and were in pieces. A very definite hole was central in the ground. Not even parts of the water fountain remained. It was nothing but an abundance of shattered cement.

The moon, which fought against the gray clouds, presented itself finally. Tonight, it was luminous and bold, capturing my attention as I stared up at it. I wondered if I had died at this spot, if I would've spent my afterlife here and be just another member to haunt the remains of this world. As a hunter, it was not something we often questioned as we were programmed to not fear death and truthfully, I didn't believe in anything past it.

"Come along, Esmore," Chase said softly, offering his hand to me. Without realizing, I had been fiddling with his necklace around my throat. Slowly, he grabbed one of my hands, still watching me in case I jerked back from the action. I still wasn't entirely sure how committed to this role of pet I should play in an effort to gain more knowledge. I wanted to run away as much as I wanted to stay. It was too easy for me to escape now, so easy that I knew it was a test or trap.

As soon as his fingers intertwined with mine, it was like taking a breath I had needed for so long. When he touched me, I actually *felt*. It was as if I had been incapable of feeling ever since my mother's death. Not even James helped me feel. Although he had tried in many ways, I was repulsed by his lingering neediness. Whereas here, right now with Chase, these feelings came to me like a wave of refreshing water. And it was a very hard slap to the face. These were unexpected feelings, ones that I could not understand, and it made me uncomfortable.

In the moon's glow, with his hand holding mine, I was torn in a mixture of confusion. I was so absorbed and mesmerized by his every detail. His chest looked so pale and beautiful at the same time. He was angelic in every way. For all his oddness, quirkiness, intensity, and cockiness, I was drawn to him in ways I could never understand.

"This was once the world's most known bridge; it was called the 'Golden Gate Bridge.' Thousands used to travel over it every day in the technology era," Chase informed me. A lot of things had lost their titles and became irrelevant when the world changed so horrifically. Humans at some point gave up on the chance of restoring everything that once was.

"This part of the bridge is still stable. When the bombings happened, the bridge was unaffected, and three hundred years later it still stands. It goes to show the strength of the foundations the humans used," he said in admiration.

We came to the end of the bridge. There were cracks along the road, and it was littered with rusty vehicles. My eyelids batted a few times in awe. I tried to imagine a different world entirely. As Token Huntress, I didn't have much time to discover such things or admire our surroundings when we went on raids. My kind had very little curiosity for the past, but with Chase, it was as if the world had opened up to me, and I wanted to learn of its beauty and origin. Chase made it feel like time had stopped, and I had a brief moment to breathe. I could consider the endless possibilities of the world and what they once may have been.

"Chase, you were once a part of this era, weren't you?" I asked. I recalled him saying he was four hundred and thirty-one years old. It seemed so unnatural, considering he looked to be no older than his mid-twenties. He slowly pulled me down to sit next to him on the edge of the bridge's road. I stared beneath us where very little water streamed through. Although murky, the moon's shine made it seem beautiful. The fog hovered over it, adding to the surreal, mystical atmosphere. I could only imagine that once it was glorious. Did the humans of that day regularly admire it or had they forgotten its glory because they were so accustomed to it?

"I've lived in a few eras," he announced. "But yes, in the time of technology and such, I was there, amongst them. In the time that I was turned, it was not like this; life was valued. People had a sense of purpose that they valued above their egos."

"Who turned you?" I asked inquisitively. Was he turned against his will or was it something he sought out?

He gave a shy smile, looking at me and then back to the water's edge. It was when he looked to the water that I could see the true depth of his pain. Like he always did to dispel a serious topic, he tried to make the situation humorous. But already that fake humor had vanished from his eyes.

"My mother, actually," he said quietly. He grabbed a piece of rubble and threw it into the water. His other hand was still holding mine, and when he continued, he held it tighter. "She was turned against her will when I was younger; my father had died in the war before that. So, my mother and I were left to fend for ourselves. My mother was very beautiful—it's obvious who I got my good looks from!" He laughed, trying to ease the tension. "You know I haven't always been in this country? I've been spread over many because of that one callous vampire who turned her. I was born in the United Kingdom, and in the end, this is where we fled." My moment of silence prompted him to continue. He licked his lips and brushed through his shoulder-length black hair.

"A vampire broke into our home, and after the vampire had his way with my mother against her will, he decided he enjoyed it so much that he turned her. Of course she didn't want that, but he threatened my life, so she agreed to it if I was unharmed. The vampire was a very sick and evil man. He was an example of the vampires who had gone rogue and violent… who lacked control over their cravings and slowly would turn into sabers when they gave into that savageness. It's just too compelling for most to refuse.

"During this era, vampires were still susceptible to the sun and mostly could only walk during the night, so I became useful in his eyes to 'fetch' women for him to feast upon. I lost my mother for many years, as the darkness of being a vampire took her entirely. Eventually though, she was able to control her vampire ways and stayed true to herself for my sake. A rarity. I now understand how lucky I was she hadn't ripped my throat out the moment she was turned. I've seen it happen far too many times to those who thought they could control their impulses. But that is, in a sense, the curse. It's because of one's arrogance and internal weakness that they cannot control themselves. Usually, after that, they don't last very long and spiral. They go on a rampage and quickly become sabers themselves."

His black hair was lightly swaying in the breeze as he continued to speak. He was looking intently into the water as he brought all the memories back. "Eventually, my mother became strong, exceptionally strong for a young vampire. The vampire who tormented her tried to create some false family-like scenario. But when his mind began to alter, he slowly started resembling a saber. My mother wanted to protect me from him, but you cannot raise a hand to the vampire who turned you, it simply cannot happen. There's a weird bond and unspoken rule that you are faithful and loyal to them. My mother was bound, but I wasn't. So, when I was fifteen, and he rested one night, I silently crept up on him. Most vampires would've been alerted by being crept up on, but, when they turn into a saber, their heightened senses are lacking. I had tried it for many nights prior, to see if I could stand right in front of him without his knowing. Eighteen days straight I did so, just to make sure I could do it without myself or my mother being killed in consequence. And on the nineteenth night, I crept up on him and, like always, he did not move. So, I pierced a stick straight through his chest and killed him.

"I thought my mother would have been overjoyed, but instead, she cried. Apparently, that ghastly vampire had many followers. He was the leader of a coven. There are still a few around these days; a lot of them have been around for as long as the Council. They're ruthless and are the stepping stone between sabers and vampires. Their ways are like a drug to them, and they enjoy torturing… they enjoy the hunt. We Council vampires are more civilized and structured. When I killed their leader, his death reeked of me, and by default, I inherited his role. To become a leader of the coven you had to challenge and kill the current leader. Blood for blood. And by killing him, I was now considered the leader but very easy prey. And so, they hunted us in an attempt to kill me and take leadership. Until this day, that coven is leaderless. No one can claim the role; it is by death alone that any will be pushed through the ranks. My mother fled with me, and for years we ran from his followers. We had many close calls, but my mother protected me fiercely." His thumb began trailing over my hand absentmindedly. His shoulders were slightly hunched as he became exhausted by the thought. I placed my other hand on his, grabbing his attention. He gave a weary smile and continued. I was shocked by my action and pulled my hand away.

"My mother wouldn't turn me until she thought I was of an appropriate age. She wanted me to have time to decide if eternal life was something I truly wanted. And also, if it was a risk I was willing to take. My mother had not turned someone before, and there are rules when it comes to such things. But at the age of twenty-three, five days after my birthday, she did.

"Still, for many years, we continued on the run and faced death many times by different vampires. The ripple effect of staking that horrid creature haunted us for centuries. Somewhere out there, I imagine they still might be in search of me, if they haven't yet all died. In a sense, they're trapped in that group. There is no one to permit them to leave and release them from being bound to the coven. They probably mostly feed off one another, which is sickening. Vampires can feed off one another but only proportionally. Our blood is like synthesized blood. After drinking too much of our own kind, we become sick, even delusional. At this point, it puts us at further risk of becoming a saber. It only takes one slip to become an inhumane creature."

He gazed into my eyes then down at the ground before continuing. I'd never known the coven's had such binding rules. Drue had once taken out a small and sickly coven, but even he hadn't educated us on the extent of their hierarchy. I wondered if he'd ever known. "Are you safe because you're in the Council?" I asked. Had it become a form of protection, and if so, where was his mother?

Chase mock smiled, debating my question. "In the early years of the twenty-first century, my mother stumbled upon a young vampire. Although so young, only ten in vampire years, he was my mother's familiar." He gave me an arched eyebrow, knowing what I was about to ask. "I will explain shortly. That vampire was Fier—"

"As in Fier, who is in charge of the Council?" I asked, surprised. I thought one's familiar was a lover, so if I were right that would mean… "Fier is your stepdad?"

Chase gave an uneven smile, shaking his head lightly as if weighing up the options. "I suppose in a certain way you could claim that. He wasn't always in charge of the Council. At the time his father, Arab, was in charge. He promised my mother and me protection, which we humbly accepted. By then the world had changed drastically. Things that had once hurt us no longer did. There were a few who knew of our kind and hunted us, but they were only humans. The only things that still continue to harm us are excessive amounts of fire and silver. They're the only things that can. Once, the sun burned us, as well as blessed water. But when humankind altered, they no longer respected religion or law. They became selfish and a very dark race themselves.

"Only a few could bless water then because only a few remained pure and believed in it. The sun was thickly covered by pollution. The humans would turn on one another in war. Terrorist attacks began; planes would drop from the sky." He looked at me for a moment, realizing I probably couldn't quite comprehend what he meant. Although I had read about them, I could not fathom their size. He continued after I prodded him to keep talking. I was learning so much.

"Mankind destroyed their own beliefs and in that, their only weapon against us. It was a myth that items like a religious cross could kill us, it was something we created ourselves to witness the stupidity of humans. However, silver's elements have retained their power over us. If used correctly flames can burn us to death, but any vampire who has been around for a few years knows how to save himself from such an unfortunate weakness. However, the sabers are still affected by all those things: the sun, silver, and pure water. When they change, they regress to a more primal version of the vampire kind."

I was surprised by how easily Chase spoke about this to me. I remained silent, eager to learn all that I could.

"By this time, it made us vampires angry to watch, as we were the ones presumed to lurk in the shadows. Of course, the government who ruled over the humans knew of us. They considered us a plagued species. Yet because of our strength, elongated life, and healing qualities, more and more of our kind were being taken.

"So Arab took action and rallied the Councils which had been gathering for many years all over the world. We overpowered the humans; they were so deluded and arrogant that they thought they could beat us. But, of course, that wasn't the case. At first, we only wanted partial control, to become the government of the humans. But the humans didn't recognize their shortcoming, and what was meant to be a quick sweep of political power turned into war. We only wanted to protect our kind, who were being taken and tested upon. We wanted equal rights.

"By then we could walk in the sun. And we took what we wanted. It spread quickly; those who didn't know of the Council had the opportunity to stand with us. Within two years, we overpowered humans and took what we wanted. But the humans only retreated and continued to sabotage when they could—this is what killed the world's humanity. I killed many; I'm not in denial of what kind of vampire I once was. It's only now that I'm older that I do not torture or play games. But I did enjoy the hunt; I enjoyed the darkness that so easily consumed vampires. But the older you get, the more sentimental you become. I've found many vampires to be the same such as Tythian. I'll never lie to you, Esmore, which is why I'm telling you this. I have killed thousands, and some in not so kind ways."

I was unable to say anything. Was he in search of some reassurance or sympathy from me? Yet I couldn't argue with him for something he had done so long ago in the past or over something I had not seen him do, even if he admitted it.

"It was the government who created the first hunter from the vampires they kidnapped. They tested and studied them, creating the first of your kind."

I knew the story of our creation and heritage, but was very interested to hear of it from the perspective of someone who had lived within that time. I was entirely engrossed in his shadowed world.

"The hunters were special. They all activated gifts after their eighteenth birthday. And you were all so easy to spot because of your eyes. It was quickly realized that when you drained a hunter entirely, their gift would become yours. We vampires are not born with gifts, which is why hunters are so prized, especially Token Hunters, as they are known to be the strongest. We were to find the hunters and bring them back. Only the members in charge of the Council were to obtain such gifts, but a few of the older ones were careful enough to obtain their own. The younger ones did it foolishly and were caught for it, and instantly killed."

At this, I was surprised. It made so much sense: Token Hunters had been targeted over the years. Now I understood why the vampires often took hunters as hostages instead of beheading or killing them straight away. It was a source of embarrassment for my Guild as we had not yet figured this out. We simply thought that because we were derived from vampires that they were the ones who naturally had gifts.

"How did you acquire your gift then?" I asked, still absorbing all that he told me. Chase took on a gloomy disposition, and his fangs accidentally slipped out. It startled me but did not scare me. He apologized and closed his mouth. I had upset him with my question.

"Ten years ago, a few of the hunters, not from your Guild but another, were closing in on our location. My mother went on that raid, and she never came back," he simply said. "We had lived together for a mighty four hundred years and yet one hunter, who had only had her gift to control for a mere six years, was able to manipulate my mother so severely she took her own life and Arab's as well.

"I found that huntress and I drained her completely. Before her last breath escaped her mouth, I ripped each of her limbs off one by one and threw her into this very river." He was now looking down at the water as if the images flashed before his eyes. "Of course, I acquired her gift. Somewhat ironic that I live with the curse that had murdered my mother. Hunters are born with gifts, and so can be arrogant in thinking that they can overpower us. The hunters may be trained to lack fear, but it's what makes them vulnerable because they are still mortal and you only have a certain length of years to learn the extent of your ability. Our lifespan has been frozen, and only certain death can kill us, not age. When we acquire a gift, we have hundreds of years to develop it fully. It was the second gift I acquired, after that I did not want anymore. My first gift was a mistake entirely. That one I have locked away for a very long time, and it has lived with me for a little over one hundred and fifty years. I acquired it from the first hunter I had killed and entirely drained, and now I have to practice control to keep that cursed gift hidden. Since Fier has been in charge, and after my mother's death, he has turned hungrier as he took his father's place. Although there are a few who could overpower him, he has many gifts that we don't want to risk challenging."

I scanned over the information that he provided me with. I had searched for answers and followed instructions my entire life. And in this past twenty minutes was the revelation I had always seemingly wanted without realizing I ever needed it. I allowed myself to absorb this for a moment before asking my next question. "So, what exactly is a familiar?"

His eyebrows shot up as if he were surprised that I'd finally asked the question or didn't already know. "A familiar is something very rare and something I never thought I'd find in my lifetime." He took my knuckles and kissed them gently, caringly. "A familiar is someone you hope to have the chance to meet in this lifetime, no matter what form they might be: human, vampire, *hunter*..." he let the word linger. "They are your soulmate, and in every life, you may find love, but when you find your familiar, it is true love and devoted loyalty. For a vampire, it is mostly the purpose of their existence. Your familiar is the one who you meet in every lifetime. It's why you feel so familiar to me because we have already met so many lifetimes before. Call it superstition, but I've seen this undeniable commitment time and time again between others. It is in many ways everything," he said, looking up at the moon as if avoiding my eye contact in his sudden vulnerability. I wanted to mock his sentiment and silly story. But nothing lurked inside of me that led me to believe he was lying. The way he made me feel, was an openness and bound attraction I'd never known.

"If by chance both familiars are vampire or hunter, they share their gifts after initiating their long, undying love. My mother had five gifts and Fier had two. Between them, they both had the same: seven each. It is—if you ever permitted me to do so—something I would share with you someday. My first gift wouldn't cause you harm because you are not a vampire. And I could share my gift of manipulating the mind with you."

The question was on the edge of my lips. I was enthralled by his belief by the unyielding security and loyalty he professed. I was entirely absorbed. "And what must one do to initiate their undying love?" I asked, my voice coming out husky, and surprising me by the entrancing tone it had taken.

He kissed my knuckles again, looking at me with his beautiful gray eyes that glistened in the moonlight. "Become lovers, claim one another as only theirs. That is what binds familiars officially. I know you may shy away from this, Esmore, but I cannot explain to you how hard it is not to touch you, to not be with you. For heaven's sake, I don't know how Tythian has done it all these years. He has made sure not to touch Whitney as she is waiting out her days. They can both sense and feel that they are one another's familiar and their bond is deep. But never have they been able to connect on that far deeper level that familiars crave: to become one with one another. If she and Tythian were to make love, it would change her entirely, which is something she has never wanted. Tythian respects her and her wishes." The air was thick with tension and longing. "You, Esmore, I crave more than anything." His hand trailed up my arm and gently caressed the back of my neck. He stared at me for a while, waiting for me to pull away or slap his hand away. When I didn't, he slowly pulled me in, and I could feel myself leaning into him in anticipation.

"Since vampires have existed, it has always been questioned whether they have a soul. But I believe it; we were, after all, born human. Finding you has provided answers to the many questions I've asked for all these years. I will protect you forever, and I will love you even into the next life until we meet again. My love for you will never die," Chase said, his words becoming a whisper as I closed my eyes, ready to embrace his soft lips. I could no longer deny my desire for him. And as he explained everything, I felt that it was all so true. It felt like a lullaby that I had been waiting my entire life to hear. I couldn't confront my jumble of feelings just yet, but I could commit to one kiss, just one was all I pushed for.

Chase's lips gently brushed past mine. Snarling noises broke our trance.

Chase jumped up immediately, standing in front of me protectively. He tilted his head as if listening in the distance. I stood up behind him trying to hone in on our surroundings.

"A spotter has just located two hunters nearby. They are circling them now and taking them hostage," he claimed, reaching out for my hand. My lips parted as I feared who those two hunters might be. Reality crept in, and I ignored his extended hand. Pain streaked across his face. I was a jumble of confusion as my body ached to pull him into me and my mind held weakly to be stubborn. I was a hunter, and he was a vampire. Folklore or not, I had to fight it with every fiber of my being because there would be no going back.

"They've caught them. From the description...," Chase continued to listen in and locked eyes with me. "Two males... one with shoulder-length black hair and the other with a short buzz cut and bulky frame."

I skipped my next breath. I think that's Dillian and James.

CHAPTER 19

B
Y THE TIME we found the other vampires who had reported the capture of the hunters, the two had already been taken to the Council. I was too late to intervene. Though I might not yet have been tied up and tortured, I didn't have the same confidence for the others in their handling. Chase took me to his room so we wouldn't raise suspicion by following the small group of vampires who had a hold of the two hunters.

"Calm down and trust me," Chase said. "We can't just barge in there, and I especially can't bring in my human. It's stickier now that they're already in here. I'll figure something out." I wanted to believe in him, but I only ever trusted my own actions. Though it aggravated me to admit, he was right. I had to for now, lay complacent in his room until I had my chance, which I would find. I needed a plan, but I didn't even have an estranged clue as to where they might be held captive.

Chase paced back and forth a few times in the room, devising a plan. I wanted to scream at him to tell me more so I could help him, surprised that I was even accounting Chase's actions as the forefront of my plan. He was the only one I could depend on helping me to find their location. A small concern peaked as I analyzed the situation and the best way to go forward. What would become of Chase if he helped me aid the escape of hunters? If he stayed true to his word as to what he told me on the bridge, then he was the only vampire I could ever imagine doing such a thing. Our kinds were enemies, and yet, for me, he would do this. I tried to push that thought down. I didn't want his safety to be my concern. I didn't want to believe or be distracted by his words on top of the bridge. I internally growled at myself. I had to stay focused.

"I have an idea, trust me," Chase said, and before I could ask how I would be involved, he vanished from the room with lightning speed. I went to run after him but thought better of it. If I snuck around like I had previously and followed him, I could be putting myself in jeopardy, and I wouldn't be of much help to anyone. The vampires would be on high alert within the Council after catching two hunters. I fought with myself as to whether I should follow him, deciding I could utilize this time to guess at where they might be hiding them. If he didn't return soon, I'd craft my own way to get them out, especially now that Chase had shown me how to escape. I didn't like having only one form of escape but the rest we'd have to improvise.

Within a few minutes, Chase returned. I was pulled toward him, making sure he was okay and he had a plan that I could act on. "I can only buy you a few minutes. Please understand that," he said strictly. "Any longer and you'll be sentencing me and those involved to a harsh punishment and possible talk of treachery. Without question, I agreed. I understood the risk Chase was facing if I was caught talking with the prisoners. He gathered me into his arms, breezing through the halls with lightning speed into a foreign room in a section of the Council I had not yet explored. His pace was so fast that I knew he was worried about us being caught. Standing on guard, outside a closed door, was a vampire whom I didn't recognize. He looked at me, unfazed, and held out his hand to Chase who placed something in there. By the look they exchanged, it seemed to be payment of some kind.

"I'll be back in three minutes," the guard warned. "I hope this is worth it for you."

Before he had completely vanished around the corner, I hurriedly opened the door. I expected to see unfamiliar faces and peer into the eyes of hunters I'd never known. Instead, I was gutted to reveal a very near unconscious Dillian and James. *It was them*. They both wore tightly knotted blindfolds with gags in their mouths. Both of them had their ankles and hands tied to the wooden chairs they sat on. I removed Dillian's blindfold and gag. He looked up, terrified, only to realize it was me. He looked at me, baffled. His mouth was dry as he tried to speak. I took James' gag and blindfold off. When I did, Dillian hesitated to speak as soon as James' eyes started feverishly searching over the room.

"Esmore," James whispered desperately. "I've been looking for you everywhere."

Dillian was exchanging a pained expression with Chase. It wasn't one of disgust or hatred, but urgency.

"Take this off my wrists so I can hold you in my arms," James said fiercely.

"I can't right now. I need to figure out how I can get you out…"

"What do you mean, you 'can't'?" James shouted, angrily jarring toward me.

Suddenly Chase was by my side, nudging me out of the way and standing protectively in front of me. I looked between him and James, shocked at the sudden outburst. James had never tried to raise a hand against me.

"That's what you left me for, so you could be with a filthy vampire! You are mine, and you ran away to soil yourself by—" James was cut off by Chase, who held him around the throat. He lifted both him and the chair to his eye-level, missing the usual spark of humor he so often wore. His eyes had turned into a stormy gray as he stared at James with complete contempt.

"You do not speak to Esmore like that," Chase said slowly and deliberately. His fangs were now out, and he looked at James' throat with consideration. Before I could say anything, Chase took James out of the room at a pace I could hardly follow.

"Chase!" I yelled angrily behind him.

Before I could run after them, Dillian called out to me from behind. "Esmore! I hoped he'd remove him from the room. We don't have much time." His face was badly bruised, and his lip and right eye had been busted. Two bite marks were on either side of his neck.

"What are you talking about?" I asked. Had Dillian and James deliberately been caught?

"I knew you hadn't died in the blast. Not much can get past my eyes, even if my body cannot follow at such a speed. I saw him take you, and after the last few days, I hoped he would keep you safe. I can't explain it, but I had the impression he meant you no harm. After the ambush, I figured out he'd been the one injecting thoughts and visions into my mind. That's beside the point. Esmore, you cannot come back to the Guild."

"What are you talking about?" I asked, now coming to his side. I wanted to somehow ease the pain or heal his wounds for him; he looked terrible. I'd never felt so sensitive or tender toward anyone. I had always felt obliged and task driven to keep them safe, but I never held any fierce concern.

"We haven't returned to the Guild ourselves yet because James has become obsessed with his mission to save you. We were all on board with it until cracks began to show within only hours after he took your place to lead. We've been hiding and trying to figure out how to track you. I came today in hopes of being caught so that I could speak with you and warn you."

"Warn me? Dillian, that was a stupid idea, now you're tied up and held as a hostage," I said, irritated that I couldn't cut his ropes now. If I did, it would jeopardize Chase's ability and effort to get them out safely. In the meantime, it would also put Chase at risk with his Council. I was torn.

"James… he's become obsessed with you. You're not safe if you return, something in him has snapped. And I mean it Esmore. His personality changed as soon as you vanished. When you were in the Guild, he could control and monitor you. But as soon as you were out of his grasp, he became violent toward the other hunters. He's half-crazed and desperate to own you.

"I assumed after the fight that vampire, Chase, brought you here. I wanted to find a way to get to you before James did because I was scared of what he might do. If you come back to the Guild, I really do believe Campture will kill you. I don't know what's going through James' mind, but his ramblings have advocated he won't defend you to Campture, even though you've done nothing wrong. He truly has a suspicion you've left him. Not that you were kidnapped or almost killed. He thinks that you're trying to escape being his.

"I never knew he was like this. I should've picked up on it sooner. The signs were so obvious with his need to control you, but we didn't take it seriously. I don't know what will happen to me now but, Esmore, I came here in hopes that I could warn you. Don't trust the Guild. Something is happening. As soon as you weren't around and James took charge of the team, all but Teary I couldn't trust. Something's happening with the Guild, Esmore, this ambush was only the begging," he said desperately. "I've replayed it in my mind and wonder if Campture sent us back to the city because she considered the risk that we might not return. What if it was a calculated risk?"

"James has always—"

"No, Esmore, I mean this. He isn't of a healthy mind anymore. He hasn't slept since you've been taken. It isn't because he misses or worries for you. The way he rambles… it's as if his property has been stolen from him, and it's his personal mission to take you back to Campture. He thinks you are his. He's been calling you a traitor amongst your raid team. He wants to return you so he can 'fix' you. Esmore, I swear I am not lying. I swear it," he said pleadingly. "I know you are amongst vampires. But if this old vampire, Chase, is willing to protect you right now, you need that to hide from James and Campture. You know he has great influence in the Guild. You must stay away," he said unrelenting.

It was so much to take in. Why would James try to turn my team against me? They would've seen me take that grenade and risk my own life to protect them. So when they saw me vanish amongst the dust alive, why would he even think for a moment that I tricked him? It had only been a few days, how had he changed into a mad man so quickly? If I couldn't return to the Guild then where would I go? I didn't doubt Dillian, I trusted him completely. I had so pointedly thought I was gaining intel to take back to my Guild, that I never even considered the twisted views my kidnapping might evoke.

I considered Dillian's warning, snapping myself out of the current circumstances. Even if I was in danger, I cared more for Dillian's safety and escape than my own life right now. He truly was my best friend and risked his life in the stupidest way on the off chance that he might be able to pass the message along.

I took two of the daggers from my garter, placing them in his hand in an upward position. "There is only one guard for the time being. Most vampires will not wake for another few hours. You must escape or they'll kill you, I'm certain of it. You know me, Dillian, I can look after myself."

"You don't understand," he whispered.

I pressed my finger to his lips. "You are my friend, let me do this for you," I instructed. I would risk my life repetitively for Dillian. I valued our comradery to know he would do the same. I gave him specific instructions on his route for escape. The rest I would figure out myself. I couldn't just leave him as bait.

Chase entered the room with James who was now raging, pulling back and forth on his chair. He was spitting angrily, like a saber out of control. It was startling to see such a transformation within him. Dillian's words sunk in as I realized the extent of James' possessiveness. The thought lingered. If he could not have me and control me, then he would most likely try to kill me.

"You filthy tramp!" James spat at me. "You belong to me! How weak you are in mind, how easily you spread your legs for anything…"

Chase sharply backhanded him across the room, smashing him into the wall. James began to bleed from his head. Chase's speed was far too fast for James to have protected himself with his metal skin. But as Chase advanced on him again, his skin then turned. "Utterly filthy! You will return to me."

"She is not *yours*," Chase hissed angrily. "You do not own her."

My own anger built at the accusations he threw at me without knowing what I had gone through. How dare he attempt to twist my team against me in the shadows as I gathered intel for our Guild as a whole. I risked my life to save him, and in return all he could consider was that I was shacking-up with vampires. He had always been controlling, but I never realized the extent. He would never let me go. And as his control of me slipped out of his hands, he slowly turned into the hideous beast he truly was. We all had our own demons to face. I felt the stir of darkness roll within my stomach again. At this point I wanted to follow Chase's lead and hurt James. I wanted to force him to retract his words. The creature continued to stir as I beckoned it to go, trying to pull myself apart from it. I felt as if I couldn't breathe, and as it rose, I wanted to hurt James, to… *kill* him.

"Esmore," Dillian said cautiously. My eyes flickered to him. I now realized I had my arms crossed and my nails had been clawing my skin in anger. Chase looked at me worriedly, now no longer fixated on his hunger for James.

"Breathe, Esmore," Chase soothed. His voice whispered like my father's used to when such desires came to mind. *Count to ten*, my father used to say. I proceeded to do so, just as he had taught me. I contained the creature as Chase's gaze pooled into mine.

I swallowed hard, walking over and kneeling in front of James. I wouldn't give him the satisfaction of knowing he had made me feel something because of his words. I would kneel in front of him with minimal expression. It was only Chase who was proving to make me feel anything other than hate and bloodlust. "We are done, James. I do not belong to you, and you will never own me," I said bluntly.

James' metal forehead smashed into my nose, head-butting me. I fell back into Chase, who then held me behind him with one arm and lifted James by the throat with the other. "I will kill him," Chase promised.

I, too, wanted to make James pay for what he'd done. He had broken my nose. Whatever we had once shared in our younger years vanished as I now saw him for the despicable man he was. And yet, as I looked into his eyes, I pitied him. A raw emotion I'd never known before.

We all turned as the guard opened the door and stepped into the room. He focused on Chase. "You know Fier will punish you if you do something so reckless," he said, blasé.

"Chase, let's go," I whispered to him softly and tried to pull him away. We had to play the part. I'd given Dillian what he needed to offer him a fighting chance of escape. I couldn't do much more for now. Chase was hesitant, but slowly he let go of James and watched him slither to the floor, choking.

I gave Dillian another wary look. "Be safe," he mouthed.

The guard followed us out, watching us as we walked down and turned into the white hall. "Erase their memory of this location," I said briskly. Chase was the vampire who had the power to blur and contort people's minds. I knew he could do the same to Dillian and James. I never wanted James to track me back here or anywhere again. I anticipated they could escape of their own accord. And when they did, I hoped it looked like they made it out of their own doing. They were hunters after all.

"Already have. Why? What did you do?" Chase asked. I remained silent. How could I confess I'd jeopardized him? When I saw Dillian tied to a chair, I couldn't fathom any other choice. I couldn't let him die, and I was confident in his ability to escape.

I was suddenly swept off my feet before moments later, Chase set my toes down on the cool ground of his room. He assessed my nose carefully. His fangs slid out of his gums, and he bit into his wrist. "Drink this," he said, offering his wrist to me. "It'll heal your nose." At my hesitation, he added, "Your broken nose will not go unnoticed by other vampires."

I was hesitant to agree. But I didn't want to raise any more attention then I might've already, especially considering I'd possibly endanger Chase in the process. I also wondered how reliable the guard's bought word of silence was. I slowly took Chase's wrist and pressed my lips to it, letting the warmth of his blood flow over my tongue, teeth, and down my throat. I had tasted blood before after many hits to the face in both training and in raids. But Chase's blood tasted different: it was sweet and comforting.

Chase pushed back my golden fringe, pushing it out of my eyes. I released my hold of his wrist, feeling the after-effect of a slight buzz. I felt my nose crumble and knit together, bone meshing within seconds. I rubbed my finger over my nose and retracted it, there was a small smear of blood, but it felt normal, not even a lump.

"I have something for you. Dillian was carrying them with him," Chase said, vanishing into the bathroom. After only a moment of silence, he came back, presenting my Barnett crossbow and sword. "He knew you were still alive and that he'd find you." I took them swiftly, looking at them in awe. I thought I'd never see them again.

"Thank you," I said earnestly. These weapons had so much value to my status. Did I have any right to still use them? I was a huntress, a Token, yet Dillian just warned me not to come back. What purpose would I have if I couldn't return?

"Are you okay?" Chase asked, interrupting the very dark thoughts that consumed me. I looked away so he couldn't gauge my inner thoughts. But he'd already seen them. My expressions and emotions were always so hard to keep from him. I didn't even know how to handle them myself after so long, harboring an emptiness. He brushed his hand over my arm. At his touch, I suddenly wanted to cry. What reason did I have to live if I was no longer a Token Huntress with the purpose to work within my Guild and protect my people?

"Esmore," he said soothingly. "Look at me." I felt vulnerable under his gaze, so I stubbornly continued to look at my weapons. Chase's other hand gently held my chin and lifted it. My gaze met his. "My Esmore, you are far too beautiful and powerful to look beneath you. If ever you feel insecure about anything, look to me. I will be yours forever, and my counseling is the least you can ask of me. But I selfishly ask you to let me make you *feel*." He exhaled. "I would risk anything for you." His breath was hot on mine as he slowly leaned in. His lips brushed past mine, and I could no longer fight the need I had for him. It was only with Chase I felt something, anything. And right now, I desperately wanted to distract myself from the chaos of my world.

Chase kissed me, his tongue leading mine. I let my weapons clutter to the floor, brushing my hands under his leather jacket to feel the cool touch of his chest. My hands trailed down his abs, embracing each and every muscle. The lower I got, the fiercer my nails dug into his skin as I knew what was soon to come.

Still kissing me, Chase, lifted me and wrapped my legs around his waist. I fumbled for what I was so desperately after, and that was his belt. Within an instant, Chase had thrown me face-down onto his bed. I clung to one of the posts as he came up behind me, kissing the back of my neck, which sent shivers down my entire body. He made me feel as if I were flooding with warm energy like we were radiating together. I couldn't handle his sweetness as he delicately kissed my neck rolling waves of shudders through me, I wanted more. I wanted to see his savageness, and I wanted him to fill me with that hunger. Reading my mind, he tore the back of my dress open in a clean sweep. Slowly, he began kissing down my back.

At each kiss, my nails clung deeper into the wooden post, until I could no longer be teased. I turned to face him, and one of my torn sleeves slid over my shoulder to reveal my breast. He looked at me lustfully, licking over his lips as he stared at my exposed body. He took my lips again, more hungrily, tugging on my bottom lip as we parted. I tried to fumble for his jeans, feeling the heat radiate from him. He took my hands, gathering them above my head and pinning them to the post. He kissed me fiercely again, his fangs accidentally sliding out and nipping my lip. He pulled back for a moment. His lustful expression had turned to worry.

My body overflowed, and I needed to relieve myself of such heat. I needed to be with Chase. He was staring at my exposed neck, swept away in the moment I nodded my permission. If this was all that he asked from me, I would give it to him. His beautiful gray eyes went hungry as he kissed my lips again before biting into my neck. The feeling was both terrifying and erotic at the same time. In a sense, I felt even further connected to Chase. It was another way of being able to be with him. He arched his head back, embracing the taste of my blood, before wiping his mouth on his jacket. I so desperately wanted to clutch for him again but was unable to as he still had my hands pinned above me. He was teasing me, which only made me more desperate to have my own thirst quenched. I needed him inside of me.

His hand slid over my dress, ripping the front of it apart. He kissed down my neck, creating a moan that rumbled from the core of my stomach. His lips brushed over my nipples, kissing me gently on both as he lifted me higher on the bed. I loved the pain it caused when he pushed me back against the post.

He looked at me hungrily before kissing me again. He whispered into my ear, his words a warm flush. "You are so beautiful, Esmore." When he said my name it came out more like a growl. Feral. Powerful. Intoxicating.

I kissed his neck, not wanting to suffer under his torment any longer. I wriggled my hands free and glided them beneath his jacket, fiercely taking it off and throwing it away. The mere pleasure I had in touching his shoulder blades forced another moan from my lips. I clutched for his belt, sliding it off quickly and unzipping his pants, desperately trying to grab hold of his hard shaft. My fingers brushed the tip of it, and I was pleased by the size.

He held my hand firmly for a moment, looking at me fiercely, wildly even. "Esmore, what is mine will be yours, and yours mine." I took his lips for my own again. I was tired of all the warnings. In this moment I was certain this was all I wanted. I gave way to caution. Chase was not the monster of stories I'd been told. Chase was something that I would agree to for the rest of my life. For better or for worse, I only cared for this moment right now. My hands went through his hair wildly.

He tore away my underwear and lifted me over him. I kissed him again fiercely as I slid over him, accepting his enormity. At first it hurt, but as he slowly began pulling me further onto him, I became intoxicated by him. Kissing his neck fiercely, our speed heightened. Moans tore from my mouth. I had never felt anything so fulfilling. I pushed him down, wanting to explore his full length on my own. I went down harder on him, causing me to moan louder. Chase couldn't handle that, and with speed, he swept me from the bed and had me on the desk.

Every time he thrust into me, I moaned louder and louder, almost ready to peak. I couldn't handle his speed or might much longer, yet I only wanted more, almost pleading for it. I clung to his shoulder blades desperately, my nails etching into his skin. I couldn't hold such pressure within me anymore. I moaned loudly as we finished off together, releasing the build-up that had heightened us so feverishly. Breathing heavily over my shoulder for a moment, he kissed my neck gently, lovingly. The wood creaked beneath us, and we both collapsed onto the floor as the desk snapped and shattered. I fell on top of him, awkwardly. We both looked at one another in surprise and then laughed at the damage we had caused. My own laughter was a foreign sound to me. But as he stroked my cheek chuckling alongside me, I was certain in every way it was right.

I moved on top of him, my chest pressed to his as I played with one of his hands, staring at it in thought. I felt different after being with him. After all my resistance, I was right to be with Chase. It felt like everything clicked in to place, and the stubbornness I held against him never made any sense at all. The word familiar rolled around in my mind. I didn't believe in superstitions, but this and everything Chase embodied was something I couldn't deny. Chase combed through my sweaty hair, pushing it aside from my face. We lay there contentedly, enjoying being with one another.

"I understand now," I said. I could feel him smiling as his breath got hotter on my face.

He kissed the top of my head in reply. "I will be yours forever, Esmore. You are my purpose."

CHAPTER 20

WHEN I AWOKE still on top of Chase, I found we were lightly swaying. I realized then that we were in the hammock and Chase was gently rocking us back and forth away from his collection of bobblehead dolls. He had covered us both with his silky beige sheets. I hadn't even noticed him moving us onto the hammock, and I'd slept so deeply that I hadn't stirred once. The reality of being together with him only hours before slowly dawned on me.

I wanted to argue with being claimed as his familiar, but I couldn't muster much resistance. Everything had changed, so much so it scared me. But, resting with Chase, I was at peace. It was like he once said, our souls did feel familiar. It was as if we had swung on this very hammock for years already together. My instinct was now to fight anything that threatened our ability to be together. I didn't feel tormented like I had in the relationship with James. I wasn't losing my freedom but almost felt like I would be finding myself through Chase without a lack of identity. He accepted me for what I was, and in return, I had to do the same for him even if we were natured to be enemies.

Chase was gently pushing back my golden hair, gazing at the top of my head contentedly. I looked into his beautiful gray eyes before kissing his smooth chest. *This chest will be mine forever, every inch is mine,* I thought possessively.

I was distracted by one of the bobblehead dolls. *Though, his collection was still creepy.*

They are not, they're cool, Chase's voice interrupted in my mind. I looked up at him, baffled.

Can you hear me? I felt stupid for asking the question in my mind. He had mentioned his gift would become my own, but it was the oddest of sensations. He had never mentioned telepathy being part of his perk. It was like a pool of whispers, and I could hear Chase's voice over all the rest, which made no sense to me. I wondered if they were the voices and thoughts of all the other vampires and humans who dwelled within the Council. I thought back to Chase's interjection and removal of James where they had been held captive. I wondered if he and Dillian had spoken in private. So all those hateful words I had toward him... he would've heard them all.

He smiled at me. *I pick and choose when I want to listen,* he said internally chuckling. *You'll learn how to use it and control it soon, but yes, my love, telepathy comes with the package. You'll quickly learn how to manipulate people's minds, and you could even start reaching people in their dreams. I can teach it all to you.* He swept his hand through my fringe again. *You are so beautiful.*

Never was I vain, nor did I care much for my appearance, but when Chase said it, I welcomed the compliment. *But not as beautiful as you, right?* I asked with a wicked smile. He arched an eyebrow in challenge, pinching at the sides of my ribs and trying to tickle me.

An echoing bang on the door forced us both to jolt upright, as best we could in the awkward hammock. I had been so absorbed by Chase that I'd dropped my guard.

"Bring your human out, Chase!" Gardar bellowed from the other side of the door. Chase threw me a look. He didn't even need to ask me what I had done.

You gave them a way to escape, Chase projected into my mind.

I couldn't just leave them there, I answered, defensive at his disappointed tone.

He sighed and somberly looked over at the door. "Get some clothes on," he said, gently lifting me. I wrapped the sheet around me, watching as he fluently stepped out of the hammock naked. He walked toward his closet, his behind so desirable. His muscles lightly rolled beneath his skin as he walked. Never had I noticed how toned every inch of him was. Feeling my gaze, he shot me a devilish stare, raising a suggestive brow. I smiled, having the same desire as he did for me, despite the grave situation we were in. I pooled over with heat for him once again, but the enticement broke when the banging continued at the door.

"Don't make me break this door in!" Gardar raged.

"I'll be two seconds. My heavens, calm yourself!" Chase bellowed. We both looked at the heap of clothes on the ground. They were shredded into bits.

I gave him a sheepish smile. "I suppose you only brought me one garment?" I asked, pulling the sheet higher up my chest.

He gave me a half-smile, gesturing for me to come to his closet. "I guess it can't be helped then, you'll have to wear something of mine."

Unfortunately, Chase's clothing didn't exactly fit me. He presented me with one of his white buttoned shirts and a long leather jacket, in an attempt to conceal most of my legs. He tightened the leather jacket around me so tightly it took my breath away, then gave me a wicked smile. The temptation was far too great, and I had to bite my lip to discourage myself from pulling him closer as he stood naked in front of me.

Another bang forced us to move. I tied my leather boots within seconds. Already Chase had pulled on jeans, a belt, and a leather jacket. I went to grab for my weapons, but he gave me a warning glance that motioned for me not to. *Whatever has happened, you cannot go in armed. Let me do the talking and remember, we were here all night. Don't worry about me. Fier will most likely threaten me. But don't worry about that, I can take care of myself,* he explained.

Before I could show my obvious discomfort with this, Chase opened the door. The barbaric vampire looked at me, uneasily. Chase grabbed his cheeks to refocus his eyes onto him. "You look at me only," he growled, deterring Gardar's lingering gaze. Although he didn't remember attacking me, it seemed the same interest danced in his eyes.

"Fier wants to see you both. By the sound of it, you messed up, and as a consequence, your human is as good as dead. Familiar or not," he smirked with a very hungry appreciation, his fangs slipping out. Chase threw him into the hall and against the wall. He came back at Chase just as quickly. Both of them grabbed one another's throat in a tight grip. I looked at my Barnett crossbow and sword, which was in the center of the room.

Don't! You're supposed to be human. Chase raised his voice in my mind.

"The fact that you're Fier's second-in-charge and your mommy was his familiar doesn't mean much to me. Fier's pissed, man. He knows you were involved with the hunters' escape. They killed eight of our kind. That's on you." Gardar finished, smiling maliciously. He released his grip on Chase, who did the same, straightening out his coat. The vampire sneered at me and then stalked through the hall.

"Come along, Esmore. It'll be okay. I'll handle Fier and protect you," Chase promised. I would not rely on his protection alone, but I took his hand anyway. I had to keep up the pretense that I was only a human or it would put Chase in danger as well. And I'd already done enough of that.

Chase led me anxiously through the halls, though on the outside he looked perfectly calm. As I hovered my mind over his I could feel that he was darting between possible outcomes. I had put him in this position. Unless the guard had squealed, there was no way they could know it was me specifically that aided their escape. But somehow, it had been linked back to Chase.

Perhaps Gardar was throwing his own assumptions about. But it also confirmed that I hadn't gone unnoticed in the short time of being within the Council. Chase was doing quick maths on the variables and what-if outcomes and how he should best interact. I couldn't make much sense of his thoughts as this ability was still new to me. I only caught bits and pieces like tuning into an old radio for only a second before losing the signal again.

We walked past the water fountain, turned right, and then walked toward the large wooden doors where it was a rave room only hours before. The doors were already open; they had been waiting for our arrival. Chase tightened his grip around my hand as we entered. Fier was pacing the room. At our entrance, he savagely swung around, holding his finger up. His blond hair was messy, and his eyes were wild. The first few buttons were undone on his silky white shirt. He motioned for the other guards to surround us in a complete circle. His fangs were savage as he spoke, spit flying. "You dare betray me after my father took your sorry life in and protected you… after pledging your loyalty to me?" Fier demanded of Chase.

Chase was unflinching. He stood there as a hard statue. He swept his gaze over the numbers surrounding us. There must have been one hundred vampires here, easily. Was this how they trialed their vampires? Were these witnesses or warriors? Looking at the ones closest to me, I knew I could disarm them quickly in hand-to-hand combat. Fier's eyes were bulging in madness.

"Fier, would you like to state what this is about? And why so many vampires? Have you convicted me of an unknown crime already?" Chase asked. His deep, threatening voice caused the other vampires to shift uncomfortably and look amongst themselves. Although Chase was not the oldest vampire here, they evidently feared him. And much to our advantage, they didn't know I was a huntress. If we had to, we could fight back to back our way out of here.

Fier pulled a shiny object out of his back pocket. To my disbelief, it was one of the daggers I had given Dillian. He must have dropped one as they escaped. Chase heard my thoughts, and he tightened his grip on my hand. He now completely understood what I had done.

"A little birdie told me that you were the one who specifically took these daggers from the weapons room. You know I have eyes everywhere within this compound, and I'm surprised you could be so stupid as to think you would get away with betraying me," Fier said smugly, and as if all-knowing.

"So, it was one of two options: it was either you or that damn human you hold so dearly. And don't dare try to tell me you were set up. I want answers now!" Fier looked like a creature with rabies; he was almost frothing at the mouth in rage. The frown marks in his face cut deep into his skin. Wind began to stir in the room, causing objects to creak. Fier's anger was manifesting through his gift. When Chase said nothing, only idly watching the vampires who shifted from foot to foot beside us, Fier snapped once again. He didn't take kindly to moments of silence and not being answered.

"Kill all the humans!" Fier announced harshly. There were a few mumbles amongst the vampires. "If my men's loyalty has begun to falter because of some human attachments, then we will be rid of them all. You will all find new ones. They are only meals!" Fier roared. The wind began to surround us, and vampires pushed together, unsettled.

"It wasn't them!" a faint voice tried to shout over the wind's loud howls. Suddenly the wind stopped as vampires pushed aside for Whitney to wheel herself in. She gave me a weak smile.

What are you doing? I asked her in my mind.

I hadn't even realized I'd done it until I could feel the sensation of her mind receiving me. I thought I could only share my gift with Chase. But then I considered when James and Dillian were captured, and with silent words, Dillian had requested that Chase remove James from the room. Having no gift of my own, I didn't know how the best way to reform or understand this new profound ability. And I shuddered to think how many thoughts Chase had listened in on, yet unlike Campture, I didn't feel like he was prying. It just simply felt like a natural connection, an extension of myself even.

Whitney looked at me warily, though she didn't seem surprised that I could now speak to her in such a way. *Esmore, I think your coming here is an important thing, and I want to protect you. I'm dying, and I can guess I only have a few more weeks if not days. I know you saw the blood yesterday that I coughed into my handkerchief. My body has been shutting down for a long time, and I'm in pain. So if I can do something right and make a difference before that, then…* she murmured and hazed out as I tried to refocus on her. *Tythian and I cannot live together forever, and it pains me to leave him. Right now he is on a raid, and when he returns, he will be furious. But if I can help save many people's lives, then I will. I had a feeling Fier would go on a rampage at some time or another, so if I can make a difference, I want to.*

"What do you mean, you weakling?" Fier spat at her feverishly. Chase held me firmly as I stepped forward.

I'm okay with this, Esmore, Whitney said to me, as if she knew what was about to come. *After I have gone, please talk to Tythain. I fear that with no one to talk to, he will forsake his sanity.*

"Kill all three!" Fier roared.

I couldn't reach Whitney in time, but as I stumbled forward, Chase covered my back as vampires began to run for us. Fier was in front of Whitney, and with one clean slice, he slit her throat with the very same dagger that had assisted Dillian's and James' escape. Gasping for breath, Whitney choked and closed her eyes. It all happened so quickly. For whatever purpose she thought she'd created, I could only manage that she'd been taken out of her misery. My mind brushed over hers. I could feel the shadows of death reach for her. And yet a smile still pressed on her lips. Her pain was not for long, but I suffered it with her.

Admiring his work, Fier looked from Whitney to me with cold eyes. The movement around us seemed to blur. I roared with hatred and pain, swept over with guilt. Whitney's death was now on my hands as well.

One vampire came at me with a large wooden spear. I grabbed it, flipping myself over her stick and over her back. Behind her, I breathed heavily, surprising her with my speed, and snapping her neck. I claimed her weapon as mine and pierced her chest with it from behind before her neck could heal.

"Hunter!" A vampire declared. Suddenly, all their attention was on me. I sliced through the first two, cutting their throats open. I didn't have a clear opening to pierce their hearts, with so many enemies in such a confined space. I could only kill the ones who gave me an easy opening, but for now, I had to severely injure and cut down as many as I could to drop their numbers before they healed and revived into masses. I would have to kill them one by one.

Two jumped from the forefront of the group. I slid under them, slicing at their ankles before they dropped. I swung my spear around in time, thrusting the blade across a vampire's eye who had tried to attack me from behind. I pierced the vampire in front of me through the chest, jumping into him as he keeled over and took me with him. I took the motion, flipping over his corpse and jumping onto a vampire's shoulders. I placed both of my hands on the ground, throwing the vampire's weight over me and into the oncoming four vampires.

My rage only burned fiercer, and the wild beast that I too often tried to hold down was now gathering itself again. I could not fall away from it. I could not resist the pull of darkness. Blood was all I wanted to see. I wanted to kill each and every one of them in an attempt to reach Chase. I was in a bloodlust frenzy.

A vampire came at me with two swords. I dodged the first, ducking to the side, and then twisted around him. I grabbed hold of both of his arms, plunging my feet into his back and pushing into it. I heard a snap that busted both of his shoulder blades. Letting go, I flipped myself behind him, retrieving the two swords he dropped as he shrieked.

My movements were fluent as I fixated on reaching Chase. I needed to get to him so I could stand by his side and protect him. I sliced through the many vampires who came at me: their throats, chests, stomachs, faces, and ankles. Nothing would stop me from reaching Chase. The old grotesque vampire, Gardar, now ran for me. A smile pressed at his lips as he arched his neck back with fangs showing, thinking it would be so easy for him to rip at my throat. I dodged him, jabbing for the side of his stomach, but he was already gone. I couldn't track his movement. I breathed heavily and tried to focus my senses on him while other younger vampires attacked and distracted me. Still slicing through them, I attempted to focus on that one old vampire.

The back of my hair was grabbed. I tried to kick my leg back, but I was heaved up by my hair as the vampire behind me held firm. As I scanned over the vampire's mind, I realized it was Fier. He jarred me onto my knees. He whistled an ear-piercing pitch, and a tunnel of wind blew through the room, blowing away vampires from his path until he had a direct vision of Chase. He was panting heavily now, standing alone. He looked into the direction of the whistle, noticing my capture.

The anger swelled inside of me as once again, I felt useless. I was one of the best, a Token, and yet I couldn't even defend myself against a mere hundred vampires. Where I was held was next to the pooling blood of Whitney. It only jerked my rage further as I once again looked into her glassy dead eyes, the blood from her slit throat already congealing near my knees. Why had she interfered? She hadn't made any sense, and now she was dead because of her involvement with me.

"My dear, Chase, you've been holding a huntress as your familiar," Fier said calmly. "I wonder which would hurt more: if she were to watch you die first, or if you watched her die an excruciating, humiliating death."

Gardar stepped forward hungrily at Fier's words. Chase's feet moved at lightning speed, but already twelve vampires held him down. One of them was Gardar, who looked at me and unstripped me with his eyes.

Revulsion spread through my veins and power possessed my thoughts. One held a blade to Chase's throat, waiting for the command of Fier. No longer could I bottle the beast that held itself inside of me. I remembered my father's words as a child, telling me to shoo the monster away, but I could no longer respect his wishes. There was no point, if whatever it was could protect Chase, then I welcomed such darkness. As soon I accepted that darkness, my whole body shuddered in pain.

My throat felt as if pins swarmed up from my stomach, and a small grisly growl passed through my lips. My gums burned, and my blood began to feel hot as if boiling beneath my skin. My mind felt like it was being torn apart to make room for the darkness to seep through. When I felt as if my body could expand no more, a lightness overtook me, and weight was no longer what grounded me.

A ghastly, domineering noise came from my mouth as the darkness from within claimed me. It tainted me and my thoughts. I felt powerful and all commanding within the room. Like I could kill them all in an instance. This darkness had my tongue rolling within my mouth with pleasure. I opened my eyes, no longer hiding from the change I felt within me. I was confident and vengeful.

My sight was hazed with a light purple. My huntress's eyes had returned. I no longer felt like I was immobile by such a slow speed. My goal was to get to Chase, and now I could do it. The power that surged through me was intoxicating, lustful, and unexpected by those who thought they had me captured.

Still, with blades in hand, I plunged behind me. My neck cracked back, but not enough to snap it. This darkness made me stronger, less fragile. Whatever was surging through me was the reason why Fier couldn't break my neck, though he tried, as I turned on him viciously, slipping out of his grip.

I threw my blade at the vampire who held the knife to Chase's chest, nailing him straight in the heart before he even knew what had happened. Vampires took a few surprised steps back from Chase as I advanced on them. Whatever they saw, they feared. Another frightening noise left my mouth as my breathing felt heavier. I simply walked up to Chase, power emanating from me. Whatever the others saw, they stepped back from it, not willing to attack me. Chase looked at me calculatingly. His voice was the light that separated me from my darkest thoughts. All I could make from his summons was *retract*.

"She's a vampire," someone gasped. I snapped on the person instantly, only to realize it was Fier. "But how?"

Slowly I raised my hand to my gums, which now felt somewhat sore. The dark that surrounded me began to deplete at my sudden realization that Chase was safe. My finger touched a sharp point—I had fangs. I hid my confusion, looking at them ferociously instead.

Chase? I asked, almost scared.

This is not of my doing, Esmore, this is you, he replied. His voice was distant amidst his own confusion.

I thirsted for blood; I ached all over with an eminent craving for it. It was the hardest of sensations to push away. I looked at Chase hungrily, and he immediately recognized my feral hunger. My feelings were heightened; my desire for all things hot and sticky like blood and sex swarmed over me. I thirsted, I needed blood as if I had been starved my entire life. I wanted to kill more. I stepped forward, letting this instinct sweep over me. *I will kill them all.*

"No, Esmore," Chase said, grabbing my wrist firmly and pulling me back. "Come back from this. Pull it back in. Don't let it devour you, trust me."

If it weren't for his eyes piercing into me like light into darkness, I don't think I could have resisted the temptation.

"She's always been a vampire?" Fier asked, astonished.

"Yes," Chase lied. Had Chase always had an inclination of the darkness that swarmed within me or was it a swift calculation as to how we could use this to our advantage? When I swept over his mind, reaching out to him, I could feel the uproar of confusion and caution around me. He wasn't scared of me, but for me.

"What is wrong with her eyes?" Fier demanded in bewilderment. Thinking quickly, I interjected, adding to the lie that Chase was fabricating.

"It's a gift," I said. My voice sounded hollower, darker, and deeper. I took Chase's advice and painfully pushed the darkness down forcing it to retract. It was not only my force that sobered the beast, but Chase was wrapping my mind with his warmth and calm, aiding me to push the darkness away. Slowly my fangs slid back into my gums. My hazy purple eyes vanished, and I inhaled deeply as if it were the first breath I had taken in a long time.

"We didn't do it," Chase said. "We had no reason to. Your culprit admitted to it," Chase said, pointing to Whitney on the ground, though he wouldn't look at her directly. He didn't let her sacrifice go in vain. "There is no reason for—" Suddenly, a commanding presence swept through the room and took Chase with him. Tythian threw Chase into the furthest wall, then went to Whitney's side.

He gasped, tears pouring from his eyes as he dropped to his knees to scoop her up into his arms. He touched her face delicately. "No," he howled, looking up to the ceiling. "No, no, no. Come back to me," he pleaded. "No, this cannot be." He held her in his arms tightly. Chase cautiously walked back to my side to stand in front of me gallantly. No one removed their gaze from Tythian, on edge as they tried to gauge the furious explosion that might collapse this room and everyone within it. He was the oldest vampire here. If he twisted his grief to vengeance, we were all doomed.

"Tythian," Fier said cautiously, slowly stepping away from him. "If you try anything, you will be killed."

"You did this to her!" Tythian accused angrily, spit flying from his mouth. I felt Chase inserting influential thoughts into Tythian's mind. He wanted to kill everyone, especially me as he felt I was much to blame for her death. Then he would kill Fier. Chase overwhelmed him with continuous influential thoughts: *Bury her, that's the place you need to be. Take her to safety. Bury her. Bury her.*

Tythian's sizeable fangs slid out as he angrily stared at Fier. "I will make sure you suffer for what you've done." Tythian's eyes glowered with hatred, and a black hole appeared beneath him. This was the first time I'd seen Tythian's gift of teleportation used. In the black hole that swallowed them, suddenly both he and Whitney had vanished.

There was an awkward shuffle in the room followed by howling wind.

Fier stared at the spot Tythian once threatened him gravely, his eyes bulging as he became on edge. A few of his guards gathered around him warily searching the room as if at any moment, Tythian would swallow them as well.

"You three, round teams and find Tythian. If he's been compromised, I want him disposed of immediately," he ordered fiercely to the nearest vampires. I had no doubt Tythian would pursue the consequences of Whitney's death. He was undoubtedly a force to be reckoned with, and I found it disarming that the Council itself, so tragically feared one of their members. "Gardar and the rest of you stay with me. And you," he turned back to Chase, his lips pulled back savagely over his fangs. "What sort of mutt have you brought into my home?"

Chase stepped forward, snarling. I grabbed him. Though we might've gotten away with the element of surprise, we were still outnumbered. I never wanted to see him caught and threatened again. "Watch how you speak about her. She's my familiar," Chase angrily warned. Fier acted like a scared child, throwing fits of rage within his manor that was crumbling disorderly around him. He wanted to make a show of regaining power.

"And yet she has the fangs of a vampire and smells like a human," Fier seethed. "And how long did you think it would take until I discovered this? Did you think you would just play happy family for ever more? If that girl has any worth or power, I own her, she belongs to this Council and my order!"

"No one owns me!" I said angrily. Chase would protect me, for better or worse, but I also had a voice of my own. I was tired of playing the role of weak human to appease the masses of my own leaders, and certainly wasn't willing to accept it from this vampire. In our predicament, I had to solidify that Chase wasn't the only powerful being they were opposing. In unison, we would fight them if we had to.

Fier licked his lips impatiently. He looked at Gardar who stared at me with hungry eyes. Fier grumbled under his breath and then began to laugh like a mad man, raising his hands as if being applauded in all his audaciousness. He pointed to Chase. "Well, Chase, I don't know what to say. Your familiar has much fire in her; I do love that about her," he said hungrily. Chase growled in a threatening manner as Fier considered me indecently. "I will make you a deal, little golden vampire," he began. "You prove that you're worth a seat at my table and I'll approve of this ill-fitted behavior, from my second in charge of all people. Chase was my best, and yet you come in here and sweep the rug out from beneath his reign of power. I don't even know who I can trust around here anymore!" Fier screamed, his fit echoing throughout the entire room. Vampires looked uneasy amongst one another as wind began to howl through the room. And then once again, he laughed to himself maliciously. "And, Chase, if you can't keep your little girl in line—no," he changed his threat and pointed at me. "If you turn my best against me and prove you have no worth to me, then you will become my leading hand in other matters."

"She is *mine!*" Chase roared, stepping forward with a knife in his hand, one I hadn't even noticed he'd collected. I grabbed his wrist to pull him back, and Fier laughed, egging him to do it. He wanted us to act out of order. Now it was a challenge. He wanted to humiliate Chase in this room of vampires. Yet he lacked the courage to take Chase front on.

He's crossing a line, there's an unspoken respect for those who have familiars, and he is stepping over it! Chase snarled at me internally.

Then let him make threats. His greatest mistake is to underestimate us. I entwined my hand into his, offering him comforting thoughts. *He will never lay a finger on me. We need to retreat for now, and we'll figure out a way to get out of this mess.*

Chase wanted instant gratification. He desired to go head to head with Fier for trying to kill us. There was a flash of a memory—a beautiful woman who strangely looked like Chase. The warmth he felt for her edged me to believe it was his mother. She held an indifferent expression. She sat beside Fier bored, holding his hand as he casually feasted off a human. I felt Chase pull back from his hatred. He and Fier had history and a binding relationship. Though he would protect me to the end of days, he wasn't ready to face cutting off his connection to this Council entirely. Not yet. He fatigued into himself and couldn't muster any calculations as to what might happen next. He wasn't ready to meet that end today.

I will follow you anywhere, Esmore, even to death, he said hesitantly as if relinquishing into the appeal that leaving this Council may be our only option. Killing Fier right now would only complicate our escape. We had to leave the Council.

Which is why we'll find a way, I said to him in reply.

"Well, little golden vampire?" Fier pushed.

"Let me assure you no such thing would happen. Never would I waste my time on such *small* commitments," I said, staring at his package.

He set a twisted smile. "Neither of them is to leave the premises. They are in lockdown. If they try to leave, you are to use any means necessary to kill them." Fier edged the threat and stepped closer to Chase, standing in front of him with chest puffed. Gardar traced his steps. Despite the knife in Chase's hand, Fier pressed his forehead close to Chase. "Out of the love I held for your mother, I won't kill you now. But so help me if you step one foot out of line, I will bring the same Council you helped build, down on you. Don't test my patience."

Don't. Chase slammed a jolting message through me. I couldn't move as I attempted to lunge for Fier as he threatened my familiar. My inner beast moved on impulse. *He's scared,* Chase said with some smug amusement. The almighty Fier was terrified of Tythian who would now hunt him.

"Sometimes, Fier, you threaten the wrong people," Chase said in a low tone. "Now, if you'll excuse me, my familiar and I will return to my room." Fier was enraged, flashing me one flustered glare before exhaling and shouting demands across the room.

"I mean it! They're not to leave this compound!" Fier screamed from behind us. "And for God's sake, start moving. I want Tythian found!"

CHAPTER 21

C HASE AND I remained silent on our walk to his room. On looking vampires watched us suspiciously. Now we were both prisoners, and it would only be a matter of time until we were in shackles and called upon once again. My blood still felt as if it were on fire beneath my skin, like at any time it would boil over once again and entirely consume me. And I wanted it to, the powerful feeling was intoxicating, and I wanted to embrace it willingly.

No, Chase said, still pulling me toward his room. We were still within hearing range of the others. *You mustn't let it take over,* he urged seriously.

He led me into his room, taking on a somber demeanor, so unlike his usual free spirit. "How are you a vampire?" he demanded. I gave a sour look, unable to explain any of what just happened. I was just as surprised as he was. My head was splitting as it searched desperately for answers. There was an overpowering beat that thrummed within me, an instinct that wanted to act rather than think. I had become the monster I'd hunted all my life.

Every part of me craved to feed the darkness which corrupted my body. Suddenly, I was in need; my skin tingled for Chase to be inside of me. I couldn't handle such cravings, I thirsted for him. I sensed him sweep his mind over mine. At my predator-like movement, he took a few steps back, trying to control himself. He felt my desire for him.

"This is serious, Esmore, you don't understand what this means," he said worriedly.

"I want you," I said, walking over to him and pulling at the ends of his leather jacket. Craving him was the only thing I could feel right now, and any questions could wait. "I want you inside of me, now," I said, brushing my lip against his ear. Everything in me burned. I needed him to cool me. He needed to fill my craving. I couldn't explain my sudden savageness.

"Your senses are heightened," he said almost in a whimper, as he tried to resist me. I nibbled on his ear, rubbing myself against his leg, my chest against his bare one. My lips kissed down his neck and to his collarbone. "As a vampire you—"

I cut Chase off, slamming him into the wall with my hand around his throat. "Stop talking," I said with a dangerous smile. The strength of my desire consumed him, and his gaze finally snapped into a lustful darkness. I would not be denied any longer.

His hand swept up me, brushing over the parts of me which desired him the most. He tore away the leather coat and shirt I wore, looking over me hungrily. I reefed his off as I hungrily looked over his perfectness; he was already hard and ready for me. I was like an animal, only wanting one thing to fill me, and that was Chase. There was an emptiness inside of me that I so eagerly wanted him to fill.

He kissed down my neck, raising his hand to my nipple to caress and then pinch it. With vampire speed he took me to the bed, throwing me on my back. I bounced with a slight jolt from the impact, enjoying it rough. And with his wicked smile, he knew it.

He slammed into me hard. I hadn't even time to prepare myself. The pain only riled me. I was able to consume all of his size, moaning in pleasure as he went into me harder and faster. I pulled his neck down to mine, holding him tightly. I now wanted to be in charge. I wrapped my thighs around him and flipped him over. I didn't let him escape as I sat on top of him, groaning in pleasure as I now dominated him on top.

As I rode him, pleasuring both myself and him, there was something that just wasn't meeting my center, something that I still deeply craved. Chase sat upright, still pounding me from beneath. He kissed the side of my breasts and grabbed my lips, pulling at them hungrily with his teeth. Every kiss that lingered sent a trail of flames through me. Another moan passed my lips as he bit into my neck. It was now so pleasurable that I had to contain myself from erupting in that instant.

I wanted him as he had me. I wanted his blood. Without even thinking, my fangs had slipped out, and I bit into his neck clumsily, but still the flow of his warm blood swarmed my mouth and filled me with such great pleasure. Chase's moan swept through his throat and into my ear. Neither of us could handle the heat and climaxed together. His hand trailed up my spine as he continued to fill me entirely. A moan passed my lips as I felt his blood drip over my naked skin. But I was still hungry and wanted so much more. He pushed me closer to his neck as I went to pull away.

"It's okay, Esmore," he whispered. With his permission, I continued to drink from him. The heat spread through my body, and again I wanted Chase. I clung tightly to his neck and drank more. It continued to arouse me. It didn't help that only after a minute, Chase began trailing his fingers lightly up my inner thigh.

"I just want to keep drinking from you, and fucking you," I said. Instantly I put my hand to my mouth, shocked at what I had said. I took my fingers from my lips, looking down at the blood smeared all over them. Chase's neck was a messy pool of blood. It looked like an animal had attacked him. But again, the urges crept through me.

Chase chuckled, relieving some of the tension from the situation and soothing my brewing guilt. "Whatever happened triggered your vampire self to come forth. If you had been turned, I would've known, so somehow, you've been part vampire for a long time, if not even from birth. I've never seen anything like it. And for all these years your inner vampire has been starving. It's hard to recognize the line between sex and feeding, they are both just as pleasurable," he said with his fingers still trailing up my leg, closer to my warmth. I shivered, unable to be disgusted with myself as I still craved him.

Already the bite marks on his neck had healed, and he was ready for round two as I looked down. I couldn't help myself, as still every part of me was on fire. I tried to resist him, but his beautiful gray eyes consumed me. I pushed away the thoughts of everything that had happened. There was almost a desperation to claim him again and again as mine. To remind myself that he was here, with me and no matter what, we would make it out of this alive—no matter what monster I might be walking out as. I was simply riding the wave of action and pleasure because in this moment, it was all that would suffice my hunger. Reading my mind, Chase smiled.

"Vampire or not, my Esmore, it is my turn to make love to you," he said, pushing me down onto my back. His hand trailed over my ribs as I impatiently exasperated my frustration while he teased me. My hands clawed at the sheets as I felt him near my inner thigh, but never further.

He kissed my hip and then the bottom of my stomach, trailing up. As I tried to pull him in, he grabbed my arms, pinning them above my head with an arched eyebrow. "No, Esmore, you can wait," he said with a confident smile. But already I whimpered for him. I was already so wet with the expectation of him inside of me again. "You are just so beautiful," he said, amongst kisses.

He continued kissing up my stomach to my chest, teasing my nipples. His wet tongue trailed to my collarbone, then my neck, where I felt the graze of his fangs. I whimpered for him to bite me, knowing I would explode with pleasure, but he brushed past it with a gentle kiss. I grunted impatiently, and he only laughed. He studied me for a moment, enjoying the toy he played with. He edged slightly up. I could feel the tip of him on my heat, my toes curling with the expectation of him driving deep into me.

But instead, he brushed himself over me until he was hovering above me. I tried to squirm out of his tight hold, but to no avail. His fangs scraped up my arms. He bit into my wrist gently, making me groan in pleasure and need. His chest was a little too high for me to be able to do the same and engulf him entirely. I began to whimper, my thighs rubbing together impatiently. He came back down over me, now biting into my neck. I arched into him in pleasure, my whole back driving up.

I felt as if I were entirely connected to Chase. That I was his as he drank from me. Gently, he pressed his hand down on my waist, pushing me down as he licked the bite marks he had just left.

"I love you, Esmore," he whispered feverishly into my ear.

I knew then that no matter what happened or what would eventuate from our unexpected circumstances or my form changing, that I loved Chase and would forever be his. "I love you too," I struggled to gasp through hot breaths. It was in anticipation that he would no longer taunt me and fulfill me as I had already given in. He then drove into me, forcing the loudest moan I had ever heard erupt from my core and through my lips. He felt even harder and larger, if that were possible.

Still on his knees, he lifted me from the bed and held me against his stomach as I bounced on him, accepting the entirety of him in pleasure. He offered his neck to me, and with gratitude, I took it again, biting as deeply as my fangs could go.

His blood flowed into me again, dripping down my lips and my chest. Never had I tasted anything so divine. I could no longer hold myself back. Chase was simply too perfect and both the sex and the blood I could easily indulge in. And so, I did, thirteen times. Chase was right, the fine line of sex and blood were two things I could not tell apart. But what I did know was that I was hot for it and I couldn't stop.

I expected to wake up very sore, but much to my surprise I felt incredibly refreshed and far more level-headed. We must have fallen asleep at some point, and again Chase was lightly rocking us both in the hammock. I admired how innocent he looked as he slept, washed away from all his cockiness and oddity.

I glanced over at the bed, mortified. It looked like a massacre had occurred. There was blood everywhere over the sheets and on the floor. I wiped at my neck, retracting dry blood. Tiptoeing out of Chase's grip, I walked to his closet to secure a shirt that ended above my knees. I then snuck into the bathroom to look at myself in the mirror.

My golden hair was clumped in masses and matted with dry blood. My throat and neck were coated in red. My body still held its muscular womanly frame, yet I looked at myself with a new set of eyes. I had become tainted. Somehow, amongst all the chaos of events in the last few weeks, my life had changed in a completely undetermined direction. And I had no control of the tumble I was swept through. I had no time to catch my breath, let alone reflect on my next plan of action. I could only act on the offense.

I flashed my teeth searching for the fangs, but they weren't there. I didn't want to try and manifest them in case I couldn't control my urges again. Already it had taken me so long to curb my desire: a day full of sex and drinking blood. I had feasted off Chase. There was a sensation in my stomach that didn't ease well with knowledge. It was so wrong. It was against everything I had ever believed and trained for. I was, in fact, my worst enemy. And yet, I was unable to think about it until I quenched my thirst and hunger.

Chase had been right, I still didn't know if it was the sex I craved or the blood. I had no answers for anything. I knew I was definitely born huntress, so why now did I have the signs of vampirism and why had it been triggered? Was it part of the reason why I didn't have a gift as a hunter? All of this was a confusing blur, but I accepted it willingly. My mind was reluctant, but my body acted of its own accord. This darkness had never been separated from who I was. When it appeared to defend Chase, it felt as if I had only allowed it to breathe for the first time. This evil I'd oppressed for so long had always been a part of me, but now I knew what it was in its ugly truth.

I slammed my fist into the bathroom basin, agitated that I had no answers. I was never like this. I was always in control and accountable. I had been lured into the city so Chase could drag me away from the Guild. I thought I was gathering intel to relinquish all that I'd learned to my people, and yet; Here I stood, as the very monster we hated. I couldn't cure vampirism. And then a light sparked in me, almost the remaining ghost of what once was good in me hoped there was a way out. Or could I? A part of me, so different to my usual controlled self, desperately hoped there was a way to reverse this awakening. I wasn't made into a vampire so surely there was some other key to the puzzle. Or would I always be thirsty for blood and turn into the very beasts I had thrived on hunting my entire life. What purpose would I have then?

The room suddenly felt colder. I looked around with an unnerving impression I wasn't alone. A black hole opened beside me, and before I could understand or react to what I was looking at, Tythian's hand reached for me in the abyss of darkness and pulled me in. I was teleported into Whitney's room. Tythian lunged for me, throwing me across the room. I hit the ceiling hard and landed on the floor face first. I coughed once. He had already grabbed me and thrown me across the room again. I hit the wall and bounced onto the bed. His hair and face were marred wild with bits of dirt and leaves through it. His usual clean clothes were spoiled by mud and torn into shreds. His eyes were crazed and purely focused on me.

"This all happened because of you," Tythian growled. He was no longer the formal Tythian, but a wild mess. His fangs were intimidating in size, reminding me that in this instance he was the predator and I was his prey.

"I didn't kill her! But I was the reason she lied and told Fier she'd done it, she was protecting me." I didn't want to fight him. It was because of me that Whitney had died. It was only now that I could focus my racing thoughts on imagining her dead body that he cradled so dearly. Everything rushed into me at once. As a Token Huntress, my prioritized goal was to make sure none of my team came to harm's way. And yet, she had been killed in front of my very eyes, just like my team had endured. Whitney had taken the fall for the crime that I had committed, and there was no way I could ever return that debt.

He silenced me, irritated when I spoke. His speed outmatched mine. I hadn't the chance to defend myself against him as he grabbed my throat. He was so close to completely crushing my windpipe. I gasped, gripping his arm. This reminded me so much of the first time Tythian and I had ever met. He had me in the same hold wanting to kill me then as well. I looked around the room, trying to find a way out. A red ribbon caught my attention. On top of the shelves in his walk-in closet, hidden amongst all the shirts, was a boxed and wrapped present. That had been the same box Whitney had once shown me. "I have something for you."

"I need nothing from you!" He growled savagely, firming his grip.

"It's not from me, but Whitney!" The mention of her name pulled him out of his feral state. His eyebrows furrowed deep in confusion. The mention of her would be the only thing that would bring him back to reality, and hopefully his salvation.

He released me, and I slithered to the ground. I gasped an excruciating breath, moistening my mouth. After a moment of recovering myself and looking back into his expressionless face, I slowly walked around the edge of the room and into his closet. He watched me warily, and I made sure not to make any sudden movement in case he snapped once again. There was blood all over his shirt which I assumed was Whitney's. I found the hidden shirt that she had begun designing for him.

"She started this a little earlier this year," I said. This was the last gift he would ever receive from her. He still watched me warily, looking at the object I presented to him. His jaw was tight as he snatched it out of my hands. Though I could sense the rolling waves of turmoil ferment from him, I left him to his thoughts. I didn't want to glimpse into Tythian's mind. I assertively put a block between us, hoping that natural feeling to do so, was indeed the right way to use this ability.

Chase had explained to me earlier in the night that to read someone's mind they had to be partial to us already. We had to receive permission from them. I doubted Tythian would ever allow such a thing to happen nor did I want it. Sure, I had a heightened sense of his emotion and could try to manipulate that, but the mind was more complex. And even if I knew how to control this gift, I wouldn't do it to Tythian.

Chase best described his ability as a puzzle; if I guessed the piece correctly, I could easily manipulate my piece to fit in next.

Slowly, Tythian pried the box open and took the material between his thumb and index finger. Whitney had finished it since the last time she had shown it to me. He maintained a hard expression. With small steps, he wobbled over to the edge of his bed. Tears began to shed as his grip tightened on it. One of the oldest and possibly most powerful vampires in existence and he wept over a human girl.

"I never meant for this to happen," I said, stepping toward him cautiously to sit beside him. Every inch closer was a risk. "I know you don't like or trust me, but if I could have protected anyone, it would have been her. It just all happened so fast. I cannot, in any way, make amends for the damage I have caused. I struggle to show sympathy, so I hope presenting this to you can offer you some sort of comfort." I realized my words weren't the greatest, nor were they probably what he wanted to hear.

"Before Fier killed her, she asked me to look after you in her absence." Tythian flinched under my words. "I know you don't trust me, and to be honest, I'm still fighting against my entire upbringing by not killing every vampire in a massacre here. But if any of the members on my raid team asked something of me on their deathbeds, I would keep to it. And this is no different from that. I will mourn my comrade's death with pride and dignity. So, I won't let you derail yourself into a saber because it may seem easier."

There was a long pause. Tythian said nothing, only staring at the odd material of the shirt. "I don't understand, why do you follow Fier when you are obviously the oldest vampire here?" Again, he didn't respond, ignoring me as he stared at the shirt. My eyes caught a glimpse of the light pulse of his neck. I straightened my back, uncomfortable with this new craving.

"Ah, yes, that's right, you're a vampire as well. The cravings are hard at first, aren't they? You probably just want to dive into my neck and feel my blood ooze over your lips," he said mockingly. I was disgusted in myself for being so transparent. He stood up, and my nose followed his scent as he walked. My fangs had already slipped out with my lack of control. I placed my hand over them, revolted in myself. "Fier serves his purpose and will pay what is due in time," Tythian gritted out as if holding in his angst and hatred for the vampire. There was a hidden leash that was somewhat pulling Tythian back. If anyone could end Fier, it was Tythian. It didn't make any sense as to why he wouldn't, and I wasn't willing to press on the matter in case he again turned that frustration on me. I briefed a glance at the door. Even if I ran for it, I'd never make it. No matter how civil he was acting now, I was sure there was a reason why Tythian brought me here. I would've already been dead if he so desired it.

He reached for two glasses and a bottle of blood. He poured one glass and gave it to me, his blue eyes sweeping over me as he assessed my fangs. I cautiously took it. This was a very different discussion to the reception I had only moments ago received. He was willing to kill me, and yet, now he wanted to share a beverage with me instead. I couldn't read or calculate Tythian's motives, or anyone's within the Council for that matter. I took a sniff of the blood, almost gagging at the bitter smell.

"It doesn't smell good does it? Only fresh blood is flavorsome. The blood of your familiar, however, is oh so sweet, as I'm sure you've discovered. I can smell Chase all over you. It's hard to tell the difference between sex and blood, isn't it? It adds a hypnotic erotic sense to the pleasure. Although not healthy, you can't simply live off one another, it would eventually make you both sick. It does, however, make sex that much more pleasurable," he sneered. He was openly mocking the revolt I held for myself. I still didn't understand why he had brought me here, especially audaciously under the nose of Fier who had teams out looking for him.

He continued. "Let me ask you the questions now, huntress. How are you born huntress but part vampire and yet reek of human? By the size of your fangs, I'm guessing you've had them your entire life without realizing. And why is it only now you discover such truths about yourself? Tell me, do you know how your abomination was made?"

I stared at him, digesting the word 'abomination.' His eyes rimmed with red as he stared at me, waiting for a reaction, almost welcoming it. I wouldn't play into his game. "I thought maybe as one of, if not the oldest vampire, you might have come across a similar case," I said, not appreciating his tone.

"Please, child, don't be daft, there are far older vampires then me." He peered into his glass, indifferent by the liquid. It felt like he had forced himself into this conversation. He was a cunning vampire who acted quickly. "What would you say if I were willing to offer you a deal? I will teleport you once, to anywhere you desire. And in return, you will owe me a favor. Quite simple, no?"

I hesitated to reply. It was only moments before that he had tried to kill me. Why would he drag me from Chase's room to strike up a deal, and what value was it for him? "Why do I need your help?"

He put his glass down, no longer pretending to have an appetite. "Well, little huntress, I'm certain you're already aware of your predicament. While Fier might be distracted by my whereabouts now, he'll soon focus his attention on you and Chase. And being the very monster you hate, I doubt you can return to your own kind. As much as I would like to kill you myself, I can make use of you yet. Fier will not let you so easily leave. I'm the only person who can help you and your familiar." He folded his arms as he leaned against the bench. "So, what do you say, huntress?"

Chase wasn't even involved in Tythian's consideration. For all he cared, he was willing to let Chase rot within the Council if Fier commanded it. It only strengthened my appeal that there was no loyalty amongst his treacherous kind. But thinking of my Guild, I felt cornered almost in the same light. Some would act on my behalf and in my favor. I wasn't entirely sure who, but if Dillian so desperately pleaded me not to return, then wasn't I at the same disadvantage.

There was a lurching inside of me that still wanted to see it with my own eyes. That the reality was, I no longer had a home to return to. Now that I'd taken a vampire as a lover with inseparable binding, I'd be walking into my execution. If the Guild ever found out about this apparent darkness that had surfaced, of my vampire self, then worse might even happen to me. I focused on Chase and what I would have to do to make sure he was safe.

"What would you make me do?" I asked. I wanted to ensure Chase's and my safety, even if it meant making a deal with the vampire I trusted the least.

"I want you to help me kill Fier. Not now. But when the opening presents itself. When all is said and done, I'll give you the signal as to when."

"But why? You can kill him yourself?" I said, confused. He could do it right now. Sneak into his room and do it. Unless Fier held more power then I realized. As Chase once told me, he had seven gifts, and I had only ever seen one.

"I have my reasons and motives. And besides, I still intend to hold my role here within the Council. Fier would rather have me by his side than lose me, and I will work that to my advantage," Tythian stated. He had his motives, his own game he was playing in the power-hungry struggle of the Council. I had to focus on only mine. "I will offer you and Chase your freedom once. As of right now, I am letting you live in good faith. And if you want your familiar to live you will keep this as our little secret as well."

"Chase will find out, he can read my thoughts," I counteracted. It was a small error in his cunning plan.

"Not entirely true, you will learn in time how to develop your shared gift." He paused for a moment in thought. "It's not as hard to keep secrets as you think it is. Much like you've blocked yourself from reaching my mind, you can shadow this entire conversation from your faithful familiar. You can only let them in if you permit it." Tythian paused for a moment in consideration. His gaze snapped on me sharply. "If you are part vampire, then what happens to his other gift you inherited, The Descendant?"

"The what?" I tried to envision Tythian's suggestion. If I were serious about helping Tythian, I needed to block this conversation from ever being read by Chase. I wanted Fier dead for what he had done as well, but in knowing that, I considered it might hurt Chase. They were bound through Chase's mother, and though he hesitated to raise a weapon against him, I didn't harbor the same reservations as my familiar. I focused on our conversation, the subject matter we discussed and felt a fuzziness rub against my mind. It was slippery but quickly clicked into place. A wave of nausea swept over me. I don't know if what I did was right, or if I'd used the gift in the manner it was meant to be shaped.

"It must now be a little under one hundred and fifty years since he blocked that gift. If you've received that and are partial vampire then…"

The door slammed open as Chase stood at the door, panicked. He was standing there naked. My eyes bulged as he walked in angrily in all his glory, glaring down at Tythian.

"You do realize you are walking into my room naked. I don't understand why your head is still held high," Tythian said, raising his glass and having a sip of blood. His demeanor had totally changed from the anguished lover only moments ago. Tythian had slipped into an articulated suit, shielding himself from the reality of what he had lost. He was all business, and in a way, it made him all the more lethal.

"I did have a sheet wrapped around me, but it fell off when I ran here. What were you thinking, Esmore? Tythian could have killed you."

"Well, as much as I do enjoy the theatrics of two familiars fighting, I will pass. If you don't mind, I would like to be alone for a while," Tythian said as he looked down at the shirt he still tightly clutched. "And huntress, I'll give you twelve hours to make your decision. When I come to you next, know it will be your only chance. I will not offer this twice."

"What are you talking about?" Chase asked, looking between us.

We'll discuss it privately, I telepathically said to him.

I put the full glass of blood down on the dining table, following Chase as he held the door open for me. He begrudgingly glared at Tythian. I stared at his behind, trying to disguise my lust. I suppose if I had a body like that, I would have no shame in showing it off either.

Before Chase closed the door, Tythian grabbed his attention. "And, Chase, do consider the other gift she may have contracted from you. You may want to teach her control and get her in to check. If she is part vampire and The Descendant is active, you've already sealed her fate." Chase went pale before closing the door with a curt nod. He grabbed my hand, rubbing his coarse thumb over my knuckles. He was worried.

"*I know what you're going to say,*" Chase protested. "*I don't own you, and you can do what you want. But making deals with Tythian is never worth it.*" We spoke telepathically, cautious of who might be watching us and if anyone saw us exiting Tythian's room. We walked past one vampire who offered a quick appreciative glance over Chase who walked in his confident stride. This familiar of mine had no shame in all his glory.

"*I wanted to offer my condolences,*" I replied. I had the ability to get Chase and me out of this mess, at a price of course. The worst part of this deal was not knowing when Tythian would call me in on this favor. Or if Chase even wanted to leave. I would do anything for Chase, and I believed he would do the same for me. But the reality was this was still new, and although I knew I could trust in him with a binding I'd never known before, I didn't understand how bound he was to his people here.

Thinking of leaving my own behind and abandoning the Guild's mission, still to me, was incomprehensible. In the back of my mind, I always felt like I'd be waltzing up to the wooden doors and entering my home in no time. Attending classes until I was thirty and hunting vampires as I was born to do. Except everything had changed since then.

Everything has changed for us both, I said to him, tightening my grip around his hand. We only had a few hours to figure out what we would do if we were officially outcast from our respective compounds. I was an abomination, and I was dragging Chase with me.

After a long moment of silence, Chase broke the tension. "*You've concealed your conversation with him from me. Are you already hiding things from me?*" My stomach dropped at his pained expression.

"Sometimes, it's better if you don't know." I only hid it to protect him, if he knew I was in cahoots to kill Fier I was scared he wouldn't stand by my side. If anything, he'd prove to only be another obstacle. This was the only option I considered that would protect us both. I blocked out any emotion that continued to try and swarm me. I no longer knew what I was doing, but killing Fier felt right, and it would be the end of his reign in the vampire Council which would make them weak. I was satisfied to regain some kind of composure as my Token Huntress status in all its former glory- for better or for worse. I needed to hold on to some part of my previous life before considering giving up on it entirely.

CHAPTER 22

E VENTUALLY, WE STUMBLED across the bed sheet that was crumpled on the floor. Chase collected it and tied it around his waist as we walked silently back to his room. We didn't cross paths with any other vampires. It was only when we entered the cold room that we turned to one another. "What did you and Tythian talk about?"

"What is The Descendant?" I asked at the same time.

He didn't seem surprised by my question, and I tried to avoid answering his. Chase let out a dramatic sigh in defeat. He caved in answering first. "What has Tythian told you about it?"

"Nothing, he just left the subject suspended in the air, giving me no real answer at all. It seems to be a common thing around here."

He sat on the edge of the hammock, gesturing next to him for me to sit by his side. He was tense. He could sense that much change was to come and this may very well be the last time we have a place to talk and discuss freely what our next move was. Within hours, we would have to put plans into action, whatever that looked like. I needed to know if he would stand by my side, or… or turning against his own would be the divider that would once again put us on either side of the fight. He grabbed my hand, smoothing over it in a comforting manner. After my conversation with

Tythian, I had steadfastly learned that I could keep some of my thoughts secret from Chase. And although he couldn't read my mind or listen in to my dialogue, he could sense that something was wrong.

Chase gently kissed my knuckles in a reaffirming manner. "About one hundred and sixty years ago, we struggled against a particular Guild. Their Token Huntress was near to impossible to defeat. She had an extraordinary gift which we called The Descendant. To best describe it, it was godly. She had so much power, strength, and speed. When she used it, two enormous white wings protruded from her back which is why we appropriated its nickname. When her wings manifested, we were weary because the extent of her lethalness amplified. She was dangerous before, but when she used her gift, there was little likelihood of us opposing her or surviving to tell the tale.

We'd encountered and fought against her for over five years, and when the opportunity came, we were finally able to take her down. I had watched so many vampires killed, even old and lethal within our own hierarchy by her majestic gift. I was so in awe of her gift that I wanted it for myself. I knew that for any vampire who acquired it, it'd be a game-changer. Only twenty-three vampires remained alive after going head to head with her in that final battle. And when she dropped to the ground, all of us turned on one another trying to get to her, to acquire her gift for ourselves. It was a maddened and desperate frenzy. I killed twenty-two fellow vampires to be the last standing, I drained her entirely and took my prize." I couldn't imagine the care-free Chase to be so blood-hungry and savage, but I hadn't known him for long, and better yet, much past this room.

"Of course, Fier's father, Arab, who was in charge at the time, wanted to kill me, as it goes against our rules. It was the Council leader's right to drain the hunters so they could greater their own strength. And you cannot steal a gift from another vampire. There is no way you could completely drain another vampire. Before being anywhere close, you would sicken and go mad. It was my mother, of course, who saved me from the death penalty.

To this day, I regret being so selfish. It was a mistake. A hunter is like light, they kill vampires who are only darkness. The first time I triggered The Descendant in battle, well, much of it was a blur." He hesitated, his hands and head dipping near his knees, ashamed. "The Descendant isn't something I could or can control. For a vampire, it took on a form more like a curse. Our very core is dark and consuming. The Descendant only amplifies that. Imagine the hunger and lack of control you're finding yourself at now times a million. But now with your strength, speed, and everything else enhanced. For three years I slaughtered and destroyed aimlessly. I don't recall much of it at all. I completely lost myself. At some point, I must have gone into hibernation after I was wounded.

Eventually, my mother and Tythian found me in a cave, one country over from where I had started. They said that I'd looked glorious and godly with my black wings covering my entirety as I slept. I'd cocooned myself from the outside world. But it took them a very long time to bring me back to humanity and to pull away from the power of that gift. There's no way to control it, not for a vampire. It brings out the worst in our kind, of all the things that we try to conceal and tame, this is the worst. There are no boundaries or sense of morals. I'm lucky I somehow didn't spiral into becoming a saber. If I have passed that onto you..." He didn't even dare finish the sentence.

I placed my hand on his back in reassurance that he had not hurt me. "We can work through this. I won't use it. Ever. I'm still a huntress, maybe I won't be cursed with black wings or an unquenchable thirst," I said, not entirely sure I'd be able to tame the hunger I already had. But I had grown up all my life oppressing the vampire within me. Perhaps I could have the same amount of control on The Descendant, unwilling to let it spiral as I had my vampire self.

Since the day I first encountered Chase, I realized that it was my vampire self that was stirring from within—reacting like to like, power to power. That darkness that constantly crept beneath my skin was waiting for its chance to rise. It was the very creature my father made sure I wouldn't reveal to those within the Guild. Had he known? Surely, he must have if he trained me to never let it escape.

If I now had to relearn to control that, I was certain Chase and I could find a way. I had to find answers, and if possible, I might be able to find a cure for this vampirism. Or maybe something had gone wrong in my genetics. After all these hundreds of years since hunters were crafted from vampires, maybe we were changing. Or perhaps I was mutated. I wouldn't be welcomed back to my Guild, but I couldn't come to terms with being the very monster I'd grown up hunting. I was swept away in the moment and lack of control when it surfaced, and I hated knowing that entity and form had been slumbering within me for so long. I was disgusted in myself.

"Esmore, you know I think you are beautiful. I hate it when you think you are anything less. Even as a vampire, it does not change who you are," Chase said, answering my thoughts.

I rested my hand gently on his, wanting to offer him comfort and security, especially considering what I would soon ask of him. To leave this place forever and the safety of what he'd known, for a life on the run with me. "Chase, I've become everything I hate and despise. It's in my very nature to kill vampires, and I have no intention of stopping that. I am a huntress, a Token Huntress. You know I don't want to leave your side. But I am no safer here than at the Guild.

Tythian offered me a deal. He will help us leave this place and teleport us to our desired location. It's selfish of me to ask, but I want you to come with me. It's not safe for us here anymore."

"Fier won't lay a hand on us. We're too valuable to this Council."

"You're too valuable," I quickly corrected him. "This place isn't designed for me, Chase. I am part *hunter*. Asking me to stay here would be like me asking you to stay within the Guild. It's not possible."

I still needed to see with my own eyes that I could never return to the Guild. An anxiousness grew within me. What if the Guild would receive me again? What if Dillian had been wrong and I should be returning to my role and reporting all that I'd witnessed here. But even within myself, could I ever rest easily knowing I was hiding this sickly thing inside of me. What if next time I disobeyed Campture it erupted to the surface? My life within the Guild walls felt like an alternative reality, and a distant memory that no longer felt like mine. But maybe they could offer me something that would help me understand what I was becoming or I could return to make sure my team was okay. That they survived from the last mission I led them through, and leave my post, falling into the shadows of the world like I'd never existed. I would be replaced.

"I should return to my people. It might be futile, and I might not be able to fix myself. But I need to find a way. I need purpose."

He looked gloomy as I spoke. I grabbed his chin and lifted his gaze to mine. "Fier will only ask questions that we don't have answers to. The only reason no one has come for us is because they are preoccupied with Tythian's next move. When that is over, they'll point their attention toward us. You've already risked so much for me. I don't want you to have to protect me. I cannot stay here, you know that as well as I do. Nothing has changed, Chase, I am still the enemy. Come with me." The request sounded more of a beg. I didn't realize how desperate I was for him to stay by my side.

Chase stared at me for the longest time and then to his bobblehead dolls, considering the privilege and power he might lose by leaving it all behind.

This Council was what had kept him and his mother safe for so many years. And here I was selfishly asking him to come with me. I needed to leave the Council, this pretend safe would only last a moment longer, and if I didn't get out now, I might never have the chance again. But I couldn't imagine being separated from Chase either, there was a stubbornness within me that never considered that as an option. We could never be apart.

"He'll track us no matter where we go. And I cannot go to the Guild or let you return there. Esmore, they will kill you."

"No, they won't," I said reluctantly. Though I knew I had my differences with the hierarchy in my Guild, and Dillian pleaded for me to get out. I had no other place to go. There was no other foundation I knew of where I could find answers. I had to go to my origins. No matter how poorly I was treated upon arrival, it had to be a risk I was willing to take—much like my gamble with Tythian's deal.

I had dedicated my entire life to the Guild. There would be people who would vouch for me. It would be no easy task to write me off and if that was their intentions… I went blank at the thought. I didn't know what I would do after that. Where else would I go? "I know you think you understand my kind. But you don't. We might lack empathy, but I offer power to my Guild. They're not so easy to throw that away. I need to return to my people Chase; I am not safe here anymore. We were almost killed only hours ago. I don't want to be content staying hostage in a place I despise with every fiber of my being. It's taking me every second of every day not to kill as many as I can within here before I fall on my own sword. I want to make sure my team is safe. I need to make sure Dillian and James returned safely."

"Why do you care for them?" Chase's voice rose angrily. "James treated you as if you were some monster that needed to be fixed. I would kill him and have you angry at me for a century before listening to him speak to you in such a way, or raise a hand against you ever again."

"You know my heart doesn't rest with him." I pushed aside his protectiveness. This wasn't about James. "I need to make sure Dillian is safe, and the rest of my team. I've been worried ever since Fier and his army ambushed us. Since losing my mother and being Token, my team has been all that I focused on. If it were just me, I wouldn't have cared. But I won't allow their ears to be corrupted with years of untruths and stories about my treachery. My honor is all I have left."

So many things bubbled to the surface. Chase and I had the same concerns for our foundations. Our union put us both at risk, and neither of us could return to the life we'd know simply by association. But I had to put a close on my life. I had to see it for myself that the Guild was no longer my home, and that Dillian who had risked everything to come here for me, on the off chance that I was still alive, was safe. I had to do the same for him.

"If your anguish is over your team, then I can show you how to contact them. I can show you how to reach out to Dillian. You don't have to return to the Guild. They'll drag you in to your prison cells where you'll rot. We can run away Esmore and find answers. It might not be all that I hoped to offer you in this life, but if this is what you want to pursue, then I'll stand by you," Chase said desperately, trying to convince me from returning to the Guild. "I'll show you how to use your gift. Though, we'll have to be in reasonable distance to the Guild to reach out to him. When Dillian is asleep you can contact him. My ability is limited in distance." He paused to think for a moment. "It'll be hard to get out of here. Fier will have eyes on us everywhere. If we take Tythian up on his offer then we could be teleported close to the Guild. If we do this and you can reach out to Dillian and find that your team is safe, please promise me we won't have to go any closer. We'll sort the rest out as we go, but, Esmore, if we do this, we'll be on the run from both Council and Guild. There won't be a day where we aren't looking over our shoulders. Trust me when I say, vampires don't simply forget being betrayed, especially Fier."

"Nor does Campture," I said grimly.

Dillian will convince you not to return to the Guild. If this is the parting you so desperately need to leave it at bay, then I will help you, Chase telepathically said.

I rubbed my hand along his smooth jawline. He closed his eyes, leaning into the cool touch of my hand. In all of this, he only cared about *my* safety. My thoughts and emotions were a constant wave of the perplexing outcome. And yet having Chase, as if he had always been by my side, grounded me. I was so erratic in ambition that he helped me clear through the mess of my own complexity which enabled me to have complete trust. I'd never held such unyielding faith for an individual besides Dillian. If he truly believed this was the way, then I would listen to his words. I doubted the transition would go as smoothly as he hoped, but I also had utter conviction that between us we had the strength to take down armies.

I needed to make sure Dillian was okay, with my own eyes. If my team were okay, then I would know that my last mission as a Token hadn't failed—except for my own disappearance.

"Whatever it is you and Tythian discussed, for whatever reasons you won't tell me, please be smart about it. You don't know Tythian as well as I do or how he was before Whitney. He may be in mourning now, but I fear he'll so easily revert to what he once was. So please be clever around him. Don't trust anyone," Chase said strictly. "If the returned favor he's asked for is too great, we will find another way."

It shamed me that he didn't press for more information. He trusted in me enough to let me hold dear to my secrets, despite the stakes that were already on the table. It was yet an added element of something that could go wrong. Chase was so different from James. He let me make my own decisions, and although he didn't support them, he would still stand by my side. I rested my head on Chase's shoulder, tired. I just needed to make sure my team was okay before I tried to pursue anything, especially aiding Tythian in finding revenge for Whitney's death. And I didn't even know if that was something I could pull off or why I had been so compelled to do it. I was dancing amongst monsters, making deals that could very well end my existence. And yet there was an edginess to me that was almost gleeful at the impending challenge.

But for now, I had to focus on the first step. "I can handle Tythian's deal. It's not out of my reach to succeed at. If it guarantees us leaving here freely, then I would sign my name to any deed."

I pressed my lips to Chase's gently. I oppressed the sickly monster within me that wanted to frenzy and heat the moment. I wanted my time to be delicate, to appreciate his softness that was molded and built for me. It terrified me to know how much I would do anything for Chase. How far I would go to amount this passion I had for him. If something would happen to him... I couldn't imagine the thought. There was nothing past Chase for me.

Let's take some of your ugly dolls with us, I offered. *We have twelve hours before Tythian strikes on his deal.*

I knew I was making a selfish request that was difficult on Chase. He was leaving behind everything for me and branding himself a traitor. Yet, at the same time, I had to check on Dillian and make sure the others were safe. I felt that perhaps these circumstances were pushing us into the direction we needed to go. I had said at the start, I could not stay for long. And no matter how much Chase tried to convince me otherwise, my beliefs remained the same, even if I was now part vampire.

No matter what step I took, I knew I would be looking over my shoulder. The only difference now was that Chase would be right beside me doing the same. Because as much as I wanted my life to revert to as it had been, I couldn't imagine returning to the Guild. I would be empty without him.

Are you sure this is what you want? There is no coming back from this; we will be chased for as long as we breathe. It's a form of betrayal, and they do not let that go lightly, Chase whispered internally. The white walls of the Council were not something I wanted to see every day. By being born a huntress, that decision was made for me a long time ago.

I only want to make sure you are safe, and we both make it out of this alive. We'll figure out the rest as it comes, I replied. Whatever afterward looked like, we would figure it out. If humans could still survive the harshness of the outside world, then surely so could we.

Chase pulled me into him, cupping my face and kissing me fiercely. His tongue slid over mine passionately, leading me and burning my senses. My hands touched his bare chest and hips. There was a desperation that hung between us. An uncertainty of raw power and anxiety that we needed to disperse.

His hand slid up my inner thigh as I squirmed with anticipation for him. Already my fangs slipped out, and I was moaning at the thought of enjoying one last time with him in his room. He bit into my neck, sliding his hand under my shirt to caress my hard nipples. Another moan left my lips as he began pleasuring me.

"I will protect and love you forevermore, Esmore," he whispered into my ear before letting me dive into his neck.

A whirl of exotic taste danced in my mouth. "And I you, Chase," I said with heated breath, enjoying the taste of his skin on my tongue. I would do anything for him.

CHAPTER 23

W E PACKED TWELVE of his favorite bobblehead dolls he wasn't willing to part with. I now felt comfortable with my Barnett crossbow and sword strapped closely to me. We were limited in what we could pack, which consisted of two bottles of blood, bobblehead dolls, daggers, and knives. Though I hadn't eaten much in the days since being here, both of us were equipped to hunt. Neither of us was willing to step out of the room, engaging in any on-looker's speculation.

I wore a white sleeveless shirt of Chase's, which was baggy on me, and a pair of his dark blue jeans. I tightened a weapons belt around them so they wouldn't fall. I wore one of his long leather jackets, which trailed to the top of my leather boots. Chase wore his pale blue jeans with only a leather jacket, of course, without a shirt.

Four hours before our agreed time, Tythian appeared in the corner of the room, closest to the broken desk. "Chop, chop. Looks like Fier is moving on you a little sooner than anticipated," Tythian hurried us along.

"What do you mean?" Chase asked, not surprised by his sudden appearance.

"Well, you see to keep my place at Fiers table, I might've alerted them that I saw you both suspiciously walking around. Not a lot of faith in you two it'll appear and oh—" He went quiet listening out. "They're almost here. So, do we have a deal?"

Before either Chase or I could argue with his sleight of hand, I focused on our objective. "I need to be close to the Guild. In the forestry north east from here. We can manage the rest."

Tythian held out his hand to me. "Then we have a deal." I shook his hand, the cold chill of skin, prickled up my back, and then we were enveloped by darkness. I reached out for Chase, dragging him along with me as Tythian took us from one part of the world and into the next. My body pounded and my stomach lurched from being teleported. Suddenly, we were surrounded by fresh air and depressed trees. I dropped to my knees and vomited onto the ground. Chase leaned over me, holding back my braid as he angrily looked up at Tythian, who smirked.

"Good luck," was all he said, and then he vanished into darkness once again.

"Are you okay?" Chase asked. I wiped the back of my hand on the vile taste. It took me a moment to get my bearings. I looked around, panting harshly as I caught my breath. I hoped I'd never have to use Tythian's gift again. It felt like my insides had been lurched out of my skin and scrambled within. "It's not easy to get used to."

I looked up at Chase who stood robust and searched our surroundings. "It won't take us long to be in range. Maybe an hour or two. Be on alert though, I have no doubt Fier will send out scouts," Chase warned. The cold breeze swept on my face, splashing the throbbing of my stomach. I enjoyed it for a moment, relishing the night's air. Somehow being out in the open made me feel free and myself for the first time in weeks.

"I'm sorry you didn't have more time to say goodbye," I said as I wobbly stood up. Chase assisted my stance.

"I don't need to say goodbye to anything, Esmore. I have you, and that's all that matters. Now, let's find you closure in your goodbyes." He pressed a gentle kiss on my forehead and streaked his hand through his shoulder-length hair as he searched the trees. "This way."

I was hesitant to find comfort in him knowing the exact position of the Guild. He was the only vampire who knew of its location. If we had remained enemies, the Guild would've been attacked already. But I followed him, knowing that all of this was for me.

It had been the first time I was able to test the extent of my heightened speed now that I'd awakened to my vampire self. There was a notable difference, and it brought me much relief to look through the purple haze of the colored eyes I'd been born with. The comparison of my speed versus what it was now forced me to ponder the bigger question at hand. As hunters, had we only survived for so long because of our gifts?

I tried not to distract myself with questions as I followed Chase's lead. After a great deal of time, we hid amongst shrubbery and trees. The fog misted over us, only opening slightly when we ran through it. Cockroaches sprang to life and fled the log as we crouched beside it. We'd run close enough to the Guild, with a decent space between so we wouldn't be detected by any of our usual security checks. Once I could connect with Dillian, and make sure my team was safe, I would have to make my peace with the demon I'd become. I had to make sure they were okay, and then I'd walk into a new chapter of my life, abandoning all that I'd known.

Chase explained to me how to find Dillian's mind. With a lot of concentration and fumbling, I could sense him, but couldn't connect with him as we'd hope. Because he wasn't yet asleep, I couldn't speak freely with him. Chase advised it was easier to speak with one in their dream state and also that from where we sat, we were too far away to try and hold communication with him while he was conscious. And if we crept closer, we would give away our position. We could only communicate with people if they allowed us to. It was like tapping on their mind for permission; they could either accept or shut us out. But the distance between Dillian and I would be too long even for that. A conscious person had a natural protective layer over their thoughts, whereas when they slept, they became more vulnerable and unaware.

We waited for many hours in silence, edgy, and on guard until finally, I felt Dillian's mind fold over into an unconscious state. Finally, he was asleep. It was tiring focusing on him for so long, maybe because I was new to learning how to control this gift.

It gets easier over time, Chase chimed in. *I'll help you ease into this. I'll be there with you. Think of any place manifesting around you. When you call upon him in a dream state, you must actively create a physical place surrounding you within the mind. When in someone's mind, it's just darkness; you need a physical area to ground both you and them into one location. If you were to have a conversation with him in darkness, you may not come back from it. You always need to make a connection with something on this earth to do so. So just think of our surrounding trees. And think of Dillian with us.*

I focused on Chase's instructions without hesitation. I closed my eyes and imagined myself being connected with Dillian, bringing him to this exact same location. Minutes flickered by, and I was irritated by the lack of response. I felt as if I wasn't getting anywhere. Suddenly, I felt Chase's hand on my back, and I opened my eyes. There in front of me was Dillian, looking at me just as amazed.

"Is this a dream?" he asked. He'd recognize this area and realize how close we were to the Guild.

"Kind of. It's a long story. But it's me, Dillian," I said, slightly desperate. I tried to get up quickly, but wobbled at the sudden movement. I was lightheaded by the amount of concentration it took me to hold our conversation. Chase grabbed onto my leather jacket to help me keep my balance.

"You seem different," Dillian said and narrowed his expression onto Chase. "The Esmore I know would not desperately speak; she talks in a monotone with a lack of empathy." He was weary and skeptical. I wanted to release a shaky and crooked laugh. I'd gone through so much, to hear my best friend say such things about me. I had to convince him. I thought of something only both he and I would know.

"When you were thirteen and sparring against me, I was swept in the moment and bit your ear!" I clicked my fingers as if finally finding it. "Julia and you didn't have your first kiss until your five-month anniversary, where you spotted a flower. But when you gave it to her, it had a deadly spider in it and it almost…"

"Esmore," he whispered and searched around wide-eyed. "No, you cannot be here, if Campture listens into this, then you've doomed us both."

"She cannot interject. I'll block this conversation from her," Chase said dismissively. Dillian starred at him wearily. Though Chase might've understood his angst within the cell and the importance of removing James, by far, Dillian still didn't trust him. He was a vampire, and although he might've been my familiar, he was still the natural born evil we were raised to kill.

"You must flee, Esmore, and don't return," Dillian said, walking over to me.

"No, I need to know that you are okay first," I said worriedly. He seemed different, almost timid.

"I'm okay, now you must go," he said, crouching with a slight wince.

"He's lying," Chase revealed. Dillian looked at him angrily. "His physical state in reality is not faring well. It's easy to cover your appearance in the mind and make yourself look like something else. If he willed it, he could appear as any other creature. It's like a separate attachment to our reality and physical presence. He's hiding his real physical condition. But another's mind manipulation even in the dream state is something I can easily remove."

"No, don't," Dillian pleaded, but it was too late, whatever cover-up Dillian had used now vanished as Chase willed it away. This was, after all, his created world, even if in dream state. Dillian's clothes were ripped to shreds. It looked as if someone had taken a whip to him and lashed at him. Bleeding gashes endeavored to sow together in an attempt to heal. His eyes were battered and black. Both were swollen, and the pink of his eyes could hardly be seen. His breathing was uneasy as he gasped for breath. There were marks around his neck that indicated someone had choked him. His black hair was damp and plastered to his neck with dirt. By the looks of it, someone had been drowning him.

I tried to hide my anger as I felt the fury of fire in my gums. My fangs wanted to slip out with the impurity of my vampire self. I wanted to protect Dillian. They slipped out, but Chase was able to hide them as if it had never happened. It was only in the physical world that they were present. When my fangs slid out, both happiness and anger excited my inner dark self.

"Who did this to you?" I asked. He looked to the ground, embarrassed by his state. But I knew he would not avoid my questions if I had already seen him like this.

"Mostly, James," he admitted quietly. "Ever since we returned, he has convinced Campture that you are a traitor, but only because this vampire has manipulated your mind." He gestured at Chase. "He's gone crazy, obsessing over you even more, claiming when they find you, he'll nurse you back to health, but keep you within his home as you are a threat to everyone else because you are unstable. They thought I was involved in it somehow. And when Campture detected that my mind had certain blank spaces, it didn't go down too smoothly," he said with a small smile. "Despite James of course having the same lack of knowledge."

I clenched my jaw. It infuriated me to see him in such a way, Dillian didn't deserve this, not by the very same people he'd served his entire life and would do anything for. But because of me, because of his desire to help me and make sure I would survive, he had taken my place in the beating.

"What do they plan to do to you?" I asked. I was so angry with James. His obsession was far worse than I had ever realized. I never knew how far he could go. Possessive, yes, but this was a sickness.

"They plan on killing him," Chase revealed slowly. Dillian said nothing, but his eyes confirmed the truth in Chase's words.

"I'm coming for you," I said to Dillian. It wasn't a question or a doubt in my mind. I would not let him die like this. I cut off our connection before Dillian could argue.

A screeching noise echoed in my mind and dropped me to my elbows on the ground. When I came back to my own reality, I was sweating. Suddenly, I vomited into the dirt, unsteady, and uneasy. Chase patted my back cautiously, looking around.

"You came out of it too quickly," he said. I wiped the vomit away from my mouth, trying to gather my wits and balance quickly. "We're not alone."

I gathered my sword and Barnett crossbow, preparing myself for a fight. Had the Guild already suspected our presence? But I was sure that their lookout didn't reach this far. No matter what, I had to get Dillian out of there. If he had been accused of conspiracy and treachery, it wouldn't be long until they sentenced him to death.

Aiming for where I sensed the presence sneaking up on us, I shot an arrow. Quickly jumping to my feet and hiding behind a nearby tree, I dodged a dagger that was thrown at me. Chase took the other side, quickly circling the trees to close in on them.

I sensed someone next to me, running beside the tree. I struck my sword at them, but their own long knife counteracted it. My sword's handle was punched out of my hand. I dropped it, hitting at the woman's face before registering the familiar scent and long golden-blonde hair. My vision collapsed on me as all fighting spirit left me unguarded. My mother stood in front of me, as beautiful as she always had been. Her exotic orange eyes stared at me.

"Mom," I choked in shock. There was no mistaking her.

"Esmore," she gasped, suddenly desperate as she hugged me. Her thick golden hair smothered my face as I nestled into her neck, still in shock. Was this a trick? I embraced my mother dearly, clutching onto her in case it was a fleeting dream. Just a few more seconds. She had aged slightly with a few wrinkles and gray hairs since I had last seen her. But she was still as beautiful as ever. When she touched me I began to sob. For the first time since I had been told she died, I cried. So many emotions overwhelmed me. When she did look at me again, she gasped, almost frightened. I realized I was staring at her neck with my fangs out, ready to take a taste.

"I'm sorry." I took a few steps back, tripping over a log, ashamed of myself. Why did my mother return to me to only see me like this?

"What do you want me to do with this one?" a rough voice interjected. I was startled and appalled to know that in my moment of reunion with my mother, I had forgotten that Chase had charged on elsewhere. There was another person with us. He threw Chase in the center of a few trees, presenting him as if he were some meal.

"Chase," I said, scrambling toward him. He was badly beaten up. I hissed at the unfamiliar male, hunching over Chase protectively. The male with rough red hair looked between my mother and me. His gray eyes studied me seriously. He was a bulky vampire; his fangs were larger than Tythian's. No wonder Chase had been overpowered so quickly.

"No, Esmore," Chase said, gathering me behind him. I held my Barnett crossbow, shooting at the man. I ran for him, picking up the dagger that had been previously thrown at me. With speed I'd never challenged before, he was beside me, putting his foot out to trip me. I skidded hard on my face. I quickly collected myself, zipping through the trees to chase him. I wouldn't let him harm Chase again. I lost my sense of direction and circled back to Chase, where the male was already standing beside my mother. His speed was the fastest I'd ever witnessed, even faster than that of the fallen hunter, Pac. Still he stared at me, a smile pinching at his lips.

"So, this is my golden treasure," the man's deep voice spoke.

"Esmore," my mother's soft and fragile voice interjected before I again chased after the vampire that threatened Chase. "This is your father."

I stared at the vampire, baffled. But my father died when I was ten… he had taught me to count and to breathe and to concentrate. He raised me to keep the monster at bay. An avalanche of thoughts bombarded me. But my mother would never lie to me.

A pinprick thought jabbed at me. Maybe I had been born as part vampire as well. Perhaps my father knew all along that I wasn't entirely huntress and that's why he focused on keeping my rage in check. That had been my father, not this vampire.

A light breeze swept around us. Chase's wounds had already begun to heal, and he was now sitting upright. "But he's vampire," Chase said, rubbing his jaw tightly. Although everything had healed, it was his way of trying to brush away his tension. He was speaking on my behalf because, for some reason, my motor skills had shut down. I was stunned.

"And is she not part vampire?" the man who claimed to be my father scorned. My mother shot him a look which made him retreat from his arrogant status.

"Well, that is something we've only just discovered as of late," Chase snapped. "It's a shame you weren't there to see it ey, Daddy-O?" He seethed with a sarcastic smile.

My mother stepped in front of the burly man before he could retaliate on Chase. "My darling, Esmore, I've missed you so much." My mother took a few steps toward me. Her leather attire was dirty as if her clothes had not been cleaned for weeks. Yet her hair still glowed with its mesmerizing blonde. She was the one who taught me how to plait mine. So many memories flooded back. I had never believed that she'd died. Nor did I ever think I'd see her again. I had been left behind to lead my raid team. To be a Token. I had been left behind with this curse, and she had known.

"Campture told me you were dead! And my father is dead! This isn't my dad. He is dead!" I exploded with sudden rage. Chase was now standing, offering his hand to me, so I too could stand. I was in shock. I struggled to comprehend anything.

"Shall we sit for a moment, Esmore?" My mother indicated for me to sit on a nearby fallen log. "Please, my dear, there is much I need to tell you."

"And who is this boy to you?" The man who claimed to be my father asked arrogantly.

"I'm her familiar!" Chase said sharply through a growl.

The other vampire gave out a monstrous laugh. "You'll never be good enough to be my daughter's familiar. You are tiny, nothing but a pretty boy flashing his bare chest."

I held Chase back, my head swirling. Instead of accepting the challenge, he slowly walked me over to the log, ignoring his indifference. I felt nauseous. So strange considering I'd never been ill before.

"Cesar, stop!" my mother snapped at him, and quickly the large vampire ceased his antagonizing.

"But my father is dead," I whispered, trying to understand.

Chase sat me down, and my mother knelt in front of me, shaking her head. "Let me explain to you from the start," she said, patting her hand on my knee. "Cesar, here is your biological father. We first encountered one another in a raid. His group of vampires was much older than our hunters, and most of us were killed. But Cesar took me to safety so I wouldn't be harmed. If this young man claims to be your familiar…"

"I am four hundred years older than you, easily. I was turned in my twenties. I would be careful as to who you call young," Chase said, showing his fangs.

"I'll rip those fangs out of your pretty mouth if you don't watch how you speak, boy," Cesar challenged, already his hand placed protectively on my mother's shoulder. Yet neither of them stepped forward as my mother and I gave them harsh glares to stand down.

By the way this vampire protectively stood over her and studied our surroundings for any near danger, it dawned on me. "You're familiars," I said in a quiet tone that sounded nothing like myself.

"The pull was far too great to deny, as I imagine only you would understand," my mother said, almost somewhat shameful. "Miraculously, you were conceived, I think perhaps because of my particular gift, the impossible came to fruition. Because of my ability, we were able to protect you as a child within my womb, giving you all the nutrients you needed.

"By then, Tyler, who you know to be your dad, had seen us together. I had stayed at my post within the Guild for years before conceiving you, and met with Cesar as often as I could. Until Tyler, who was my best friend, followed me one evening. He caught us. Cesar and I had become complacent in running away together. He could have reported it. I would have been humiliated and beheaded. But instead, he gave us a chance. His condition was that Cesar and I could no longer see one another. And although Cesar offered us protection, you my unborn child, I feared leaving the Guild, it was all I knew. So, we parted ways. Even though I wanted to be with Cesar, you were my child, and your protection was my absolute concern.

"The night you were born, much relief swept over me because you had huntress's eyes. I thought maybe you would have come out of this unscathed and live a normal hunter life. However, Tyler was skeptical, and because you always had a temper, he tried his hardest to train you to calm yourself, just in case that rage was something else entirely.

"We had ten amazing years together. Tyler kept our secret and raised you as his own. Although we were only friends, and he was good at keeping such a long-time secret away from Campture, it was hard not to think of the treachery we played around her. We avoided her at all costs, and kept our minds busy with other trivial thoughts if we crossed paths with her. But she had her suspicions, and we were closely watched. When you excelled at everything, they thought you a prodigy. But I had my fears of it being something else."

I was breathing in and out slowly, staring at the ground as I practiced the exact same thing my father had taught me, which was suppressing my urges and darkness. My entire upbringing had been a lie. And it was only until I was within the Council and Chase was threatened that I broke that seal.

"It seemed you were living a very normal life, you and James were…" She fell silent, looking at Chase as his lips tightened angrily around his fangs. "You had made it onto a raid team."

"I am now a Token Huntress," I interjected with my eyebrows raised as if it were the only silver lining to our dire conversation. She smiled proudly at that.

"No doubt, Miss. Campture named you as a Token Huntress. The closer you came to your eighteenth birthday the further you excelled. Your superiority was hard not to notice," she said problematically. The silence eerily fell between us. My mother, who was so strong and superior in many accounts didn't meet my gaze. The question loomed in the air.

"What happened?" I asked with so many questions around her disappearance. I never fully believed she died the way Campture informed me, but I was struggling to believe she was standing right in front of me right now, alongside a vampire who claimed to be my father. "Where did you go?" I asked, all but leaving out the main question, 'why did you leave me?' My mother's gaze struck mine.

"You really don't recall any of it, do you?" She asked sincerely.

"Remember what?" I said, growing in confusion and anger. There were so many answers I wanted with so little time. My mother sighed heavily, she was almost hesitant to begin.

"Leading to your eighteenth birthday and when your skills began phenomenally excelling, I had a slight concern that it might've been from a different part, that possibly, there might've been some form of your father in you." She looked at Cesar. "Since the day you were born, I had my concerns, and so I watched you closely. You're my only daughter, and I would've done anything for you. I prayed you would be simply an exceptional Huntress, but a mass in my stomach unfurled every ticking hour that closely approached your eighteenth birthday.

The night of your eighteenth birthday when you were sleeping, I watched over you. At midnight you began to mumble and shift uncomfortably in your sleep. I stood up to aid you but when you opened your eyes," she was hesitant. "You attacked me. And when you touched me, my skin began peeling away in waves of miasma as your gift began to come to fruition."

I watched her agape. I went to say something but couldn't. What? I didn't remember any of that. That didn't make any sense. I didn't remember any of it.

"That night your fangs revealed themselves for the first time. You went into such a trance that you didn't even know who you were or who I was. The small creatures of the night screamed around us and the cockroaches within the room around us weltered into a puff of smoke as if they never existed.

When you attacked me your huntress's eyes vanished. It was like your vampire self was eating away the purity of your Huntress self. It was all-consuming, and in that moment, I realized I would lose you. That you would kill me and be worse than any saber that ever rampaged the earth. On your touch and in your very presence you would take down colonies of creatures, whether it be hunters, vampires, or humans. I feared in that moment, as your miasma peeled away the skin and rotted the bone of my left arm, as I held you back, that you could single handedly destroy everything that came to be on this earth; aimlessly walking and killing simply by your presence. So, I did the only thing I could think of, I removed your heart and replaced it with my own energy." There was a swirl of nausea that circled in the pit of my stomach. *My heart?* I could barely comprehend what she was telling me.

"As hunters, our gifts derive from our heart and passion, if you ever had the chance to practice with your ability, you would've learned that. We aren't so different from the vampires when it comes to the importance of our heart. Life and death, energy and flow. I knew there would be consequences for having violated you in such a way and taking that away from you. Although my gift works to replace other organs sufficiently, the heart is different. Though I might be able to temporarily replace it, I can't replicate the same. If your real heart stopped beating, then so would you. So, I knew I had to keep your heart hidden. When I removed it, and you dropped to the floor in a deep sleep your purple huntress eyes vanished. It was as if the remains of your huntress self was being eaten away by your vampire self. By removing your heart, the source of your hunter gifts it only left further room for your vampire self to grow and conquer. I never understood the destruction a vampire counterpart could have on a hunter, until I saw it devour you within seconds. I was scared about the shell it might leave you in, but I had to act in the moment. I didn't want to lose you, and it was the only plan I could fathom for the time. I panicked," she admitted honestly.

My legs felt weak as I just stared at her numb. What kind of monster was I? I had attacked my own mother? My mother who had a contingency plan for everything had faltered and been panicked? And worse of all, I couldn't remember any of it. What it did leave behind was the remains of taking the last of my empathy, of my passion in being a hunter and nurtured the presence of my vampirism that I'd silenced for so many years.

"But why didn't you take me with you?" My question was a small desperate rasp of a child that felt abandoned. Was I so broken and was she so scared that she didn't want me to join her on this quest? Was she worried that when I woke, my loyalty to the Guild would overpower my love for her?

"I didn't want to leave you," my mother said uncharacteristically desperate. Cesar put a hand on her shoulder in reassurance. It seemed to calm her. I placed my hand on my chest, suddenly feeling so empty. It made sense as to why I felt very little emotion. I'd always thought it was because I was a huntress. But in truth, I literally had no heart. It was only when I was with Chase or that he touched me that I actually felt. The rest of me reacted in heightened expression by my vampirism.

Chase wrapped his hand over mine, watching me warily. *Are you okay?* He asked me telepathically. I had an overwhelming emotion of abandonment and desperate pain that wanted to claw out. I was almost certain, that maybe tears would be evoked.

"Then what happened?" Chase said on my behalf, saying the words out loud that I couldn't conjure. I needed to hear this. I wanted to know the severity of my deformity and the answers that would affect me for the rest of my life.

My mother looked from Chase and then to me. Who would've thought the day would come where both my mother and I would take a vampire as a lover- as a familiar, when we'd been crafted and trained to kill their kind.

My mother's voice broke as she found her strength. "In my panicked state, Campture was aware something was amiss, she'd read my mind and was close to our home at the time. I had to flee. I couldn't take you. It would've drawn their attention to you, and I wanted her attention purely focused on me. I don't know how much she knows about your gift, but when I saw her, I ran, and they gave chase. Anyone who knows of this, Esmore, will hunt you and your heart down collectively. Vampires will try to gain this power, and the hunters will try to use it to their gain of eradicating the vampires entirely. You are my only daughter," she said desperately and dropped to her knees in front of me to rub my jawline. Both Huntresses, in all their might and glory, crumbled in front of one another. "And I couldn't watch you die. I panicked and fled with every intention to return to you. I threw out erratic thoughts of having tempered and experimented with you while you slept. I painted myself to be crazy so they'd think corruption lay only in me. I barely escaped with my life.

Thereafter, other Guild's had been informed, even vampires of unknown origins began to trace my steps. Because of my gift which is renowned, they wished to hunt down the sole traveling huntress. This world may be vast, but things like this spread rapidly. I knew I could turn to only one person and that was your father, Cesar. It almost cost me my own life on numerous accounts, but I was determined to keep you safe, in the only way I knew how. I wanted to find him and make sure we found a safe place to hide your heart and then I would come back for you. No matter the cost."

I sat glumly. My eyebrows were furrowed as I tried to consume every word and point of direction. I truly was a monster. Cesar spoke, "We had to find a hunter who had the gift of concealment to hide your heart. It's a lot harder than it sounds, especially when the man we needed could conceal his very presence," he said, rolling his eyes. "But eventually we found him, and I drained him to acquire his gift, so I had full control of concealment. It's hidden in a place no one will ever find."

I tried to fathom my mother's reasoning in a logical manner. There was one tipping point that didn't make sense, and so I looked at her deadpan, almost angrily, thinking of myself lying on that floor, exhausted on my eighteenth birthday with no recollection of what had happened or the abomination I'd become. So much loathing bubbled, in both me and toward my mother. No matter how much I wanted to believe in her and understand she did this all for me. I was angry.

"How did you know I wouldn't be killed? What if Campture turned on me?" I demanded of her. After they gave chase to my mother, they could've killed me. She left me on the floor, vulnerable.

"I knew my escape would raise enough suspicion within the Guild for her to create a backstory. I had powerful allies within the Guild. If they'd found out about my sudden escape they would've questioned further, and so I was adamant, in true Campture fashion, she would lie and cover her tracks. In a split moment I had to weigh up the options. If I'd taken you with me, I would've only put you further at risk. Exposure to the outside world but also if I carried you on my back, I wouldn't have been able to defend us both as we escaped. That, and I was assured if anything happened to me that certain Hunters would look out for you. I'd created alliance well before the time I left. I was confident that those certain Hunters could be trusted.

And besides, Campture couldn't properly explain what she overheard or saw when she read my mind or gave chase to me unsuccessfully. Stringing me in front of our fellow hunters wouldn't have bided well within the Guild. And so, I'm not surprised to hear she'd crafted a story about me being dragged away by sabers."

It'd all been a calculated gamble that could've ended in tragedy. But that was the role of our kind, only I was the centerpiece that could've been punished in consequence for something I didn't even know about or understand. Everything could've played out so differently, but it made me understand why Campture had kept me so close and kept a blazing gaze on my back the entire time of my rein. All because I was something that shouldn't be possible to exist. I was born this way.

And are still beautiful in every way, Chase interjected into my mind. I looked up at him, startled by the amount of warmth and love he spread through to me, soothing my tumbling thoughts.

"I know I don't deserve your trust anymore, Esmore, but please know that I did everything I could to protect you. I came back for you. If you return to the Guild, they'll kill you," my mother said seriously.

"I'm not fleeing," I said defiantly. I was so angry with my mother. She'd left me behind with every chance of me openly displaying my vampirism within the Guild. I could've already been killed by now. But when I looked into her beautiful florescent orange eyes, I couldn't hate her for what she'd done. I only hated myself for not figuring it out sooner. "They have Dillian. I'm going back to save him. They've pushed a death sentence on him for being in alliance with the vampire Council and me."

"Dillian." My mother winced at his name. She knew who Dillian was. She had always been fond of him and thought for a long time that we would end up in marriage. "Campture ordered this?"

"James is not who we once thought he was. He's gone ill in the head and from what I can gather, he wants me dead or to keep me hidden for himself. He's grown obsessive, and I fear leaving Dillian in the current state James is in. He's already hurt him so much. I can't just leave him."

"No hunter is worth risking my daughter's life," Cesar objected.

"You've only been involved in your daughter's life for two minutes, you do not get to make such declarations," I snapped just as quickly. My fangs slid out in anger, and I again covered them from my mother, ashamed of my lack of control. My eyes hazed in their huntress purple. It was only a reminder that this was the spark of my huntress self my vampirism selfishly devoured within the few seconds it had. That without my vampirism on display I couldn't even showcase the one physical trait of being a hunter. After a moment of Cesar staring me down, he let out a monstrous laugh.

"Ha," he bellowed. "She is my daughter. Well, I do like a massacre at a Hunter's Guild, so let's go kill them."

"No!" my mother and I both growled at the same time.

"We rescue both Dillian and his girlfriend Julia, and then we flee," I ordered. Dillian wouldn't leave without Julia, and if he were taken they would suspect her as well. After what happened to Whitney, I couldn't have Dillian's and Julia's blood on my hands, no matter what challenges that might bring me. The rest of it, I would deal with as aftermath. Right now, I could hardly focus on standing, floored by everything I'd been told. So instead, I focused on one task at a time. *Dillian. I needed to save my best friend.*

CHAPTER 24

T HE GUARD OF the Guild wall was prepared. Because of the announced execution of Dillian, I had no doubt that Campture would have raised the number of those guarding the wall while so many others within the walls would be preoccupied. I suspected they had Dillian tied up in the same room that she'd imprisoned me in. He would probably be executed upon morning. The hardest part would be finding Julia. I wasn't overly familiar with where she would be. She might even be in hiding.

We waited impatiently and very quietly in our awkward group. Hours had gone by as we stretched through into day. We needed the cover of night before getting closer to the wall. The forest held an eerie atmosphere to it, more so than usual. A lot of animal blood stained the ground. I could smell it in the air as my own cravings wanted to be satisfied.

I was fiddling with a dead leaf when I deliberated over my conversation with Dillian, and his intention to propose to Julia. After everything that had happened, I very much doubted he'd had the chance to ask her. I threw the leaf away, somewhat agitated. The air seemed to be far hotter than usual, and I was starting to feel very hungry.

I looked at Chase's neck as he sat at the base of a large tree. Its bark looked dead and its roots unstable. He had his eyes closed, but I knew he was awake as I hovered my mind over his, and he scattered over various ideas. A cocky smile pressed on his lips as he noticed my mind scanning his, and then his gray eyes flashed open. "Don't be so greedy, you cannot drink from me anymore. It'll eventually make us both sick if we continue doing that," he said with a sly smile before stretching himself awkwardly against the tree.

"Why not?" I asked, extremely disappointed. I thirsted so much it burned my throat. I flushed, still hot. "Why is it so hot?"

"The sun still irritates us to a certain extent, my Esmore. It mostly immobilizes the sabers, that's why they lurk in the shadows." Chase took my hand and began drawing light circles in my palm, which alone was enough to arouse me. His simple lingering touch was like a drug. "Because we are both vampires, our blood is in a more synthesized state. After drinking the same blood for a while, it becomes toxic to us. However, I don't know if that's the case with your blood because you are part huntress. But if you kept drinking from me you would become very sick." He kissed the palm of my hand, sending a trail of hot flames up my arm. I bit my bottom lip in response.

"Stop, or I'll take you now, and I don't feel the most comfortable doing that in the presence of your parents," he said, antagonizing me as he rolled his tongue in his mouth playfully. "I would love the chance to have you in the wild, though."

I quivered erotically at the thought. The hardest thing to control besides my lust for blood was my tingling body that wanted Chase so desperately. Not jumping him was taking every ounce of control. And it seemed as if Chase had more control than I could ever conjure.

My mother was sitting not so far away and speaking with Cesar. I felt different toward her, now knowing what she had done. I could understand why she'd done it, but I still clutched at my chest where I should have a heart, instead, there was nothing. It explained the constant emptiness I felt. Somehow, I felt as if I were deprived of something and it had been my mother who had violated and taken that from me.

"So, where do we go after this?" I exhaled evenly, trying to calm myself.

"Where did you both come from? The Council?" Cesar interrupted, who must've been listening in on our conversation. If I'd known him as a father figure sooner in life, I may have been embarrassed at the exchange he might have overheard. But instead, he seemed only like a very rowdy and old vampire. The only shared quality I could see in both of us was arrogance. And that's what I disliked about him most.

It saddened me to know that the man who raised me was not at all my father. It perplexed me even more to know a hunter could adopt in a child not of their own and raise them. I trembled to know that all his years of raising me and claiming me as his child might have simply been a ruse. He was all I knew as a father and I still thought of him as my dad. So how could Cesar so quickly expect me to discard such memories and fondness? He was not my father, even if he did partake in creating me. My father was the man that raised me, and I would stay true to that belief.

At first, I simply ignored Cesar, because I didn't want to participate in conversation with him. I found myself rebelling. I grew harsher at the thought of him being my actual father, and a vampire at that. It was my mother who raised me to kill them and yet here we both were, our familiars vampires. Under my mother's watchful eye, I then spoke.

"From the Council," I said. "My raid team was ambushed by the Council's forces there, and Chase took me in from the wreckage. It has only been a short time since I was last at the Guild, but a lot has changed and been revealed since."

"An interesting choice for a daughter of mine. I would never align with the Council," Cesar deflected. "I even had one of the vampires I turned infiltrate there so I could find out what all the commotion was about and why it was so interesting. I don't think he likes it very much."

I didn't like his casual tone. As if we were bonding or enjoying polite conversation. "Let us get one thing very clear before you aid me in freeing my friend. The man who is my father and raised me as his daughter, is dead. I will remember him for the time he put into raising me. You cannot come here suddenly to announce that you are my dad. You sacrificed that option the moment my mother and you parted for eighteen years. I'm *so* happy you found one another, at the cost of yet again abandoning me. And letting me discover on my own that I am part vampire when this whole time I lived in a Hunter's Guild." I had angrily raised my voice. He was so arrogant, it frustrated me so much.

"Esmore," Chase whispered, waving calm thoughts over me.

"Your eyes have returned to their purple," my mother gasped, coming closer to study me. I placed my hands to my fangs, irritated that yet again they'd slipped out without my knowing. I couldn't control my temperament. The gnawing darkness within me only wanted to spread further. I wanted to fight them both. But it was Chase's pooling gray eyes that told me not to. His mind hovered over me, gripping tightly to my humane side before something else pushed over. After a moment of silence and ignoring my mother and Cesar who studied me seriously, I calmed myself enough to sit beside Chase again and retract my fangs.

"Lost time isn't something a vampire of my years has to worry about, my dear. We have an eternity to fix things. I am however, disappointed in your stupidity," Cesar provoked me.

"Cesar," my mother growled.

"Well, we have been sitting here for what, two hours now?" Cesar demanded from her. "I commend you on waiting until dark; it seems like a smart tactic. But have you forgotten that your mother and I have the gift of concealment to infiltrate the Guild? I wanted to let you lead this little mission because I thought it was cute. But it's a massive oversight."

A subtle breeze swept through us, spreading a thicker mound of fog over my knees. I bit my tongue so I would not spit harsh words at him. "And you only mention this now?"

"Well, my long, lost, ever-brooding daughter, you never asked," Cesar taunted in response.

My mother warily looked between us, giving Cesar a harsh glare and forcing him to wipe the smug expression from his face.

"And you didn't want to mention anything?" I asked angrily of my mother.

"You needed to calm your thoughts about all that we discussed. But it seems you've already made your mind up on it all. At least we won't have to worry about your recklessness. We can conceal all four of us. Your father and I will look for Dillian. I cannot recall Julia. So you'll have to find her."

"No, I need to be the one to find Dillian," I discouraged them. We had to infiltrate the Guild so we could collect both Dillian and Julia. But I felt responsible for Dillian's safety and urged that it was me that protected him.

"My daughter, please be smart about this, you know you can trust us to get him out safely. It's the only way we can get them both out alive. But be wary, the concealment gift doesn't hide one's physical presence. If another hunter has heightened senses, it'll block them from noticing us. But if someone physically sees us, they will sound the alarm. It's like blocking the smell of us from vampires, but if they see us, they'll know we're very real. It only takes away the sense that we are there. No one can read our minds, feel our presence, or locate us."

"Just don't get seen," Cesar said. He had a large ax strapped to his back.

"Yea, I get it. Don't be seen," I grumbled to him. He infuriated me so much. My mother was still holding onto the same sword from the last day I had seen her before my eighteenth birthday. She was always fond of that sword with the gold trimming. I gathered my sword and Barnett crossbow. My mother was right, if we didn't have Julia, Dillian would never agree to go.

"Fine, we head for the north wall, closest to where Dillian is imprisoned," I agreed.

I didn't feel overly different after Cesar put a veil of concealment over us. It antagonized me that somewhere out there in the world, my heart had been hidden using a gift such as this. It was only when Chase placed a hand on my back that I realized I was overwhelmed by the thought of not actually having a heart. I felt violated. To make it worse, the only time I could feel emotion or be tortured by my deepest thoughts was when Chase was touching me or when he was with me. He was my only real connection to empathy.

We followed a small trail that my mother was familiar with. We were wary of our surroundings and froze at certain times, straining our ears for sounds. We reached the wall where Dillian and I often stood guard. Now there were another two guards that I wasn't overly acquainted with.

It dawned on me that Campture might've set up Dillian's execution in an attempt to bait me. If there was something Campture hated most besides vampires, it was traitors. Staring at my mother's long golden hair, I questioned whether Campture was still searching for my mother. I had my suspicions that she also knew she wasn't dead. And what was I to do now after learning that my heart had been hidden? No matter what my mother's intention, having no heart really did make me feel empty. I had always felt as if I were missing something. Now that I knew, I desperately wanted it back. I wanted to know love and be with Chase. I felt cheap and that the love I offered him was only erotic lust. But how could I ever explain that to him? I knew that I must have loved him, but the feeling was caught in a very hollow emptiness in my chest. Like my mother said, hunters' passion is derived from their heart, so what did I have to live for or offer him? All I knew now was darkness, anger, annoyance, hatred, thirst, and sexual desire. And when I was with Chase, sometimes remorse and anguish.

Cesar stepped forward to take the two guards out, but Chase raised his finger to him. As I tapped into his thoughts, I realized Chase was manipulating the guards, convincing them they urgently needed to collect water because one of the wooden sheds on the farm was alight. I imagined he used this very same tactic when he lured me in to first meet him. Cesar hmphed in response.

We weren't far from where Dillian sat unconscious. I could feel him in the same room they'd thrown me into. I indicated to my mother where he was; she nodded with determination. Cesar came to her side, offering his clasped hands. She placed her boot in it, and he flung her over the wall swiftly. She touched the ground silently. Cesar offered me the same gesture, but Chase brushed him off with his shoulder in a show of strength, no doubt. Just as swiftly, I was flung over the wall, landing quietly on my feet and crouching with my Barnett crossbow aimed. The guards were all gone. I could sense Chase looked over his shoulder at Cesar smugly, impressed by his handy work.

My mother was also crouching low to the ground and walking toward the imprisonment area. Cesar and Chase clambered the wall and were by our sides within seconds. My mother parted with Cesar, and Chase and I ran toward the huts. We were cautious and expected more hunters to be patrolling the grounds. The ones that were didn't glance in our direction, proving Cesar's concealment abilities. After two fellow hunters strolled past with weapons in hand, we rolled out from between two huts and continued walking toward where Julia lived. She and Dillian had now been together for a long time, so I knew the location of her hut. Much to my relief, when I came closer to their home, there was only a single mind in there that worried about Dillian. She sobbed for him, feeling useless.

Looking on both sides, I flicked my fingers to Chase to stay guard where he was now. I needed him to make sure no one entered as there was no place to hide in any of our homes. When he crept back toward the shadows, I sneaked across the damp ground. I hurried inside, holding my hand over her mouth before she let out a terrified scream.

She panicked until she recognized my face, her sobs ceasing. I was hunched over her awkwardly on top of her bed, where she had been crying into her pillow. I pressed my finger to my lips, indicating for her to be silent. She nodded vigorously, her long wavy brunette hair shaking as she did. I slowly released my grip on her.

"I'm here to take you and Dillian away. There's no other option; they will kill him. And I won't let that happen. If I leave you behind, they'll act on it and will kill you instead. Grab whatever belongings you must, we leave now."

"Is he okay?" she whispered, wiping tears away from her watery eyes.

"I don't know yet, but we'll get him out alive," I said earnestly. "Is there anything you need?"

"No, just Dillian," she whispered. "And this." She grabbed a small wooden carved box from beneath her bed. There was another single bed, and double behind her where her parents and brother slept. I understood how hard it was to leave the Guild, where she was leaving family and safety. But for Dillian she bravely wrapped herself in a cloak. She was prepared to see the light of a new day with him. It was a strength I was embarrassed not to have. We were so trapped within our own world of killing the vampires and retrieving the humans we had forgotten about love and peace. After taking Dillian and Julia, we would be embarking on a new day and world. One where I hoped I could find some peace within myself.

CHAPTER 25

I OPENED THE door, cautious when Chase was no longer there. The day had taken on a very sudden darkness to it as nightfall approached. I searched for his mind but to no avail. Cesar's gift was working against us. I couldn't find him anywhere. I searched both corners before realizing that he was no longer within the shadows I had left him in or anywhere nearby. I panicked.

"Is everything all right?" Julia whispered behind me. I heard a noise and held her firmly to the wall. The hunters walked straight past us. A smell teased my nose, and my fangs felt hot, wanting to emerge from my gums. With all my might I restrained it, but the smell of blood was so thick and beautiful. I could smell so much blood both in and outside of the walls.

The throbbing of Julia's neck artery caught my attention. I was so hungry, and her neck looked so salty and clean. My fangs slipped out as I stared at her throat. I just had to have one taste.

"Pull yourself together."

Cesar's large hand shook me suddenly. Before Julia could see my fangs, I hid my face in the shadow of Cesar's large frame. If it weren't for Cesar, I would have happily fed off my best friend's girlfriend.

Julia screamed and fled at the sight of Cesar, but he'd already grabbed her and knocked her unconscious, dragging her limply back to me. "We have to go now; something isn't right. The clouds are covering the sun and night is soon to come. There's a lot of blood out there beyond the walls. I'm guessing sabers are outside. I can feel their movement, and they're close. Someone within the Guild's lost a lot of blood. If the sabers pick up on that, we have more to worry ourselves with. Come along, your mother has your friend," Cesar explained.

"I have to find Chase first, you both go ahead," I said, walking past him through the two huts.

"What do you mean you have to find him?" Cesar asked, grabbing my arm. His fangs slipped out as he smelled the air. I, too, followed his lead, picking up a familiar scent. I recoiled at the panic that stabbed my stomach, but I knew immediately the one who was bleeding heavily was Chase.

"Take her now," I said, breaking out of the grip he had on me. I ran into the direction I could smell Chase's blood. When I looked back, Cesar had already vanished. Sticking closely to the hut's walls, I was surprised by how few hunters walked past me. Where were they all?

"Esmore!" James' voice quivered. My head automatically jerked in the direction he spoke. A hut was positioned between us, but I saw fresh black droplets of blood, dragged around the shelter. I kept close to the shadows, following the steps of the blood that smeared the ground. When I looked around the corner, most of the Guild surrounded James and Chase as onlookers. Chase was tied up by silver ropes. Kora and Kasey were close to Chase. They must have trapped him as he was hiding in the shadows waiting for me. We didn't go as unnoticed as I had hoped. The smell of blood still swept through the air from the outside of the walls. I could now sense movement. I feared Cesar was right, and for some reason, a pack of sabers was drawn here.

"I know you're out there, Esmore!" James called angrily. He had changed much since only days ago. It looked like he hadn't slept at all; he looked crazed. He was walking around the pit of hunters. Four hunters were holding the silver chains wrapped around Chase tightly, as he could hardly stand. Campture and Kelf were standing behind James. I searched the many faces of those who encouraged him to flame the foul vampire.

I had never considered moving against my people, and I never wanted any harm to come to them. But that had been before they harmed my familiar. I now realized the side I was on. I hated vampires and days ago would've also called for their blood. Even now I still would. But my beautiful Chase would always be my one exception. He couldn't suffer such a fate, especially after I had brought him here. Guards no longer stood on the walls. They were all surrounding Chase, twinkly-eyed for their grand capture. I noticed Teary and Tori, who looked around at the group uneasily. Had Chase guessed correctly? He once said they were the two who would resist my beheading, and from the way they were reacting, he might've been right. Chase knew that this predicament would happen, but never did I realize he would be the bait.

"Esmore, sweetie, if you don't come out now, I'll kill him," James called. He pushed the flaming stick into Chase's face. Chase screamed as his skin began to melt. I picked up a bucket of water, diving into the center of the hunters and pouring it over Chase, who looked at me helplessly. His expression told me that he wished I'd never come out. I kicked the flaming stick out of James' hand, jumping on him and slamming him to the ground.

"There's my beautiful Esmore," James said, raising a hand to my cheek. I jumped off him, disgusted that he would try to touch me so affectionately after torturing my familiar. I tried my very best to restrain my vampire self. If they witnessed that I was now a vampire, then there was no chance of escape. I looked glumly at Chase, knowing already we were outnumbered. I had no idea how I could outwit all of the hunters that surrounded us. They stared at me with a mixture of hatred and disgust.

"Behold, our traitor Token Huntress," Campture announced beamingly. "Bedding a vampire. Such filth."

I ignored the many insults that were called out to me. All of it built such angst within me that I struggled to oppress the swirling darkness in the pit of my stomach. I felt trapped, an unfamiliar reality. The smell of Chase's blood encircled me. But further past the wall I could smell an odor that could only be carried by sabers. As Cesar had said, they might've been closing in on the Guild.

"There are sabers out there!" I shouted at my fellow hunters, now brushing my hand through my hair. What was this anxiety I felt? Where were my usual calm and collected self? I had no heart so why did I suffer at the very thought of the situation?

"We are a Guild of Hunters. Don't doubt our skill, you filthy monster," Campture hissed.

"Esmore, my love," James stretched his hand out to me.

I stepped away from James as I struggled to contain the acidic sensation that tore through me. I tried to keep myself calm and push down the darkness that wanted to claw its way out. Chase stared at me worriedly, now tugging at his chains as he tried to get to me. I was standing directly across from him, panicking.

"Stay with me and let me aid you in getting better. We can destroy this monster right now who has taken your mind. You will find peace, my love," James said. "Be mine, you always have been. You are *mine.*"

"And if you don't, you will die right now," Campture added quickly. I loathed the huntress, who even now still tried to play mind games. Pretending that she would reward James in such a manner as if I were some prize. She knew I'd never go to him, and in it, she would be victorious in making an exception out of me. Did she hold such hatred for me because I resembled my mother in so many ways? To what extent did Campture suspect my mother's betrayal?

Chase tugged on the silver chains viciously in an attempt to get to me. He knocked one of the hunters from balance, dragging him slightly through the dirt. Another hunter came from behind him, shoving a wooden spear into his leg and dropping him to his knees. Chase's scream broke everything within me. The silver tip was planted in his skin, eliciting constant pain.

His scream broke me in ways I'd never thought possible. I snapped, my fangs came out. Large growls came from me as I hunched my back. I could feel something take over, and I happily accepted it. My vampire self had already spread throughout me. There was something deeper that lingered and hungered. I would do whatever I could to protect my familiar. As I felt the change begin within me, I couldn't move. I was frozen there for a time, hunched over like an animal as this darkness took its true form.

"Kill it!" Campture hissed.

Shards felt as if they were passing through my back. I heard a cracking noise. My hunched figure echoed with pain. Two large white wings sprouted from my back as my pain slowly receded and was replaced with a lust for death and chaos.

James pulled something from behind his back. At the end of it was a large explosive fixed to a stick. I had no time to move as I was still rearing from my come down of pain and elixir all at once. He speared me through the chest, and as soon as it touched my skin, the explosive reacted and blew my chest open, traveling straight through me.

My eyes widened in shock. Everything fell silent. Chase tore from his chains, beheading the hunters around him who fought back. Hunters attacked him, overpowering him quickly. My knees dropped to the ground as I stared.

The slow ringing of screams began to pierce my ears as I saw shadows streak over the wall. There was a serene sense of peace in the dawning underworld. Maybe if my time had come, I wouldn't suffer as I had. Maybe there would be nothing. But what I was most certain of, was eventually there would be Chase.

Rain began to thunder to the ground. One by one I began to feel tiny droplets on my face, suspended on a line between death and life. In a clean snap, all my senses became alert once again. The shadows that were piling into the Guild were sabers who had climbed the wall. They smelt of fresh blood and flames. Hunters confronted them in a hoorah of holding their own fort. In front of me, one saber leaped onto a hunter, ripping at his lips hungrily and then diving into his neck. His screams startled me into realizing I could be next. *Get up.*

James stormed toward me, slicing through two sabers in his path. His skin had turned to metal. Past him, I could see Chase struggling against the eight hunters who kicked into his stomach. Still on my knees, I took another breath. I looked down at my chest, where slowly my skin sealed over my wound. As it did, my once beautiful white wings slowly folded into my back, not having the energy to offer me any power. I hadn't time to appreciate its magnitude or glory. And maybe I'd never know the sensation of how to fly. I knew it was The Descendant that had come forth. As my wings receded, a black spread over the beautiful white coloring on one of my wings. My near-death had tainted such purity.

When I felt it sink into my skin again, a part of me felt even darker and more twisted. Like all that had once been pure within me, such as my hunter beliefs, they were now only half as my vision of cruelty and vampirism crept over. James grabbed my chin, looking at me with disgust. "How nice of your eyes to go purple now. I saw you first. I loved you first. It is me who owns you!" he spat with hatred. "All I want to do is look after you, Esmore; just me and you. I can still make you better."

At my silence, his eyes glowed with rage, and he backhanded me across the face. Still my chest hadn't fully healed, and I was incapable of moving. Having no heart may have been the only reason I survived. But taking such a fatal wound left me weak. I coughed into the muddy ground, where rain sloshed in puddles. The small wooden parts of the Guild had descended into flames. Screams from hunters and high-pitched squeals from sabers eroded the purity of the grounds.

"You always thought you could do better, didn't you, Esmore?" James went to kick my stomach but hesitated when he looked behind me. A deep, meaningful growl tore through the air. Within seconds, James was grabbed and flung meters through the air. I couldn't see where he landed.

"Come here, daughter," Cesar's voice tore through the commotion. His fangs dripped with blood as he cradled me in his arms protectively. "Tythian, stop taking your bloody time!"

Suddenly Tythian was by my side, wrapping me into his arms. He bowed to Cesar, gentleman-like, and looked down at me. "I think the little vampire is realizing she's more special then she once thought," he antagonized.

I didn't even have the time to question why Tythian was here or how he knew Cesar. But I was certainly glad to see him. "Please, Tythian," I gasped dryly. "Chase." Blackness swallowed me, and I was in a pool of emptiness, before resurfacing beside Chase. Tythian backhanded a hunter fatally who had tried to spear Chase.

"Esmore," Chase whispered, dragging himself over to me. He looked as severely beaten as I did. I used all my strength to tear at the silver of his chains. The silver burned and made my hands bleed. I tried, but the blood only loosened my grip. He cupped my face.

"Esmore!" Campture roared, walking toward me. My mother intervened. The look both of them shared was one of pure hatred. "Trinity, why am I not surprised? You think you kept this from me. I've known for a long time what your daughter truly is," Campture announced with smugness. That explained why she wanted to lure me back to the Guild and take me hostage. "Our battle may not be today, vampire whore, but it will be soon. As soon as everyone knows about the gift your daughter possesses, they'll search for her. You cannot keep her safe."

My mother threw a dagger at her chest, but James intervened, pushing Campture aside. A large bang erupted, breaking everyone's stance. Tythian was knocked toward a nearby burning horse carriage, just missing the open flames. My mother was flung toward the brick foundation of the tunnels. I realized the bang had erupted from the weapons room, and within no time at all the explosions would go off. I needed to move. My chest hadn't entirely closed, but I needed to *move*. I held Chase tightly in my arms, trying to stand, but my legs buckled.

My mother ran to my side, snapping the silver off Chase. She was the only one of us who could tear through them without being affected. Flames poured out of the tunnel, reaching for us like snakeheads. I felt the gentle touch of Tythian's hand, and suddenly darkness consumed us again.

A breeze now swept between us as we stood on a grassy ledge

overlooking the Guild. I witnessed the blast which could have claimed all of our lives if it weren't for Tythian, who had teleported us out. The Guild was up in flames, and from here my sensitive ears could hear the screams of many of my comrades falling.

"Esmore," Dillian's voice interrupted me. He looked badly battered as he stood behind me, holding Julia. I had no words, my mouth was parched. I was so drained and exhausted that I couldn't will anything. I felt limp. The further I was wounded, the hungrier I was. Yet right now I was incapable of moving. I was so hungry that I could have preyed on my best friend. It was joy in the immobility I felt that lessened my temptation.

"Oi, Tythian!" Cesar shouted from nearby as he ran up the hill toward us. "You couldn't give me a lift as well?"

"You are the oldest vampire I know. I knew it wouldn't take you long to return to us," Tythian said, bored of Cesar's theatrics. We all continued to watch the flames as the sabers' squeals pierced all of our ears. Tythian continued, "You know it was the Council who lead that large pack of sabers to the Guild. They've been living within the city for some time now. Fier wasn't fooled by you at all, Esmore. You led them to the Guild. This was Fier's first attack on the Hunters' Guild. He had simply played you into being a distraction."

Neither Chase nor I could say anything. I flashed a look into Tythian's way. And what if he were involved? How had we not known we were followed? How did we not know we triggered this battle?

"I'd suspected he might've been keeping tabs on me," Chase admitted. *When I first saw you, Esmore, I came here often just to be close. I suspect this has been thought out for a while now. Perhaps Fier didn't confide in me as much as I thought.*

"It looks like Fier is being clever and conserving his army. Is the World Leadership Council soon to be held?" Cesar asked of Tythian.

"That's a ridiculous name," Tythian scorned, but he answered him. "In a few months now. It looks as if Fier is serious about trying to outmatch the other Councils and take further leadership of more land. As you suspected," Tythian praised.

I let that information sink in. So Fier planned to overpower the Council surpassing his division?

"I suspect they already know," Cesar responded as we watched the crashing flames in the distance. "This next Council meeting will destroy many of our kind and maybe even other covens. They are no different from the human wars. There are always men who want more."

I tried to numb the mounting questions. For today I only wanted to rest, and then worry about it in the new dawn.

"How do you two know one another?" my mother asked.

"Well, Tythian is my first son of course," Cesar said with a proud smile as he pulled Tythian in for an embrace which then turned into a headlock. "Well, so to speak, he was the first I turned into a vampire."

I wanted to feel shocked or overwhelmed, but I was far too tired. Even as my body tried to rejuvenate, it struggled. So Tythian was the vampire Cesar spoke of placing in the Council. And I now understood why: because a secret war had been brewing. The Hunter's Guild knew nothing, we had been so out of our depth this entire time, and in it, my arrogance boomed thinking I could ever match them. But that was no longer a battle for me to fight. Or was it? Right now, all I was concerned with was that my team would stay safe.

"Esmore," Chase coughed. Slowly I watched the burn marks on him heal. He now had the energy to fully lift himself and hold me in a tight embrace. He almost pushed me over onto my back because he held me so firmly. He kissed my lips hungrily. "Thank god, I thought I'd lost you," he whispered into my ear, holding my hair tightly to him. He kissed my ear again. I wanted to be sad for the hunters who would be killed tonight. But we were a diligent breed; I knew some, if not most, would survive. I couldn't mourn as they so quickly turned on me and left me for dead. I wasn't sure who I was fighting for any longer. But I was certain I was where I was meant to be, and that was by the side of my familiar, my mother, and my best friend.

"So, what do we do now?" Tythian asked. My mother looked at Cesar worriedly.

"Perhaps her heart isn't as safely hidden as we first thought," my mother said. "Word of her ability will spread, and her gift will be highly sought out. They'll want to use her as a weapon against one another."

"First, we get them out of here, we need to retreat," Cesar said, placing his hand on Tythian's shoulder. Cesar was directing him to teleport us. Tythian held his hand out to Dillian and Julia, waiting for their permission before transporting them. Apprehensively, they accepted and vanished into a black hole.

"Esmore, you're literally the definition of an immortal," Chase teased with a smile. I gave a faint and uncertain smile in response. Chase had not changed at all; it was me who had changed entirely. And with the knowledge

I now held, I wondered how long it would be until the next smile would spread along my lips.

"Others will come looking for me. I don't think I could survive a beheading," I said, now understanding the war I was amidst. I would be the token item vampires and hunters would search for. After all, we were all creatures who grew to survive and thrived in power. They would come for me, all of them.

Chase kissed my lips, pinning back a piece of my golden hair behind my ear. "I will not let them touch you. We weren't prepared this time. But the next, we will be. I will never fail you again."

I cupped his face, "You have never and will never fail me."

Suddenly Tythian was standing behind us. "Little vampire," he stated. "Do not forget your promise to me, either."

Darkness consumed us as I waited patiently for the place where he next transported us. A smile spread across my lips. I thought I would be hungry and vengeful after all that had happened. The hunter was now the hunted. But I was relieved to find that, because of Chase, I would fight for the *right* reasons. Instead of killing vampires and finding humans to protect, I would now selfishly fight for my individuality and existence. Chase was my awakening to that, and I would not let him go. He was my only connection to emotion and love until I found my heart. And when I did, I would no doubt give it to him entirely. He gave me a reason to live, and this new thirst gave me a reason to search for power.

Keep reading for a preview of
Token Vampire, Book Two in the Token Huntress Series

T✹KEN VAMPIRE

FROM INTERNATIONAL AWARD WINNING AUTHOR
KIA CARRINGTON-RUSSELL

CHAPTER
I

What hit me first was the damp and muggy air as I tried to breathe. My body pressed against the cold stone floor. My heart pounded, and my stomach lurched from being teleported. My sight took a moment to readjust to the darkness that surrounded us. I sat in the dark; the stone flooring beneath us cooled my fingers when I brushed them along it. Goosebumps pricked my skin. I was used to being underground in the Hunter Guild, but this was far deeper into the network of tunnels than I had ever been. Tythian had teleported Chase and me, his hands still rested on our shoulders now as we all struggled to regain our composure. Only seconds before, we were watching the hellish scene of the Guild burning to the ground. My fellow hunters who'd turned on me were screaming in the distance. I didn't know how many survived. I couldn't even feel guilty for not caring. My emotions remained stagnant, like they always did.

Chase and I clung to one another for support as we tried to get our bearings. We were both exhausted. My mouth was parched as I inhaled the scent of blood, imagining its warmth filling my mouth. I knew it would restore the energy that was stolen from us during the ordeal with James and Campture. Relief rushed through me as Chase's fingers trailed over my cheek, grabbing my attention. It was only at his touch, or my mother's, that I could truly feel and it was overwhelming. One thing screamed out at me, and that was the fact that everyone I loved was now safe. I looked to Chase with simple relief; my Chase, my familiar, whom I would die for. He brushed my cheek with a smile, a wicked glow in his eyes. *I need to drink some blood*, I confessed to him telepathically.

His smile widened. *I know Esmore, I'll find us something*, he replied.

The vampire lifestyle was not one I could get used to anytime soon. My body screamed for blood, but the other thing that was heightened, despite my exhaustion, was the torture of not being able to ravish Chase then and there. We had both almost died today. I had my chest blown out and yet, I'd survived. I watched the man I love be tortured. All I wanted to do now was to shred the clothes from his body and devour him, to claim his as my own again. Another smile spread across Chase's lips. He knew it, he could sense it from me.

"Are you both going to just sit there all day?" Tythian interrupted with his hands behind his back as he looked at us impatiently.

We were interrupted by a sound. I heard Dillian's voice in the distance followed by a scream. It was enough to startle me out of my stupor, and I immediately ran into a narrow dark hall. When I turned the corner, I came to a rocky circular room lit by candlelight. The wooden chairs and tables were spread about. Above was a small chandelier with candles. I quickly scanned the room, assessing the occupants.

My mother and biological father, Cesar, watched me from the corner, alongside two unfamiliar male vampires. One had black hair and blue eyes. He eyed me coolly as he leaned back in his chair so far that the front legs balanced in mid-air. The male beside him watched on with a childish smile. He beamed as if toys were being presented in front of him. His hair was long and blond. He wore no shirt, but there was a large wooden cross adorning his chest as a necklace. His eyes were the same color as the wood, which contrasted nicely against the light tan of his skin. His body was covered in various black tattoos.

To my right, huddled in the corner, a larger male vampire stood over Dillian, baring his fangs. Dillian stood in front of Julia protectively. The hood had fallen from her head, revealing her sheer terror as she cowered behind Dillian.

"Just one taste, eh, boy?" the vampire mocked. He was Dillian's height, if not taller. His black hair was cut short, and his green eyes shone like a snake's.

Neither Dillian nor Julia had weapons to protect themselves. Dillian could hardly stand after being so severely beaten. I took only four steps forward at my most heightened speed, but the vampire seemed to have vanished. Instantly behind me, his rough hands brushed over my plaited golden hair.

"Mm, you smell yummy," he said. Before I realized it, I'd turned and grabbed the vampire by the throat, lifting him from the ground. Growls swept past us, but the loudest was my own. I could sense Chase behind me. I kept my eyes on the vampire savagely.

"They are mine!" I said, remembering how Chase had to objectify me in such a way within the Council. "And if you ever touch me again, I will break your spine into small shards and feed it to you."

I dropped him to the ground, and he slithered toward the other men angrily. Chase walked around the vampire with his hands in his pockets and a smirk on his face. It was both he and Cesar who had growled. *Shards of spine, really?* He spoke to me within my mind. I felt the touch of a smirk on my face as well. My aggressive instincts shattered when Chase looked at me in such a way. Chase obviously realized I didn't need him to protect me.

"Be good to your sister, the lot of you!" Cesar bellowed, kicking his boot into the vampire who had threatened Dillian. Dillian was still on guard as he hugged Julia protectively.

"Their what?" I hissed. The thought of being connected to these vampires in such a way sickened me. My mother also looked around, somewhat shocked.

"Oh, so you're the little sister we've heard so much about," the blond-haired male with the wooden cross on his chest said while standing and stretching his hand out to shake mine. "Call me, Yolo."

Yolo obviously sensed my disdain because he pointed his outstretched hand at Chase. Chase looked down at his hand, his hands still in his pockets. He raised an eyebrow at the gesture and looked at him tiredly. "Yolo. *Seriously?*"

"Hey man, when I turned vamp I could choose whichever name I desired. I was a new me, thanks to Cesar. So, Yolo, right. You Only Live Once." He said it with a cheesy grin, but the smile faltered somewhat when he realized Chase wasn't going to shake his hand. He withdrew it hastily.

I looked back at Tythian, who still stood in the doorway. His expression mirrored my contempt. I turned to Yolo and couldn't help but glance in confusion at the cross that rested against his many tattoos.

He smiled again as if my gaze alone was all he needed to initiate conversation. "My parents were Catholic, you see. So I keep to that. I love my mom and dad, even after their passing. I never had the chance to see them again after I got turned. It took over one hundred years to be able to contain my thirst, so Cesar didn't let me near any humans or civilization."

"One hundred years?" I choked, thinking of my own burning desires. I was struggling to keep myself from indulging in the necks of Dillian and Julia right now. If it weren't for my exhaustion and determination not to get any closer, I shuddered to think what might happen.

"Connor took the longest." He pointed to the dark-haired male who had been balancing on his chair. He seemed timid, and he looked at Tythian for reassurance. It forced me to question if he was mute. "Connor was found in 1936, during Hitler's reign. He had the blue eyes but not the blond hair," Tythian said as he walked over to him. He spoke affectionately of Connor. Despite being an introverted man, I could see the respect he held for Tythian. "His family was murdered. Connor was left for dead, except Cesar turned him. Connor never forgave any human after that. He got a little twisted and saw the vampires as a more heroic race and the humans as parasites and beasts. It took a while to dilute that hatred."

I looked to Connor as he leaned shyly forward, assessing us. His blue eyes were piercing and held so much sadness. He continued to stare even when our eyes met.

"And that's Balzar!" Cesar bellowed with a monstrous laugh, pointing at the vampire who had threatened Dillian. "My daughter is only eighteen years of age, and you are over one hundred and fifty, yet you still get your rear-end handed to you!"

"Yeah, would someone like to explain that?" He tsked under his breath. "She doesn't even smell like a vampire." I looked at my mother, who seemed just as uncertain as the others. At first I thought she might've been familiar with them or this location, but her tense body language indicated otherwise.

"Well, when a daddy vampire and mommy hunter love each other very much," Cesar continued, rustling his hand through Balzar's short hair. "They create a vampire-hunter baby girl who is stronger in everything because of that. The end."

"You suck!" Yolo laughed and pointed at Balzar. Balzar grunted under his breath at the insult before pouncing on Yolo. Both of them ran down a hall childishly.

"And you also forgot to mention that she carries the Descendant gift within her which is perhaps the biggest cause for concern," Tythian said, now standing with his hands strapped across his chest in an unscathed dress shirt, despite the ordeal we'd been through.

"Why have you brought us here?" I asked, not wanting to waste my time with stupid introductions any longer.

"Because you are safe here, and you can build your energy back up. You'll need it," Cesar said, resting a hand on my mother's lower back.

"In the next few months, a war will begin. And this time we, our own coven, will not step aside and let the humans or Council rule," Tythian began.

"You're a coven?" I narrowed my eyes on them in judgment. They were at times no better than the sabers. Yolo and Balzar returned after hearing my raised voice.

"Not all covens are bad, Esmore." Tythian brushed me off.

"We've just chosen to live more freely from the start," Connor's rough voice interjected, surprising me. So, he wasn't mute.

"Cesar turned all four of us, so we were indebted and bound to be a part of his coven. But we would have stayed even if we had the choice to leave. We are family here. And there are many other covens around the world we're aligned with that think the same way. Of course, not all agree or care," Yolo said, shrugging his shoulders.

"So why attack the Council?" I asked.

"It's not just the Council, my beautiful daughter," Cesar bluntly stated. "The humans too have been gathering power. We cannot live in a world where there is another war, and the Council takes further control and power. They demand one ruler. If all are combined under one Council, it could be a free-for-all hunt on the covens. We hit them from the side before they gather that power, which is why I had Tythian infiltrate Fier's Council. They've been gathering numbers for a while now, and his father, Arab's displeasure with covens has been known since the day they tried to rally us all against the humans."

"You met Arab?" Chase asked.

"I did," Cesar confirmed smugly. "And I met your mother as well. Who was far nicer than you, might I add, pipsqueak."

Chase growled under his breath, enraging Cesar. When Cesar's demeanor changed, both Yolo and Connor growled in support.

"Stop with the macho dance," my mother interjected. "Cesar, tell her about the humans."

"I …" His attitude dissolved at the request of my mother. "The humans have been hiding. You hunters lost contact with them, but the government of the humans has been functioning. They're trying to create a new form of hunters. Stronger ones to overcome their predecessors and by extension, the Council."

"I don't know why they don't let it go. I mean, the world has already turned to shit. It won't be like the good old days of the early 2000s," Yolo said, stretching back on his chair.

"How do you know this? Do you have proof?" I asked.

"Yes," Tythian interjected in a quiet yet angry tone. His jaw was quivering, and his hands were still across his chest. "Whitney was one of their victims. When I found her, she was left for dead." I shivered at his words, and I felt Chase straighten beside me.

"But Whitney had been dying from cancer. You saved her from a pack of sabers when her father was killed," I said, repeating Whitney's story. Chase's fingers brushed past mine, but I refused to accept his hand. I could sense the guilt rolling off him.

Tythian exchanged a look with him before continuing. "It's what we made her believe," he said under his breath.

"I don't understand," I said. Slowly it clicked together. I stared at Chase accusingly. "You tricked her mind?"

"Only because Tythian asked me to. Esmore, with enough suggestive thoughts people can forget their darkest nightmares. I spared her that pain. It was Tythian's familiar, and his call." Chase tensed. He was trying to smile, and I could sense that his mind was thinking of something funny to say like he always did to dispel serious situations. I felt the rumble of darkness within me tap lightly in my stomach, like butterflies trying to escape. Only Chase could create this feeling within me, and I hated it. But I was too weak for rage to sweep through. I hated how close I stood to him. I was able to feel the betrayal, lies, and pain he had caused.

"I asked Chase to do so," Tythian confirmed. "I found my love—my sweet, beautiful Whitney—abandoned beside her dead father at dusk. It is true sabers attacked her, which I didn't lie about, and that her father died at their hands. But where they had come from was a secure place for humans … where technology remains highly advanced. They are trying to create stronger beings. According to our research, the injection killed most; and in Whitney's case, the disease spread through her for many years. I was feeding her my blood every night without her knowing. I could have never turned her into a vampire because of the parasite disease, even if I tried. However, after so many years of my blood rejuvenating her, it stopped working."

"It was her brother who injected them both," Yolo spoke up now,

245

allowing Tythian to slip into a subdued silence. Now I knew if he had the choice he wouldn't have respected Whitney's wishes. He would have turned her anyway. But if that were to happen to Chase, I would have done the same. I could not judge, yet I felt sick by the lie.

"How do you know all this?" I retorted.

"Yolo, here is a part of that human group," Cesar interrupted. "He was the only one who could infiltrate them."

"How?" I demanded. How had the Guild been so left in the dark about this kind of intel, with so little inclination?

Yolo stood up tall. I could see a lightly quivering mist surrounding him. Within seconds a human woman with long blonde hair in a tight skirt, shirt, and high heels approached me with a velvet voice. "Because I am Jenn Cadolwadt: engineer and specialist at the Human Activist and Regaining Existence Movement," she said, holding out a hand for me to shake. Yolo even smelled like a human woman with a strong smell of flowers.

"He can bypass all the scans. He comes up as human," Connor spoke from the corner of the room.

"Why a woman?" Dillian asked from behind me. It had been the first time he'd spoken amongst this mess.

The woman gave a sheepish smile in response. One that made my whole body cringe. "Well, mostly because of these," Yolo said, grabbing hold of his bountiful chest. "It is a pretty nice rack, if I do say so myself."

My stomach turned. "I think I'm going to be sick."

"She needs blood," Chase growled, ending the conversation. "She's lost too much."

"Of course, sorry for having not noticed sooner," Cesar bellowed, evidently irritated that Chase had noticed it before him. "Connor, if you would be so kind as to show those two to their room, and Tythian, can you show the two other hunters their room?"

"No!" I said savagely, looking at Balzar. "They stay in the same room as us." I would protect them no matter what.

After much hesitation, Cesar agreed. "Very well, but you only have a day's rest until you are to come out and meet the rest of my coven." He dispelled us within moments, and the others went their separate ways as Tythian escorted us silently through the rocky and cool halls.

ABOUT THE AUTHOR

Kia grew up in the Darling Downs Region in Queensland, Australia. Graduating High School, she pursued a career in freelance journalism. In 2014, having always had a passion for writing fiction, she decided to follow her dream of becoming an accomplished author.

Now living on the Gold Coast, Australia and travelling every spare minute she gets, Kia is constantly searching for new inspiration for her writing and filling her heart with adventure, one country at a time.

OTHER BOOKS BY KIA CARRINGTON-RUSSELL

Mad Hatter Vampire Prince:

A PREQUEL NOVELLA TO THE TOKEN HUNTRESS SERIES.
CAN ALSO BE READ AS A STANDALONE.

Kyran Klaus is the prince of Grand Klaus, his reputation honoring him the title of the Mad Hatter Vampire Prince. Crazy, deadly, lustful, and utterly bored with life.

Sasha Pierce is one of a kind. Having been experimented on by her mother as a child, she's become a human weapon who's looking for answers beyond the walls where her kind aren't enslaved to vampires.

When the Mad Hatter Prince takes a sudden interest in Sasha and her work, she scarcely begins to cover her tracks and hide her secrets. What she doesn't anticipate is being a pawn in his most sinister performance yet.

Disturbingly Wicked! This novella is not for the fainthearted. Lust, Gore, Wit, and Malicious Humor. Prepare to be deliciously tainted.

Token Vampire

The world within the Hunter's Guild has turned into chaos. Esmore, Token Huntress, has been outcast, targeted by her Guild, and is on the run. Now reunited with her mother and true father, Cesar, Esmore is hiding within Cesar's coven with the family she didn't know existed. With her newly found vampirism, she must learn to control the heightened urges and emotions that consume her—blood, lust, vengeance, protection, and love.

Armed with only a few allies and her familiar, Chase, they must strive to find a place in the new world when the rules that guided them once, now have no meaning. The darkness inside Esmore is bubbling below the surface, threatening to consume her, and Chase must teach her to rein it in, for if she doesn't, he may lose her entirely or worse, watch her turn on those she loves most.

Esmore is soon to learn what she is and most disastrously the danger she's become.

The Shadow Minds Journal:

In this world, there are creatures lurking in the shadows. As a child, I once played with them. As a teenager, I began to fear them and became victim to their attacks. As an adult, I now realize that no matter how much I try to escape the grasp of this world, I was inevitably born into it.

Now reborn as a Guardian in the year of 2986, Vivian Lair must uphold the treaty between Angels and Demons on the human world and city of Shabeah. Contracted to seven demons who she can shift into while taking direct orders from the Underworld Lord, Haymen, it wasn't exactly her ideal rebirth. Involving herself with the Angel of War, Gabe is even worse.

Still fighting those who try to possess her during her sleep, Vivian must now record and try to hunt the Volv through the Shadow Minds Journal. Now stuck between the hatred and lust of two of the most powerful entities in all worlds, Vivian is involved inevitably in the upcoming conflict.

Blood. Lust. War. She must kill before being killed.

My Escort Collection:

A collection of the Best Selling contemporary series that includes: My Escort, My Exception and My Expectation. Clover is personal assistant to Debra Coorman, the merciless boss of Candice fashion magazine. The bright lights of New York are dim for Clover, who is tormented by a work schedule like no other. Debra is relentless in her determination to demean Clover. For once, Clover dares to play Debra's games, and intends to prove her wrong at the next glittering event. With mixed emotions, Clover contacts a male escort, Damon. If his velvet voice over the phone is anything to go by, Clover knows her money will be well spent. But when Damon appears at her door, something unexpected happens. The taunts and the games begin. Who is truly going to win at this game?

Aroused: Taming Himself

"Remember my name because you will be begging me for more. This is my promise to you."

Meet Hayden Zilch: entrepreneur, sports manager, investor. Cocky, tantalizing, and an utter womanizer. He is a man who loves pleasuring women. He can show you a world you have only fantasied about.

So what happens when this sex-mad womanizer decides to finally find The One?

Starting off with a list of five women, Hayden sets out to learn the difference between lust and love. His adventures have him laughing, crying in pain, and begging on his knees as he battles to tame himself. Can Hayden really control himself around these five beautiful temptresses?

Taming Himself is the first in this five-book series which tells the story of Hayden's search for both love and pleasure.

Phantom Wolf

A book that is so dynamic and can pull my emotions free so easily is a 5 star novel.
★★★★★ - *Paranormal Trance Reviews*

Sia is a Phantom Wolf. Neither dead nor alive--and rotting from the inside--she is on the edge of her curse. Once a Phantom Wolf has been created, they hunt their blood pack and slaughter all their loved ones. Except for Sia, who woke years after her death to find herself rampaging through the land on a lonely path.

She continues to run from the rival pack that hunts her because she is a Phantom Wolf. Attracted to a scent, Sia finds her old best friend, who is now a grown woman. Having once saved Keeley, Sia takes the role of protector yet again, despite Keeley's involvement with the mysterious Alpha, Kiba, and his kin brother, Saith. An ambush separates the pack and the four of them blindly fight the new warriors that attack them: desperately needing to find out where the attacks are coming from, as Sia has vowed to protect Keeley. But at what cost?

Now being chased, Sia finds herself conflicted by the mortal and spirit world while trying to protect her kin. Sia must confront her fears, as well as the human lover who killed her many years before. It is not only survival Sia contends with, but her own façade that must be broken so that she may find peace within herself once more.

The Three Immortal Blades

Contains the entire Award Winning Collection. Karla Gray is an ordinary young woman that is taken from her mundane life into a world of blood lust as she begins to struggle with a unique ability. Karla is a Shielder; an exceptional fighter born with the rare ability to project a Shield for protection. However, Shielders are not the only kind that possesses such a talent. The Shielders battle a war that has been raging for centuries against Starkorfs, who harvest humans and Shielders alike to obtain a near immortality. Alongside the charming Lucas and selfless Paul, Karla must unravel the purpose of her curse and battle an unknown presence manipulating her thoughts; a mysterious woman who may be dormant for now, but has every intention of possessing Karla- mind, body, and soul. Within this new reality that Karla faces the search for the Three Immortal Blades begins.